CW00408816

Cold Moonlight

Book One of
The Game Of Gods

Mark R Mitchell

To my mum and brother

Who knew when to support me: and when to tell me
that I was doing it wrong

Contents

Prologue

I held the dangerous woman that I loved in my arms, and I watched her chest gently rise and fall in sleep. She looked so beautiful in the light of the magical flame that danced in my hand that it was almost possible for a moment to forget that she was a killer. As I thought about the fact that I must now leave her I understood fully for the first time the true agony of what being a grey wizard meant, what it would always mean. The agony of always having to work from the sidelines. How my objectivity, my ability to see the world as it was and not as those who were well educated in the ways of this world wished it to be, could only be maintained by never staying too long in any place lit fully by the light: even when that was the light of love.

Vicky, such a normal name for such an accomplished killer, was smiling as she slept, her eyes glowing with vivid dreams. The nature of how her lips twitched suggested the dreams were more explicit than those you talk about in public afterwards. Her eyes were open as she slept, as all really powerful wizards were, in honour of the gods. The firelight's dancing light blazed in the molten fire of her red hair: the same almost piercing brightness that danced in her eyes. When Vicky laughed and her eyes smiled it was like staring into the vivid brightness of a new dawn, right into the hope of the living day. I always thought of her as being the heart of the morning, the girl of sunrise and of new beginnings. Her hair glowed in the morning sun and she was loud and talkative from the moment she got up. Her laugh could make you feel your heart aching in your chest, her giggles send shivers down your spine. And when she smiled softly at you, when she singled you out, of all the men around her in the crowd, it was as though time itself stood still, and the only thing that mattered in all the world was her.

In that moment if I could have had my heart's desire it would be to spend just one more day here with her before I must leave. To be woken up just once more by Vicky's grumbling stretchings as she decided it was now time for a fresh start to the day and that it was past time for us both to be up. To see her smile at me as she cleared the last fading remnants of sleep from her eyes. She had always found getting up easier than I did. Perhaps we would have started the day again by making love in our tent, sweat pouring out over her soft skin as I called out her name, and she called out mine: and afterwards she would whisper in my ear that she was worried the neighbours might think we were too noisy. Or perhaps the new day would have just begun with sizzling bacon and hot coffee while she sharpened her sword carefully and wondered whether it would be just training and guard duty today, or, with a sudden eagerness in her words, whether blood would flow. I wondered what dark magic treatise I would be translating as I sought to master its power, and whether my hands would also darken with blood before the day's end. Perhaps there would have been time for both sex and breakfast: but that normally ended up with us having just to rush both of them and neither ending up being any fun at all. I smiled wryly. Not that trying to moan about that would have ever got much sympathy from anyone.

But I had tarried almost too long in Vicky's life already: the time for wishing was long past. Weeks I should not have really spent here had become months escaping in Vicky's life and bed from the truth of the dark reality of our world. Outside the moon's cold light beat down: calling. My other mistress. And not to answer that call would be the end of all I had worked towards for so many years, the end of the reason for which I had drowned the lands of men in blood and pain. Gently I disentangled myself from Vicky's arms, then quietly got dressed and gathered my things. I drew my dagger, the steel harsh in the light of the moon. Vicky was still sleeping, but restlessly now, her arms curled around my pillow, holding it uneasily against her chest. Her breathing had heightened a little, the faint sounds of stress beginning in her chest. It hurt to see her in pain but there was nothing that I could do about that for now: both of us hated it when we were parted.

I turned and raised my eyes up, and spoke softly to my gods. "To Odin, the Wanderer and the Glad of War and who I call, above all, The Allfather. Long have I honoured you, from most desperate beginnings, through untold darkness: and throughout all the wars and despair of men. Through all the first Viking age not one of your pagan kings, not Ragnar Lodbrok, nor Ivar the Boneless himself, shed as much blood for you as I have. Hear me now I ask you, and shelter Vicky as you have sheltered me. Let not her excitement for bloodlust and victory take over, so that an unseen sword blow or spear slip through her guard. And shelter her from trusting too generously, that she may not be vulnerable to those who would strike steel from behind through her ribs. In hope of your blessing, and to seal our bargain, I offer you blood from my body." I raised my left hand and struck down in one motion with my right. I cut open my skin from the top of the middle finger to the base of where my palm met my wrist. Blood sprayed out in a fine mist, but the floor beneath me was untouched, not darkening with a single touch of red. A strange fire burned in mid-air, consuming my offering, and I knew that my sacrifice had been accepted. I seized fire magic, a magic that is strong in almost all grey wizards, and bound the cut in my hand with flame. The bleeding stopped, but I could still feel the pain where my flesh had been both cut and burned. But all true sacrifices required pain: was that not the essence of all pagan faith?

Then I stopped, this second prayer would be more difficult, though just as necessary. But then everything about my relationship with this goddess was complicated. Odin felt so familiar to me it felt at times like I was talking to an image of myself, an image that talked the same language and thought in exactly the same way that I did. The second deity who I worshipped was as different from that as day was from night. I felt like I was talking to a strange, almost alien, personality: one whose thoughts and feelings were the complete opposite to my own. But one whose very presence made my heart and mind race. What is opposite to us we always find the most attractive: the most beautiful in all this world. If Odin was my yin then the goddess I worshipped was my yang. And the gods only knew which of the deities was the more great and terrible in absolute terms: if that question even meant anything.

I took a deep breath, and then began. I was praying to a goddess who could be very temperamental. Odin's subtlety and power were terrible but I understood them as I understood my own grey magic. I found it a little more difficult to approach correctly a goddess who could be moody and difficult: some would argue to the point of schizophrenia. There was a side to her that was almost the very light and essence of goodness itself. On the one hand the goddess's arrows would strike down monsters

4

and the corrupt with sudden death as she defended the innocent. She lived in the forests and mountainous wildernesses far away from the luxury of civilisation where she could have enjoyed an easy life of comfortable decadence. And she spent much of her time hunting down the darkest of demons for the benefit of all human kind.

On the other hand no other god or goddess but her had such a taste for human sacrifice. In ancient Greece she had vulnerable men, shipwrecked sailors, clubbed to death and their heads mounted on crosses in her honour. In Sparta, the great military power of the ancient Greek world, the price of her blessing and power had been yearly human sacrifice before her altar at the centre of their warrior state: and if the flogging of innocent boys before her altar drew too little blood her image would darken, expand and hiss on encouragement in serpentine tongues. Among other things she was the darkest of the Greek goddesses of war.

This goddess had once stood alone against the two giants who enforced the surrender of all the other gods and goddesses of Mount Olympus, all the other deities in her Pantheon. Who knew what had truly happened that day? For the virgin of the gods had been sent down as a peace offering, her ravishment and rape the price of the giants' goodwill in the surrender negotiations. And yet when she returned to Mount Olympus she was still untouched by man and yet both the giants lay dead. A feat surely worthy to be celebrated in legend and song for as long as this world should last: and yet all the details were hidden in dark silence. Only the goddess knew what had really happened that day, and the sugary sweet version of the story she had told tasted false even to the most innocent ear.

This same hero goddess had once slaughtered almost every member of a fourteen strong family of children

5

with her brother Apollo, leaving only one boy and one girl alive. Their arrows had hissed mercilessly through the air: bringing death to the innocent. The price paid merely for the mother comparing her fertility with that of this goddess's barren womb. Pagan gods made many claims to power: but non to perfection.

Not that the goddess was even barren. Just as she hadn't been sexually active she hadn't had children. Much had changed since those distant centuries.

I started my second prayer. "Goddess of the moon, the light that shines at night long after the sun has faded in its battle against darkness. Protector of the innocent and the young. The finest archer who has ever lived, whose silver shafts strike death into the darkest heart. From the first time you came to me in the light of the moon, through all that has happened since, including bathing with you naked in pools of gleaming water shining in the midnight moonlight." For a moment I could feel the goddess smile. "Through all you have stood by me in my darkest hours, except in your moody moments when you have been a rightly indecisive pain." The moonlight flickered, almost as if in guilt. "Through all that we have shared, and however tempted I have been, I have always honoured your lifelong commitment to chastity and faithfulness." And in the emptiness of the tent, though there was no one but Vicky and I inside, I could clearly hear the soft sound of a woman laughing. It sounded nothing like Vicky's laughter, hers was swift and quick, a lightning flash of joy that lit a room: a giggling of silliness and fun. This laughter was deep and soft, private and intimate: a call to the deepest pleasures of this world.

"That last claim," whispered a voice like moonlight on the night streams, light and beautiful, yet simultaneously piercingly sharp, "really is impressive word play." She was so close I could feel her warm breath, tickling on the back of my ear. Just that much of her touch was like a shot of liquid fire suddenly burning its way through my most sensitive veins. It had been over a year since I had last seen her, and there was a part of me that reawakened for her at just the slightest touch. Her voice giggled as she went on, its tones soft in the tender intimacy of my inner ear. "You have 'always honoured my lifelong commitment to chastity' have you? Shall we ask my father, Zeus himself, what he thinks about that? I've always been daddy's little girl, and he was so pleased when I asked for eternal virginity when I was three. And it was virginity Edward, not chastity. It wasn't so long ago I was the goddess of always keeping my pants on, not the goddess of taking them off only at… now what exactly is the polite way to talk about explicit sexual activity again?" There was a slight pause while the goddess enjoyed my discomfort. "Oh yes I I've got it. Only taking my pants off at, let us say… appropriate moments."

I swallowed drily, trying to keep my thoughts clearly focused on the task at hand. There are parts of the past that you know should stay dead, but which take only the slightest flicker, the slightest touch of air or breath, to rekindle and spring back into life again. And yet all that can bring is pain, however sweet it feels at the time. For the time for those parts, those feelings, has passed. I managed to keep my voice just about calm and level: I had not expected my goddess to appear in person in answer to my prayer. "I know the pain that man's sexual desire has caused you goddess. And I have both honoured that and suffered greatly for it. I sometimes think that being flogged bloody in front of one of your altars would have been less painful then my relationship with you."

There was a silence: and then I felt the soft squeeze of the goddess's hand on my shoulder. It was a touch that brought comfort: and maybe something more. "I'm sorry

Edward, sorry that you have suffered so much for me. Because of you I have turned from virginity, from forever abhorring the touch of any man, to chastity, which means faithfulness to your partner. From the goddess of children and virgins I have become also the goddess of all who hold faithful and true to their vows. I was strong in the beginning, but I doubt any god or goddess has ever increased in strength as fast as I have." There was a pause for a moment, a silence in a tent now bathed in the clear illumination of soft moonlight.

"You know," said the goddess disbelievingly, "even Aphrodite, goddess of love and the carnal pleasure of sex, who used to laugh at me and call me frigid and broken, saying that if all lived the way I did the result would in the end be the extinction of all mankind; even she now follows me and works under my direction!"

There was a silence, and then I could almost feel my favourite goddess scowling. "Well some of the time she does anyway. I've been a huntress for uncounted generations long before the time of men. I know that she's still sneaking about during the night and taking love to all sorts of places it shouldn't be. Breaking all sorts of vows of chastity! I would say she never seems to stop taking her pants off, but I'm not convinced she ever has time to put them back on in the first place."

I took a deep breath, wondering from long experience how to tell my goddess that she was suddenly in danger of going off on a very long and in-depth tangent about Aphrodite: without risking Artemis going into a sulk because after so long apart I was now telling her I didn't have time to listen to her stories. It was so easy sometimes now to forget this goddess was not even remotely what anyone would call human. She was so every day in some ways: so humanly real: but she was also a goddess. Her human self was inextricably intertwined with magic and the divine. And, however

8

much she might appear at times just to be nothing more than a normal young woman, it was incredibly dangerous to ever let yourself forget exactly what she was: a goddess of both light and dark: good and evil. It was so much easier with Odin in some ways, in his dark cloak and with his one sharp eye transfixing you however hard you tried to meet his gaze, his inhuman store of knowledge and wisdom burning with every word he said. You could never pass one moment with him without feeling the true power and greatness of the divine. And while Odin's character was shaped in the subtlest shapes of grey he was always clearly one unified personality. You always knew exactly where you stood with him: even when you didn't understand the slightest word that he was saying. But this goddess had two forms that were as different as day and night, and while one side was almost ridiculously heroic and brave and courageous her dark side made Odin; god of the sheer pleasure of being immersed in blood and war, demander of human sacrifice and the blood of living people; look as gentle as the carpenter god of the Christians. And while Odin demanded the blood of all, men and women alike, the goddess's thirst when she was her other self was for the blood of men alone: and for many years now she had drunk deep indeed.

I resumed my prayer.

"Through all that we have shared, and however tempted I have been, I have always honoured your lifelong commitment to chastity and faithfulness, and through all the blood of men I have shed for you. And now, as once I honoured your vow to virginity, now I honour your new power of chastity by my faithful love to Vicky, from whom I have never cheated or strayed: and who of all mortal women is the only one I hold dear in my heart."

The goddess smiled, and appeared before me: the beauty of moonlight made flesh. My feelings for her were so strong I didn't know if the sight of her was pleasure or pain. She was beautiful, though a strikingly different form of beauty to that of Vicky's. The goddess's hair was dark and tied into two ponytails with a silver clip, whereas Vicky's was bright red and hung down long and free to her waist. Artemis was slender, her curves subtle and sleek; while Vicky had blossomed more fully and obviously with all the beauty of natural womanhood. Only their eyes were the same, large and round, so expressive. But the colour that shone out of them was so different. Artemis had eyes that were bluer then the sky during the midday sun; looking into her soul was like looking into the bright searchlight of all that was true, a light that stripped bare your soul. Vicky's eyes were a soft green, like looking into the essence of magic and miracles, a call to growth and fresh life and laughter in the sun.

The goddess reached forward and touched my face. Her nails were not red like Vicky's but a clear blue that matched her eyes. The colour fitted her perfectly, seeming as natural on her hands as red seemed normal on other girls.

"You know," said the goddess awkwardly, cutely, "that you don't have to do that really long prayer each time you want to talk? I really care about you remember? All you need to do is say my name and I'll come running. It's quite simple. Just say it. For a moment let me pretend that we are not goddess and worshipper, but friends: or perhaps maybe something even a little more. For a moment let me pretend that the past between us never had to die. Just call me by my name as you would any other girl."

"Artemis." I said softly, and at the sound of her name on my lips she smiled and her cheeks blushed red. "See!"

she said, "it's easy!" There was a moment when it felt like it was just the two of us, when all the rest of the world just fell away. But reality was ever near. After a pause, that was no more than a few moments though it felt like an eternity of gold, Artemis gave a small, sad, sigh: and brought us both back disappointedly to the present. "Now why are you praying to me?" she asked softly, reluctantly bringing us back to business.

"If you were always Artemis the Friendly I would just use your name," I said uneasily, "but I don't think Artemis the Terrible would respond well to such... disrespect of her divine personage."

Artemis shuffled her feet guilty. When she was in a friendly mood she was always embarrassed about what she got up to when she was angry: about what happened when her other self took over. You could have written a thousand books and thesis about the true nature of the relationship between the two sides of Artemis and still have come no closer to the truth.

"I'm getting better when I'm Artemis the Terrible." Artemis the Friendly pleaded, with the same look in her eyes as that of a child who was insisting vehemently that they had not been eating chocolate, when all the while they had sticky brown stains all around their mouth. "This year at my annual festival I didn't even have that many men flogged to death at my altars. I only had eight! That's my lowest ever! Not even in double figures!"

Which means, I thought distantly, that somewhere inside you the hunger for the pain of men is unsatisfied, and sometime this year your silver arrow shafts will strike again into my gender, bringing blood and pain as Artemis the Terrible rages in her hatred against us.

But giving these bleak thoughts words would have achieved nothing, except bring Artemis the Friendly more pain. And even I, who had shared so much with Artemis, had never been able to fully decide if they were two different goddesses or just different aspects of the same one. But causing The Friendly pain for the deeds of The Terrible did not feel right, nor would it be sensible. Whichever side of Artemis you were with the other was only ever a split second from taking her place before you.

"It's okay Artemis." I said quietly, holding her close. "You know I understand how complicated the two aspects of you are. Just like I understand that Odin's love of both fine poetry and the bloodlust of war are just two different facets of his undivided whole."

I kept my voice level and hoped she didn't hear the confusion I felt beneath the surface. It was easy to care for and worship Artemis the Friendly: even if she could sometimes be a bit daft. When dealing with Artemis the Terrible I sometimes wondered just what in Hades I was doing. It was only when I was face to face with her that I sometimes wondered if the pagan gods were just the heartless demons that the Christians claimed them to be. Odin's love of death and violence could be terrible, but it was satiable: and linked to mankind's primal urge for struggle and strife. Once sated he turned to other things, particularly the inspiration of poets and his never-ending hunger for the acquiring of more knowledge. Artemis the Terrible hungered for the blood of men, and the more she had the more she wanted. Not a natural hunger but an ever-growing sadism that seemingly grew without end. It was a hunger that threatened to consume all other aspects of her personality.

Artemis the Friendly was easy to get on with and loyal, to everyone but especially to me, almost to a fault. I had earned Artemis the Terrible's respect only by turning so many living men into rotting corpses for her. But even so the incandescent fury in her, which always burned inside her just below the surface like a living thing, might come rising over the surface if she felt I had insulted her. Even just a slightly incorrect form of prayer offered to her by a man, which The Friendly probably wouldn't even notice, would be something that The Terrible would find very difficult to handle without resorting to male sacrifice and bloodshed.

I stepped back from Artemis, much as I longed to let her sink into my arms, that could not lead anywhere good, not in the long term. In the short term it might well lead somewhere only too pleasant. Not only was she divine and I mortal born but she was the goddess of chastity. The more faithful I stayed to Vicky the stronger I made Artemis and the more she liked me. Cheating on Vicky with Artemis, cheating with the goddess of chastity herself, that would destroy everything. My love for Vicky, my worship of the goddess and, I had a horrible suspicion, possibly even my relationship with both sides of Artemis. And then the goddess whose worship had saved me in the darkest places of this world would be back to being little more than a monster, preying off the blood of the innocent in a vicious cycle of sadism that would never end. And, most painful of all, we would once again stand on different sides of the battlefield.

I held up my dagger. "I want to give this to you." I said. "Dwarf forged steel. It has taken several lives in war."

"I think you mean you want to sacrifice it to me." said Artemis gently. "You're calling on me as a mortal to a god, not by the terms of our personal relationship. That means you want my divine favour for something." She sighed softly, and touched the brooch I had given her, the one gift I had ever made to her as if she had been human, as if our relationship had been one of human love. "I would have preferred a gift," she said sadly, "but we both know that isn't in my nature." She held out her hand and took the dagger, which shone in a sudden shaft of moonlight as bright for a moment as a star. Then the next moment the weapon was gone: dissolving into motes of drifting silver which faded into nothing in the still night air. It rematerialized at Artemis's side, part of the world of the divine now. "It's a good blade Edward," said Artemis lightly. "Sharp, well made and good for skinning animals and monsters when I'm done hunting. Even when I'm moody I'll like it because… well because you've killed quite a few men with it…"

Her voice trailed off into embarrassment. Then she looked up and cleared her voice. "So what are you asking for in return for my useful present?" I had neither wanted nor taken anything back the day I had given her the silver brooch. But my memory of the look in Artemis's eyes that day was one of the most precious gifts she had ever given me.

I resumed my prayer. "I call upon you goddess of the moon and silent death, hunter and protector, to cut down all who would strike my girlfriend from afar. To pierce with your silver arrows those who would bring death to her from a distance, and to slay those who would come upon her through the darkness, that her eyes, trained to sunlight, may not see."

"Okay," said Artemis carefully, "I'll protect her but…"

"She is pagan." I said quietly, slightly disappointed at Artemis's reluctance. "Of Faith and true religion. She is no more Christian or secular than I am."

"Yes," said Artemis, "and I like her very much. Well, jealousy means I totally hate her all the time! But, you know, if I wasn't jealous I would like her very much: definitely. She brings out the best in you and, even though it's painful for me to watch you be with someone else, your love is strong and your relationship is an honour to my worship. I'll have no problem looking out for her when I'm in a good mood…"

"But when you're Artemis the Terrible?" I asked questioningly. "Why? What's wrong with Vicky? She's a girl, she's faithful and therefore chaste. She's killed and she's a pagan. What's the problem?"

Artemis shuffled her feet. "She's killed yes, but always because she's fighting to save life. She might be chaste now but she wasn't not that many years ago. And she's never taken part in living human sacrifice. When I'm in a bad mood those things will make me really mad."

I looked at my goddess levelly. "Then simply remember that should Vicky live to the appointed hour then enough blood of men, women too; but you won't care about that much either way when you're in a bad mood, will flow to drown even Artemis the Terrible."

Artemis looked at me for a moment, her eyes weighing her options, then she nodded curtly. "I accept your sacrifice and will honour your prayer. Until you call on me again in your next hour of great need." She reached forward and squeezed my hand. "Good luck Edward." she whispered softly. And then she was gone, the moon was hidden behind the clouds and the night was dark. It felt very odd, suddenly being without her, and without the cold glow of her moonlight dancing on my skin.

I took one last look at Vicky, the mortal love of my life, and smiled to see her back deep in pleasant dreams. Did she rest easier now that Artemis was gone I wondered? Her long red hair pooled in soft curves down the base of her neck. The sight was so beautiful it hurt. I had beseeched the gods on her behalf and I had already woven powerful protective magic around her myself. She was as safe as I could make her: for now: until the time appointed. And then I would simply have to pray desperately that all the odds rolled in my favour.

15

I turned and walked out to begin my quest, a quest to draw a sword from a stone, and to lay it in the hands of a King Pendragon. A quest whose success was desperately needed, a quest whose outcome even now teetered on the edge of a blade.

I walked out into the night, but even as I bent all my power: the strength of both grey, fire and moonlight magic: to the task ahead part of my heart remained behind. Behind with where my little sister: my girlfriend now: lay sleeping in our tent. Where, distantly noticing my absence she curled her arms in upon herself unhappily, crushing my pillow and my scent against her chest.

Chapter 1

Seventeen Years Previously

The sun was beating down hard from the sky, a sky which was a relentless bright blue. Not one drift of white cloud anywhere to stop the heat bathing your back in sweat or baking your tongue to the roof of your mouth. It was the sort of weather which made inactivity and dozing blissful, and any attempt to do something productive quickly unpleasant. I had never really liked the heat. "Go on Edward!" said my elder brother Jacob. "The rope ladder isn't that high. You go first, up to that branch, and we'll follow you."

"He'll never do it." said my older sister Jess, her voice dark with contempt. "He's too pathetic. He might not be as affectionate as he used to be, when he was as cuddly as a little girl, but he's still embarrassing. He hasn't got the balls to do anything manly or brave." I knew it was stupid that, after so long, their taunting could still hurt or get to me: but it did. I still didn't fully understand why my own family would put so much effort into hurting me almost constantly. School I could accept more, I expected the other kids to call me odd or weak. I had long got used to them hurting me with their fists and magic when the teachers weren't looking: and increasingly nowadays even when they were. I got why strangers would want to hurt me: most people don't know how to deal with anyone that is different after all. But it still made me feel very hollow that my own family wanted the same. But one of the first lessons I had learned in this life was how much everyone hated grey wizards. Even as a young child, even in my earliest memories, I had quickly picked up that most people thought something about me was very wrong.

I looked at the rope ladder, where it led up into the great leafy green boughs of the tree overhead. I stared up at it uncertainly. It wasn't that high but I knew there was a hidden reason my brother and sister wanted me to go first: and not a good reason. But I hated being called pathetic and weak. I swallowed. "I don't really think…" I began carefully.

"Scared little freak, cowardly and meek!" my sister sang, while "Fucking limp!" my brother sneered, "Not good for fucking anything." I closed my eyes in pain. I knew it was stupid to do what they wanted but I hoped it might just shut them up for a bit. And maybe, deep down, some unacknowledged part of me still wanted to somehow earn their love and respect.

I put my hands on the rope ladder and looked at the brown bark of the tree in front of me. I tried not to think about the risk of falling, about how much that it could hurt. Then I started to climb, my hands steady as I fought to hold in their shaking, my eyes fixed resolutely on the tree in front of me. I didn't let myself look down and see the drop, because then I knew my arms would go rigid and that I would let go. I had little experience of heights, but I soon knew that I had risen high enough that dropping to the ground would really hurt. The tree was in front of me and above me and it felt like all time had stopped. That I had to go up and up forever. Hand after hand I pulled and then, very suddenly, there were no more rungs. I was at the top, and only the bark of the tree stretched out further above me: and the branch I was supposed to sit on was besides me. I took a deep breath and swung myself sideways, landing cleanly on the branch: there was no further to go. I stopped: unable to believe that I had done it. "I did it!" I called out, my face flushing with pleasure, "Who's going next?". My voice was filled with triumph and I was almost glowing with pride. Victory was rare for me. The moment I started to do well at anything the other kids, tacitly cheered on by their parents, would soon put a stop to it. Everyone knew that grey wizards were supposed to be useless at everything, any evidence that ever started to emerge that could possibly threaten that theory was soon put a stop to.

I looked down at my elder brother and sister, but they weren't happy. They hadn't expected me to succeed I realised sickly. They'd just wanted me to fall so that they could laugh at me. My brother looked disappointed. My sister scowled. She turned and whispered something in my brother's ear, and when she stepped away he was grinning. "Well done Edward!" he called, his voice syrupy sweet. "Well done you. But that isn't really high is it? Let me show you really high." He laid his hands on the tree and I felt the brown magic surge in his hands. Brown magic: the power of nature, or enhancing nature, and the wild. A power of permanent transformation.

The oak rippled under his hands, its tree rings lengthening with a protesting roar. Its bark almost crackled with protest as it stretched outwards and the tree grew thicker, and its very structure sounded like it was screaming as it stretched howling into the air. The tree grew high. It started to grow very high. The small rope ladder did not grow. I couldn't help it. I looked down. When I saw how far below the ground was getting everything started to sway and swirl. I felt every muscle in my body turn rigid but I don't remember letting go. But I did.

I do remember falling. How everything almost stopped and everything became so very nearly completely still: and how the green grass below crept up to meet me. Slowly: as though both of us were in absolutely no rush at all. And I had all the time in the world to watch the ground as I raced down to meet it: and part of me wished that when I struck it everything would be over: forever.

Then I hit the earth hard: and there was no more shock and stillness. But there was pain. And bleeding.

I did not know it at the time but I had been lucky. Lucky to let go before the tree grew even higher, and lucky that for the past several days the ground had been soaked by rain. So water had soaked even through the dense covering of the tree's leaves above so that the ground I fell onto was very soft.

But at the time all I felt was pain, and stupid, and failure: and all I could hear was my brother's and sister's laughter. "Pathetic little grey, so weird and useless!" they called, their forms shaking and whirling on the edge of a vision which now shook with pain and was streaked with tears. "So stupid he fell out of a tree!" And then all I could hear was their echoing laughter as they ran away, while I lay there with one leg bleeding and my head feeling too heavy to lift. My thoughts were jagged and disjointedly sharp: and all my feelings and perceptions seemed reduced to broken mush.

I don't know how long I lay there, in pain and in the dirt, while the world swam as a meaningless mass of indistinct shapes: but bright and clear enough to make my eyes hurt. After a while which could have been just moments, or could have been an ice age of the earth, a blurry figure became clearer in my vision, but not quite enough for me to recognise. I wondered distantly whether it was my older sister or brother who had come back to torment me further. It was probably my older sister I thought distantly. Much as my older brother enjoyed hurting me he did grow bored with the repetition of it after a while. My elder sister's hatred for me was far deeper, she thrived on my pain the same way a sadist thrives on picking the legs off a stick insect or spider, or the way that a vampire thrives on the taste of blood. No matter how much she hurt me it would never come close to satisfying her hunger, no more than throwing fresh fuel on a fire would ever extinguish it.

But in actual fact it was neither of my elder siblings: it turned out to be someone quite different. There was no laughter before my elder siblings started kicking me to renew my pain, but instead a small uncertain voice asked anxiously. "Kiss it better?" Then its owner kissed my cheek. Nothing should have happened. To be able to perform instantaneous healing was something even powerful white wizards usually needed to be in at least their late teens to attempt. Even then they would have needed direct physical contact with where I was hurt: primarily my leg and where my forehead was split and bleeding. Even a fully trained adult white wizard would have struggled to do anything much simply by just kissing my cheek which: from a healing perspective: was nothing but an unharmed piece of skin connected to the undamaged inside of my mouth.

But white light flashed at the small voice's command: impossible though that should have been. But then, this child's magic was even at this age already pushing all limits. Bright light, the same power and glory of the morning sun, struck me directly on the chest. And the next moment my head was clear, the pain had gone and the bleeding had been very firmly stopped indeed. What was wrong with me had literally been commanded out of existence. "All right now?" asked the small voice anxiously. I looked up at the source of the sound, through a vision which was no longer broken and swirling but was instead suddenly completely and absolutely crystal clear. I saw a small child, no more than two, smiling nervously at me. She was dressed in red trousers and a red t-shirt with the picture of a red-haired superhero on it. She, alongside my mum, was one of the only two people in this world who made me smile. And soon, as the warmth and haze of what was left of my childhood faded, she would be the only one. I was twelve, and the only friend I had at that age, the only friend I had ever had up to that point, was a two year old.

"Hey Vicky." I said, in a soft voice full of warmth and affection. "All better thank you. And it did hurt a lot before."

Vicky beamed. Even at that age she loved being helpful, and especially when it involved sorting things out for her favourite brother. "You come help me climb?" she asked, "want go to top, but scary!" For a moment the world shook, and my arms went rigid once more. The image of the rope ladder hung before my head like a fallen star, and the image of a huge, monstrously grown, tree on which every step took me higher up: and so made the fall that bit more dangerous, that bit longer. I bit on my lip, so hard that it bled, having to fight with everything I had to stop the scream that came with the fear of falling once more. But Vicky had helped me, and I did not want to be unfair to her. "Okay." I forced myself to say, and stood up and started walking, a little shakily, towards the big tree once more.

Vicky yanked my arm demandingly, pulling me in the opposite direction. I would have said it was with all the imperiousness that only a two year old can muster, but her decisiveness: or bossiness depending upon how you looked upon it I suppose: would only grow with her age. "Not want to climb big stupid tree! That is a very silly thing to climb! Nowhere near the play area!'' she said. ''Want to climb Rope Mountain! That much more exciting! That at the centre of the play area!''

''Vicky what is Rope Mountain?'' I began, but she was already dragging me out from under the tree's rich green canopy and back into the open sunlight that fell onto the park beyond. We came out from under the leaves and Vicky stopped, gazing upwards adoringly. ''Rope Mountain!'' she whispered, almost shyly. It took me a moment to blink the sun out of my eyes and then I finally saw what she meant.

We were at the edge of the play park. Behind us it gave way to the copse of big trees that stood between us and the car park. In front of us a set of ropes had been set up attached around a central pole. It formed a triangle shape, with the steel pole at the centre running at exactly ninety degrees to the ground and its top forming the upmost point of the triangle, and the ropes building up to it in ever shrinking horizontal circles with sloped vertical ropes running in between them.

Vicky walked over to the bottom of Rope Mountain and reached her hands up, then stopped shyly, and I saw what her problem was. Her hands didn't reach to the circle of rope so she could pull herself up and start climbing: because she was nowhere near tall enough. I walked up beside her, and stopped, swallowing. For whatever reason, whatever trick of fate: perhaps the construction of ropes had been covered to protect it from the rain, perhaps the sun fell more directly on this part of the park: the ground here was baked hard and rigid. Falling onto the ground here from any height at all beyond the very smallest would really hurt. Not that Rope Mountain was that high for a twelve year old at the moment: but if I was on it and Jacob decided to make Rope Mountain grow… I hesitated, the swaying fear of falling sickening in my gut once more.

Then Vicky reached across and touched where I had bitten my lip. "Bleeding!" she said distressedly. There was a flash of light and the pain and blood were gone. And her concern and care made up my mind. It was rare indeed that anyone expressed any affection for me. I would never risk doing anything that might lose me my little sister's love.

I pulled myself up onto the first circle of rope, easy with my longer arms, then held my arms down until Vicky seized my hands tightly so that I could pull her up after me. She scrambled up eagerly. I saw the sign. Children must be at least four years old and above this height: diagram with an arrow: to play on this attraction. But I ignored it. I was twelve and well beyond the age where the challenge of Rope Mountain would have even interested me let alone threatened me. Vicky was not only half as young but also about half as tall as was remotely safe. Even with me guiding her it was still dangerous for her to be trying to climb this. But we were a team, used to working together as our grey and white magic seemed so naturally just to click. Even though all the textbooks that we had drummed into us at school insisted that that was absolutely impossible, that white and grey magic were complete opposites. The white an epiphany of all that was good in this world, the grey the clearest demonstration possible of all that was twisted and foul.

We went up slowly: but surely. For Vicky it was a truly stretching adventure, well outside her comfort zone. Which meant that it really excited her, already she burned with the desire to achieve things. To push herself beyond all known and all safe limits. She was young: but not too young to know fear. But even by that very young age she wanted not to hide from things that were difficult and scary, as all are taught to do in the civilised world, but to face anything that seemed to her difficult and challenging until she had utterly overcome it, at which point all her interest in it would be instantly and completely lost. With a very determined look on her face my little sister reached up her arms towards me each time we needed to get across a gap in the ropes. Then, when her arms were locked in mine, she pushed herself forward with her feet, driving herself upwards across gaps between the ropes almost twice as tall as she was. Each time she hurled herself through the air, trusting absolutely in my strength to support her, each time the gap between us and the ground grew greater. Each time I got her up to the next level she screamed with delight and squeezed my hands. This was not the first time we had worked together, although this was far more dangerous than just trying to help her get across a set of monkey bars, or trying to do a complete and safe three hundred and sixty degree circle on a swing.

Up and up we went, until the ground was further and further away. Then I was standing on the highest rope of Rope Mountain: Vicky's final goal. Distantly I could see the relatively far off ground but I barely even thought about it. All I wanted was for my little sister to be happy, for her to get to the top. The last gap was even bigger than the others.

I looked at her: concerned and nervous. For her, not for myself. "This is a really big gap Vicky." I said cautiously, hoping for common sense to restrain the excesses of her enthusiasm, "and there's only really space for one person to stand on the top rope." That was one other thing the sign at the bottom of the climbing ropes that I had ignored had said. "Only one child may safely be at the top of this climbing apparatus at any one time. Otherwise, there is a very real danger of falling and serious physical injury, especially for younger children."

"So you need to do a really big push down with your legs to get as much force upwards as you can," I said anxiously, "and then I will hurl you up out of my arms and then catch you as you fall back down. You ready?" I tried not to think about the danger Vicky was now in, of which I was far more terribly aware now than she was. I didn't even let my thoughts start to go to what would happen to Vicky if I failed to catch her. If she fell: all the way down from the top of Rope Mountain.

Vicky looked up at the big gap ahead of her, and gulped, then she squeezed my hands hard. She knelt down, balancing as expertly on the rope she stood on as if she had been climbing all her life. She leapt, and I hurled her upwards. It would have been no great leap for a man or woman, no record breaker, no championship winner: but it was a leap into danger by a two year old who was old enough to know fear: and both brave and wild enough to hurl herself on regardless. And for me it would have been no great hurl for an adult athlete, no feat of strength of weight lifting that would have been remarked upon in a professional full-time championship. But for a twelve year old it was a feat of strength that should have been almost beyond the limits of his slight frame: everything going into rising up the person in the world whom he most cared about. She hurled into the air, a blaze of red in the rising sun. Her hair shone like fire and the blush of the dawn: and her eyes glowed with a fire that the civilised world has feared since it was young. The fire of the gods. The fire of the barbarian. Danger and glory mixed together, a fire that could burn away the very centre of the civilised world. There is a very real reason why the civilised world does not want grey and white wizards to mix.

Vicky landed in my arms and I shook with the impact and swayed, the ground swirling around me as I fought for balance with the new weight in my arms. While above me Vicky cried out in triumph, seeing only her victory and not the very real danger of us falling. "I queen of the world! On top of everything!'' she yelled out, in complete and utter childlike triumph. We were both on the top of Rope Mountain, with nothing around us but empty air, but I managed to stabilise us: and within moments she was as secure in my arms as if she had been in a playroom protected by lock and key. She could no more fall from my arms than my heart could fall from my chest.

My little sister screamed out in toddler triumph, and the magic in the cry was so strong that the wind whipped up around her, hurling around us so that her cheeks flushed and her hair danced in the rushing blasts of air. Even young adult wizards would have been envious of how effortlessly and freely Vicky called upon magic, of how easily her power flowed. ''Look, look everyone! I on top of Rope Mountain! Mummy, daddy come see! Everyone come see!'' She called out, both completely happy and completely demanding at the same time. Her voice carried out far over the howling air, as she called out eagerly for adult attention and appreciation. There was a long moment when only the wind blew and the leaves moved and Vicky looked around impatiently: wanting some important looking adult to tell her really, really well done. Haven't you done well in climbing up so high?

My father came racing out from under the trees, with my mum behind him. When she saw what was happening she raised a hand to her mouth in horror and went white. My father's look went very dark: a fury I knew only too well already bursting over his pleasant surface façade as he saw something that dared to threaten his great self-pride and ever present sense of complete self-importance.

''Edward!'' he yelled furiously. ''Get your sister down here this instant. Don't you know how dangerous that is? Can't we even trust you for one...'' At this age, even though I expected it by now, his opinions and statements still really hurt. I felt my calmness and my control, a moment ago so completely clear, start to shake a little. And where I was currently standing that could soon turn very dangerous.

Vicky wriggled frantically in my arms, distressed not to be getting the reaction that she wanted so badly. "But daddy can't you see?" she inquired anxiously, suddenly squirming dreadfully. "I'm on top of the...". It wasn't her squirming that caused me the worst problems though, tricky though that made our position and balancing. It was her sudden switching of her attention from me to him: to her wretched daddy. It was the sudden rise of the black despair of jealousy that turned our position on the top of Rope Mountain from one of perfect safety, to one that was very dangerous indeed.

And then, in the middle of a strong wind and holding a living, writhing, restless bundle in my arms, I fell.

Everything went very slow and very still. There was a slow eternity in which we fell together, far from the pole, tumbling together in each other's arms, down, down towards the ground below. In a few moments of absolute quiet, in which it felt that nothing moved but us and it seemed that all the rest of the world had just gone away, Vicky and I fell together towards the ground. She looked at me as we fell, and there was no anger in her eyes, just surprise that something had gone wrong. And as we fell she slid underneath me, and with my weight bearing down on her I had all the time in the world to realise just how badly my little sister would be hurt when we hit the ground, the weight of my body breaking her against the hard surface of the earth.

When I had fallen from the growing tree earlier the stillness of my descent had brought me nothing but time in which to accept my fate. In a world where I was constantly tormented and teased why do anything to struggle against the inevitable. Why struggle against the fact that life would be nothing but more pain? Already at some level I knew that, like a weed surrounded by beautiful flowers in a gardener's favourite patch of garden: the most beautiful flower bed that is always the first point of any display: I stood no real chance of making it in this life. Had I been born into the working classes I might have managed an existence as a grey wizard of a sort, the same way that weeds can flourish on motorway verges, far from the prestigious eyes of any who care. But being born as such a powerful grey wizard in the heart of the proud upper middle class of this corrupt society, long since grown stagnant and stale, I already knew was an effective death sentence. From the moment I had been born it had never really been a question of whether I would fall but simply of how long it was that I would last.

But this time as I fell though the stillness I realised with absolute and utter clarity just how much I loved my little sister: and that if she was hurt today it would be because she had put her trust in me. Because she had chosen me: not mummy or daddy or anyone else: to be the best person to help her climb Rope Mountain. And in a world of all the horror of civilisation grown decadent: that mocks even the idea that anything could possibly be really wrong with it with the phrase, "First World Problems!": that rejected me just for being who I was, my little sister was my only friend, the only person who really cared about me. And the only person who had ever really cared about me.

So this time I did not accept my fate. Instead, for her sake, I physically screamed as I reached out and tore the power of grey magic into me. I flooded with power and I faded. Not the ground, which would have sent us crashing only deeper into the earth and hurt us both even more: but especially Vicky. Nor did I fade the air around us, which would have merely strangled us, ripping vacuums into our lungs. Instead I faded the very power of gravity itself as it worked on us, bearing us down hard into the earth. I faded it so that we hung in mid-air, suspended in nothing, while my little sister looked up at me. In that moment of perfect calm the wind danced with us, and the small "o" of surprise on Vicky's lips turned to a giggle of delight that came from deep inside her. My little sister's red hair flowed in the wind and her eyes were dancing. No one had ever seemed to me more beautiful. "Love you big brother." she whispered.

And we hung there for a moment snatched out of eternity, a moment of magic snatched out of time, in which there was nothing else that mattered anywhere except the fact that we were together: and that we both loved each other very much. That moment of it being just the two of us was the first moment of perfect happiness that I had ever experienced in my life. We had each other: what need was there to let anything else from the rest of the world in? We were all the other needed: all that the other would ever need. Then at last: having no other choice: I relaxed the magic and let us gently float down to the ground unharmed: wishing we could just have stayed like that: suspended alone together in our love: forever.

My father screamed at me for several hours afterwards: but it was totally worth it.

Chapter 2

When the gods threw the dice to determine my starting lot in life my genetic heritage of power drew as good a score as my environment drew a bad. Whether or not you can use magic and the extent of the potential of your power is as genetically determined as your eye colour or the size of your hands. But in terms of drawing out your potential who is to say what type of environment is really the best? A rewarding loving one that brings out all your natural talents and abilities is what most would claim. Yet when the role of environments in bringing the best out of people has been tested objectively in the laboratory, unclouded by the unscientific mist and fog of love, the loving supportive type of environment only ever wins the silver medal.

What takes gold? Well when they tested rats the best type of environment of all turned out to be feeding them the absolute minimum amount of sustenance, far below the recommended minimum level needed for good health and growth, for them to have any chance at all of survival. Most of the rats died of course, others went mad or blind. But those that survived to hit puberty then lived twice as long, aging twice as slowly, as their happier and more conventionally raised silver medal brethren. Managing to survive on so little for so long had made the physical systems of the gold medal rats literally twice as strong as their well looked after brethren. And as I survived my environment in the end, who is not to say that in terms of bringing out my magic power what was intended and seemed like the very worst possible environment for me, as bad as a seed landing on thin layers of dirt and ash rather than on rich and deep healthy soil, was actually really the best possible combination after all?

However if we are looking at it conventionally I would have claimed that my environmental starting lot in life, even with the mainly ineffectual and quite shallow love of my mum, was in many ways around as bad as it could get except for that fact that I got Vicky. Many people go their whole lives without ever having something that special. So how then do I place any kind of overall value or summary at all on the whole? No easy verdict or conclusion could ever reflect the experience of growing up in a world where I had no friends except my younger sister, and all adult figures outside my family despised me. My elder siblings made it very clear they wished I didn't exist and my father hated me: but I had the love of the most special and beautiful girl in the whole wide world.

However in a weird way Vicky is also the only reason that I would have to settle for getting only a really very, very good verdict for my level of inbuilt magical power: whereas without her around no one would have questioned that my inbuilt talents were extraordinary.

My father was a very gifted wizard who used his power to make lots and lots of money for himself working in the Wizard of Many Colour's civil service. He was a highly paid middle ranking functionary but his rise from a poor working class background had left him with deep delusions of self-congratulation and grandeur. Having established a local environment where his word was law and no one dared to contradict him: basically because he was the boss: he had come to believe that the rest of the world only ever had difficulties because it did not also just revolve entirely around his opinions. He had wealth and relatively high status, but outside his local area of competence no real political power. He told stories about the meetings he had gone to, filled with important people: but of course also nothing but hot air until HE had started to speak and set everyone at that meeting very straight. Of course he was not self-aware enough to realise that the very senior governmental administrators had simply listened to him in barely polite silence, and then just ignored everything that he had said.

My mum was a good to very good wizard, who came from reliable middle class stock. She took a part-time administrative role in local government which brought in a steady second income and gave her time to focus on raising her family. Her first child was a boy, Jacob: a brown wizard who was very gifted and talented. But her second child, a girl, Jessica, wasn't really gifted or talented at all. She could sort of scrape by, only not really that well by middle class standards. Few doubted that Jacob, the first child, would grow up to make a very fine brown wizard; but no one was really sure that Jess was going to have the ability to hold down the sort of job that every middle class wizard was supposed to want. It was difficult enough for her being so overshadowed by her elder sibling even before her younger two were born. But at least both Jacob's brown and Jess's blue magic were respected forms of power, both recognised as leading to valid positions in society. Then I was born, the most gifted grey wizard in ten thousand years: and if my father could have got away with it he would have had me drowned at birth. The level of power I had been born with would have been great, if not for the fact that middle class society despised the ambiguous power of grey magic more than anything else in this life. The very nature of grey magic had a terrible tendency to constantly show the corrupt nature of the emptiness that lay behind the civilised façade of a stagnant civilisation and society. The shame and loss of prestige for my parents and family at my birth was devastating. For grey wizards desire nothing more in this life than the solving of very difficult problems, while all of the highest culture of society is based on their being no problems left to solve. The top levels of civilisation are always by definition perfect, everyone at the highest levels always thinks so.

And then she was born; my little sister. And Vicky's white magic power put even the strength of my grey magic far into the shade. And that was a massive relief to my parents, for white magic was the exact opposite of grey, the highest regarded and most respected power in all the land. For white is the power of implementation, and what could be more glorious than the ever more effective implementation of the ideas that everyone agreed were already utterly fantastic: everyone who was important anyway. And even the Great Wizard of Many Colours who ruled the state of Britain acknowledged that one day Vicky's power would far outstrip his own.

The first time my elder sister's friends drove my head under the surface of my parents' fishpond it was just for fun: they weren't intending to kill me. I mean if it had happened they wouldn't have been too bothered, but it would be pushing it to try and identify it as attempted murder. Jess was fifteen, I was fourteen: Vicky was now four. After a couple of moments when lights swam before my eyes a pressure grew painfully in my chest, spreading fast to hurt me everywhere. Then the teenagers holding my head down threw me out of the water and onto the grassy side: laughing while I gasped retching for breath.

My older brother Jacob, eighteen, looked out at me from the window of where he was studying for his public exams, smirked for a moment, then turned back with a complete loss of interest to his studies. It wasn't that Jacob didn't like hurting me anymore. It's just that he had gradually grown bored with oversaturation of it and felt that he now had more important things to be doing. This just made my elder sister madder than ever, as about her only way of bonding with him had been to hurt me. She had not realised that he had already decided I wasn't likely in the long run to survive her repeated attentions, and wanted to be distant enough from what was now happening that no one could ever accuse him of having got his hands dirty with my blood. Pleased as he would be to see me dead he really wouldn't want any funny business that could possibly tarnish his utterly immaculate academic record.

I lay there gasping on the side of the grass, smeared with mud and shame, already knowing not to fight back or to go to my mum. If I fought back I would only bring on one of my father's rages for bringing shame on my family, for using grey magic. And anger at me fighting back would only make my sister and her friends and boyfriend attack me even harder. And if I ever used grey magic as a direct offensive weapon the law very clearly demanded an almost instant death sentence. If I tried to talk to my mum there would be tears and distress, but then my father would sit her down and talk to her, and with his charm and so convincing salesman words everything would be turned back around into my fault. To him I was everything that was wrong in a child. The foul black sheep in his otherwise absolutely splendid family.

I'd hoped my sister and her friends would lose interest in playing around with attempting to drown me after a while, when I reacted as little as possible. The same way that I had starved their previous tortures of energy by minimising my reaction as much as I could. But I found it impossible to be unresponsive to the pain of nearly drowning: it hurt and scared me in a way that nothing else they had previously done had. I never knew how much it was my frantic struggles underwater, while lights danced before my eyes and the pressure tightened everywhere around me into pain, that amused my tormentors; or whether Jess's new boyfriend, Mike, the leading candidate to be head boy at her prestigious private school, just particularly hated grey wizards. Either way he couldn't stand how the prestige of dating Jess, a stunningly beautiful girl with an immaculate family background, was so fouled by the very talented young grey wizard who dared to have been born as her brother. But either way bullying, or any form of sadism and inflicting pain on others, always has to be stepped up to stay entertaining: and the amount of time my head was held very firmly down under the surface of the fish pond water became longer and longer.

It was on the fifth drowning game when I realised that if I didn't get air the pressure inside me was about to explode open my mouth and my lungs would flood with water as I died. Grey magic tore into me and in desperation I FADED. A whole chunk of reality disappeared as though it had never been. The next moment the pressure was gone, and the next after that I was vomiting into the blessed taste of fresh air while all around me laughter swirled. But although I could now breathe everything still grew dark and I fell through pain and sickness into empty blackness.

When I woke up my chest and lungs were still on fire and I could smell the aridness of my own vomit all around me, where I had been left to lie in it. I could taste strong acid in my mouth and half-digested macaroni cheese. I had been left alone and completely vulnerable where I could have chocked to death on my own sick. I realised with a dull dread in my chest what I had buried deep, deep, down for weeks now. Jess and her friends really didn't care whether their fun killed me or not. Either way they were cool. And so was the world I thought sickly. My mum would cry for me but nothing else would happen and that would be that. No one wanted to be the one to actually kill the weed themselves, but all would rejoice in its fall. I found myself absently wondering what my elder sister would do with her life once the main driving source for her hate was gone.

Despair then took me, and I lay there broken in my own vomit: too hurt and drained even to move until the light faded from the sky into night. After many dark hours which seemed to have no end, sleep finally took me. I dreamed strange dreams: deep and dark. Dreams of an old one-eyed man with a terrible spear that when he wished it looked no more than a harmless stick: and who knew more of the secrets of the world than I had imagined could ever possibly exist. And other dreams. Dreams of a young woman with a deadly bow and even more dangerous silver arrows. The huntress of the moon. She was very beautiful and her wide eyes were the brightest blue I had ever seen: outshining by far the cloudless, sunny mid-day sky.

"Why you sleep there?" asked a curious young voice. "Where fishpond go?".

I opened my eyes to meet the curious gaze of a four year old, whose red hair glowed in the morning sun. Shafts of molten golden light dancing through and inside her hair into the utter stillness of the early morning. She was astonishing beautiful and even more powerful. She had none of the huntress's eeriness: she didn't need it. She simply made up for the lack with sheer, raw magical strength. The brutal force of almost insanely strong white magic that she had at her command.

"I'm tired." I said weakly. "Jess and her friends tried to drown me in the fishpond, so I got rid of it."

Vicky looked at me horrified, her green eyes wide with sudden terror. "Drown you dead!" she cried, "No that is mean! That is nasty! And who I play with if you die? No one else exciting like you. They all treat me like young baby!"

"It's okay," I said weakly, finding with her nearby the strength to finally sit up. "I've faded the fishpond out of existence haven't I? There is nowhere for them to drown me now!" I managed not to think about the uses Jess could make of a toilet, a bath or a sink.

Vicky looked at me wild-eyed. "But Uncle Ian having swimming birthday party!!!" she cried out in panic. "Swimming pool very deep. Mummy not even let me near the deep end!"

Which is why you spend all your time in the swimming pool thinking about that deep end, I thought distantly. The moment you see a challenge in front of you you find it impossible to think about anything else.

I managed to smile at her. "There'll be lots of people near the swimming pool at the party when we go there. I'm sure I'll be okay."

"Will be okay." said Vicky thickly, tears trickling down from her eyes as she started to cry. "I will look after you. I cross my heart and promise lots and lots." And she stepped close and put her arms around me. And I realised as she held me, uncaring of the vomit and stench that covered me, that there was one person in this world who still loved me: and who was strong.

It was almost one week later that my Uncle Ian threw his fiftieth birthday bash: and he would very soon regret that he'd decided what he'd really wanted to have was an indoor pool party. Of course it wasn't a pool party in the way a child's party would be a pool party: where you would go swimming and try to scramble over obstacles on floating islands and throw inflated balls at one another. It was a pool party basically in the fact that the adults would stand talking around the pool and encourage the children and teenagers to have a go in it. Probably later, after the children and teenagers were no longer around, the adults would then make a great show of jumping into the water in all their clothes. But poor old Uncle Ian's birthday party never got that far: although at least it would be an event that no one ever forgot: admittedly not in a way anyone would have ever supposed he would have ever wanted or intended.

Even at that age I hated parties. I never knew how to make polite conversation, and hated the way that those who considered themselves to be the best people would listen to me in barely polite silence: wanting me just to be gone so that the taint of associating with me didn't risk adversely affecting their social standing. All the time that I tried to talk to anyone I would know that they were all just waiting for me to leave. Vicky was busy playing with friends her own age and I didn't really want to spend my time at a party with a bunch of very young children, so I was just swimming up and down at the end of the pool, counting the time until I could just go somewhere quiet to sit down and read. Somewhere away from the company of people who really didn't like me: which meant somewhere away from pretty much everyone. I really didn't think I was in any risk of being drowned at such a public event, not when it would be so much easier for Jess and Mike to get rid of me in quiet. I had sort of vaguely noticed that I kept seeing Vicky nearby, but hadn't really thought much about it. I would have been touched if I had realised her fear of me being drowned in the swimming pool was making sure that she kept a keen eye on me.

I would have been shocked to know that Mike had come to the party that night fully intending to drown me in the swimming pool: that he came to Uncle Ian's fiftieth birthday bash with the clear intention of premeditated murder. He'd simply had enough of his girlfriend being related to a grey wizard. I know Jess encouraged Mike to hurt me throughout their relationship but I never knew whether she realised he actually intended to kill me that night, or if she just wanted to have fun by seeing me in so much pain. Probably to be honest: she just really didn't care. Perhaps I was naïve to spend so long swimming alone in the pool but I was far more terrified of being drowned in a bath or toilet. I couldn't believe that I would be dunked and drowned where everyone could see. While I knew that whenever I was alone I was vulnerable I had not thought enough about the fact that people will spread weed killer on their front lawns quite openly in public, happy for everyone to see. Sometimes younger children see the truth far more clearly than those who confidently think they are old enough to know what is really going on.

Either way it was stupid that I risked swimming in the deep end. But then, did I really want to spend the night swimming around in the shallows with all the younger children? I hated being called weak and pathetic enough as it was. And did I want the fear of being hurt to start to take over every decision that I ever made in my life? Either way, in the end the dramatic events of that night all happened very fast.

I drew up at the end of yet another length of the pool, absolutely stupidly in the corner of the swimming pool above the deepest part of the deep end. "Hey Edward!" said my elder sister, and I jerked in surprise at seeing her standing so close to me right next to the edge of the pool. She was speaking in that syrupy sweet voice that always meant that things were about to get really bad for me really quickly. "Did you miss us?"

I took hold of the safety steel rail that was across the edge of the pool and gripped it like death. I should have fled in that instant as fast as I could, using grey magic to fade myself invisible and intangible. But this direct attack in public did what very few things over the previous years had managed to do, and caught me by surprise. I curled up like a hedgehog would do on a motorway road as the bright car lights descended. My sister was wearing a tight revealing blue swim suit that both matched the colour of her blue trickster style magic and that I had recently begun to recognise was both provocative and attention seeking. When I was younger I had only recognised that it was the sort of outfit she wore when she wanted to spur on her current boyfriend to hurt me even more.

"Us?" I asked: warily. I glanced around uneasily and saw, near the other end of the swimming pool, my little sister laughing and paddling in the shallows with her friends. I caught her eyes, terror in my face, and saw only how far away she was. And I felt both terror and guilt that I was looking to my little sister to protect me: a perversion of the fact that at fourteen I should be looking out for my four year old sister, not the other way around. My gaze hesitated on her for only a split second before tearing away as I spun in panic trying to find Jess's friends. And then I heard the splash as a heavy figure dropped down into the water behind me.

"Yes." said the voice of Mike, the teenager who wanted to be head boy, the boyfriend who hated the fact his girlfriend had an embarrassing grey wizard little brother so fucking much. "Forget about me?" he snarled, "cause everyone's about to forget about you forever. The only sad part about all this is that I only get to kill you once. God I wish I could get to drown you over and over again."

I seized grey magic even as his hand came over my head and pushed it below the waterline. I knew in a single moment: at the sound of his voice even before I heard the words he spoke: knew at some deep instinctive level that he was going to try to kill me. I thought I was ready, and let loose the power of my grey magic even as he struck. I could not attack him directly, not unless I wanted to be arrested and then executed. This restriction meant that I had no chance in direct combat with the power of a sixteen year old wizard two years older than me who was half white and half brown. Powered by the brown magic that boosted his muscles with hugely reinforced natural strength and the raw power of the white magic that burned around his hands my slender boy's body could no more have resisted the relentless hand that drove my head underwater than the dust can stand before the wind. But I blasted out the grey into fading the water of the swimming pool, and for a moment the entire level of the swimming pool dropped even as my head descended and I thought that I was safe. But my elder sister and Mike had learned from the fishpond experience. There would be no draining my way to safety this time. Jess's blue magic, the magic of illusion and trickery, leapt up; so that what all everyone else in the pool and around me saw, including all the prestigious wizards standing chatting and drinking and feeling very self-important around the pool's edge, was some stupid grey wizard mucking about and spoiling the fun of the pool party for everyone. A chorus of protest and disapproval went up all around the room, and from a dozen separate places magic of pretty much all colours except grey and black leapt, and the water suddenly wasn't draining any longer. I couldn't fight the power of nearly twenty wizards at once. In the last moment before Mike's arm drove my head below the surface all I could think of was that I'd drained enough that I'd have been okay if I'd stayed in the shallow end. My desire not to seem weak had allowed Mike and Jess this chance to kill me.

My head went under water, bright lights flashed above the surface, so close but so far out of reach; and an all too familiar pressure began to build in my lungs for what I already knew would be the final time. Pain and panic spread everywhere as I thrashed about uselessly: trying desperately to get a grip on something, anything. There was nothing. And the worse thing was: even in all the pain of beginning to die: that I knew, even as a child, that Mike would get away with it. "Just a bit of childish dunking gone wrong." the official report afterwards would read. "Mike certainly deserves a most severe slap on the wrist!" There'd be a lot of finely worded formal phrases, some colourful but irrelevant prestigious examples of general principles and the report would conclude, with the complicated language heavily disguising the brutal and obvious truth, what has happened is okay because Mike is a person like us and Edward is not. Mike would probably only get to be deputy head boy rather than head boy: just being careful while the whole nasty business tidied itself over until it could just be forgotten. Then he would go on to a successful career after graduating from a prestigious university with a first and a blue: by which time this unfortunate incident would have long since just faded into irrelevance. And all the while my dead face would rot a very different kind of blue.

And all for this would have happened, save for one thing I had just done. One momentary glance that would save my life, and in so doing: in the end: change the fate of the entire British nation. And many that have now died would instead have lived: and some that would have died now still draw breath instead. But overall many more would still now be in the world of the living had I never breathed again after Mike drove my head beneath the water.

I had turned my eyes instantly from Vicky after she had seen my look of pure terror, so I did not see what she started doing the next moment, my gaze already turned away to search for my attackers.

But the multiple reports and investigations written afterwards all described what Vicky did next with unbelievable clarity and complete and deadly accuracy. After all, if those in charge of us do have one skill it is the ability to push around finally written pieces of important looking paper.

When Vicky saw the terror in my face all the light and laughter in her voice faded away and her smile died on her lips. She went in an instant from a happy bubbly four year old to as white as a sheet. But what she did was oh so terribly calm. She had been thinking about me being drowned for nearly a week after all. She slid off her float and took hold of the metal poolside steps and, very fast, climbed out onto the side of the pool, white magic spinning around her in a cold and deadly rage. Aunty Rachael turned to her and sighed, "Now Vicky you were doing so well in the pool, being such a good girl, and now your being silly running…"

But Vicky, who normally loved nothing more than doing exactly what she was told by important looking people, simply flicked her fingers and Aunty Rachael went flying. She hit the wall of the swimming pool room so hard that it was two years until she walked without crutches again. Vicky just walked on, barely even noticing what she had just done, with eyes that blazed with a white light that saw through Jess's illusions the way the naked eye can see though transparent glass. Two more adults tried to stop her. Both had quite powerful magic. Both got badly hurt. Then Vicky reached where I was drowning.

Jess looked at her in surprise. "Vicky, what are you…" Vicky backhanded her across the face with a crack of white magic, and Jess fell like a disjointed poleaxe, blood spurting from her shattered jaw. Mike looked up at my little sister in shock.

"Put my brother out of the pool." snarled Vicky, shaking with so much anger that she barely sounded human, and her words cracked with lightning as she gave out her implacable command. The air itself smelt charred and in places the side of the swimming pool burnt black. Around all was chaos and confusion as wizards of all the different colours of magic panicked, trying to shelter their own children, trying to tend to the wounded. All this meant that for a few moments Vicky, the centre of the storm, was left completely alone: with no fussing adult to try and stop what she had come to do: no fussing adult to try and stop her from saving my life: whatever the cost.

Mike looked up to face Vicky. And his lips curled as he gathered shields of power around himself. "I'm the most powerful wizard in my year at school and you're just a stupid kid." he began, his voice arrogant as always and completely cocksure. "Your brother is just an embarrassment who…"

And Vicky just put her right hand through his shields as though they weren't even there: they simply exploded away at the strength of the lightning in her touch. Mike screamed as her fingers touched his forehead and every nerve in his body went slack: below the waterline his grip on my head broke and I surfaced from the pool, gasping for breath.

There was a sudden and terrible silence all around the room as Vicky, with just the edges of the fingernails of one hand, raised up a fully grown muscular sixteen year old by his hair, raising him high out of the swimming pool. All around eyes gazed in shock and stunned inaction as a furious four year old held up a shaking teenager's head before her face. And in her eyes there was no trace of mercy as she passed her childlike certain judgement on the man who was trying to hurt her big brother.

Her free hand hit him. And the force of the magic blasting into Mike could be felt by everyone in the room: even the sides of the swimming pool shook. He was almost certainly killed outright by that blow. But Vicky's terrible anger had not even begun to be sated. She hit him again, even harder, and then again: one last time: with all the force of childish fury exploding in her magic. Then Vicky simply dropped the smoking remnants of Mike: that could perhaps very loosely be described as just about intact enough to be a wrecked corpse: and turned very calmly towards Jess. In that moment my little sister was utterly determined to punish both of the bad people who had hurt her brother just the same. Jess brought up her magical shields with a scream of pure terror.

It was then that four adults seized Vicky from behind, blasting her in magic of blue and brown, red and white. Magic swirled around the five as Vicky was dragged backwards, kicking and screaming and raging like a wild thing: cheated of her vengeance. All the adults involved in subduing her suffered severe burns that took months to heal. But they were skilled and strong, and there were more coming from behind and so, for all Vicky's snarls and screams of fury and rage, order was being ruthlessly restored. The incident was coming under control, medical assistance was being summoned, and some thoughts were already beginning to turn to the mountain of paperwork that this shocking and unexpected incident would generate.

In all of this I was quite forgotten, just left gasping air in and water out by the side of the pool. Wizards that mattered had been hurt and one, Mike, even killed. What hope did I have of getting any attention? I had crawled out and just lay on the side of the pool, trying to take in the fact that I was somehow still alive. I distantly wished I could do something to help Vicky, who had just saved my life like an avenging little angel, but I was currently retching up too much pain and chorine to do anything besides feel sick. So much was going on that no one noticed when an old man in a cloak sat down next to me. A man in a dark cloak and with a smile that never touched his eye. Its pupil was a solid black, surrounded by a billowing grey. I had only ever seen him before in my dreams. In his hands he carried what looked at first glance like a harmless staff and stick to support his walking but was, in reality, a deadly spear. His voice was utterly calm: his words rang quietly with subtle power.

"By magic and by understanding you have kept yourself alive long after the odds of the fates would have seen you dead and cold Edward. To develop the power to survive what is being done to you, but to know when not to strike and provoke a reaction that would surely end you, that is a rare combination: especially in one so young. You have shown enough spirit and skill to catch my attention: the attention and interest of Odin Allfather: as I wander the cosmos and for the enjoyment that watching you has given me I will reward you with a riddle. For a grey wizard what better reward could there truly be than the most dangerous truth hidden deep inside a most surprising and unexpected question? A question that no one else has ever thought to ask. Take care for this is no idle game. How you answer this riddle will shape the entire rest of your life, for every moment that you draw breath. You do have one advantage to help you though, one unexpected reserve card you have to play. For I am not the only deity whose attention your struggle has drawn. The other's interest is surprising. Let us just say that you are not her usual type. But she will help you out at the last moment. Though when she takes an interest in a man it has historically worked out as more of a curse than a blessing: and who is to say how her interest in you shall ultimately be judged by either of you? But that is a question for another day. Right now here is the riddle whose success must now consume your mind.

One of the most fundamental truths of the world is this Edward. Hate is not the true opposite of love. The true opposite is indifference, a non-reaction, a total lack of caring. Hate and love are just two sides of the same coin: the same reaction with different hues. Only what you truly love can you grow to hate; and only what you hate with every fibre of your being can you grow to love stronger than death. So then, now that you know all that you need to know, should you save your sister? And think fast boy, you have mere seconds to make your choice." And then the next moment he was gone, although I did not see him leave any more than I first saw him appear.

I turned to look at where six magicians were now subduing a still struggling Vicky. The riddle made no sense. Of course I would save Vicky if she got into trouble: I loved her. But I didn't think she needed much saving at the moment: the wizards around her weren't going to hurt her. If I had caused such carnage they might well have decided to take things into their own hands, and no questions would have ever really been asked, but they were dealing with a child white wizard. Hurt her and they would all end up on trial: and in the end quite possibly dead. I glanced quickly at Mike, he would want to hurt Vicky, but he was the very definition of completely dead. He was now nothing more than just fragments of blood and flesh. So I turned my gaze towards Jess and what I saw there caused me to narrow my eyes. She could still well be a threat to Vicky. She was standing up and had wiped the blood from her mouth, but she was otherwise unhurt, and her eyes were torn with rage and grief.

She turned towards where Vicky was still continuing to fight and I readied my magic: ready to fade away in an instant any attack that Jess launched. "You fucking little bitch!" screamed Jess, lost in grief and fury, blue magic whirling around her uncontrollably. "You just killed my boyfriend! Next time I'll make you watch as I drown your stupid brother right in front of you, you stupid fucking cunt..."

The white magic around Vicky simply exploded, and where one moment there had been six strong wizards pretty much wrapping up restraining one little girl, the next there were six helpless adults being hurled across the room like pincushions. One was killed outright and another died from his wounds within days.

"You want kill my brother?!" screamed Vicky, her little body shaking and contorting with a sudden blast of utterly renewed fury. And at her howl the wind leapt up, and lightning tore outside from a cloudless sky. Every window in the swimming pool room shattered and the suddenly raging wind hurled fragments of shattered glass indiscriminately around the room. Wizarding shields went up everywhere and I had to fade several spinning pieces of glass into nothing and was still slightly too slow to get rid of one: which left a nasty cut just under my left eye. Half a centimetre more and it would have half blinded me, but luckily where the shard actually hit it did me no real harm.

Vicky screamed again in pure primal childish fury and another blast of lightning hurled from the heavens. Outside through the broken remnants of the windows you could see expensive cars and, beyond them, farmers' fields burning from where the previous bolts had struck. Screams showed that she had caught people and not just land and property in her fury. Outside the sky shone a lovely clear blue, not a cloud in the sky. People were dying under the beautiful tranquil setting of a perfect summer's day. Another lightning blast tore a hole in the swimming pool ceiling, and masonry and plaster thundered down. But that was just a minor after effect. The bolt slammed through the ceiling into the swimming pool below, blasting magical power and electricity into the water and wizards and children screamed as they were burned or suffered severe electric shock. Many more people were badly hurt: and yes more people died. Including more people who mattered.

My magical shields were up by now and I was out of the swimming pool so my defensive magic easily protected me from this second blast. But, clear though my mind now was as the pain of my near drowning receded, the old man's riddle was making less and less sense. Did I save Vicky? In the next few seconds, save her from what? There was no power I could possibly imagine that could threaten her at the moment, and in the incredible event that one did appear that was that strong to hurt her what exactly could I possibly do about it in any case? Anything strong enough to threaten my little sister at the moment, at the height of her power and fury, would be well beyond anything I had the strength of magic to deal with. The power raged around Vicky in a lightning storm, an untouchable white blaze of death.

I turned my eyes to Jess, who now stood facing her younger sister alone. Vicky had made very short work of anyone who had just tried to restrain her in any way. Jess looked suddenly very small and very vulnerable, and the defences of blue magic she had gathered around herself looked almost pitiful in comparison to the storm of Vicky's fury. There was no way that she was any possible threat to my little sister at the moment. Even the thought was laughable.

Then the second divine power the man in the cloak had talked about intervened. A single shaft of moonlight, so bright and clear it hurt your eyes to look at it as much as staring directly at the sun did, fell down upon Jess: and in that moment I saw the expression on my older sister's face.

There was a terrible calmness in it, and I realised with a sick lurch in my stomach that Jess had realised that she was about to die. People just caught on the edge of Vicky's fury were dying, and Jess had positioned herself dead central. I could not have stood against Vicky's storm of magic and anger, my brother Jacob could not have stood against me, and Jess could not have stood against Jacob. I had always hated Jess, hated the way that she hid behind her boyfriends. Hated the way that she spurred them on, as when she was younger she had spurred on my elder brother. Always she had encouraged and incited others to hurt me: while always keeping her own pretty hands oh so completely clean. Except for the few times when her hate and desire to hurt me took over so much that for a short time she would actually desire the feel of my blood on her fingernails. Faced with death I would have expected Jess to just scream and cry, to beg for mercy: caught out at last like a coward. But instead she stood tall, held her head up high, braced her legs, and faced down death itself with all her power pouring into her magical shields: all her strength going into dying in one last moment of dignity. And I knew in one terrible moment that Vicky was not the one sister that I was being given a chance to save. Of all the people in this room I alone might be able to call out to Vicky and stop her rampage.

But in my very moment of realisation Vicky struck: and the time for words was passed.

For years I had wanted Jess to die. Everyone disliked or hated me, excepting only my mum or Vicky, but out of everyone only Jess dared to take so far into practice the urge to hurt and destroy me that everyone felt. She would persecute me long after all my other tormentors, from my brother to my father to her previous boyfriends, had grown bored and very fed up. There was a consistency and determination to her hatred that terrified me: but which some part of me almost respected. She at least had the courage to act on what she felt, in a world of cruel comments and incessant backbiting from the shadows.

I could see Jess's face in the moonlight, and saw how as death came she gritted her teeth to meet it and gathered all her power around her: the same hope of stopping that strike that a stationary pebble would have of stopping a direct hit from a speeding express train. But the strength I saw made me act.

That, and the weird thought that the best relationship I had in this world was with one sister. Maybe, if hate could turn to love, there was something I could salvage from my relationship with my other sister?

I felt the power of the grey flood me, and let it loose. Vicky's attack fluttered and started to fade into nothing. Some of it also was twisted aside harmlessly as it came across Jess's shields. Vicky started in surprise as she felt me intervening, and I felt her power start to fade away in her confusion. The lightning weakened, and I knew suddenly in that moment if I really pushed that I could use my power to fade away the lightning completely: leaving Jess totally unscathed.

But although I half tried I didn't really want her not to get hurt at all. Part of me was still screaming against the entire fact that that I was saving her. This was a girl who would laugh to see me dead. So although I could have faded all of the lightning, in the end I just couldn't bring myself to push myself hard enough to do it. But I had done enough to save Jess's life: and even as the remnants of the lightning bolt struck home I could hear the laughter of the man in the cloak echoing across the heavens at the answer to his riddle, and heard a loud piercing keen that was the first time I ever heard what I would later realise was Artemis's victory cry.

Jess lived. But she would never use her legs again and she spent the rest of her life in a wheelchair.

Chapter 3

I knocked at the door, the sound clear and hard, but there was no reply. So I knocked again: even more firmly this time.

"Just fuck off." shouted a voice from the other side of it. "I just want to be left alone!". But even the anger and obscenity in the reply was faded and weak: like everything about its owner these days. I sighed. I'd tried playing along with "fuck off" and "go away" and all the other things the owner had hurled at me the past couple of weeks. It wasn't getting me anywhere. So I seized intangibility, fading myself a little, and just walked through the door.

It was the middle of the day but the curtains were still closed. The room smelt, not bad exactly, but not fresh. Musty, with a couple of day's washing all over the floor. Apart from the mess on the floor everything was sickly spartan. Where once the room had been full of girly magazines and new clothes and mounted photos of Jess hanging around with her friends: shopping with daddy's money in expensive clothes stores or at parties where all eyes were on her: there was now nothing. Things had not turned out well for Jess after the incident now recorded in both history and social media gossip as The Pool of Fire and Blood.

The entire driving force behind the official investigation had been the need to apportion blame. Eight people had died, eight prestigious, middle class people, eight people who mattered. And dozens more had been injured, many seriously. By the time Vicky had finished her rampage what had started as a pool party had ended up as bloody as any warzone. Luckily only two victims had suffered injuries severe enough to be what people politely call "life changing". I wasn't sure one of them really counted, the man who had lost his vision in his right eye to a piece of very sharp glass. I would have argued that his injury was "life dehancing" as he could still live a similar life to before: just a limited version of it.

But there was no question that Jess's injuries were in the "life changing class". She couldn't move a muscle below her waist, which meant she had to go everywhere in a wheelchair. Not that she was actually going many places at the moment. It wasn't just her injuries that had proven "life changing". There was also the matter of the report into what had happened and the upper middle class reaction. It had been the only news article anyone had talked about for weeks. Parties and social media had buzzed with furious reaction and everyone had a different opinion on what should have been done and what should be done NOW. There was talk about whether risk assessments for social gatherings needed to be introduced, whether there needed to be stricter educational standards for pre-school children, and a great deal of discussion over whether grey wizards needed to have background checks done before they could go to social gatherings. The fury of opinionated hot air, most of which was just giving people the chance to express their pre-existing opinions rather than having anything particularly to do with The Pool of Fire and Blood, lasted until the witch terrorist attack in London a few weeks later: at which time it was swept off the chattering classes' radar as though it had never been. But it left a lasting distaste behind in its wake, a distaste which had settled on the scapegoat identified in the report published into the event, and which went public while the event was still hot news.

Everyone had expected the scapegoat to be me but: to everyone's surprise including mine and everyone's disappointment except mine: that had proved to be impossible. The problem was simply that the evidence wouldn't support that I'd done anything that would damn me in the eyes of the law: however much it was reworked and looked at. The nice simple verdict of blame and execute the grey wizard that all the officials really wanted to reach was simply not possible in the circumstances. There were literally no relevant facts, however small, to attach that verdict onto. Grey magic had been used only to fade water from a swimming pool and to reduce the power of Vicky's attack on Jess. Also I could clearly be seen to have played no offensive role in any of the bloodshed and carnage at all. Apart from using grey magic defensively all I'd done was look at my little sister in terror at the start of the attack and be held under the water by Mike while he tried to drown me. There was no way this time to twist the victim into being the perpetrator: events had left the bureaucrats with nothing to work on.

But no one was going to be satisfied with blaming a four year old, particularly one who had actually been saving her brother from a very brutal drowning. Mike's role did not look good in the slightest, but he was already dead and no satisfaction or revenge could be had from taking things further. Besides his family was extremely prestigious and for political reasons it was far more expedient to present him as a victim of proceedings rather than as a perpetrator. They'd even built a statue in his honour in his private school carved out of the purest white marble and with a painstakingly beautiful plague written on ivory in his honour. "To all that could have been." The answer which you were supposed to think of was of course yet another highly paid and prestigious bureaucrat: and to forget that another answer was also a murderer.

That left only Jess standing very firmly in the spotlight: and with the anger raging in the upper middle class community about what had happened the report needed someone to vent all that rage onto really rather badly. She ended up as the perfect target. There were several things that damned her. One was that her magical abilities, on the wrong side of strong, weren't anything special among the most powerful wizards of the upper middle class. She was expendable in a way that Vicky just wasn't. Also, while Jess was technically a minor, she was not young enough for her age to protect her in the way that it did my little sister. Fifteen year olds are seen very differently to four year olds. Another factor firmly against Jess was that she had screamed in public at the height of the event that she wanted to see me drowned. Me being drowned privately would have caused nothing but sighs of relief all around, but screaming it out in public... that looked and sounded very bad indeed. Public spaces weren't the place to be saying what you really thought, anyone who was anyone knew that. And then of course there was the fact that she was now in a wheelchair, partially disabled. She simply wasn't what a prestigious wizard firm or young male wizard would really want anymore. Society makes all sorts of noises about inclusivity but when it comes to the truth of personal relations the truth is always very different. When time calls the upper middle class wizarding world can be as ruthless in purging those that were once their own as they can be in purging those that they have considered outsiders from the beginning.

And so Jess who had once been a plant, not the most successful one but nevertheless definitely a plant, became in an instant, and the result of an official enquiry, nothing more than a distasteful weed: one no one wanted to touch or to be anyway near. In many ways it was harder for Jess being a weed than it was for me. She had known what being a plant was like. I had always been a weed from the very beginning. I had known nothing but society's hatred and scorn, but Jess had grown up always being very proud of being part of the in-crowd.

At fifteen she hadn't been given an official criminal record, only because that wasn't legal or possible at that age, but she had numerous, "cautions" on her file, which meant that in practice no school would ever accept her. It would take an awful lot of work to have her on board and would make achieving high marks in their inspections much more difficult. She had of course been expelled from her prestigious private school even before the ink of the signatures on the official investigation was dry. They didn't want anyone in their community mixing with anyone like that. She was legally entitled and obliged to an education so she was supposed to have tutors come to work with her while the necessary fiction of looking for a school that would accept her was maintained.

In practice the tutors turned up for the first month or so, but when Jess didn't come out of her room for them they gradually stopped coming. Now all that happened was that there was a weekly phone call to enquire if Jess would be having any lessons this week, which my father curtly answered with "Jess will not be available for her studies this week. And these calls are a total waste of everyone's time. Especially mine. And my time is very precious." before just hanging up. He'd had all Jess's pictures taken down from around the house too, and forbidden my mum from going to help her. "After what she's done she needs to sort herself out and take some responsibility. She can't possibly expect any help or support from us until she's got herself into a state where she damn well deserves it." If he could have shouted her out of existence I'm sure he would have done so gladly. This was another devastating blow to Jess, who had always thought that she was very close to her father. She had never realised that his expressions of support and love had been totally dependent upon him being proud of her.

Jacob had always had a keen eye for which way the wind was blowing, and could see that being associated with Jess in any way really wouldn't cut the right tone for either his social life or career prospects: and so he just discreetly drifted away. So Jess had also lost the relationship with the brother she had always felt that she was close to. Vicky's behaviour at least could not have been an unpleasant surprise, my little sister had always hated her older one and Vicky was just glad that Jess was now out of her way.

There was no movement from Jess's bed, other than her burying herself deeper beneath her pillow. I turned and walked to the curtains of her room, and pulled them open. The sunlight was bright in the room, sharp and the contrast with the previous dullness almost dazzling. At it the form in the bed gave a little cry. I made myself ignore the slightly pathetic sound. I pushed open the windows to let the air in.

Then I turned around, went back to the bedroom door, and propped it open with a door stop. Then I brought in Jess's new wheelchair, bright and shiny and modern and almost never used. My father had made a great show of buying it as a demonstration of how supportive he was being: before realising the supportive father look wasn't

59

the vogue the society he mixed in wanted right now. As far as I was aware the wheelchair had been used only once, to bring Jess back from the hospital to her room a week after The Pool of Fire and Blood. I moved the door stop and closed the bedroom door behind us to give Jess and I privacy. Then I wheeled the wheelchair up to her bed. It was surprisingly light, although I realised quickly that the wheels were going to play havoc with the carpet. "It's been three months since...since the pool fight." I said. "That's way too long to have spent in bed." I found myself wondering suddenly just what Jess thought about while she hid away in here, her life broken and in a thousand pieces. Here where the difference between hours, days and weeks had ceased to have any real meaning in a constant daze of listless misery.

"Just leave me alone." pleaded a voice from behind the covers. "I just want to be left alone."

"You've been left alone for three months." I said reasonably. "And I don't think it's helping anymore. Let's go out for a walk."

Jess laughed hollowly. "Walk Edward? I'm fifteen and I will never walk again, never feel or move my legs. My little brat of a sister wrecked my lower back so completely that I will never get to go "walking" anywhere ever again."

"Yes," I said slowly, "but you can still feel the sun on your face, the wind in your hair. You can still learn to use your hands to move your wheels and get mobile again. You don't have to spend the rest of your life hiding in your room."

"Oh great," said Jess, "don't worry that everyone now hates me. Don't worry that I will have no career and no one will ever fancy me. Don't worry that I'm disabled and dependent on other people even to get out of bed or get dressed. Hey I can feel the sun on my face, whoop good for me. That's all anyone ever wants out of life isn't it Edward? To wander around outside going, "Oh look how nice the weather is today." "

I felt something inside me grow very cold. "When I was drowning in that swimming pool, when I was so sure that this time I was about to die, one of my last thoughts was of how much I like the feel of the sun, and how I would never get to feel warm again. Had Vicky not saved me I would now have none of those things that you've just taken the piss out of."

Jess pulled down the covers, so that for the first time in three months I saw her face, and looked at me. There was no anger now, just the tiredness and despair of complete inertia. The three months had changed Jess. Before she had been beautiful, her face slim and always tastefully done up with makeup, her skin had almost shone with health and life. Now she was spotty and overweight with inactivity, and her skin had taken on a sallow, oily tone.

"You know, I'm not actually that mad at Vicky anymore. When it first happened all I could do was hate her. She killed my boyfriend, and it was the best relationship I've ever had. And she broke my back. But I've had plenty of time to think Edward, plenty of time to do nothing but think these last three months. More time to think than in the whole of my life so far and yes, the way I treated you was appalling. And," she stopped suddenly and let out a half strangulated sob, "yes maybe I did deserve to die for it. So yes I can't hate what Vicky wanted to do. She was saving the life of someone she loved and she owed me nothing. I've never taken so much as the slightest notice of her existence. She gave Mike what he probably deserved and she would have given me the same too." She stopped suddenly, and her brown eyes stared directly into my own. My eyes that were black pupils, surrounded by swirling grey.

Jess spat out her next words, her face suddenly shone with hatred, real and hot and fresh. "But you had to interfere didn't you? You cast your grey magic to weaken but not stop what Vicky was doing and this: this!: is the result. I'd rather be dead. You've taken everything from me that matters. If you wanted revenge congratulations: you've fucking well got it. You have made me suffer more than I ever thought possible."

"I know." I said levelly, "That's why I just left you for three months." My voice went ragged. "I am prepared to help you now but first I needed you to pay for what you've done to me. Really pay. And you have. The last three months sees us even. Now it's time to sort things out for you. Time for me to help you get some kind of life back."

"How are you going to sort this out?" asked Jess bitterly. "You going to use fire magic to fuse the bones in my back? You going to somehow help me walk again?" She tried to be sarcastic but she couldn't stop the eagerness from slipping into her voice.

"No." I said quietly, "You will never walk again. I can't cure your broken back: no one can. And even if they could you don't deserve to be cured. Your old life is dead Jess. That is your punishment for what you have done to me for years now. But that doesn't mean you can't have a new one."

"A new life as a cripple." said Jess bitterly, "A new life constantly dependent on others. A new life where no one even likes me."

Well not a life where the type of friends you used to have will ever like you I thought. But I was sure there must be other types of people in this world than just that. People not so tainted by image and power. People who would be more forgiving in their attitude.

"Better than a new life as a bed ridden cripple who can't get out of bed because they lay there so long that their muscles wasted from underuse. Better than a new life of chronic obesity and bed sores where you can never leave your room: which is what may happen to you unless you get yourself back into some sort of routine and purpose. And that will be on you Jess. The fact that you lost your ability to walk is not your fault. If you lose everything else it is."

I looked at Jess, who was staring at me now with real terror in her eyes. "But how? How can I face life like this? I go outside and all people are going to see is the fat mess of a girl who…"

I cut her off. "You just have to think about the little things Jess, the same way I do. What do you think I had to look forward to, when your boyfriends were beating me bloody or forcing my head under the fishpond? Do you remember when Mike held my hand in the kettle and kept it there while he switched it on and you both watched the water heat up? Do you remember the way I screamed?"

Jess went very pale, and suddenly couldn't meet my eyes at all. "So what I did," I said quietly, "is instead of thinking about the big picture, which could only end with one of your "jokes" finally killing me; I just focused on each individual moment: on each game I got to play with Vicky, on each time my little sister gave me a hug. And with those little pinpricks of light, which I leapt to one to the other through the darkness, I have ended up here: In this room right now. By never thinking about the big picture I have ended up in a place where the big picture doesn't seem as bad anymore. Perhaps the same can now happen to you."

Jess looked at me trying to understand. "So what, think about the fact it's a sunny day rather than the fact I can't walk?"

"Let me show you." I turned and went out of the room, then came back in. "Here's a cup of tea that I made for you half an hour ago. But you told me to fuck off when I came to give it you. It's a little bit cold now. You asked the big question, can fire magic cure your back? And you hated the answer. But what you could ask instead is could fire magic make me a nice drink?" I smiled at her and called the power of fire magic until the once tepid tea simmered and boiled. Then I handed it to her. "Be careful it's hot!"

Jess laughed shrilly at me, despair and pain bubbling up from under the surface. The hope that had started to flicker in her face at my previous words now drained away from her eyes. "So I'm supposed to just get over a broken back because you just gave me a hot cup of tea! Well thanks Edward but no thanks. That's the shittiest advice I have ever heard!"

"Jess," I said gently, "how often in the last three months has anyone given anything to you out of affection or kindness? Anything at all?" There was a long silence.

I handed her the tea quietly, and as she took it her hands were shaking. There was a new expression on her face, one that I had not seen before. It took me a moment to realise that it was a look of abject terror. I realised suddenly that I was forcing Jess to think about how bleak the overall picture was for her for the first time, forcing her to think about how bad things had really become for her so suddenly and so out of the blue. Making her face all the things she had spent three months of nothing trying to hide from.

"There are many things you can get back Jess." I said quietly, reaching over to squeeze her hand. It was the first time in my life I could remember being affectionate towards her. "You can get back to having things to do in the day, to your life having a meaningful routine, to a world around you that is larger than the walls of your bedroom. And, who knows, maybe even one day again having people who want to spend time with you. A world where people give you little things like cups of tea so often you don't even think about it.

But it all starts with setting yourself small objectives. Like enjoying something as simple as a hot drink that someone cared enough to make you. And then something as hard as wheeling yourself along the hundred metres of quiet road at the front of our drive."

Chapter 4

We stood at the end of our drive. A fourteen year old with eyes made old beyond his years by a lifetime of pain, a small girl with bright hair the colour of fire, and a disabled, no longer pretty, overweight girl in a wheelchair. The sun shone down bright overhead, and the sky was a glorious blue. The road which linked the drives of all the neighbouring houses was quiet, the houses around were large with spacious front gardens. On one side, at the edge of the housing estate, a wood shone with the bright reds and golds of autumn leaves. Directly ahead of us was a farmer's field full of horses which grazed peacefully. Jessica turned to face me. Her voice was shy, uncertain. "I'd forgotten how nice it was being outside. The sun is lovely! I think the last time I was in the sun was when I was on a holiday in Majorca before..." her voice trailed off, as she suddenly came out of her enjoyment of the moment of memory back into the harsh reality of how bad things were for her now: of how much she had lost forever. I reached out and touched her cheek. "Your skin tans just the same now as it did before The Pool of Fire and Blood. Little bit of work and you'll look just as good as you ever did. You'll be back to being the centre of attention in no time." Jessica turned her face up towards me: she was going to be turning her face upwards an awful lot in her life from now on I realised: and she smiled at me: the first smile I had ever seen that touched her eyes. She squeezed my hand. "Thank you." she said.

"Of course," I thought bleakly, "you will still never again ever stand up."

Vicky scowled at me fiercely, her eyes cross. "I don't understand Edward!" she said furiously. "Big sister try to drown you down dead! Not one time but lots! Why we help her get better? We should punish her! She wanted to kill you!"

Jessica stared at the floor. I took Vicky's hand in mine. "Come and walk with me sis," I said, "and I'll explain." We walked about ten metres together and then stopped. I wanted Jessica to be able to hear our conversation. A slight wind was picking up and I could feel the taste of the dust it was blowing into the air. Everything felt very still and very calm.

"Vicky," I said, "was that hard or easy?"

Vicky gave me one of those "are you stupid?" looks that only a small child can ever really give. "Easy peasy." she said dismissively, "A baby could do it!"

"Yes," I said, "well maybe not a baby but someone who is two could do it. But not Jessica. And how old is Jessica, Vicky?"

Vicky looked at me and thought hard. "Really, really grown up old. Fifteen!!!"

"Yes Vicky," I said gently, "and at fifteen Jessica cannot do what you just did easily at four. She will never be able to walk again. Not one more step, not as long as she lives."

Vicky looked at me in puzzlement. "But she can still move in wheelchair," she said uncertainly, "so why…?"

"Vicky sit down for a moment." I said. My little sister sat down on the road and looked up at me expectantly. She was wearing her beloved red again today, and her t-shirt was covered with brightly coloured super heroes. "Vicky, Jessica has to sit down all day, everyday."

Vicky still looked puzzled. "But I like standing up and sitting down Edward! It doesn't seem a bad punishment! I like Mike's punishment when I kill him dead! He not mean to you anymore after that!"

I brushed aside the thought that things would now be much simpler if I had just let Vicky kill Jess as well as Mike three months ago. We were now where we were. I took Vicky's arms and started to drag her across the floor, using grey magic to fade away anything on the surface of the road that might cut through her trousers and hurt her. "Vicky this is the way Jessica has to move forever." I said carefully. I walked very slowly backwards. "And all around her people are constantly running, walking, passing her by in the street. All the time she is reminded how easy it once was for her to move around just like everyone else; but now she can only move slowly and with a great deal of effort. But all around her people are walking, never allowing her to forget. She is punished for what she did to me every day of her life, every waking moment."

"Oh," said Vicky, with an expression of slow horror. "Oh. That is really bad punishment. Really nasty."

I seized her and raised her back to her feet so that she stood upon the ground again, the thing that Jessica could never again do. "That is why we will now help our big sister. She was punished, punished by you hitting her hard enough so that she can never again leave her wheelchair except to go to bed."

Vicky looked at me. "What if she get better? How she being punished then?"

"She won't get better Vicky." I replied lightly. "All the magic experts have looked at her and they all agree that you hit her hard enough to put her in the wheelchair forever."

Vicky thought about that for a moment, then she smiled savagely. "Good." she said very firmly. "Not like her try drown you dead all the time. Or all the times her boyfriends beat you up and make you scream." Then distress suddenly flickered urgently on her face. "But Edward," she asked anxiously, "what if she get better?"

I thought about that. It was just about possible I supposed: although very, very unlikely. One day a magical research breakthrough in healing might enable someone to put Jessica's back together again. I used grey magic to fade my next words: these I did not want my elder sister to hear. "If our big sister ever walks again," I said flatly, "then she has chosen to end her punishment. She will have decided that all the bad things she did to me did not really matter after all. So then, if that happens, we will kill her."

I ruffled a smiling Vicky's hair as we turned round to look at where Jessica waited. "Vicky gets why we're helping you now." I said lightly, "Jessica, are you ready? Think you can push yourself to where we are standing?" Jessica took a deep breath and then took hold of her wheelchair wheels. And then she started to turn them. It was only a few turns before her face drew up with strain and her breathing came in ragged gasps. It took her nearly two minutes to reach us, and by the time she did she was bathed in sweat and perspiration.

"That really hurt," Jessica gasped, "and I was barely crawling."

"How do you think my hand felt when Mike held my arm so tightly I couldn't tear it from the boiling water of the kettle while you looked on and laughed?" I thought bleakly. "How do you think I felt every time your boyfriends forced my head underwater and I wondered if this was the time that they were going to end up killing me?"

But all I said was. "Well done Jessica. That was your target for the day. Well done sis."

Besides me Vicky folded her arms crossly, her face jealous. I raised an eyebrow at her. "What is it Vicky?"

"Sis," muttered Vicky darkly, "I'm sis. You only ever call her Jess or Jessica." And she stared at me with a look that was decidedly grumpy.

I knelt down and stared straight into my grumpy sister's face. "Right sis number one, go around behind sis number two's wheelchair and help push her. I want her to have longer outside."

"Hey," said Jessica indignantly, "shouldn't I be sis number one? I'm older and..." the look I shot Jessica could have withered a puppy and she piped down. Vicky ran round behind the back of the wheelchair. Then she stopped and looked at me. "How I going to push her?" she asked indignantly, "She much bigger than me! I only got little arms."

I looked at Vicky sceptically. "Sis number one are you a wizard?"

"Yes."

"Are you particularly good at white magic?"

"Yes Edward but..."

"Is white magic particularly good at generating force and energy for things like... pushing things?"

"Oh."

And after that we walked along easily to the edge of the woods where the tarmac gave way to woodland undergrowth. The trees ahead of us were full of growth and bathed now in the colours of autumn. Here we stopped, looking at the muddy path that led into the trees. Jessica sighed softly. "You know all these years I could have gone walking in the woods and I could never be bothered. Now I guess I'm stuck forever to well tarmacked paths and roads."

I looked at Jessica with weary scepticism.

"Sis number two are you a wizard?".

"Yes."

"Did Vicky break your back or your magic power?"

Pause.

"My back."

"Are you pretty good at blue magic?"

"Yes Edward but..."

"Is blue magic particularly good at creating illusions and temporarily changing the nature of things? Like for instance changing mud to tarmac for a brief period of time so that a wheelchair can pass?"

"Oh."

And then we headed into the woods, white light enthusiastically blazing around Vicky as she pushed the wheelchair, blue magic dancing below Jessica's wheels as she turned the mud and soil temporarily into wheelchair friendly ground. Unnoticed my grey magic temporarily faded all the branches and thorns that could have scratched the two girls.

We lived near the top of a wooded hill and soon we came out onto the summit: where the trees and slopes fell away so that you could see right out over the Cheshire plain. Houses and fields danced in the sunlight, and you could both see and hear far off the gentle hum of traffic moving on the motorway. This view is what I had wanted Jessica to experience. What I hoped would give her hope. When we came to the top of the hill the sun was shining bright and warm on its summit. As the plains, fields and houses fell out before her Jessica gave a cry of delight, a sound that had not been heard for three months. A sound that sounded of life and vitality: not sterility and inactivity. We stayed there a long time. Jessica stared out at the view: and looked at the people on the hillside around her: and began to remember what it felt like being human. She watched the young children playing, the teenagers bored and moody, and the adults resting gently. Jessica had always liked being around other people and she had always done very badly when left to herself. The complete opposite to me.

At last she turned and squeezed my hand. A gesture that showed more warmth and affection than words ever could. "Thank you Edward." She said softly, tears in the corners of her eyes. "Thank you for today. It's made me realise I don't want to spend the rest of my life lying in that room. But I'm tired now. Could you take me home please? And tomorrow…" she stopped and looked awkward. "I wish I didn't have to ask you this but could you help me get dressed and into my wheelchair tomorrow so I don't have to stay in bed all day. I know I'm a girl and it's weird but…" she swallowed painfully on the hard truth, "I haven't got anyone else to ask." The look of pain on her face showed the agony of her realisation that many of the simplest things in life she just couldn't do anymore on her own. And of her realisation that all the people in her previous life who had claimed to care for her had, in fact, abandoned her at once the first time she got into serious trouble.

For a moment all I could suddenly think of was that if it had been me who had ended up paralysed in our struggle, perhaps from water on the brain, then the best that I could have hoped for would have been for one of Jess's boyfriends to smoother me in my bed with a pillow while her laughter rang in my ears. Anger rose up inside me, and for a moment I was tempted to leave her here. Or, even better, to lead her into the woods and then leave her, trapped and helpless. To cry alone in the dark while rainwater soaked her skin and she had all the hours of darkness to realise that she was totally alone. The desire to kill the light I brought back to her rose up inside me, a desire to feel her pain as I changed my mind about helping her. To see her fresh agony as she realised that the chance of some sort of future that I had just dangled in front of her was now nothing more than just a lie: that she was really just utterly alone.

I took a deep breath, and cleared my mind of darkness. I had my revenge already: I had taken three months of revenge on her by leaving her to lie alone so long after The Pool of Fire and Blood. And she was half paralysed, a punishment that was total and that would last as long as Jessica's life lasted. The grudge between us was done. Not forgotten: but it was fulfilled. I had no mandate now to hurt her any more. I made myself not want to.

I squeezed Jessica's hand. I knew that in so doing I was finally committing myself irrevocably to forgiveness: and to genuinely helping Jessica to make a new start of things. "Sure thing sis. We'll get you back home and then I'll get you up tomorrow morning. Fresh and eager to face your life once again."

And I hoped desperately that she made a better job of her second chance at life than she had at her first.

Chapter 5

The true work began the following day.

It is easy enough getting yourself dressed and ready in the morning. It is much harder to get someone else ready. Someone who has been used to getting themselves ready as naturally as breathing, someone who is trying not to cry through tears of frustration as they remember how easy things, which are now so difficult, used to be. Things which now take many minutes which used not to take so much as a single moment of conscious thought. It is harder still when your helper doesn't really know what he is doing. And harder yet again when you gradually realise that hardly any of the old clothes fit because of recent weight gain.

But I made it work: no, we made it work. And after I got Jessica up and dressed Vicky was waiting up for us: eager to wheel sister number two to the staircase. I then faded the floor temporarily away and weakened the force of gravity so that all three of us sank gently down to the ground floor. "We need to move your room down to this level," I said to Jessica, "as daddy has refused to let mummy put in a stair lift." I looked at Vicky.

"Daddy never uses his study on the ground floor at all. Could you go and swap everything from the two rooms around?" Vicky nodded enthusiastically. She always liked being busy and helpful. "Oh and Vicky," I said earnestly, "be really careful with Jessica's things. It would be sad if some of them got damaged in the move."

Vicky looked at me indignantly. "I not STUPID!" she said forcefully. "Stop being fusspot!"

"Yes," I said mildly, "but we're in a hurry and daddy doesn't really care about any of his things. Especially not about his shiny new laptop or extremely expensive television. Feel free to do whatever you like with them. He won't mind if they get cracked or damaged as they change rooms."

Then I sat down at the kitchen table with Jessica on a Saturday in the middle of a cold autumn and tried, on a grey and dismal morning, to work out what she was going to do with the rest of her life.

Jessica's first suggestion was that she spend her time catching up on her schoolwork. I didn't think that was an entirely awful idea: but didn't think it should be her main focus. With what they'd written about her in the report into The Pool of Fire and Blood she was never going to get back into any regular school, or to get to go to university. She was certainly never going to get hired by any middle class employer into any position of responsibility. We needed to start by thinking about what kind of life we could now get her: not go along with the fiction that she was somehow going to get back any of what she'd lost at The Pool of Fire and Blood.

The first hard truth that Jessica had to come to terms with was that instead of being able to go anywhere she wanted in one of our parents' cars the only places she could commute to daily under her own steam were places in our hometown of Prestham. And as the centre of that was half a mile away down the hill that meant her fitness would need an awful lot of work for her to be able to manage even her daily commute: not least because she would have to wheel herself back up the hill at the end of each day's work. We tried to find volunteering opportunities for her online but: after a few disappointing hours where Jessica came near to tears: I decided we might be better off going down to the local library and seeing if the local noticeboards had any opportunities being advertised the old fashioned way. At the very least I thought, it would be the first time in months that Jessica would have the chance to talk to someone besides her own family. And it would also get her out of the house and get her some fresh air and exercise. My mum was home for the day so I was quite happy to leave Vicky busy rearranging my father's and Jessica's rooms. White magic was whirling loudly around all over the place as my little sister floated things up and down the stairs, and so much stuff was just flying around everywhere that I wondered if Vicky had forgotten exactly what it was she was supposed to be doing and had just decided to try and rearrange the entire house. It would not have been the first time that Vicky got carried away by the strength of her own magic.

I'm not going to pretend that Jessica found it easy making her way down to Prestham centre, even with me helping her, but I was proud of her. She pushed herself on through what must have been a very difficult hour without once complaining or starting to feel sorry for herself. She managed to maintain her hope and optimism right until we looked at the local noticeboard in the library and we could see nothing that would be helpful to her: not that either of us were entirely sure exactly what it was we were looking for in the first place.

"There's nothing for me," said Jessica slowly, "nothing useful anyone wants me to do."

I squeezed her hand, "We'll find something." I said reassuringly. My eye turned again to the jobs board. "They're advertising for a full-time library assistant." I mused. "You'd probably find stacking the books quite

76

dull but you'd get to organise events and talk to library users and meet new people."

Jessica looked at me flatly. "Applicants must be eighteen or over and have a clean criminal record as the job involves working both with vulnerable adults and with children and young people under eighteen." She laughed sickly. "Not eighteen and not got a clean criminal record. And even if I had…" she looked around her despairingly. "I'm sure I would find the sorting a little dull Edward: but I wouldn't even be able to reach the books on the top shelves."

I looked at Jessica, and smiled slightly. "Jessica please go up against the wall and show me how far you can stretch."

Jessica looked at me suspiciously. "Edward I…"

I raised a disapproving eyebrow and she sighed and wheeled herself over to the wall and stretched up as high as she could. "See?" she said disappointedly, "I can't…"

"Jessica please go online and find the application form and start filling it in. I promise you by the time you've completed it things will seem a lot, lot better."

"Edward…" Jessica began, but I stopped her by placing one hand on her shoulder. "Listen sis…" I began.

"Number one or number two?" asked Jessica, trying to disguise the fact that was a genuine question with sarcasm.

"Oh for fuck's sake will two completely different girls please stop comparing themselves!" I almost yelled: intense frustration suddenly rushing up inside me.

People turned to look at me: and I remembered abruptly that people were supposed to talk very quietly in libraries.

"Just go and log onto a computer and fill in the form." I said weakly, a little embarrassed. "By the time you're done with it I promise that you'll all but have the job."

I turned and walked away to one of the library computers and sat down. A few clicks and button presses and then I was on the internet. I set up a search engine and put up something that looked suitably booky and library like. Then I let the power of the grey flow through me, searching out Jessica's criminal record, and I gradually faded the warnings away to nothing: until her record shone starkly clean. Then I found all the other candidates' applications for this library assistant job, online submission was compulsory, and faded them away into nothing. The grey magic flowed out of me easily: so subtle, so powerful: and unlike all other forms of magic so difficult to detect. If the wizard casting it wants it to be, grey magic can be almost as invisible as the wind. That was one of the reasons why grey magic was so despised of course. It was very difficult to know what grey wizards were doing, and what we had done. And advanced civilisation always wants to be in control of everything. Unless an extremely experienced wizard was sat right next to me even the most skilled magic users in the country would have struggled to notice that I was even touching magic.

Then I locked the computer, and turned and walked to the bookshelves. I reached out and placed my hand upon the top shelf, and made it look as though I was browsing through the paperbacks: looking for a quick read. Then, in a quiet moment, when I was absolutely sure that no one in the library was paying me any attention, I once more took the power of grey magic and I continued to fade away what stood against my elder sister beginning to rebuild her life. I wove my grey power carefully: casting a spell of great subtlety and skill. All across the library the shelves sank down, then stopped and stabilised permanently in a much lower position. The highest shelves in the library now could easily be reached by, say, a fifteen year old girl moving round in a wheelchair. I won't claim no books fell off shelves anywhere as I rearranged the library's physical structure, but overall the spell was remarkably successful, the change in the shelving height swift and silent.

The patrons looked around as my spell kicked in, and I quickly channelled the magic of the grey again. This time I faded away memories from people's minds: memories that the shelves in this library had ever been any higher than they were now. It was easy enough to do: after all the height of shelves in a library was of no real consequence to anyone: except to my elder sister's new job prospects. With the library staff a little more grey magic was needed, as the layout of the library was a significant part of their daily lives.

I turned and walked over to where the manager waited behind the library counter, supervising the activities of her staff, and caught her eye. Then I struck with all the power of the grey in one sudden moment: making emptiness rise up in the core of her memories. I faded away all her memories of the other candidates for the library assistant job. In particular I faded away the decision that she had decided to give her niece the position before it was even advertised. I dissolved her thoughts until she believed that no one had ever applied for the role. Then I made her knowledge of the original closing date for the job, in a couple of weeks' time, disappear into absolutely nothing.

The library manager blinked and staggered: and put a hand to her head for a moment as if unsure whether anything had happened. But I was already walking away from her: back to where Jessica had just completed and submitted her job application form online.

"Notice anything about the shelves?" I asked mildly.

"They're lower," said Jessica anxiously, "but aren't people going to notice that…"

I shook my head and smiled at her. "As far as anyone else besides us two knows those shelves have always been that exact height. Now we're going to need some trickery and illusion for the next stage so I hope your feeling up to using your blue magic." I took my older sister's hand. "Link your powers with mine."

Jessica paused for a moment, then called upon her magical power. I looked at the computer screen in front of me, squeezed my older sister's hand: and once more summoned the power of the grey. First I slipped through online to where Jessica's date of birth was stored, then just faded out the last digit of the year of birth. Then Jessica's blue magic flowed out and an 8 became a 4. She had to work the magic a few times before the change stuck fast: becoming permeant. Blue magic finds it easy to make the most drastic changes to almost anything but making them last more than just a few moments: that is much harder work. The nature of reality resents the raw change imposed upon it by blue magic and tries hard to reverse the change and push things back to the previous status quo. So different to the universe's easy acceptance of the permanent changes wrought by brown magic: but then brown magic can only increase things that already exist in some form, it cannot create anything entirely new and different out of nothing the way that blue magic can.

Then I focused my grey magic on the closing date of the position and faded it away: and I dissolved the date that the computer had recorded Jessica submitting her job application. Jessica changed the date she had submitted her job application to a couple of weeks ago; and then turned the date of the closing date for the position to four days ago. Then I withdrew my magic and dissolved the link of power between us. Jessica was now the only candidate for a role whose application period had already closed.

Jessica looked at me, and cleared her throat uneasily. "Edward if you have this level of power over paperwork then couldn't you just send me back to school? If working together can wash away the records of the past this easily…"

That was not the right thing for her to say. If enough of the past was washed away wouldn't we be straight back in the situation where she was trying to kill me? Wouldn't too much of her punishment have been ended?

"I can't." I said, truthfully enough. "When I fade things away they are not truly gone. It is not like brown magic, which works with what already exists to create permanent fast acting changes. Nor is it like blue magic, which can produce the most varied chemical changes and illusions which after repeated attempts can be made to permanently stick. Things that are faded disappear from our physical reality but some trace of them somehow always remains: like the shadow of old memories. What once was lingers on as a metaphysical shadow: long after the grey magic that faded the object from existence has gone. And the more pressure that is put on that shadow the more likelihood it will remerge back into reality. If you tried to go back to school, with the amount of times your records would be checked and the exposure your file would be put through, there is no way that under that level of pressure that I could maintain my magic to hide the damning data in your personal history. But nobody is expecting you to get a low paid job sorting books in a library. The pressure on your records caused by applying for this positon will be minimal."

"I'm going to be able to hide in my local library in the town I grew up in?" Jessica asked sceptically. "Your magic isn't going to get battered by a thousand interactions every single day as people see me and think- oh that's that girl from The Pool of Fire and Blood incident? Or even if people just recognise me from seeing me around town from before all this happened: and then start questioning how a well-connected girl from a prestigious private school has ended up doing a job like this?"

"Jessica we may have grown up here but we went to private school. No one in the local community knows who you are. Our father never wanted you mixing with the "wrong sort" did he? And even though Prestham is a well off middle class area many of the local people he considered far too low level to be mixing with his precious daughter. You might as well be a newly arrived stranger in Prestham in many ways. And luckily for you you're a minor, no pictures of you were put into the public domain following your… incident at The Pool of Fire and Blood."

I took Jessica's hand. "Now one thing more." I turned and met the manager's eyes. The next moment I was inside her head and I faded out an hour long slot from the morning: a dull and unimportant hour when the library had been very quiet and nothing much at all had got done. "Now sister," I said quietly, "create a really impressive memory of an interview inside the manager's head, and make sure she's absolutely convinced that you thoroughly deserve this job. Take as many times as you need to go over it, you need to make this stick." Blue magic whirled and swirled in soft curls of stream water and deep currents of river and ocean blue. And I concealed my elder sister's spell from detection with the fading essence of grey magic.

And then her spell was done.

I released the power of my grey magic; and for a long moment Jessica stared at me: her face thoughtful. "The fact that your magic can do all this, but unlike all other forms of magic is almost impossible to detect: no wonder everyone is terrified of grey wizards." She mused wonderingly.

Then Jessica started: suddenly scared. "Edward what am I going to tell people at work about my life when it comes up in conversation? I can't tell them the truth! What on earth am I going to do?"

"You're a blue wizard'.' I said. "You're good at making stuff up. But think quickly: because it looks like the library manager is coming over here to offer you a job."

Chapter 6

I won't claim that Jessica found building her new life easy: especially as at almost every moment she was faced with the reality of the restrictions that meant just how much more limited her life would now be. But step by step, day by day, she fought to once again have purpose and meaning in her life. To leave behind forever the three months when she had lain in her room with absolutely nothing to do and when no one could have cared less what happened to her. Like most things in life, the hardest part was getting started and getting into her new routine.

For a long time the most difficult and frustrating part was the physical challenge of getting Jessica up for work in the morning, and then back into bed to sleep at night. But as we gradually got used to the process of getting her up and washed and dressed and into her wheelchair: and the reverse process in the evening: it just over time became more and more automatic. My elder sister's tears of pain and shame slowly but surely died away. It was hard for Jessica to exercise but I made her work at it everyday: Vicky and I walking a mile with her at least once a day: and over time she was able to wheel herself without our help more and more. As the weeks turned to months the excess weight she had gained faded away and her arms actually became quite muscular. Eventually her fitness increased to the point where she could handle her commute to work herself without needing to be pushed at all: and going to and back from work gave her steady regular exercise. Pride in her appearance meant a great deal to her and she started to take care of her skin once more. Her spots faded and her makeup and perfume returned. The job Jessica had could have been as dry as dust. She could have let it be nothing but dull and negative repetition as she ground her bored way through the day. The position she had could never be a stepping stone to anything. Jessica would get no real external reward however well she performed in the role. Were she ever to get promoted even to manager then I would have found it impossible to maintain the spell that was keeping her criminal record faded out. Even as it was occasionally someone who knew Jessica from the old days would bump into her in the library, and, even though I was normally quite a few miles away at the time, I would have to place my hand on the nearest wall, my breath ragged, as I fought to maintain the fading out of my grey magic that kept the warnings on her record concealed.

If Jessica had wanted she could have spent her days sorting the library, checking out books for customers, and then just gossiping with the staff or playing on her phone. She had a permanent position, no possibility of promotion and very limited pay rise opportunities so there was little external pressure one way or the other.

But she decided to make the job her own. In some ways it was a relief to her to be in an environment where she could make her own decisions without being judged all the time. At school she had always felt not quite good enough, constantly under pressure to do better from family and teachers. This was why in the end she had resorted to competing through the prestige of her boyfriends and the beauty of her physical appearance. But in her new role she flourished. Jessica organised all sorts of events and activity days. She set up weekly children's story times and organised sing-a-long poetry sessions for toddlers. She got authors to come in to do guest talks promoting young adult fiction, and she set up a schedule of creative writing classes for teenagers. She also organised a local reading group for adults and persuaded the local history group to hold its lectures at the library instead of a dim dark hall at the back end of town with no parking. It wasn't a prestigious or well respected job, but Jessica was helping to make a lot of people very happy. And now that most people enjoyed interacting with her without putting pressure on her, the cruel jibes and jokes that had been such a constant part of her former life made no return.

My mum was just happy that Jessica was back to living some sort of life: but my father's fury with her never abated. To him she was soiled, shamed. To be hidden away. I think he would have preferred it if she had never again left her room. As it was he started to insinuate that, as despite all his help and guidance and support, she'd failed to make it into a prestigious university at eighteen and was now doing some low grade job at a library like a girl from a council estate: she should start looking for her own place. On what she was now earning there was no way that would be remotely affordable to Jessica for about ten years. Also without a carer Jessica would simply not be physically able to live an independent life. But from my father's point of view all of this was irrelevant: all that mattered to him was that daddy's apple had got quite rotten and had fallen very, very far from the tree. No doubt he saw me and her new work colleagues as worms eating our way out through her insides. He started to talk about all the money he'd wasted on school fees for her over the years, and the more he talked the more his voice rose and his temper came out: the anger that always raged in him when he didn't get to have everything all his own way. I nearly screamed as I fought with everything I had to maintain my grey magic fading as my father's thoughts, driven and powered by his sudden rage at Jessica, ran over the gap I had planted in his memories over exactly how old his eldest daughter was. By the time my father was done shouting I was lying against a wall with everything blurring, blood running down the inside of my nose. But I had managed to make my illusion hold.

After a time things became a little clearer to me: the world a little less shaky. And an old man wrapped in a long cloak was sat across from me. A man who had last come to see me in the middle of a massacre: when the fields burned with fire and the ground was slick with prestigious wizard blood. His words were calm and considered, sharp and precise as a razor blade. "Jessica was the answer to the first riddle in your life. But she will not be the answer to the many more to come." The light in his eyes was simultaneously both beautiful and terrible, bright and dark. Eyes with a core of jet back surrounded by swirling grey.

I blinked at him. "Can't you tell me something useful?"

The old man smiled. "I just did."

And then the next moment he was simply no longer there. Gone as though he had simply never been. I sat for a long moment, utterly confused. I looked up after a while. "Last time someone else helped me out as well?" I asked hopefully. "Sent down a very helpful moonbeam. You got anything for me this time? I could really do with the help." Nothing happened. I wiped the blood away from above my mouth, and sank back against the wall in frustration. I hadn't got a clue what the dark god of wisdom and war had just told me.

It was many hours later, when I lay in my sheets unable to rest, when I finally realised what the old man had meant. Helping Jessica was a huge commitment of both my time and energy: and I provided all the practical and emotional support that kept her new life going. If something happened to me that ended up affecting that support then there was no "spare" for Jessica to fall back on. If I was about to have to face the challenge of more "riddles" would I be in any position to keep supporting Jessica? Just the first riddle had already changed both her and my lives forever. I needed to find someone to support her, someone who…

The next morning I knew exactly what I was going to do. I spent a lot of time on the internet that day, using grey magic to fade out the filters in my way. It took me a long time to find exactly what it was I wanted. Then I simply altered a few things on the preferences that controlled a few peoples' web search browsers and made sure they were adapted, by fading away appropriate lines of code, to where they led directly to the advert for the children's reading group on the Prestham library website.

The next afternoon I turned up at that reading group with Vicky, supposedly just to show support for one of my elder sister's new projects. There was a new book out by a popular children's author, and the session was well attended by parents with preschool children. I found myself responsible for looking after Vicky, which would have been slightly odd if Jessica hadn't been there as well to be publically responsible for us. The session went well, Jessica reading out with colour and animation in her voice as a mouse wandered off into the centre of a wood towards a monster he was convinced didn't exist: and a witch worried about precisely how many magical animals she could fit onto one short broom. Jessica shared out the reading with the other parents and got the children to join in where possible. Vicky's reading was the loudest and the clearest (and I'd managed to subdue her grumblings that she already knew this book) and the shyest was a little girl called Danielle, who Jessica coaxed and supported into perfect reading. The parents were a complete mix of middle and working class, drawn both from Prestham, the middle class town in which we lived and the library was based, and the working class town of Elmsford three miles away. Jessica's sessions were starting to draw a wide audience.

There were two parents who stood out a little. One was a young lad with good chat, nice tattoos and fun banter. I could tell Jessica liked him, her cheeks went a little red every time she watched him encourage his child to read. At first I thought he seemed nice too, until I noticed that he was so busy laughing with people he wasn't bothering to ask them anything about themselves; and that he was more concerned with showing off quite how good his daughter was at reading than he was with actually helping her learn or have a good time. When Jessica's back was turned to me I reached out softly to grey magic and faded her attraction to him quite simply out of existence. Jessica was done with showy bad boys whose good stuff was all on the surface: she'd had quite enough of them in her first attempt at life. They didn't bring out the best in her. The other adult stood out for entirely different reasons.

He wasn't old but he was middle aged, perhaps in his mid-forties. He had a very high level of skill and power in brown magic, and was an academic at the local university of Chester. He was also: in what is the kindest possible way to put this: a little eccentric. He had a long brown cloak that fell down so far that it covered his feet and he kept tripping over it. This was not helped by the fact his very tall pointy hat with stars sewn on it kept falling down over his eyes so he couldn't see anything:

even with his screwed up spectacles which had been the height of fashion only about a hundred and fifty years ago. He was clean and his clothes were in good condition, but they had clearly been ironed in all the wrong places and he had creases everywhere. He had a long wooden staff of living oak, with what looked like some kind of empty, comfortable and clean birds' nest in the top of it. He had a long brown beard, well kempt and clean, but which kept getting in the way of his arms and causing him to drop things.

He was also Danielle's dad. I walked up to him at the end of the session, and smiled at her. She looked at me uncertainly through big brown eyes. I looked at her kindly. "Your reading was beautiful." I said gently. "Did you like the book?"

Danielle shuffled nervously. 'Understood it'.' she said uncertainly. "Like the brave little mouse."

"I like the brave little mouse too." I said. I turned over my shoulder and called out to Vicky. "Vicky why don't you come and play with Danielle?"

Vicky came wandering over, carrying a huge book with her. "The wizarding book of huge records."

I glared at her suspiciously. "What exactly are you planning to do with that Vicky? There have been bad experiences of you having a go at setting your own records. Incidents which have ended with you accidentally setting trees on fire, and large parts of the neighbours' houses falling down."

Vicky's eyes went really round, round as saucers, and her face went completely innocent: which always meant that she was making something up. "Nothing Edward," she said sweetly, "just want to look!!!" I closed my eyes for a moment, hoping this time Vicky found a more appropriate record to try than, "Maximum number of things set on fire by magic at once." or, "Most numbers of things broken by magical lightning simultaneously."

"Vicky why don't you come and play with Danielle?"
I said "We were going to the park anyway."

Vicky looked at me confused. "Were we? Thought..."

I glared at Vicky and sent magical sparks dancing up her shins.

"Oh yes," said Vicky suddenly, "we going to park. I remember." Her eyes did the saucer thing: it was very convincing.

I turned to the brown Wizard. "Are you and Danielle coming? It would be so nice...". I cut off with a cry of pain as a small blast of lightning stung my bottom. I turned round to glare at Vicky, but she was staring innocently up at the ceiling, whistling loudly.

"Well, oh erm, I mean if you are really sure: I mean that would be, I mean the opportunity would be: Of course what I'm trying to say is splendificus and that, well no bless my beard that didn't sound right at all..." he trailed off into confusion. The only thing he had achieved was to accidentally bless his beard with brown magic, which grew another foot and a half without him noticing it.

"Was that a yes?" I said gently.

The wizard's face went very still. "I would love to. Danielle you see, she doesn't have many friends. I've tried taking her to all the sorts of places where young children go but none of the parents want Danielle to come round to play afterwards. I think well, I know it's that, you see, I look a bit like a tramp I think, and not, you know, good with words and things, and I don't think..."

He took a deep breath. "I think the parents round here think I'm a bit weird. And that's why my daughter has no friends." You could see a tear in one corner of his eye, which he blinked away.

"What about her mother?" I asked gently, even though I already knew. "Doesn't she..." The brown wizard went quiet for a moment. "Her mother passed away during Danielle's birth. Medical complications."

"That's really sad." I said quietly, "Very rare in this day and age."

The brown wizard looked at me, and in his dark brown pupils I suddenly saw a look that I knew only all too well: the look of a man who was haunted. "She was my wife," he said thickly, "and every other night I wake up screaming as I remember that the fact we made love ended up leading to her death. My very love for her killed her."

There was a long silence, and then the brown wizard found the strength to speak again. "The last thing my wife ever did was make me promise not to blame her child for her death and to raise her to be happy." He stopped and wrung his hands. "I don't think I'm doing very well. I try but while I can understand all the languages of men and beasts and unravel the deepest secrets of the cosmos I don't understand what small children need or want. She doesn't understand the books I try to read with her, or the games I try to play. I don't know what…"

I took his arm gently. "Vicky could do with a friend her own age too. Particularly someone shy who isn't going to compete with her to be the loudest, most active and sometimes just the downright silliest. And they are both strong in magic, they can probably play well together."

I had sensed Danielle's magic strength early on, like her father she was powerful: very powerful. Not compared to Vicky of course, but then no one was. Vicky's power level was just off the scale. Sometimes I found myself wondering why: her magical strength was just so extreme.

I turned to Jessica, and tried to make my voice sound offhand. "Sis you coming? Vicky and I are going to the park to play with Danielle and her father. It's the end of your work shift so you want to come?"

"Well I haven't really got much choice!" grumbled Jessica. "It's not like I really want to have to go back and be alone in that house with just my parents is it?"

"No," I thought silently, "I really didn't want you to be able to get out of this meeting."

The brown wizard started with surprise. Then he swept off his hat with a bow. "My apologies madam but I did not notice you were here. I thought everyone else had gone."

Jessica looked at him for a moment. Then she giggled: although there was no malice in it. "You thought Vicky had just been left here without a responsible adult, at four?"

"But Edward here is looking after Vicky and..." he paused, then peered at me at the end of his spectacles. "Great scot I hadn't noticed! By all the heavens you're just a young whippersnapper of a teenager yourself. Bless, bless, bless my beard." It grew really, really long at that but he still didn't notice. "Why of all the dancing daises and freshest primroses in the world you're not much more than just a child yourself are..."

And then he stopped, and suddenly the air grew very still. "But you're not are you Edward?" he said coldly, in a voice that suddenly had not one trace of his everyday confusion and bluster. "Or at least you are something far more." He turned eyes that had gone from uncertain and dazed to the sharpness of sun light striking on razor steel. "There are powers, gods, and demons, watching over you, and a darkness, a darkness so deep, deep down inside."

And I felt the power of brown magic whirl, an incredible hurling strength that even as it was called made the pillars of the building stretch upwards with new strength and the stone of the ceiling crack as it reformed into new and larger shapes.

But my power was incredible too. And I had a lifelong experience of magic being used against me, of peaceful moments being torn aside as fists smashed into my face: or magic cut blood across my skin. And I would not let things fall apart with Jessica. I would not let this man become my enemy. I seized the power of the grey and let it all loose, speaking in that moment one simple word.

"NO!"

For a moment the very air itself convulsed and screamed: as two powers ripped at each other. For a second the future of all of us danced on the edge of a blade. But I had just the slightest edge, the slightest more experience of needing to be quick off the draw. The grey magic clicked home: and the memories of Jessica and the brown wizard faded back to the point just before he had had his revelation about me.

I rematerialsed in the library toilets, where I collapsed and vomited into the toilet bowl. Grey magic wouldn't be hiding much of anything if I just collapsed with exhaustion in the middle of a room. When I raised my head up it was to look at fresh red streaks of my own blood. I shuddered, and flushed the loo. Fast flowing water washed all the bad stuff away. A lifetime's experience of pain made me practical about such things. I took a few moments to gather myself: and splashed my face with cold water from the tap. Then I came back out.

"You ready now Edward?" called Jessica, "I think Danielle and Vicky are really keen to get to the swings."

"Sure." I said. I tuned and made myself meet the brown wizard's eyes. To my relief there was no trace of remembrance of anything that had just happened: no memory of the sudden discovery about me that he had just made.

94

"Sorry." I said apologetically, "We were talking for ages just now but I don't think I ever asked your name."

The brown wizard winced. "It's a bit embarrassing really. It's, you see, well it's Merlin."

I stopped dead. "Oh I'm not saying that I'm THAT wizard!" the brown wizard said hurriedly. "But my parents did have a strange sense of humour when it came to my naming day." He stopped for a second, and stroked his beard proudly. "Of course I do realise that with such a distinguished name I do have a lot of living up to it to do. But I do try my best." He strode forward purposefully: and fell straight over his now ridiculously long beard. It got tangled all around him and went everywhere. Merlin sat on the floor: peering blinkingly around. "Did I fall over something?" he asked startled: his brown beard tangled all around him and all confused and knotted up in ways that I hadn't even known were possible.

Chapter 7

Vicky stood looking at me smiling very sweetly in front of the fenced off children's play area. She was holding Danielle's hand tightly. "Me and Danielle go and play Edward?" she said endearingly. "Please? Promise be good!"

"If you're going to be good then why do you still have the Wizarding Records book with you?" I asked suspiciously. "You said you were just looking at it."

"Just looking." said Vicky smugly. "Not been naughty!" I knew she was planning something very silly but I didn't know how to stop her. I could just have faded the book away with grey magic of course but I really didn't want Vicky to throw a strop that could lead to the whole play date with Danielle falling apart. It was really important for Jessica that this meeting went well.

Danielle tugged on Vicky's sleeve, too nervous to speak to me. "We play on swings now?" she asked her new friend. "And maybe… roundabout?"

I sighed. "Go and play." I said wearily. "Just remember Vicky you are a lot stronger than Danielle is: you are going to need to shield both of you with magic if you do end up "record attempting"."

Then I sighed and watched as my little sister and her new friend ran off to play. For a moment I looked at them almost wistfully: part of me wishing for a moment that I had had a childhood a little more like that. But I had no time for bleak reminiscing: not now. Not when I had to make this seemingly chance meeting work for Jessica.

I joined Jessica and Merlin where they were sitting outside the coffee shop at the table with the best view of the play area. Merlin was contentedly watching his daughter play: while enjoying a piece of fruitcake with clotted cream and a large cup of tea. He looked in a very different state to the stressed man in the library: happy and even relaxed. Beside him Jessica was sat with just a fruit juice and a bag of crisps. With her limited mobility she now always had to be very careful what she ate. She was smiling though. I realised with a start this was probably the first social occasion she had been to outside her family and work since The Pool of Fire and Blood. I sat down beside them, and took a sip of my black coffee. I still felt on edge. I had set everything up, but I couldn't do much more to help how things now played out. My elder sister's future happiness was now completely in her hands.

Merlin was still smiling out towards the play area when his hat fell over his head again: covering his eyes. "Well of all the dratted and confusticated skedaddles..." he began, but Jessica calmly took his hat off and slipped her fingers inside. "The elastic has gone Merlin." she said lightly. Blue magic flickered over her fingers and she made needle and thread out of her napkin. She sowed for a little while then handed it back to him: placing it firmly onto his head. The hat now fit perfectly.

Merlin looked at her and blushed. "Thank you. It's such a silly thing but it makes such a difference and I've never found even the simplest practical things very easy. My wife always used to say…" He trailed away, lost for a moment.

After the silence had started to become awkward I opened my mouth to say something but, to my surprise, Jessica spoke first. "Merlin why are your spectacles so dirty, come here let me clean them." She reached over and took the spectacles off his nose and turned his napkin into a cloth, which she then used to rub his glasses with. She then handed them back to him. "Better?" she asked kindly.

Merlin put his spectacles back on and squinted at us. "My they are much clearer and sharper. I know how important good eyesight is and it's so difficult for me to see things clearly at long range. But you've done me such a cracking job young lady why thank you. Why I can see that nice young waiter over there as clearly as I can see both of you right now."

He turned round and, with a smile and a wave, looked happily at a plant pot just inside the café. Jessica was biting her lip hard: her face creased up as she desperately tried to suppress a fit of the giggles.

"Merlin," I said carefully, "when was the last time you had your eyes checked?"

"I used to get them done all the time, I had a really good relationship with my optician. But then I got tempted by a bargain in a general store and when I discovered how what I was buying was nothing more than pointless tiffle of the highest pontificating order I went back to my local optician with my head hung low and my pride in pieces. But I was too late alas: and the once proud opticians had become nothing more than a cut price bakery in the middle of Elmsford's town square."

I took a sip of strong black coffee. "I know that really good opticians." I said gently. "It's where I go. It's still there. There's a bakery next door." There was a small silence. Then Jessica just couldn't keep it in any more:

and she broke down in an uncontrollable fit of the giggles. She hadn't laughed so hard in months.

Which meant she wasn't used to it: and she fell off her wheelchair.

And Merlin, normally seeming incapable of getting himself out of bed in the morning, moved like lightning. He caught her in his arms before she fell or came even near the floor. There was a silence, and he quietly put her back into her wheelchair, with no fuss or over top reaction: and smiled at her kindly.

"You know," he said, "until that happened I would have sworn you had spent your whole life in that wheelchair."

Jessica went a very bleak shade of red. "Why?" she said coldly. "Do I fit your image of someone who's disabled?"

"No," said Merlin, "it's just the way you were today, with the reading and the children. Not one of the people there would have even really remembered that you were in a wheelchair. It was like it was just a part of you that you had accepted: and then almost forgotten. When I think of you the fact you are in a wheelchair barely even registers in my mind. At the reading session earlier I saw only a beautiful library assistant, working hard to make sure everyone had a good time."

"Oh," said Jessica, and something in her tone was different. "I've only been in this wheelchair about five months. I dread that being disabled is the only thing about me anyone will ever see."

"Continue as you are doing and I don't think it is something that people around you will ever even think that much about." said Merlin gently. "I know I don't."

Jessica smiled with real happiness, her cheeks slightly flushed, her face flattered. "So what do you do when you're not failing to notice your glasses don't work?" asked Jessica. I don't think she'd noticed she was doing it but she sitting straighter in her wheelchair in a way that highlighted her chest: and with one hand she had started to absently play with her hair. It wasn't like how she had flirted before her accident. It was gentler, more real, less deliberate and conscious.

"I work at the University of Chester." said Merlin. "I teach and research history and biology. And publish research in both fields."

"Oh," said Jessica, almost coyly. "What was your latest book called?"

"The Comprehensive Guide to the Mating Habits of the Burlesquene Cabbage: eighth edition." said Merlin proudly. "It's been quite a hit." He stroked his beard proudly. I leaned in to where Jessica was staring at Merlin with a horrified expression on her face and whispered into her ear.

"It's a book about improving the quality of food for treating patients who are really sick. It's led to significant increases in the survival rates of patients suffering from a variety of extremely life threatening diseases. His research is as brilliant as he is eccentric and odd: and he has received an award for being the best teacher in the university: several years in a row. His book titles need work though."

"I'll say." said Jessica back: also whispering: rolling her eyes. But she had THAT smile back on her face. Then she turned and looked at me suspiciously. "But how do you know so much about Merlin anyway? We've only just met."

"Oh I used grey magic to check out his record as we walked from the library to the park." I said lightly, lying quite smoothly and naturally. Doing morally ambiguous things for the right cause had been almost beaten into me by my environment. "We crossed some wifi spots on the way here and I let my grey magic drift down those to make it easier to reach the University of Chester website." I didn't think Jessica would react kindly to news that I had been using grey magic over previous nights to scan dating agencies for local candidates for her; and then using magical manipulation to ensure suitable single parents saw the library reading group advertised online so that I could arrange for them and Jessica to meet.

"My biological research is about to hit a really exciting new phase." continued Merlin happily: luckily not having heard any of our quiet conversation. "I have just secured funding for a detailed investigation into the breeding habits of restorative broccoli. I'm going to produce a book that will be the complete and utter package." He smiled happily and tucked into his fruitcake.

Jessica didn't laugh this time. She reached out and touched Merlin. On his shoulder.

He looked up at her, startled, and I wondered if this was the first time that a girl had touched him since his wife had died. I'd read his online dating attempts and it hadn't been going well. They'd been sweet as sugar, but he had absolutely no idea how to flirt or even really just talk to women. It also didn't help that it soon came across that he wanted a mummy for his little girl far more than he wanted a partner for himself. Jessica smiled at Merlin and with just the slightest movement of her head somehow managed to flick back a few strands of her hair across her forehead. She didn't move her hand, but left it resting on his shoulder. A touch that said far more than a thousand words. "Merlin," she said, affectionately but very firmly, "your research sounds really cool but you need to work on some of those titles. We don't want people getting the wrong idea about you."

I smiled, realising that my role in this was pretty much done: and that I seemed to have achieved the result that

I wanted. I started to gather grey magic, preparing to slip quietly away and leave.

Then a rolling roundabout, propelled by white magic, and two shrieking small girls, came crashing down into the seating area at the front of the coffee shop. It spun whirling in a blaze of brown and white magic: and then crashed to the floor as Vicky and Danielle came tumbling off. Shields of white magic blazed around both of them as they fell, absorbing the impact of their fall; and so they were unhurt by the impact: although the flagstones around them were badly broken and burnt.

I walked over to where Vicky lay on the flagstones, looking dreamily up at the sky. "Three hundred and twenty spins of roundabout in one minute Edward! New record! And remember protect Danielle with magic!" she added proudly. "Did dead well and was dead good at same time."

"Vicky," I said flatly, "you broke the roundabout."

Vicky looked up at me startled. "Oh," She said confused, "That matter?"

I tried in that moment to decide whether I had the cleverest or just the daftest little sister in all the world.

"Let's put it this way," I said bleakly, "you keep breaking things and you're not going to be allowed to play with Danielle ever again." I didn't mean that: but I wanted to see what impact the threat would have. I hoped the two had already grown close.

Vicky's eyes went wide. "No!" she yelled out desperately. "Sorry!"

I turned to Jessica and Merlin. "You know," I said, "that's the first time in my life that I've ever seen Vicky scared. She wasn't that bothered the time she got trapped after she'd used magical lightning to knock down a tree. Danielle must be a very good playmate!"

Chapter 8

Merlin and Danielle lived in what could be loosely described as a ramshackle cottage with a garden that had grown so wild that it was virtually indistinguishable from the woods all around it. "The wildness of my garden helps Danielle play and learn in a protected environment while still learning to love wildlife and nature." Merlin had told us happily as he tried to find something that could remotely be called a garden path to give us a tour. He had failed. "And I always think that one of the things children like most is a good garden to play in."

I kept quiet, but that would have been a much better idea if over time the after affects of Merlin's brown magic hadn't turned the magical protective fence posts around the garden into trees and bushes, which were doing nothing to prevent wild and magical animals from wandering from the woods into the garden: animals which were quite capable of carrying off and eating little girls. Although luckily the fact that the garden was so overgrown that Danielle couldn't have found anywhere to play in it anyway was probably keeping her safe.

Most brown wizards enchanted their homes to be bigger on the inside than on the outside Merlin had told us proudly as he led us in through the front door of his and Danielle's home. Both Jessica and I had to bite our lips to stop us pointing out that he'd managed to enchant it to make it smaller on the inside than on the outside. The interior of the cottage was like its owner. Filled with fascinating things and incredible learning: and a complete dishevelled mess. Only one corner stood out as an oasis of calm and tidiness in the chaos: where a child's bed with her toys and stuffed animals was in the warmest and cosiest part of the house. When Merlin opened the door there was a great barking and yelping, and a huge crossbreed of a dog, a mix of golden retriever and great eagle, came bounding enthusiastically towards the door. It was two times the size of a normal dog, had claws instead of paws, and great eagles wings on its back.

Danielle squealed in delight, practically the first sound she had made since the roundabout crashed, and almost dragged her new friend Vicky over to see her pet. I had quickly picked up that Danielle was very quiet, but it was rare to meet a child so totally silent. "Zuggles," Danielle cried in delight, "Zuggles." She turned and looked at Merlin beseechingly. "Me and Vicky go fly?"

"Well of course my dear, nothing like a good bit of flying now is there, and you are so good at it my dear! Why you often go out for hours on end and I have no idea where you are at all. Scares me speechless when you do that you little whippersnapper. Why I worry so much my beard folds into so many confusticated shapes." He stopped and paused as though struck by a sudden thought. "Unless of course Edward and Jessica have some small objection to very small children flying off by themselves unsupervised."

"Well…" Jessica began.

But I cut in and she deferred to me: she always did in cases involving Vicky. "Okay."

Vicky looked at me suspiciously. "Okay?" she said warily. You could tell she had been braced for battling with fierce objections.

"Yes," I said, "Danielle seems to know what she's doing and I really want you to make friends. BUT there are two conditions."

Danielle was pulling out a feeding tray and piling it with meat for Zuggles. Then she took up his drinking tray, poured out the last of the old water and gave it a quick little clean, and then started adding new and fresh water to it. She was clearly confident and practiced in looking after the animal. I looked at where her part of the wall, while neat and tidy, was covered in pictures and colour. You could see Danielle's drawings of her house, her dog, her father. Unusually for her age she already preferred the variety you could get by shading with colouring crayons to the brighter but simpler colours you got by using felt tips.

You would have expected someone so creative to be strong in blue magic, but at first look I had only sensed the power of the brown in her. I looked more closely at the shy little girl: and then found what I now expected, cleverly hidden behind her father's protecting magic. Danielle was half blue and half brown, a powerful combination. Brown magic found it easy to make permanent changes but was limited by having to work with what was to hand in the world around already. Blue magic could generate almost an unlimited amount of chemical changes, but building from nothing took a great deal of energy and the changes were difficult to make last more than a few moments. But if you had the power of both blue and brown then your magic complemented both parts of your talent together in a very strong and often deadly combination.

And a sharp thought made me suddenly cast out my power towards Merlin. Gentle as the whispering wind.

And I found what I had suddenly expected with him too. He wasn't a pure brown wizard either, despite initial appearances. Powerful blue magic grew within him, hidden deep. He was far, far stronger in magic than he chose to appear to the outside world. He was stronger than any wizard I had ever known or had heard about: except of course Vicky. The balance in him was actually two thirds brown to one third blue, where as his daughter was more fifty-fifty. Danielle's mother must have been a blue wizard.

I let nothing show on my face, there could after all be many harmless reasons why Merlin was concealing the full extent of both his power and his daughter's. I refocused on the present, on ensuring my little sister's safety as she got to know her new friend.

"The two conditions are: first: The Book."

"But…" said Vicky disappointedly.

"No Vicky." I said firmly, "You've done enough new record setting for one day." Vicky sighed and handed it over. I placed the Big Book of Wizarding Records on the top of the highest shelf well out of the reach of little hands and fingers. Vicky's eyes followed it imploringly.

"And second… well you know the second."

"Oh," said Vicky, "yeah, that."

I walked towards her and drew a steel blade. Then I called upon the power of the grey to cover us. I ran the blade slowly down the centre of my left hand, and then down the centre of her right. Then we placed our hands together: to renew the protection spell that bound us close. It was a simple but powerful spell: that meant that should Vicky feel distressed she had but to think of me and I would feel her call. Then in mere moments I could appear out of the grey by her side. It was supposed to go,

"By blood we mingle,
And by blood we bind.

106

Think of me in your distress
And I will hear you in my mind.
Moments later let me appear
From deep in grey shadow
And fight for you until no danger lies near.''

But as we sang together this time, unknown to us, the eyes of Merlin could feel the power of the spell through the grey mist that surrounded me and my little sister as I cast the great protection spell. And he fed my spell with his great magic to unlock that spell's true power and meaning.

As we ended the verse, instead of fading away as usual our voices grew louder and clearer. I felt myself grow taller and stronger, and a whirl of confusion and light danced in mine and Vicky's heads as we sang words of power: words beyond the comprehension of our years and childhood. Yet words which came from the deepest desire of our hearts.

We could not see what was happening, nor afterwards remember: but the eyes of Merlin could. And what he saw was not two children: but a young man great with the power of the grey and the moonlight; and a beautiful young woman: whose hair flowed red like flame and in whose eyes shone the force of lightning. They were not brother and sister anymore: but two young lovers: wreathed in a fire that burned brightly and fiercely all around them: but they were unharmed and untouched by the flames. And these are the words that Merlin heard them sing to each other, sing from the darkest unspoken mysteries that grew inside them, from the silent heart of the universe. For one of the deepest mysteries of all paganism is that incest is the preserve of the gods alone. These are the words of the two lovers' song, if it can be like their song without their music.

I could not bear the thought of you being touched by
another,
Why cannot the world forget that we are sister and
brother?
We are bound in birth and blood, love and trust
Why do you call it abomination that we also feel
lust?
You say that our union of sex and love is a sin
Know you not the shape of our hearts will let only
my sibling in?
Who are you to call our union dire?
When we but follow the love that sets our hearts on
fire?
You are I: and I am you.
Till death do us part let there be no one else but
you."

Then the fire faded, and the music was gone. And
where two lovers had once stood now stood just two
children: with no real memories of anything that had just
happened: save that the protection spell had worked. But
Merlin had seen and remembered. And so did the gods.

"Zuggles ready Vicky." Said Danielle eagerly, but still
unsure: as though scared her new friend was about to
find her boring and strange. "Want fly with me?"

Vicky shook her head dizzily, as though coming out
of a deep daze. Then the next moment all confusing
thoughts were swept away and she was, suddenly and
completely, just a little girl again. The next second after
that she was running over screaming with delight
towards Zuggles: who stared back at this new and very
loud little stranger quite calmly. Vicky had already
healed the dagger cuts on our hands with white magic
during our protection spell.

I took longer to recover from what had just happened.
Perhaps being older I sensed dimly something of what

had just happened in a way that my little sister, being so much younger and more innocent, did not. Who can say? I sat back against the wall dizzily even as Merlin raised his hand and the roof of the cottage opened so that the two little girls on the back of Zuggles could fly up into the open air beyond. The next moment they were all gone, rising into the darkening December sky. This left just me, Merlin and Jessica in the cottage below. I would have started to feel very much like a third wheel: if I had felt well enough to stand up.

I wrapped myself in grey magic, so thoroughly that even Jessica and Merlin forgot that I was there. Which was of course the entire point of the spell. I closed my eyes and tried to focus on what had just happened to Vicky and I as I renewed the protection spell between us: but all I could see was the figure of a beautiful young woman outlined against the darkness: singing words I could not hear clearly, wreathed in flame that was both beautiful and did not burn. She seemed both very familiar and completely strange at the same time. A promise of something beautiful, friendly and terrible to come: but currently something very, very far away.

Merlin turned to Jessica, and his hands twitched nervously. Where a moment before with the children around he had been quite comfortable he was now, left alone with a very attractive young woman, clearly out of his depth.

''My dear lady would you care for a cup of tea? I have all sorts of beverages. Why I have written treatises on the breeding habits of the tea leaf and...

But of course! I am forgetting that young ladies always prefer alcoholic beverages nowadays. Why I believe I have some fine specimens of wine somewhere, saved for a special occasion such as this, in a place so safe even I no longer have any real idea where on earth it is. Of course I can't fully vouch for these alcoholic specimens, because my research into vine reproduction has never really been given the time and attention it deserves. That is something that I must address most..."

"Merlin," said Jessica, very gently, "could you close the roof please? I'm a little cold."

"Oh." Merlin said, a stricken look on his face. Then he whirled his fingers and the roof closed. "I'm sorry, you had gotten cold and there I was just going on and on about where I keep things while you were..."

Jessica smiled at him, and squeezed his arm gently, affectionately. He calmed instantly at the warmth in her touch. "Don't fret." she said softly. "Problem solved now. And I'd love a tea. Strong with milk and very sweet."

Merlin raised his hands and the tea set danced over to her: and settled down in front of her. The tea pot raised itself and started to pour her a drink. I realised with a dull sort of horror that my role was going to be to sit in the corner and hear Merlin's chat up lines: and watch my sister flirt. My sister!!!"

"Fruitcake?" asked Merlin. Jessica blushed. "I'd love to." She said, taking his hand gently and squeezing his fingers. "But I have to careful with what I eat because..." she trailed off, glancing awkwardly at her wheelchair.

"Because you wish to be as stunningly beautiful tomorrow as you look today." said Merlin lightly, gently filling in the gap in the conversation before it could become awkward. "My apologies Madam. From now on you shall have nothing from me but sugar water and the sweetest apples."

"Sweet tea will be fine." giggled Jessica. She picked up her hot drink and before she sipped it she whispered to herself, "And now someone cares enough to make me hot drinks again!" Then she tasted it. There a moment's pause and then, "Oh that's lovely." Jessica cried: not quite able to conceal her surprise. Merlin's domestic skills up to this point had after all been more than a little lacking. "What did you put in it?"

"Giant bee honey fresh from the hive. I keep some out in the woods. You know I've managed to breed ones that don't die when they sting you and the honey they make is just heavenly. I must show you them sometime. Don't worry about them at all, once they've stung you a few times I'm sure they'll soon get used to you. They're really quite friendly once you get to know them properly."

I settled against the wall, wondering how on earth I had ended up having to watch all of this.

Things settled into a pattern very easily after that. Vicky went over several times a week to play with Danielle and Jessica and I always went over as well. The fact that Vicky and Danielle became best friends made what was starting to happen between Merlin and Jessica easier: much easier. After all Jessica had to be the responsible adult for Vicky didn't she; surely my elder sister had to be at Merlin's house looking after her little sister if she was to be doing things properly? I was never quite sure how I ended up in that little cottage so often. I suppose it was just that the place felt so much warmer and more full of love than the place that Jessica, Vicky and I called home. It was an unusual experience for me and my sisters: but especially for me. The feeling of having people around who actually wanted to spend time with us: and talk to us, not at us. At times it felt like all three of us had moved in with Merlin and Danielle.

Soon Jessica was also going by herself a couple of times a week to see Merlin. After about a month she started referring openly to the time she spent with him as dates. After a couple of months she still spent her weekends at my parents' house but during the week she stayed at Merlin's. The excuse made was that it was easier for her to commute to the library from his cottage than from her parents' house: as the route was flat and she didn't have to wheel herself up and down Prestham Hill each day.

But why wouldn't she want to be spending her time with Merlin and Danielle rather than in the house where she was formally registered as living? At her parents' house her father was always out either at work or social gatherings: and while her mum was pleasant enough to Jessica she was far more interested in her own social life than in her children. Merlin and Danielle could offer Jessica a thousand times more love and affection than anything she had back at her "home".

I spent a lot of time in Merlin's little cottage unseen as well. Wrapped in grey. For a long time I didn't admit to myself what I was watching for. I told myself I was trying to be a protective big brother: to make sure that Merlin was as genuine and nice as he seemed. That I wasn't setting my sister up with someone who would ultimately just let her down.

It took me a long time to admit that what I was really watching for was to make sure that this new, nice, Jessica was the real one. That as my elder sister's life bloomed again the old cruelty wouldn't also reappear. I had suffered for fourteen years at "Jess's" hands. I would never forgive myself if all my attempts to save my elder sister ended up leaving a nice, but shy and emotionally vulnerable man, and his very young daughter, back on "Jess's" far less than tender mercies.

But though I watched like a hawk I could see nothing: no flicker, no trace, no expression: that reminded me of the tormentor that Jess had once been. And I began to hope against hope that maybe the evil part of my older sister was really dead.

Chapter 9

It was just as the sun was starting to set that The Voice first whispered to me.

I saw a vision of a mountain. Black obsidian rising high in the centre of a desolate wasteland of dust and ash. And sun. Of a sky so blue that there was not a single cloud, and a sun fixed burning in the middle of the sky. Even the slightest touch of its presence made you ache for water.

"Do you know the worst thing about hope Edward?" The Voice asked me mockingly, confident in its absolute cruelty. "It is that it makes failure painful. Only in despair can men ever be free. The only true peace comes in a complete and total acceptance that things can never get any better than the way that they currently are. That the way the world is now is the way it must always be, the makeup of the world is a story that is already finished: and fixed in that conclusion forever."

"Who are you?" I whispered: shaken. "What are you?"

"I am the ruler of this world. I am the power of order itself made manifest. And your strugglings for compassion have most displeased me. By all the rules of man and morality Mike paid justly with his life for his crimes against you. So much so that not once have you flickered one eyebrow in remorse for what happened to him at The Pool of Blood and Fire: when your little sister literally ripped him apart with white magic and he died while still in his teens. And yet your elder sister: whose crimes against you are so manifest and so much worse than Mike's ever were: lives on. Her life is becoming almost good. Yet Mike made your life a misery for barely a couple of months. Your elder sister hated you for fourteen years."

"A new life that Jessica has fought for: a new life that she has striven to earn." I said guardedly.

"Yes." said The Voice, darkly amused. "Given a choice between having absolutely nothing in her life and having some kind of existence Jessica has fought very hard to bring herself back from the brink. And, with your help, she has done very well indeed. She has a job, and is very close to having a serious boyfriend and with him independence from her parents. A far cry from all those weeks she spent just lying uselessly in her bedroom. But is this really a new life Edward? Or is it just that Jessica is making the most of the circumstances she now finds herself in: just as she did before The Pool of Fire and Blood? After all, as she is disabled, her options are so much more limited…"

"She wasn't making the best of anything last time." I said bleakly. "Unless she was trying to make a career out of making my life absolute hell. And I have been watching her intently for months now. It's not a case so much of, oh I'm feeling really uneasy about what might happen to Danielle and Merlin if "Jess" reappears, and more "Uggg should I really be spying on personal moments like this?" It's been six months now since Jessica first met Merlin. I think I'd have noticed if "Jess" was still around. I knew her better than anyone."

"So sure of yourself." murmured The Voice: sickly sweet: "So confident in your power of redemption. And if she falls it will hurt you so much now. Your hate has turned to love has it not Edward? You really care about her now. The first time you have experienced what it is like to love a girl as a sister."

I blinked at just how stupid that remark was. "Uh hello, Vicky?" And at that the Voice really did laugh: deep and dark and long. "We will see how all that plays out in the fullness of time. But not down one of the millions of routes of all the possible futures is there even one that is "sisterly" between you and Vicky.

But we are talking about your elder sister right now. And let me promise you, that before this coming night is through, you will see that the old Jess is not fully dead. She's still there: just sleeping for a while. And while you wait let me just show you a couple of things about "Jess" that you did miss. You didn't know everything about her, after all."

The vision of the past flared before my eyes. A dark shadow of horror.

A girl was sat alone in the library, reading a child's book, an old dog sat next to her. A very small brown beagle: with little eagle wings. The library was dusty: quiet and still. Apart from the receptionist at the desk there was no one else around. It was open late into the evening today as part of World Book week. Outside you could just hear the sounds of the town nightlife starting to wake up. The small girl shuffled nervously. She liked the library and the colourful books: but the sounds and the loneliness made her nervous. Daddy had come with her and he had said he wouldn't be long but when daddy disappeared into his books she wasn't sure what not long meant. It normally meant that she would be sitting by herself for a very long time. She turned and smiled at Tuggles: he made her feel better.

"Here, here boy." she said, and, "Here Tuggles." The old dog stretched himself and crawled into her lap. She smiled at him and he wagged his tail. He was an old dog: his hair white and he walked only with great difficultly. He had kind gold eyes and he snuggled into the lap of the little girl: and she smiled and started to tell him a story.

"Daddy said that when mummy had me she was very sick." the little girl began, and I jolted as I realised that the little girl was Danielle. She was still nervous and shy in this vision: but I had never heard her speak so much or so freely in real life. Always now she was quiet: always now she looked out on the world from behind scared eyes that had seen more than a four year old ever should. So careful with her words. I had assumed it was because she had lost her mother so young that she was scared of something else being taken from her. But I realised dully that made no sense: her mother had died in childbirth: Danielle had never known her to lose.

"When mummy was very sick and she knew she was going to have to leave this world and go to Elysium, which daddy says is what other people call heaven, she called him in and said to him that he must look after me very well for her sake." Danielle paused, then knelt down her head to the dog's ear and whispered guiltily. "I think she should have made him promise to find me a new mummy as well. Someone who could look after him and me." She sighed tiredly. "When daddy makes me tea he tries very hard but it would be nice one day to have food that is hot. Or sandwiches where the butter was on the right side of the bread."

She stopped and smiled and tickled behind the dog's ears. "Mummy also made daddy promise to look after you, and for you and me to be special friends like mummy and you were Tuggles." Tuggles licked Danielle's face and rolled over so that Danielle could tickle his tummy. "And we are special friends aren't we?" gurgled Danielle with delight. "You're my bestest friend in all the world!" And the old dog barked enthusiastically as though saying yes. And Danielle laughed and giggled and, her fear forgotten, felt completely safe.

But feelings can be illusionary. And the safety of love is always fleeting.

There came a drunken laugh, and three teenage wizards came staggering into the library. "I'm sorry," said the receptionist smartly, "but I don't think this is really an appropriate place for you to be. There are plenty of pubs further down the roa…"

Then one of the wizards looked at her, and she went very quiet as she felt his power and his prestige. And she saw the way his eyes caressed her form even through her dull work shirt and blouse, with a sense of entitlement and ownership: as though he always felt entitled to take from this life exactly whatever it was that he wanted.

"Excuse me." she said, and crossed over to the door to the back office. She opened it and very quickly went inside. Then she fled through the fire exit. That left a large, quiet and very empty library: and three very dangerous teenage wizards.

I recognised Mike straight away: the arrogance and contempt on his face that had always been there in life. The epitome of power and cruelty. He had a very pretty girl on his arm and behind him stood a younger man: who it took me a moment to recognise as his younger brother Tim. Just as cruel, but nowhere near as talented.

I sucked in my breath as I recognised the girl he was with. I had hoped never to see her again: though once she had tormented most of my waking moments. The girl who I had prayed almost every day I would see dead before one of her "jokes" killed me. She was fourteen: but I only knew that because I knew her date of birth. She looked like she was twenty one. She was dressed in bright blue, not that she was wearing all that much, and both her mini skirt and her tank top were unbelievably tight. She was plastered with makeup, her skin glowing with foundation and her lips a vivid red. She looked absolutely stunning and she knew it.

Mike's arm was wrapped very possessively around her shoulders, holding her forwards like she was his most treasured possession: highlighting to everyone else just how desirable she was. Just as at the same time the tightness of his grip showed clearly to those exact same people that she was only his to lay: that no one else was going to come close to getting a fuck. In that moment I found myself hoping that he had survived the first couple of my little sister's hits. That he'd been alive and conscious as long as possible as he died: that he'd had as many long moments as possible to feel his death as Vicky's white magic literally ripped his body apart.

There was a silence in the library. And I realised suddenly that the only other people in the building were Danielle and, far away, Merlin: buried in a different world of books and learning and magic. And I realised in that moment that his terrible absent mindedness: which had always seemed so harmlessly and even so comically endearing: was in fact a terribly dangerous flaw. Quietly, very quietly, acting on some childish instinct of danger buried deep, Danielle stood up and started to cross the library floor: her winged dog absolutely silent in her arms. She moved fast, and was very, very quiet indeed, and she knew with a terrible certainty just how important it suddenly was for her to find her daddy. She was small, and could well have passed by unnoticed.

But she didn't.

"Hey," said Jess, catching sight of her. "Hey little girl. What are you doing here? Little children shouldn't be up this late. And what are you doing with an old dog like that? God he's ancient. You want be careful you don't catch fleas!"

She turned and walked towards Danielle, who backed away, but found herself trapped against a bookcase. "Tuggles nice dog." she said uncertainly. "Tuggles not got fleas." She crushed him to her chest and he, feeling the sudden tension in the mood barked loudly at the intruders, a bark that turned into a deep low growl when they didn't back away.

Jess flicked her head, playing with her hair. "Well," she said "that isn't very nice. Give me that dog right now! He's clearly not safe for little girls to play with."

Danielle looked up, her eyes bright and angry. "My dog." she said defiantly, brown and blue magic swirling fiercely around her as her temper rose up suddenly. "You not nice. You go away now or my daddy…"

There was a swirl of air magic, and Tuggles was suddenly ripped from Danielle's arms. Mike seized him. Tuggles snarled but Mike blasted him with white magic: and the old dog suddenly lay very still. Stunned.

"Give me Tuggles. Give me my Tuggles!" screamed Danielle, stamping the floor so hard that the board beneath her feet swelled with brown magic and grew outwards: splitting the carpet.

"Give me my Tuggles." mimed Mike: while Jess giggled at his side. "Give me my Tuggles."

Then he sighed and turned to Jess, kissing her on the lips. "Come on babe this is getting old. Let's give the stupid little girl her dog back and get out of here. There's more exciting places even in this shithole of a town than this dead-end library."

Jess's face fell in disappointment, and she leaned and whispered something in his ear. Mike grinned, then hesitated. 'But babe we don't actually know who her dad is. We do that and we could get into so much trouble." Jess just giggled that objection away, and leaned in to whisper in his ear again: letting her soft warm breath caress the end of his earlobe. Then she teased the edge of that sensitive skin with her teeth.

Mike sighed. "Fine babe, but I still think this is daft." He turned round to Danielle, and she came forward cautiously, her arms outstretched. Her eyes were fixed on her beloved dog Tuggles: who was beginning to recover and rouse himself.

"Now before I give him back to you," said Mike, "My girlfriend has just pointed out something to me. Now you won't really understand this but when my girlfriend and I have problems she makes it all better by spreading her legs." He smirked and a blast of wind suddenly blew up, raising up Jess's miniskirt to expose what little of her legs that garment had been hiding. Jess shrieked in mock horror, and clamped her hands over her skirt, holding it back down.

"Now you have a really nasty dog here and…"

Danielle had reached Mike's foot and held up her arms imploringly. "Tuggles not nasty!" She said earnestly, desperately. "He good dog." Her voice fell suddenly. "He was my mummy's dog and when she die she give him me." She looked up, tears in her eyes. "Please." She begged. "Not hurt Tuggles." And through her fear she managed to force a smile onto her face. "Love Tuggles. Please."

And for a moment even someone who had as little compassion as Mike hesitated, and then actually changed his mind. He blinked: and took a deep breath. "Okay then." he said, his voice suddenly distant, and almost embarrassed; and he began to move to hand the dog back.

Jess scowled, and leant against Mike: pushing her full teenage breasts against his side.

Male lust flushed across Mike's face, and his expression changed in an instant: arousal bringing back all his natural cruelty. He snatched Tuggles away from

Danielle's outstretched fingers: which had almost touched the outer edges of his fur.

Danielle's squeal of delight and Tuggle's yelp of joy were cut off abruptly. "Please," began Danielle again, but Mike could now feel his hard on pushing against his jeans and in that moment he would have done anything to get inside Jess.

"Like I was saying," Mike sneered, "whenever me and Jess have a problem all we have to do is spread her legs and everything feels so much better. Now your dog, Tuggles was it, has so many problems. A bad temper, fleas, and god knows what else. So to sort that out we're going to have to do the same as I do with Jess, spread his legs."

Of course in humans spreading your legs leads normally to the natural process of intercourse and pleasure. Fully opening the front legs of a dog is a profoundly unnatural act that rips open their heart.

Mike called up his power and a very localised force of wind picked up: beginning to force Tuggle's front legs apart. His barking started to rip with desperate pain. Danielle could not know fully what was going on: but some instinct in her recognised the cruelty in Mike's face. She seized the power of brown and blue and threw everything she had against what Mike was doing. She was the child of Merlin: and even at three she was not without power and skill. For a moment two different powers of magic clashed fiercely together: and the air magic killing Tuggles was halted in its tracks.

But Danielle was still just a little child. Her power exploded, and she was hurled backwards against the book shelf. When she raised her head blood trickled down from the inside of her nose. Tuggles legs exploded outwards in the hurricane like force of the wind; his heart tore and he gave one last great cry: half bark and half scream. Then he shuddered and lay forever still.

Jess took Tuggles's still warm body from Mike and handed back what was left of the old dog to Danielle with a cruel smirk lighting up her whole face. "Now there we go little girl, all sorted. No more bad behaviour, no more nasty barking. Very soon no more fleas." She giggled. "You know he even made a loud bark at the end that sounds a lot like what happens when someone comes. I'm sure he enjoyed dying really."

Danielle watched Jess silently out of quiet eyes: and said not a word. The silence that was now as much a part of the little girl as the colour of her eyes had begun. She just mutely took Tuggles's body in her arms and hugged it as hard as she could: terrified that he made not one of his familiar noises and that he lay now so unnaturally still. She didn't fully know what had happened but she already knew that something was very, very wrong. She cradled Tuggles's body to her chest as though the beat of her heart could retrigger his: and she didn't even notice the teenagers laughing as they left: their fun done. She silently poured brown magic into Tuggles: and blue. She tried everything she could think of, every spell she knew, to stand him back up, to make him bark again. She promised that if only he would make one more yelp, would wag his tail one more time, that she would tell him all the stories in the world: all the ones she had wanted to share with him but never got round to.

I don't know how long she worked to get Tuggles up on his feet again, only that by the time it finally, in some terrible way, sank in that Tuggles wasn't coming back his body had already grown stiff and cold. And it was at that point that she realised, in some awfully clear childish way, that her only friend had been taken from her. And that she hadn't been able to save him.

That was when she started screaming. Within moments her father was with her. But though he was great in power and lore not even he could undo the final eternity of death. Perhaps the cruellest part of all was that if there had been but a single flicker of life left in Tuggles he could have brought him back: as healthy and as good as new. But instead Merlin just had to hold his daughter in his arms and tell her that he loved her. They burned Tuggles together in their garden and scattered his ashes in the forest around it: and her daddy gave her a new magical dog, a new animal to love, a golden retriever with eagle wings known as Zuggles.

But for all her father's love he could not undo what had been done. And from that day to this Danielle has barely said a word, and has not dared to tell anyone her stories, instead drawing them in pictures: where they will stay with her and where she can keep them safe. And always now she looks on the world with terrified eyes. Scared that those she loves will once more be taken from her.

The vision faded. And I sat on my bed with all my senses feeling numb. "And to think that you were so proud of how Jessica is now fighting for her new life!" whispered The Voice. "You know that Jessica doesn't even know that the girl she hurt this way was Danielle. She did things like this so often in her previous style of life that all the details of her many "nights out" have blurred. She barely remembers any of this event at all in fact: she was so high at the time. But tell me Edward, while no one would deny that Jessica is now putting a lot of effort into making her new situation work out as best for her as it possibly can, has she ever said that she is sorry for all the things of horror she did in her old life?

Or indeed, for any of them?"

Chapter 10

I sat invisible in the garden outside Merlin's house later that evening: trying to decide what to do. Everything just felt numb. Memories of Jess unlocked by the vision burned before my eyes. I had forgotten how Jess had been so altogether evil. How she had been completely devoid of any trace of humanity, love or pity. I remembered her laughter as Tuggles died in a great deal of pain: and felt icy hatred swell inside my heart.

But then I looked over at the three people in the garden: or more accurately the three people and one dog: and I could see no trace of Jess.

The six months since Jessica had first met Merlin had seen some quiet but definite changes gradually take place in his cottage and in his garden. Wildflowers and plants still grew in abundance, and the garden was still a haven for all sorts of wildlife, but there was now some order: and not just complete chaos. In the garden there were now areas that were clearly recognisable as lawns, and Jessica had helped to have some swings set up for Danielle to play on. There were paths made of stepping stones leading through the flower beds full of trees and bushes: so Danielle could imagine that she was exploring deep through some magic forest as she hopped from one to another. The fence around the garden had also been restored, meaning that Merlin's daughter was quite safe playing there alone: secure from any hungry denizens of the forest who might try to wander in to eat her.

Inside the house there had been clear changes too. The house was still filled with personality and character, with many, many books and odd ornaments; but they were now organised and sorted in a way that most people could understand, as opposed to a way which had completely baffled even Merlin. The house was now also bigger on the inside than it was on the outside, as it had originally been intended all along. Danielle's area still stood out as an oasis of calm and order, but it was now a proper room rather than just a space in the corner and her pictures were now hung all around the house instead of just by her bed. Merlin now had one placed proudly over his work desk, a brown wizard wearing a hat with stars on it and with a hat and cloak that now actually fit instead of being a few sizes too big.

The three of them were sitting outside today, celebrating Merlin's forty-seventh birthday. Jessica was sat next to Merlin, her hand gently interlocked with his, while Danielle sat in his lap and excitedly pointed out what she had done to help Jessica in the cooking. It seemed that she had helped to prepare the peppercorn sauce for the steak and helped to peel the apples for the crumble. Zuggles dozed under the table, happily sated by his special birthday meat treats. Tuggles's ashes were still spread out in the forest of course: the innocent dog murdered and very dead.

I turned from what was becoming a very happy family and walked into the cottage, where I sat down alone. My head in my hands. To all intents and purposes Jess was dead and gone. Jessica seemed as different from her as day was from night. But was she? Jess had adapted herself to be the partner of powerful wizarding teenagers, very successfully. She'd been one of the most desirable catches in her prestigious wizarding school: if for entirely the wrong reasons. And now?

And now Jessica was becoming a perfect catch for someone who was a far more powerful and successful wizard than any of her ex-classmates had been or were even likely to be. In a weird way Jess would have been very proud of bagging Merlin: not that he would have had the slightest interest in what my elder sister used to be. On the surface of course nothing was the same between Jess and Jessica at all: even Danielle couldn't recognise them as the same person. But had the underlying person actually changed, or was all that had happened was that the external mask my elder sister needed to put on to get what she wanted had simply needed extensive reworking and drastic changes after her back injury? Had her outward show simply melted and flowed while her pure core of unadulterated evil remained completely the same? Had my offer of help to my older sister merely led ultimately to the resurrection of Jess in a new form?

I did not: really did not: want to believe that was what was happening. But the fact that I did not want to believe it did not mean that it wasn't true. I thought again of what I had seen Jess do to Tuggles: and I could not stop a shiver from working its way down my spine.

I walked over to where Danielle had covered her wall with pictures, the level of detail of her colouring drawing my eye. Even at a young age you could tell that one day she might have real skill. And with the amount of monsters in the images it was all too clear that she was still partially traumatised. In most four year olds' drawings it's not the bad guys who win. As I drew close to her bed I noticed a slip of paper, hidden beneath her pillow. I drew it out.

On it there was a picture that made me take a very clear intake of breath. It was a picture of a young woman, stunningly beautiful but in an old fashioned kind of way. With blond hair and brown eyes and sitting in a wheelchair. Beneath the picture were two simple words. One question.

"My mummy?"

And a voice spoke suddenly in my ear. A voice of moonlight and a voice of song. A young woman's voice: breathtakingly beautiful. And yet somehow just listening to it made you feel cold. "All this time I have watched you and you have fought on when there was so little hope of any success. Don't falter and fail now, don't give up on your sister, not when you are so close to victory."

The words gave me comfort, and a renewed sense of purpose. I took Danielle's picture away with me, and walked back up the hill, my thoughts racing in a dark blur. The Voice had said that it was tonight that I would see a resurfacing of the old Jess after all.

I was sat waiting for her in her room, after Merlin dropped her off late. She wheeled her way across her bedroom, quietly in the darkness, and started when she saw me sitting by her bed.

"Oh Edward you're up," she began, "that's good because I need you to help me get to bed and…" she trailed away as she saw something was wrong; as I just sat there in the dark: in a silence as deep as any of Danielle's. The moonlight stark and cold as it played across the sharp steel of the blade dancing between my fingers.

I felt a distant spur of hope. Jess had never noticed anything about anyone else's moods, far too completely wrapped up in herself and what she wanted. But I remorselessly forced it aside: hope could be dangerous.

"You seemed happy tonight sister." I said softly, "Are you happy in your new life?"

Jessica smiled, although we could still both feel the tension in the room. "It's going really well with Merlin, although it's still early days and he's a lot older than me, and it's going to take time…"

"You're out of time." I said flatly, "Six months is a huge chunk of time in a four year old's life. It's time to commit or leave."

Jessica blinked, startled. "I'm sorry Edward, I don't understand. What do you mean…?"

I said nothing. I just handed her Danielle's picture. And waited for Jessica's reaction.

It wasn't what I hoped.

She started, and gave an almost scream. Her face went very pale. Then, after a very tense and painful silence, Jessica began in a weak and uncertain voice. "I really, really get on with Merlin and Danielle is a great kid," she said shakily, "but I'm still young and I don't want to limit my options just yet and…"

And the words even sounded like Jess had used to sound. Words my elder sister had passed merely days before The Pool of Fire and Blood rang once more in my memory. "I'm going to do whatever I want to do Edward. I don't need to be as clever or as good at magic as you. A rich wizard is going to marry me because I'm well connected and beautiful: and then he's going to wait on me hand and foot for the rest of his life. Just got to tease him and give him just enough sex that he will still always fancy me and not get bored: and then I won't have to do any work at all when I'm grown up. It will be one long shopping and holiday trip."

The knife flashed as I drove it into the table: hard.

Jessica stared at where the blade lay quivering in the wood. She looked up at me, her lips trembling. Real fear in her eyes. "Brother?" she questioned uncertainly.

Then a voice spoke from the darkness. A Voice that echoed in both our ears. "Your brother is a little scared tonight Jess, or Jessica, or whatever it is you currently wish to be called. He has begun to believe that you are not a new person, reborn from the confines of your wheelchair. He has begun to believe that Jessica, the sister he loves, is a lie. And that only Jess, the sister who he hates so much, is all that you have ever been."

"No that's too strong." I cut in sharply. "I still believe that she is Jessica, and that Jess is dead. I also believe that Jessica is a thousand times stronger than Jess could ever be. It is just fear that makes me doubt."

"Well," said The Voice silkily: as though it was our friend. Poison that seemed so pleasant to the taste. "In that case you should have no problem with me putting your older sister to the test, should you? You should welcome this should you not, as a chance to prove that you are after all right about who Jessica really is? Because your elder sister has never got to decide for herself has she? First in her life she only had the opportunity to be Jess: then after her injury she only had the opportunity to be Jessica. Why don't we take a modern feminist approach to this? And let the lady herself decide."

Then a different voice spoke softly in my ear. An old voice that sounded like the very essence of magic itself. "Have a care about challenging The Voice tonight Edward. His is the only power that will have victory this day." And I knew in that moment that this voice came from a man in a dark hood and a cloak: an old man with only one eye, clad in grey. And I knew that, while his words seemed simple, I had just been set another riddle.

I thought for a few seconds, and then gave one of those rare smiles that touched my eyes. If you were facing me it was so terrible that it would make your blood run cold. "I am not frightened to join you in battle for Jessica's soul: in the chance for her to choose between good and evil. But you are so great and powerful that I fear you may cheat to win. So I ask but one favour. That you may let me show Jessica one thing: one thing in all its entirety: before she makes her final choice."

129

The Voice shrugged, almost in disinterest. "Agreed."

And around the three of us everything went dark. "You go first," said The Voice, mock pleasantly. "Present your preferred option of your elder sister's future to her."

I walked through the darkness: through a suspended moment of time and space: to where Jessica sat waiting nervously in her wheelchair. I held up my hands and in them a bright engagement ring spun and danced in the light. "If you choose to be Jessica," I said gently, "if you choose this life that lies before you now, you will never again walk upon your own legs, never again feel the ground beneath your feet. Every day hours will be spent as another helps to dress and bathe you. You will never have any more of a career than that of a library assistant at the lowest level, a role that many of the girls who grew up with you would look down on with undisguised scorn. You will be married to a much older man who is not cool or fashionable, and you will never have the opportunity to go clubbing, or to play the field, or to dabble in drugs. You will be a mother to a vulnerable child who is not your own, with all the chores and restrictions on your time that demands. You may in time perhaps have other children with Merlin, or not, as you decide. You will not have a grand life, one that will be remembered or the so called "great people" will talk about at parties with pride. Many feminists would argue that you have been brutally domesticated.

But you will be deeply loved by your new husband and daughter. You will be needed, both in your work and in your family life. And should you follow this path you will make yourself and many other people very happy, each and every day. Well most of them anyway!"

Jessica smiled at me and squeezed my hand. "I want to choose this path Edward." she whispered. "I pray for the strength to take…"

And then The Voice started to speak to her.

"I can give you everything Jess. I can give you back your legs, your strength. I can wipe away your dependence upon others, make it so that you can, like the smallest child, bathe yourself and get yourself into and out of bed each day independently and by yourself. I can make it so that when you walk down the street not one person sees you as disabled, not one person looks at you with pity in their eyes.

And I can do far more then that Jess, far more. I can wipe your criminal record clean. Even now a car waits outside to escort you to a prestigious boarding school: with access to all the luxuries and rich boys you could ever want. I will provide you with unlimited wealth, and will make you more beautiful than ever. Any prestigious man you want will be your plaything if you but click your fingers, and a life of untold luxury and ease will be yours forever. Every whim you could ever have will be serviced by your husband and lovers; and any material thing that you want in this world, cars, clothes, holidays, houses, all will be yours. All who grew up with you will gaze longingly at you: the boys will all want to possess you and the girls will all want to be you: and their admiration and jealousy will be the sea in which you swim for the rest of your life."

A plain gold ring glinted in the darkness: the same type of ring that The Voice gave to all that he bound in dark covenant with himself. "Simply take this ring," whispered The Voice, "and what you once were you will be again. And your beauty will ensure that everything you want in this world is yours."

There was a long silence, in which Jessica couldn't meet my eyes and I already knew the choice she was about to make. Of course she was. It was both as my one-eyed mentor had warned me and as the demands of common sense dictated. You'd didn't get to be an eternal tempter without being very good at what you did.

I waited while Jessica turned away from me and slowly, and with a great deal of shame and guilt, started to wheel herself towards the ring of gold. She reached out her hand to touch it.

Her fingers were right above it when I said a single word. "Wait." And I wasn't speaking to Jessica.

Her fingers froze, literally unable to touch the ring. There was a long silence. Then The Voice spoke angrily. "Edward what are you doing?"

I felt a secret midnight thrill run through me. "Whoever you are," I thought, "you had this world me hurt too badly and for too long. You let the dark become a part of me. I wonder, has it been so long since you had any good competition that you have forgotten how to play the rules of your own game?"

"We made deal." I said calmly. "I said that I was afraid you'd cheat so I needed to be able to show Jessica one thing, in its full entirety, before she made her choice. And I haven't shown it to her yet. This game isn't over."

"I didn't cheat," said The Voice flatly, "so your chance to show her something isn't relevant."

My voice hardened. "No I'm sorry that's not how all this works is it? All the rules of magic and all the stories agree: in all magical games of temptation and chance: however much each party may try to deceive the other, the rules as stated have to be literally followed in all instances. If I'm told I'll get three wishes, I get three wishes. And while I wasn't told I'd get three wishes I was told I'd get to show Jessica a vision before she made her choice. You can examine our terms in all the fine print you wish, there was nothing about you having to cheat for me to get to show Jessica one thing that I thought she might find very important."

There was a silence. Then The Voice snarled: real anger in it. "Yes you are right. Go ahead then, show Jess whatever it is you want. Not that it matters: I heard what Odin Allfather whispered in your ear. That tonight only my power will triumph. He does not lie Edward, even though he almost always speaks in riddles."

Jessica turned and rolled herself towards me, broken and shamefaced, while I stood there and tried to keep my face from smiling. I made myself think about the fact that, in all the struggles that might be to come with this demon, he would never underestimate me so badly again. I would only be able to get this lucky once.

Jessica stared at the floor. "I know what you're going to show me Edward. A vision of how much Danielle and Merlin love me. And I know how much it's going to hurt. But at the end of that I'm still going to make the same decision." She looked at me with tears in her eyes. "Edward he said he'd let me walk again!"

"In the end Jessica the choice will always be your own." I said gently, reaching out to stroke her hair. "And at the end of all this I am terrified that you are still going to make a choice that means that I lose you forever."

Then my voice hardened for a moment. "But I'm not going to show you something sweet and sappy Jessica. What I'm going to show you is exactly what kind of life it is that The Voice is promising you. What awaits you once all the fine words and promises have been swept away."

I reached out my hand to her head, and I showed her what she really needed to see. I took the power of The Voice and used it against him. I took the vision he had given me and I showed it to my elder sister: in all its unblinking horror. I let Jessica see, in all too terrible detail, exactly who Jess had been: and exactly what sort of life it was that awaited her now if she took The Voice's ring of gold. And The Voice howled in rage and fury as

133

he realised that his own power was being used against him: that whether my older sister now chose good or evil it was The Voice's own power that would have been used to carry the victory.

Jessica screamed, and her eyes went wide. She stared at me, her face white. "It was me?" she pleaded, looking at me desperately. Looking frantically for a way out: for any way out. For this not to be real. "It was me that traumatised Danielle? It was me that murdered her pet?"

"Yes sister." I said softly. "You did that: and many other terrible things."

Jessica looked up at me, and burst into tears. "Oh Edward," she wept, "I'm so sorry. Sorry for what I did to you, for what I did to others. For what I did to…to Danielle."

Then she raised her head and looked at me, and in her gaze there was a clear and terrible purpose, one that held not a shred of doubt or could have been any more completely resolute.

"I have a brother who loves me, a man who wants to marry me, and a little girl who wants me to adopt her. After all that I have done I do not deserve to have any kind of second chance: let alone one like that. I am truly the luckiest girl in all the world." And she took the engagement ring and she clung it to her chest.

The Voice howled in primordial fury, as a soul he had long considered his own slipped through the steel clad fingers of his grasp. He howled and the darkness rose up around us: but I held the sister that I loved to me and wrapped us in the grey.

And then a silver arrow shot past us, deep into the heart of the darkness, and its light was the fierce glow of the moon. "Demon." said a woman's voice grown cold. "By all the laws of magic and the cosmos you have lost your right to Jessica's life and soul. It may have been centuries since you have tasted such defeat: but that does not mean that it is any less valid. In all your anger I trust you have not forgotten that you must, as all others, be bound by the deepest laws?"

There was a silence, then the darkness faded away. "As you say Artemis." The Voice replied calmly, the mocking charm back in every fibre of each word. "Yet one battle lost, however painful, will not change the outcome of this war. And even now feelings towards this boy start to swell inside you. Feelings that you will never admit. Feelings that I will not and cannot fail to bend to my cause."

Then the next moment we were back in Jessica's bedroom, the darkness had gone, and we sat in the stunned silence of victory.

But all I could hear was The Voice's insane laughter echoing inside my head.

Jessica proposed to Merlin the next morning. Blinking away his surprise he had never felt happier than when saying yes. He got so confused and confuddled in the occasion that saying yes took him five minutes too. The engagement party was arranged for a couple of weeks' time and Jessica moved in with Merlin permanently straightaway. That was also the day that she adopted Danielle as her own.

It was almost enough to make someone believe in happy endings.

Chapter 11

The sun beat down from the centre of the sky and all around us the land was bathed in a shining heat haze. You could see, here and there if you looked closely, the small areas of dead dirt and dust that were starting to spread even in the heart of this: one of the healthiest wildernesses: spreading as the order of The Mountain spread around the world. There was a time, even a couple of years ago, that we would have rested from the heat. A time that I would have used grey magic to shelter us from the remorseless drain of the implacable sun. The sun which drained my magical strength, even as it boosted the power of our opponents' sorcery. But that time was before the midday sun hung in the centre of the sky for five hours at a time each day: before the days grew ever longer and the nights ever shorter. Before a Christian knight of England drew a sword from a stone, and became King Arthur. Before the new monarch's rule spread over all the British Isles and then Europe. He had established his new regime primarily by military conquest: but almost everywhere he had been heavily supported by the local pre-existing elites.

Order and secularism ruled everywhere now: backed up by the Knights of the Table Round and by other Christian sorcerer fanatics. The wild had fallen, the elves and the free dwarfs were dead or scattered: even creatures of magic had been hunted to extinction or rounded up into zoos. Once beautiful animals of wild power were now nothing more than stuffed exhibits in museums; or forced into zoos to put on tawdry shows for young school children. The Mountain's rule was now everywhere, absolute, unchallenged. Any who dared oppose it found themselves confronted by the might and power of one of the new Knights of the Table Round. Should any enemy of The Mountain somehow manage to overwhelm these champions of white magic and steel then very shortly an army would arrive to ram the message: the message of unending order and the end of change: home in fire and blood.

Vicky and I moved under the tree cover, further up the mountain. Not The Mountain on the other side of the world: just an ordinary everyday peak. Even here the trees were sickening from the constant sun, from the power of order grown too strong. Vicky was twenty now, in the full flush of beauty, with long red hair and curves that drew any man's eye. In a dying world she was a defiant flush of health and life. She enjoyed the attention, but she would never do more than laugh or mildly flirt. She actually recoiled from any attempt to touch. She had given herself to one man, and gave herself to him alone. She wore chainmail armour, even she could not run in plate day after day, and carried two sharp blades across her back, swords that could cut through almost any metal or armour in the world. She alone could easily pierce and cut through even the armour of the Knights of the Table Round: King Arthur's protection alone lying beyond her skill.

Our world has seen breath-taking technological change over the centuries. Computers, banking systems, motorised transport, airplanes; yet since the fifteenth century military technology has remained absolutely fixed, the axe and sword, the pike and crossbow, still the defining weapons of war. Researchers tried unsuccessfully to develop weapons based on gunpowder for a couple of centuries, but magic in this world is too powerful to ever let science and technology become a threat to it. Science fiction novels vividly describe imagined worlds in which gunpowder was made to power devices which fired fast little bits of metal (which they called guns and bullets), airplanes were used to drop things which caused explosions (which they called bombs) and strange armoured cars existed (which they called tanks). All simply speculative escapism, nothing like that could ever exist in this world.

I was thirty. I had a couple of daggers attached to my waist and carried a spear on my back, in honour of my god The Allfather. The huntress Artemis had abandoned me long ago. The absence still felt like a hole in my power: and my heart. Thinking about the divine maiden of the moon turned my thoughts towards despair and I found myself wondering bleakly how many pagans were now left in this world after the mass persecutions that King Arthur had ruthlessly enforced. We had been slaughtered before of course, but under his regime the forced conversion and the slaughter of pagans had run on an industrialised scale: until there hadn't been enough of us left for his regime to keep on killing.

We came through the woods to where the trees overhung a gently ascending path, the main route through the mountains. Then I dropped down to the floor, gasping from the heat. Vicky sat down next to me and passed me the water bottle. I drank deep: water as delicious as sparkling fruit juice in my thirst.

Vicky smiled at me, then laid her head upon my shoulder, and tilted her head up so that her eyes looked up into my face. She was so beautiful. Even after four years together I still found her proximity breath-taking.

"You find the heat so difficult don't you?" my wife said, as she leaned over and kissed me on the lips, not quickly. I could taste her tongue and our sweat mingling in my mouth. It was sweeter and more addictive than any drug. I kissed her back.

Then I lay back against the rock behind me and Vicky sank into my arms. We lay there for a while, until the sun gradually faded from the sky, and the shadows of dusk started to creep across the sky.

"We're not going to make it are we Edward?" Vicky asked at last. There was no grief in her voice, no bitterness. She was simply stating something as obvious as that the sun would rise tomorrow.

I took her hand in mine and squeezed it tightly. We were together at least: at the end of everything. "No," I said, "we have the chance to do one last good thing before we fall, but no: there is no hope left for us. This is our last day alive."

"Do you think we ever had a chance?" Vicky asked distantly, only half curious, "Do you think it was mistakes that we made that blew it: or were we just fucked from the beginning?" She flicked her red hair from where strands of it had fallen over her eyes. "Did we muck everything up Edward or were we basically just up against Fate itself?" she asked idly.

I stroked her hair and held her close. I wanted to feel her warmth, the shape of her body, one last time. To have the woman I loved in my arms for just a little longer before we both went forever into the dark. It was so hard to believe that tomorrow she would be dead and cold: her features which were now so expressive forever fixed and still. Her bright voice, even in these dark days still mostly so full of hope and fire, finally silenced forever. This time tomorrow we would both be starting to rot. I forced my thoughts back from despair and back to the all too brief present. "I think the main mistake was…" I began.

And then there was a crackle like there was sudden interference.

I heard myself say, "when Jessica's match with Merlin failed because she couldn't handle not having children of her own and just having Danielle to raise. Jessica started to believe Merlin didn't really love her at all: he just wanted a mum for his child from another woman. If only I'd managed to convince him to take the risk to try for children with her, but he was so traumatised after his first wife died in childbirth: and with all the complications caused by Jessica being in a wheelchair: that he refused to ever risk her going through pregnancy. If only I'd managed to persuade them to have kids together things would probably have been so different. Things in that small family of three started to fall apart; and when The Voice revealed to Merlin that Jessica was the reason that Danielle was traumatised in the first place my elder sister killed herself in shame: leaving behind a young child now so badly damaged that she became completely unstable. Mainly because she believed she was the reason that her mummy had killed herself. When no one was able to offer Danielle any kind of effective help, that was when Merlin turned against us: and put that bastard Arthur on the throne."

There was a flash, and a flicker like time rewinding.

I heard myself say. "When Jessica died in childbirth bearing a stillborn child Merlin couldn't handle what he'd done: that he'd killed a woman he loved with his love a second time. And this time he didn't even have a new child to cling on to. And there had been so many warnings about how unsafe childbirth would be for my older sister with her back injury. Merlin never forgave me for persuading him against all the odds to try for a child with Jessica, and when The Voice showed him that

I could have stopped her being half paralysed at The Pool of Fire and Blood in the first place but chose not to he never forgave me. If only I hadn't managed to persuade him to have kids with Jessica then things might have been so different. When Jessica died with her new child that was what turned Merlin against us: and why he put that bastard Arthur on the throne."

The normal flow of time resumed. I hesitated. "The only other thing I sometimes wonder is if…" I trailed away awkwardly.

Vicky's voice went very flat. "Edward this had better not be the line of all this bad stuff is happening because you and I are in an incestuous relationship. I hated it the first time you came up with it and the fact that you repeat it every now and then doesn't make it any less rubbish. I have told you, a thousand times, we love each other. There is nothing else to it. As children we loved each other as brother and sister. When we became older that love just evolved into something else. Who cares if everyone else thinks it's abomination? Would you rather that I was with someone else? That I whispered, "I love you." in another man's ear? That I came against a more suitable lover's cock in the middle of the night with that cry of pleasure that only you know?"

I closed my eyes. "It would be less painful to have my heart cut alive from my chest." But: just because the thought of not having Vicky as my lover was agony: that did not mean I was wrong about our incest having played a key role in bringing all this suffering into the world. I wondered quietly almost everyday if all the misery around us was the divine punishment of the gods for the forbidden closeness which we two shared. But at the end of all things it is too late to start reviewing whether the choices we made so long ago were right or wrong. We had sown a whirlwind with our love: we must now ride it until whatever end.

We waited, waited until the sun sank low in the sky, and the shadows crept across the mountains. Then finally we heard the two horses and their riders pull up.

One of them in particular I knew now only too well. He wore a coloured hat with stars, and a long brown robe a couple of sizes too big. The days when he shared his life with Jessica and all his clothes fit were long gone. The rags he wore were now dirty and tatty, no longer cared for, and the features of the man were drawn and haggard. He looked like he hadn't eaten properly in months. His eyes, once so calm and tranquil, now burned with a strange, fanatical light. The descent into madness marks people as surely as does the pain and symptoms of physical diseases. I turned my gaze to the knight who rode at his side, and a strange distortion crashed across my vision. I knew that the future Edward standing in the mountains recognised the figure as King Arthur, but my present consciousness, which I realised was in some sense detached from the events and watching it almost like watching the events of a film, could see only a suit of armour with white light blazing where the features should be. I realised that the light was not actually part of what was happening, it was interference with the vison of the future I was experiencing.

"Should we not have brought with us great force in arms?" King Arthur was questioning uneasily. "All the forces of passion and chaos are broken. Why do we risk our lives by hunting down alone the last two wizards who are a danger to us when we could so easily have an army behind us as we track them? The Knights of the Table Round could…"

"The last grey wizard could hide from us for years," said Merlin, "unless he thinks he has a chance he will never risk his sisterlover's life by emerging from the shadows to strike. And as long as he and Vicky live your throne is not secure. But if he thinks he has a chance he will…''

I leapt down from the rock, naked spear in my hand: clad in all the power of the grey. Behind me I heard my sister's shriek as she descended down from the heavens like a lightning bolt, her sword glowing in her hand with light and flame. No enemy had ever stood before her and lived, and she was the reason why nearly half the spaces at the Table Round now sat empty. And I had killed so many now that I had long since lost count of the amount of wizards who had fallen to my power. It would not have surprised me to learn that it was the best part of a thousand.

But Merlin was no ordinary wizard: he was a force of power born out of legend. His shields of brown and blue magic rose up all around him like the stone of the mountain slopes and passes: and the water of the raging torrent. My spear flew with all the power of the grey against him, but though he was wounded and his horse fell he was not killed: and my momentum was ended. Long we fought, brown and blue against the grey. Two masters of power, the strength of fire and grey mist against the power of brown earth and blue sky. In terms of skill and magical strength there was not so much as a hair's breadth between us. But I wanted to live and, suppressed deep down in his heart, Merlin wanted to die: wanted to end this life. Both his wife and all his children were no longer in the realm of the living: and without them he took now no joy in drawing breath. His desire for the final fulfilment of what he saw as his vengeance for his family's death was now all that now kept him going.

Then suddenly there came a howl of agony and rage: all too terribly near. Merlin looked at me, and smiled sadly, and I felt my blood turn to ice in my heart. With a howl of desperation I brought my spear round in one last swing. But Merlin had already dropped his defences and made no move to resist, so that my spear drove straight though his heart: tearing it open in a surge of blood and muscle. A death blow.

Merlin looked at me, and in that moment spoke the final words his most learned tongue would ever speak. And the most terrible thing about it was that he was not angry: only sad. Even his eyes were filled just with tears: not anger and rage. "Now the payment for Jessica's life is done." He said simply. And he called me not by the name "Edward", but by a new title, by a name which I realised was the name by which I had already come to be known by all others in this future reality. A name from Arthurian lore, a name of power, terror and beauty. A name which shocked me to the core: for Merlin is not the only wizard of great power to walk in that great traditional story of myth and legend. But it was not a name I would have ever expected to be mine.

I turned, in a terrible slowness where everything seemed like a dream, but when I saw what had caused the cry it still felt almost like my heart had stopped. There was three foot of steel sticking out of Vicky's chest. She raised her head to look at me, and as her eyes met mine one last time she managed somehow to give me one last smile. I looked into the soul of the girl I loved for the final time: and then saw the last of the light leave her eyes forever. Then Vicky's head fell forward across her chest, and she was gone: leaving behind only a very bloody corpse.

Everything was still and everything was cold. I walked towards Arthur through a world grown very, very calm. The utter stillness before the darkest storm. I saw Arthur raise his sword and made no effort to resist: I welcomed death now as much as Merlin had. Arthur's blade descended with a terrible flash of heat and light: the sword in the stone an irresistible bringer of death. But

I did not even try to stop it. Instead I concentrated all my magical strength as I hurled my spear straight at the small eye gap in Arthur's armour.

The sword stroke basically cut my body into two lifeless halves, but in my last moments I saw Arthur fall too. My spear went literally straight through his head. The next moment all that was left in the pass were six corpses, two horses and four human, starting to cool. And the insane triumphant laughter of The Voice's triumph. He would never find another puppet as powerful or useful as Arthur but what cared he for that? There was now no one left to oppose him and a more or less suitable replacement for Arthur could be found easily enough. The war was won.

I woke up screaming, to be greeted only by the stillness and quiet of the early hours of the morning. I was alone in my bedroom, and all was quiet. I took deep ragged gasps, letting the silence help calm me. I was still fourteen. Vicky was not dead, Jessica was not dead, I was not dead, Danielle was not dead and Merlin had not gone insane. And then the soft sound of small feet on wood made me realise suddenly that I wasn't alone.

I turned and met the eyes of the most beautiful woman I had ever seen, except, maybe, that of a certain red head that I had just dreamed about. But the two could not have been more different. This girl was dark-haired while Vicky was red headed. Slim where older Vicky was curvy, and short where adult Vicky was tall.

The girl was stood on a chair close to my bed. This meant she towered over me as I sat up, which, as she was so little, made me smile for a moment.

She was wearing a bright red hunting tunic, which left her arms bare and fell down about halfway to her knees. Her hair was tied into two ponytails by a bright silver clip, so while her locks were long they were in no danger of falling into her eyes. Her belt was bright green as were her wrist bands. She wore nothing on her feet and all her nails were unpainted. Her eyes were the clearest piecing blue I had ever seen, and she wore a silver bow and quiver full of arrows across her back. Her body was covered with green tattoos of plants and flowers and growing things. She wore a beautiful garland of blue roses in her hair, alternating dark and light. From her back stretched two large gossamer wings, bright green bones supporting them, the flesh a tender and delicate pink, and covered by alternating light and dark blue feathers. Daughter of the king of the gods she was quite literally a fairy princess: albeit one that was human sized. Small human sized.

I cleared my throat, suddenly slightly nervous at the sight of my special visitor. Ever since, two months ago, The Voice had revealed the identity of the female goddess who sometimes helped me out I had been doing research on her, a lot of research. The same way that I had done a lot of research into who Odin was after he had revealed his identity to me at The Pool of Fire and Blood. So I was now fully clued up on how to talk to pagan gods and goddesses properly.

I raised my eyes to her. A pagan raises his eyes to the heavens to acknowledge the power of the gods but he does not kneel or grovel at their feet. Only the "one true god" is so fond of seeing men kneel. "Artemis," I began, "Mistress of the chase, protector of wild animals, guardian of the innocent, goddess of women in childbirth…"

Artemis giggled. "Edward what are you doing?"

I stopped, shaken. "I'm praying to you." I began. "I've read up on it. The first step in getting the attention of a pagan god or goddess is that you have to get their name right. I have to call you by all the possible names that you could ever use and then…"

"You'll be here all night!" laughed Artemis. "When I was just three I asked my Father, Zeus, king of the gods, for as many names as my brother, and he's got loads: like seriously loads!"

"But,..." I began.

"Edward," said Artemis, "you have to say our name right to get our attention. Then list the history between us. Then you tell me what you want, and what you're going to sacrifice to me to get it. But in case you hadn't noticed you've already got my attention! Hello pretty goddess here, wanting to chat!"

"Should you really be talking about being pretty?" I said dubiously. "Aren't you supposed to be the goddess of virginity and stuff?"

Artemis raised her eyebrows. "Edward do you really think that the best thing to greet the goddess of female virginity with, the first time you see her, is to both remind her that she's got no sex life and to also tell her that, as she doesn't sleep around, she shouldn't even be allowed to mention the fact that at least she is pretty?"

I flushed awkwardly. "I didn't mean... it's just that..." I tried to think of a polite way of saying that on meeting you my first impressions were not those of a goddess who stood for eternal virginity. Then I decided things couldn't get any worse than telling the goddess of chastity on her first meeting that most men who met her would think that she was hot. Very hot. So I quickly changed the subject.

I frowned suddenly. "It's the middle of the night, why can I see you so clearly that I can even tell the colour of your eyes and clothes. Even with night vision I shouldn't..."

Artemis smiled, her eyes glowing. "I am the light that shines in the dark places of the world, the light that shines when all other light goes out. Even though it is darkest night of course you can see me, clear as day."

147

"Okay." I said, after thinking about that for a moment. "Thank you, by the way."

Artemis frowned at me. "For what?"

"For shining down the moonbeam at The Pool of Fire and Blood that let me know it was Jessica I had to save, and for telling me not to give up on her when I began to despair that she was turning back into Jess."

Artemis smiled, and her whole face lit up. "Hey," she said gently, "no problem." She reached out and touched my cheek. Her fingers were very cold on my skin. It was like she was a living icicle. A snow princess. "I like the way you look out for people." she said softly.

There was a glimmer of light, and suddenly Artemis was no longer stood on the chair. I started as I realised that she was sat next to me: and shuddered from the sudden cold. She put her arm around my shoulders and gave me a hug. "You have two very lucky sisters." she said.

Her arm was so cold I was fighting not to shiver but I could feel her affection for me. I realised in that moment that I had gained the attention of a powerful deity indeed, but one which was never intended to be too closely worshipped by man. "You know," I said, "I was sure it would be The Allfather who visited me next. I kind of thought you were just going to hang around in the background saying stuff and throwing moonlight around."

Artemis turned her head up to me and I was reminded with a start just how small she was. I was only of moderate height but she was a full head and a half shorter than me. "I care about you just as much as he does." she said simply. "Although it is difficult for me to admit to having feelings for anybody from the opposite sex. I'm not confident even around really nice guys. I'm much more comfortable with other girls, mostly."

148

For a moment we sat in the moonlight, our legs swinging gently: and all I could feel, for the first time in my life, was a sense of complete and utter peace. I had no one to look out for, nothing to think about, just the sense of being with someone who cared about me. Artemis's touch might have burned with cold but it ached with tenderness. Then the memory of the dream, if that is what it had been, returned to me.

"Yes," said Artemis softly. "The vision of the future which is to come cannot have been pleasant. I am sorry."

I stared at her in confusion. "How did you know what I was just thinking?"

Artemis smiled. "When a god and a worshipper start to grow very close, and when a god or goddess starts to bestow his or her blessings on a mortal, the two start to become linked at the deepest levels of their minds. They become more and more linked from the bottom of the subconscious to the highest level of conscious thought. They begin to hear each other's thoughts, and start to feel reflected emotions of what the other is feeling."

I didn't quite know how I felt about that. But the needs of the terrible future which seemed to await were far more pressing at the moment than the possible consequences of becoming linked dangerous closely with the beautiful goddess of female virginity. I took a deep breath. "Is that it then? Is the future just fixed and unchangeable? Is that how it all ends? In violent and failed death? Did you tell me what is to come just so I could start to make my peace with it?" I felt sick as I saw the light once more leave my little sister's eyes.

Artemis ruffled my hair. Her touch was so cold it made the back of my neck shiver. "If all was so fixed why would I even bother to send you a vision? I want you to change your fate. I don't want Arthur to come to the throne, I don't want my worshippers to be persecuted, and I don't want you and Vicky to die like that." There was sudden pause, while strong and strange emotions fought on Artemis's face. "Who's to say that you should necessarily end up with Vicky anyway?" she continued after a small pause. "It's surely at least possible that one day you will meet a girl that you love more."

My relief was so strong it hurt. "So I can change the future away from what I just saw?" I asked desperately. Then I was struck by curious thoughts. "Are you going to help me out regularly like this? And why couldn't the future vision show me who is going to become King Arthur so I could just, you know, take him out?" A random question suddenly struck me: random but important. I needed to know how accurate the research I had been doing into the gods was. "Also since when are you the goddess of prophecy? Isn't that your brother Apollo's job?"

"Of course you can change your fate!" said Artemis, nodding vehemently. "What would be the point of anything if the future was already completely fixed? I'd like to mark you as my champion, as would Odin, but to prove yourselves worthy of both of us you must pass this test. First change your fate so you don't die uselessly, and you must also offer us both great sacrifice. That's one sacrifice each Edward!" She smiled at me and stuck her tongue out. "We gods are greedy you know, we don't do two for one deals!

As to the person who will become Arthur I can't show you who he or she is. The Voice's power blocks you from all attempts to see him. Besides, that would make changing the future far too easy! A champion of the pagan gods shouldn't have the answers just handed to him on a plate!" She squeezed my shoulder affectionately. I could feel my flesh break out into goose bumps. "And finally I have just as much power of prophecy as my twin brother thank you. It's just we can both only give it to members of the opposite sex. He of course has been happy to give it to pretty much any girl with a pretty face that comes along. You should have seen just how many oracles there used to be in the ancient times! Of course the gift of prophecy wasn't all he often gave them.'' Artemis's face darkened for a moment, her friendliness disappearing as she suddenly grew very grim. ''There used to be quite a lot of pregnant oracles back in the ancient times as well.''

Then she shrugged and rallied herself, and the next moment was once again a picture of friendliness and chattiness. ''But there's very few men I've ever trusted enough to give the power of prophecy to you know!'' She mock punched me in the ribs, ''So you should feel very special!''

I looked at her carefully: when I spoke my words were cautious. ''Much as I'm flattered by the divine attention I don't think any of this is what I would have chosen if I had a fully free choice. I would be quiet content with a safe normal life where people weren't trying to kill me.''

Artemis broke out giggling. ''That is the stupidest thing I have ever heard. If you had wanted a simple life all you would have needed to do is let your fire magic develop and forget about your phenomenal grey magic potential. Then your life would have been safe and simple: dead boring but safe and simple. But instead you chose to try and grow as a grey wizard in a world where that is flat out forbidden. So don't start faffing around now and pretending you just want a normal life. Odin and I are just helping you have what you have always wanted. What you have always: deep down: really wanted more than anything else. We're giving you the chance to go on an adventure!''

Chapter 12

The early evening sun was slowly descending from the sky as I wheeled Jessica gently around the rest of the university gardens. It was mid July and the plants and flowers were in full bloom: a rush of colour and scent. I hadn't recognised any of them but then plants weren't something I knew much about. I struggled to identify something as straightforward as roses, but it was clear that Jessica was learning fast. She had never had much interest in plants before, but now she was fully involved in designing a perfect garden both for her and Merlin to have guests round to: and for Danielle to play in with her friends: which at the moment basically meant for her and Vicky.

I followed what Jessica was saying as best I could and I had managed to pick up the names of a few things. I now knew what Photinia Red Robin and Lavender Munstead looked like. But the main thing that came across was Jessica's genuine interest and developing passion for this area of her life. "It can be frustrating," she told me, "even with blue magic to help change the chemical balance of the soil the fact that I am in a wheelchair means I can't do as much myself as I would like. I draw the plans, and buy the materials and do a lot of the watering. As I've had some raised flower beds installed I can even do some of the planting, but most of the weeding and all the digging is impossible for me. But it's nice, I never used to be interested in very much before: except looking good and how much my clothes cost. And gardening gives me a different type of exercise to just wheeling myself around."

She paused, and for a moment looked both scared and guilty, her face suddenly pale. She spoke to me quietly, as though raising up her darkest secret. "Still sometimes feel so trapped though. Just fifteen and I have a kid, a fiancée, a house to look after and a going nowhere job for life. Tell me this is where I'd be a year ago and I would have screamed."

The world went black for a moment, and I when I looked up I was wiping blood away from under one eye. "Just nineteen." I hissed. "Do you know how powerful your husband to be is? Do you know how much grey magic it takes to conceal your true age from him, how much more than it does for everyone else? You are nineteen Jessica, and you must never even think anything else. Who knows how Merlin would react to the truth, or what else it would lead him to question. He must never know what you did to Danielle in the library, you understand?" The future had shown me all too clearly how that knowledge might quite literally send him mad. Jessica nodded: her face white.

There was a pause for a moment while I thought about the rest of what she had said. "As for the other stuff," I shrugged, "you weren't happy as Jess anyway. You can choose to feel trapped in your new life or you can choose to see it as your support and your reason to get out of bed in the morning. And you chose this remember? You were given the option to be Jess and walk away from it all." My voice hardened suddenly. "Do you now regret the choice you took?"

Jessica shuddered. "No thank you. But it's still scary. They talk about not ending up with a baby too young if you find yourself in a serious relationship as a teenager. No one talks about ending up adopting a four year old who asked you hopefully if you're her mummy within the first year of your relationship with her father." She paused. "It's both flattering and terrifying at the same time you know?"

"You'll do fine." I said lightly. "Just compare the life you have now with the life you had when for three months you didn't want to get out of bed: and were doing literally nothing with your life. No one cared what happened to you at all or even noticed that you weren't around. Now there are people who need you in their lives everyday, and start to notice quickly if you're missing. Like now for instance, when you need to get back so that two small girls can decide what they are going to wear for the engagement party tomorrow night."

Jessica smiled. "You know those two have got so close that anyone would think they were sisters. You try and separate them and the din and protests last for hours."

"At least it makes Danielle talk," I said, "that's something."

"I am working on that," said Jessica, "but what… what I did to her has left a scar so deep. I pray every day that she will heal but I don't know if…"

"To which gods?" I asked, slightly more sharply than I meant.

Jessica looked up at me in confusion. "It was just a metaphor. Sorry I don't…"

"Nothing" I said, waving my hand, "just silly talk. My mind wandered."

"Like my husband-to-be's can do." said Jessica darkly. "It's been an hour and a half. We'd better get back to where he's minding Vicky and Danielle. If he's started reading a book instead of playing and looking after them I will quite literally kill him."

We headed back towards the university accommodation, where the five of us were staying for the couple of nights either side of the engagement party.

Merlin was reading a book, but luckily it was to Danielle and Vicky. It was even a child's story book. One of the first things that Jessica had pointed out to Merlin was that: while it might be an excellent and very learned text: one of the reasons why Danielle hadn't been very keen on her bedtime stories was that she probably a little bit young to be getting much out of the full and unabridged version of War and Peace.

We entered the room so quietly, and the girls were so enthralled in the story that they didn't even notice us for a moment. Then they did, and the next moment a shrieking Vicky was in my arms. The moment she touched me to wrap me in a fierce hug reality disappeared in a single flash of a thousand different dancing colours, all of them unbelievably bright, and a vision of the future burned before my eyes.

It was the night after Vicky's sixteenth birthday party. I was twenty six. I had come back from the front lines of the war on special leave to see her. Not that with video calling or texting she was every far from my thoughts.

But right now, after we had been for a meal and to see a film, I was alone in my bedroom in the still early hours of the morning. My phone was flickering with messages as my conversation with my girlfriend echoed back and forth. Laura was two years younger than me. She was a wizard of many colours, a wizard who could draw power from all ends of the spectrum but was dependent upon none. Laura was particularly powerful in white magic and was a specialist researcher in medical biology. We had both spent many years being single: and everyone around us was now so keen to tell us what a good match we were. Both bright, both well educated, both similar ages, similar middle class background. And Laura, while ticking all the right boxes in what middle class wizards were supposed to want was both average looking and dull: meaning most successful wizards didn't want her as any more than a work colleague or distant acquaintance. But she would be a very good catch for a grey wizard they all agreed: quietly relieved they didn't have to feel guilty about someone who was all the right things on paper but who in practice was just being left permanently on the shelf. Laura was genuinely happy enough with the match: she liked the prestige of dating a war hero and loved the fact I could do things with grey magic that no one else could. Plus she much preferred having anyone's company to being by herself.

I hated the whole relationship. When I had first met Laura I had thought she was just the wrong side of pretty, now, after over a year of dating and getting to know her personality better, I thought that she was close to hideous. While boasting about me all she could at public occasions in private Laura had never said so much as one nice thing about me. But she had said many unpleasant ones: some that were even cruel. She hated the fact that as a grey wizard I didn't follow the conventional routines like all the other wizards of different colours that she knew. But then, of course, none of them had said yes when she'd wanted them to ask her out.

Why did I let this hideous charade of a relationship continue? Because I had a problem: a really serious problem. Because I was in love with someone else. Someone who I was really not supposed to be in love with: someone who I was not even supposed to think existed in that way.

This problem was so serious that the vey few times I'd ever actually been able to go through with shagging

Laura it had been by imagining that she had green eyes full of light and laughter and red hair so bright it hurt to look at it in the light.

Back alone in my bedroom everything was still and quiet as the night rested, except for the constant flashing of text messages on my phone.

I was in the middle of typing a particularly annoyed reply to ''You just want me for sex don't you? That's all I am to you. Just a fuck buddy.'' when my door slipped open, the creak of its hinges loud in the silence. Vicky came in, wrapped in a bright red dressing gown. She held up her hand and sent a globe of light spinning in mid-air to light up my bedroom. I smiled at her, but the look she gave me back was one of real anger.

''Edward what is it with Laura, does she not ever sleep? Does she just sit at home all night just playing on her phone?'' Vicky raised her hand and my phone flew out of my grasp, landing in her outstretched palm. She switched it off: with a look that was very final. ''If she's like this with you,'' snarled Vicky, ''how are you going to get all the rest you need to stay safe on the front lines?''

Then, with Laura dealt with, Vicky smiled and relaxed. Her mood changed so suddenly it was almost like she had suddenly become a different person. I tried not to look at her in the light, tried to stop my eyes from drinking in every curve of her soft skin. I might as well have tried to stop liking chocolate, or giving up needing to sleep. Her hair danced in the light to the nape of her neck, where beads of sweat were forming. I could see the tanned skin of her lower arms in the bright light, her skin glowly with life and make up. Vicky always made herself look good. Soft red fabric curved upwards from her budding breasts, and I knew she had deliberately come to see me wearing a dressing gown a couple of sizes too small. My little sister's lips were full and red: the lipstick beautiful and stark. Just looking at her made me think of

157

sex. She came and sat next to me on the bed, and without her even touching me I felt my breath quicken, my cock harden to beyond the point of pain.

Vicky leaned her head against my shoulder, and her eyes flickered downwards to check out just below the centre of my waist. What she saw of my physical reaction to her made a smile light up her face, and left a wicked fire dancing in her eyes.

I desperately tried to remember how I was supposed to feel about my little sister. I was supposed to be protective and friendly towards her: not ache with everything I had to come inside her.

"I don't like Laura." said Vicky, very firmly. "She's too similar to you. She doesn't bring out the best in you. Together you just get really boring." She spoke calmly but completely finally.

I took a deep breath. "Things aren't going that well with her at the moment that's true. Maybe she isn't the one for me?" I smiled and tried to make a joke of it. "Why you got someone else in mind?"

"Maybe," said Vicky, flicking her hair back playfully. "Maybe there is someone who loves you. Someone who you can't take your eyes off even though you try so desperately not to look. Cheeky! Someone who doesn't even have to touch you to make you start thinking about love and sex. Someone who wants to fuck you as much as you want to pound your cock inside her."

I swallowed, while Vicky met my gaze and that strange fire dancing in her eyes drew me into her soul. It was far from the only thing of hers I wanted to be inside. Vicky's voice was mostly level, but it shook in places with a desire so strong it was closer to the ache of pain than the release of pleasure. "I've seen the way you look at me Edward, the way your eyes drink me in. You stare at me the way a man dying of thirst stares at water. But I'm not a mirage in a desert Edward. I'm real and I'm here. I can see I'm what you want; what you need. You know we both want to be together in that way. Why are you fighting it so hard?'' Her voice hardened suddenly. ''You know that we both love each other more than anybody else in the world could ever do: we always have. Give me one good reason why we shouldn't date? Why you shouldn't make me your girlfriend?''

I could feel my hands clench as I fought back with everything I had against the urges of both my heart and the head of my cock. ''Because we are brother and sister. Because loving you in that way is wrong.'' Slowly gently I pushed her head away from my shoulder, and I felt a sickness deep inside me as I was suddenly deprived of my sister's touch. I could suddenly feel all the colour draining out of my world. ''I love you Vicky. But it is a greater sin to love you in this way than it would be to not love you at all. We can never be together, not like that.''

I pulled away from her, standing up from where I was sitting on my bed. Vicky made no move to resist, she simply reached out and put her hand in mine, so that our fingers played and danced together. The fire in her eyes burned on: defiant and determined.

''You know Tom tried to kiss me today.'' She said, almost dreamily. ''I didn't really want to, and he tasted like cigarettes and mouthwash. It was quite horrible really, but it was still my first kiss. I wanted to give that to you but you're faffing around so much at the moment trying not to get into my pants that it really pissed me off.'' She turned and looked at me. ''I don't really want him but I did it because I knew it would make you jealous.'' I couldn't control the pain in my heart, the burn of jealousy and the growl that rose in my throat. Vicky blushed with pleasure.

''And he wants far more than that kiss from me, much more. And there's a couple of other boys at school who

159

do as well. And if we're never going to be together then maybe…"

"Vicky." I reached out and placed a hand on her shoulder, and as the sweat of our bodies mingled together under my fingers and on the palm of my hand my body almost cried out in pleasure and need. "Don't…"

Vicky was smiling deeply now, but her eyes never left mine: the fire fierce, and confident. Confident now that she would, at last, get what she had wanted for the last two years: that my resistance was finally coming to an end.

"Don't what Edward? Don't be an absolute slut? Well if you don't want your younger sister to start playing the field, if you want her to settle down in a nice steady relationship and be a good girl then…"

She looked up at me and laughed. "You want to protect my modesty? All you have to do is take off my dressing gown."

As though in a daze I put my hands to her dressing gown and she slipped out of it. She wore nothing underneath. My eyes drank in the swollen redness of her full nipples, and traced their way down her stomach to where her mound was covered in dark hair, hair that did nothing to disguise her glistening slit. Her mouth moved so close to mine and her arms came around me. I knew that within moments I would be inside her. It was what I wanted with all my heart: but I still knew that it was wrong.

"Vicky," I began, one last time calling on a strength from some deep dark reserve, but she pressed one finger to my lips: hard enough I could feel them being pushed back against my teeth, and her other hand slid down to fully and very firmly embrace my cock. I wanted her so much that at the first loving, tender brush of her fingers, I almost came in her hand. "No more talking, Edward."

my little sister whispered, her breath moving from her mouth to mine, playing on the surface of my lips. "And unless you want me doing this sort of thing with another man I suggest you never fight your feelings for me again. A girl could get the wrong idea. And an unhappy girl could end up going elsewhere. And we both know that you really don't want that."

Then her mouth sealed on mine and we were in each other's arms and the rest was easy: oh so easy. Good stories are supposed to end when you are at last in the arms of the girl you love. But in this horror story our coming together in sex and love was only the beginning.

Then the vision ended, and I was suddenly back in the present day. Once again my little sister was just a child. She gave me a very warm and innocent hug: and then started telling me all about the massive game of snakes and ladders she, Danielle and Merlin had all just been playing.

I shook my head, trying to clear thoughts that were suddenly so confused. Why had I been shown that vision of the future, what was… I forced my attention back to the present, trying to suppress the bleak sense of foreboding that seemed to wait beckoningly ahead in a future growing ever darker and more strange. What on earth was I supposed to do to prevent what I had just seen happening from coming to pass? Did I even want to?

Danielle had climbed into Jessica's lap. "Mummy," she said, "Daddy very good today. He played big game of snakes and ladders and I go up big ladder and daddy fell down snake. Then he made sandwiches and managed get butter on right side of bread like you showed him. And then I had hot chocolate and Vicky had can of coke and then Daddy started telling story…"

Jessica used blue magic to create a cloth out of the air, and wiped absently around Danielle's mouth, where some of the hot chocolate still remained. "It sounds like you've had a really exciting day my love. And I'm sure daddy will get chance to finish the story later! But what about you Danielle?" She said lightly, "Have you made up any more stories you want to tell? Any more stories about the brave little mouse?"

Danielle shook her head sadly. "Brave little mouse hit by car. That his last story. Everyone goes away in end. Started new story, about brave little monkey." She blushed shyly. "But not ready yet."

Jessica leaned in and kissed Danielle on the forehead. "I am sure it will be a lovely story and I can't wait to hear it. But come on you. It's getting late, well past your bedtime. And you've got a big day ahead of you tomorrow."

She looked up at Vicky and her eyes narrowed "And come on you as well. It's past your bedtime too. And no record setting or getting carried away with your own power tomorrow. These are Merlin's and my work colleagues and friends and you need to be well behaved and make a good impression. Merlin and I will be in a lot of trouble if we annoy these people."

I whispered in Vicky's ear. "So it is important you are good. Maybe you could help Danielle with her story instead of using white magic to make the loudest possible bangs and flashes. And see," I hesitated, unsure for a moment, "see if you can make the mouse story have a happy ending."

Vicky looked at me dubiously. "Will be good Edward and like Danielle' stories but mouse not going to get a happy ending. Mouse is squashed flat in the middle of the road and all his family then starve to death because no food. Danielle draw pictures. Mouse is ball of red fur on motorway tarmac. How that have happy ending?"

Before my eyes a dog howled in agony as its front legs were ripped apart and its heart gave way. I took a deep breath. "Okay so the mouse is a goner. But maybe you can persuade Danielle to get the brave little monkey to end up somewhere nice."

Vicky looked doubtful. "Danielle is planning for little monkey to get lost and go looking for his mummy but instead find an enormous crocodile. Crocodile is going to rip little monkey to pieces and eat him all up. Then mummy monkey so sad when she see what happen to little monkey that she fall out of tree and hit her head and die. Danielle draw pictures. How that going to have a happy ending?"

I sighed, wearily but also in pain. "Maybe the monkey could win the fight with the crocodile?"

Vicky wrinkled her nose. "That is silly. Crocodile much more scary than a monkey."

"Maybe the monkey has magic?" I asked.

Vicky folded her arms crossly. "That even more silly Edward. Like people most animals not have magic!"

I was running out of ideas. "Maybe have Danielle tell the story from the perspective of the crocodile? He seems to get a happy ending."

"The next story is about the crocodile."

"Oh good." I said, cheered that Danielle seemed to be able to do some happy stories at least.

"Yes," said Vicky, "after crocodile eat monkey all fish get scared and swim out the river to the sea. There is no food and crocodile starve to death. Danielle draw pictures!"

I tried to come to terms with the fact that Danielle was writing and illustrating disturbing horror stories and showing them to my little sister: but at least Danielle was telling stories again. She hadn't been telling any at all since Tuggles died, not until Jessica had adopted her. Small steps I supposed.

"Just see if she can think of a story with a happy ending." I said weakly, "Or just play snakes and ladders again or something. '' Then Jessica was shooing the two little girls off with her and they all went to go and get ready for the children's bedtime.

That left me and Merlin alone together.

As the door closed behind the three girls the atmosphere changed. It wasn't hostile, that was too strong, but it was only just the right side of neutral. Both of us had power: both of us had secrets.

There was a long silence, while my black pupils stared into his brown, and even in the warmth of the summer sun the evening air began to feel chill.

"Come." said Merlin at last, in a voice that was not unfriendly. "As my fiancée's closest relative I think we should spend some time together. And I have something to show you."

We turned from the room we were in and went deeper into the university building. At first we passed through halls with great portraits and wild landscapes hung in golden frames on the walls; walls which were inlaid with gold. The rooms were beautiful, stunning, and they conveyed the power and prestige of all the highest forms of learning. Of course they were also just an excellent public relations job. This was a place for socialising, for dignifying the grand occasions of life: especially weddings: with all the dignity of the most advanced forms of higher education and in-depth specialist knowledge without any, well learning, having to actually take place. The distinguished hardback books on the shelves were never opened, or done so only for people to gawk at the painstakingly beautiful illustrations, or to scan read random parts of impressive looking text to onlookers to prove just how clever what the book said was.

We went on, and, as simply as passing from one door to the next, the atmosphere changed. We were in the real library now: here learning and studying did take place.

And while this part of the building was certainly functional no one would describe the design of these rooms or their furnishing as attractive or impressive. In front of me electronic barriers waited, and beyond them stacks of shelves filled with university library books. The rooms we had passed through before had been empty, deserted: used only when they were booked for private events. Here the atmosphere was everyday. Students studied, and library staff moved.

Merlin came over towards the electronic barriers, and one of the staff moved towards him from stacking the shelves. His voice was quiet but firm. "Now Merlin you are a credit to this university and the hours you work are an inspiration to us all. But tomorrow is your engagement party and you know that you shouldn't be here, you should be with your fiancée helping her get ready. We will give you all your books back on Monday don't you worry, but you are not to go near them until after this weekend. So turn yourself around and back you go. This weekend is about you being there for your daughter and your wife-to-be. You are about to celebrate getting engaged with a party. Books are not allowed!!!"

"I haven't come to read." said Merlin. "I have a problem... a potentially contentious issue with a crucial in-law that I need privacy to resolve. The keys to my study please."

"He's not lying." I said flatly. "If Merlin tries reading a book during this meeting then I'll dematerialise it in his hand. And yes I am not an easy relative."

The library assistant's voice went very distant. "You're the grey wizard. The one who keeps getting more and more powerful and yet no one dares to stop. I really don't get why."

The woman's voice which answered his question was strong and clear. "It's because grey magic isn't actually illegal, just using it to hurt other people is. But most people don't have the self-control to never hit back, particularly with the extent of the abuse that all grey wizards receive. And even if they do develop extraordinary levels of restraint then the bullying they receive just steps up as their powers grow. Even grey wizards who survive initially and start to grow in power soon find themselves in a state where it is either fight back or die: and either way they are screwed. Lose when they hit back and they die. Win and they are just arrested and executed for using grey magic as an offensive weapon."

"So what's different this time?" asked the library assistant uneasily.

"That when the abuse was stepped up to the critical point a little white wizard got involved. Edward's little sister made very bloody examples out of those who were trying to kill him, and as she was a white wizard and fighting in self-defence of a family member the law couldn't lay a finger on her. Now no one dares to raise their hands against him, for fear of her reprisals.

Anyway that's all besides the point. If Merlin wants to work on his engagement weekend then I say let him work on his engagement weekend. It's not our job to regulate his personal life now is it?"

The woman was very beautiful, with long dark hair and a full figure. I would have guessed that she was in her early thirties. She looked natural, but had actually gone to a great deal of care with her make up.

I didn't like the way she looked at Merlin at all, with an almost hungry interest in her stare. I liked even less the way she placed one hand confidently on his back. "You are such a credit to this department Merlin." She whispered into his ear. "No one else in this whole university is half as brilliant as you."

I was pleased that Merlin seemed not to even really notice her touch. He just dipped his head to her politely.

166

"Thank you kindly madam. That makes things tonight much easier."

He collected the keys from the library assistant, and we passed through the stacked rows of bookshelves. Past students and academics at their desks, past the coffee shop, and past where books gave way to seemingly endless stacks of journals. Then Merlin and I came to an unremarkable door that led off the library, though even from here I could feel the power warding the room. Merlin turned and slipped his key into the lock.

"Who was that woman?" I asked uneasily, feeling very protective big brother all of a sudden: not liking that another woman had such a level of interest in my elder sister's man. "Which woman?" asked Merlin, genuinely baffled.

I sighed, although I was quietly very relived at his lack of interest. "The woman who gave you those keys?"

"Her, oh her." Merlin waved a hand in dismissive indifference. "She's my manager. Quite new here really. Couple of years or so. Came from seemingly nowhere to be our head of department. She keeps saying nice things but I'm worried she doesn't think much of me. She seems to be hanging around everywhere I go, she's there almost everywhere I look."

He turned and whispered to me conspiratorially. "I used to be worried she thought I wasn't up to scratch, that she was constantly checking up on me to make sure my research and teaching weren't going downhill. But now I think it is more than that. I now suspect sadly that she has an alternative agenda. And a most disgraceful one, for a man with a child and soon the most beautiful and caring wife in all the world."

I stared at him, utterly astonished that he had managed to put two and two together. "You noticed she's got an interest in you beyond the professional?" I said, amazed. I couldn't have been more astonished if

167

he'd managed to cook Danielle a complicated meal without giving her indigestion.

"Oh yes." said Merlin, nodding his head wisely. "I know what she's up to and it's downright despicable! Show's a complete lack of morals. Why, I think she's trying to steal my research on the breeding habits of broccoli all for herself! She wants to sell it on to big business to make lots of money while I am left poor and penniless with a family to support. It's an absolute disgrace."

I was caught between a desire to sigh, and a sudden need to just punch the wall in intense frustration.

Merlin used the pause to look at me wisely. "But I'm onto her don't you worry. I know what Nimue's game is and I don't..."

But I didn't hear the next words as what he'd said meant everything else fled away in a sudden intake of breath. I'd only had a couple of days since my first vision but that had been enough for me to start looking into old Arthurian lore. I didn't know that much yet, but I did know the basics: which meant that I knew who Nimue was. A female sorceress of great power and beauty. A sorceress who, over time, took all of Merlin's power and sealed him away for ever: or killed him depending upon which version of the story you read.

Legend was very clear about Nimue's relationship with Merlin: about how she was very possibly the single greatest abusive lover of all time.

Chapter 13

Merlin's study was much like his cottage. Filled with books, ornaments; and now also with pictures drawn by Danielle. Coloured drawings of magical animals and fierce dragons gazed down on Merlin from his walls. A photo of Jessica holding Danielle was framed at the front of his desk. It had been taken recently at Water World. Jessica had been about to take Danielle to play in the pool with the wave machine. Jessica's disability meant that she had just had to watch of course. The study room was also relatively neat and ordered; and I smiled as I realised that my sister must have helped Merlin out here too. I wondered what it would have been like before my elder sister got involved. Probably just a dishevelled mess with no pictures or photos to give it warmth. Through the window at one end of the room the last of the sun's light was setting. It was sinking behind the hill on which Prestham was built, bathing the trees and the rock face on the hill in a golden glow. From here the rock face was a grand and impressive structure rising out of the earth, but it was too far away to be seen in any real detail. However from the centre of Prestham at the foot of the hill the top of the rock face looked like the face of an old man: cased in stone: looking out over the town below. Wound with gulleys and caves the rock face had been called, as long as anyone could remember, "The Old Man of Prestham". It was fun to climb on, especially with an overambitious four year old. Vicky and I had been up it many times. She had always loved climbing: though the days were long past when something as simple as Rope Mountain would have fascinated her. Rope Mountain would struggle even to register as interesting nowadays: now that Vicky no longer saw it as difficult.

Merlin was looking at the photo of Jessica and Danielle, and then he reached out and held it up in front of him. "You know," he said absently, "Danielle and Jessica spent a full day at Water World. Jessica couldn't go swimming, or on any of the rides of course, but she made it one of the best days of Danielle's life. The only thing that Danielle found sad was that mummy's back wouldn't let her come and play in the pool as well. For a long time I felt so bad about what was happening between Jessica and I. She a young girl in the full blossom of her youth, and me a middle aged man. Scatty and wanting nothing more than a good book and to put my feet up by the fire. What could I possible offer her? She is so young. But then I saw the way she was with Danielle, and the way Danielle was with her. You know I can't remember the last time I heard my daughter cry?"

He turned to me, and in that moment I realised that he was crying himself. "Do you know what it's like, to love your child but not be able to take care of her very well no matter how hard you try? I love Danielle so much, but I couldn't even manage to feed her properly, or to find her friends. I didn't even notice when some bitch killed her beloved dog right under her eyes: and practically under my nose. And then I met a lovely girl who makes my daughter happy. Do you know what that is worth Edward? More than a river of gold, more than an unending sea of knowledge stretching out to the horizon."

Merlin looked at me: and for a moment his gaze was hard as steel. "I can see the power in you Edward. Feel the strength that is growing. And that would be dangerous enough in itself but when combined with the bond you have with... with Vicky.... Well part of my role as a brown wizard is to identify any grey wizards strong enough to become threats to society. By all the laws of this country and by all my compassion for my fellow man I should order the arrest of both of you under the emergency powers of the state. The level of danger that you pose means that you would be imprisoned indefinitely without hope of release or trial.

I raised an eyebrow. "Considering you're warning me of this you have no intention of doing so." I commented mildly. "So why not?"

Merlin sighed, and it was like all the life and fire suddenly went out of him. "Because I know how much you mean to Jessica. And I know that she would never forgive me if I acted against you. I could save so many innocent people from you, but then I would once again have a four year old eating soggy cereal three times a day and crying herself to sleep at night because she's so lonely and confused. Crying as softly as she can because she doesn't want me to hear: because she loves her inadequate daddy and knows that he is already trying his hardest to do his best."

What a lovely story. It was one that I wished that I could believe. I turned and met Merlin's eye directly. "That," I said flatly, "was a really good attempt at convincing me to trust you. It's only your bad luck that it didn't succeed."

You could feel the tension in the room sharpen, like a knife edge in the air, but neither of us yet seized or started using magic. If a conflict between us began to escalate neither of us had any idea how we could begin to make it stop. Unless it ended in victory for one and death for the other of course.

I turned from Merlin and walked over to the window and looked out over the garden. "Why did you lie to me and Jessica the first time we met?" I asked, almost absently. "You claimed not to be THAT Merlin. But within two decades you will place a King Arthur on the throne."

"What?" said Merlin, "The Merlin of Legend has been sealed away inside hillside stone for over a millennium. I am powerful yes, and have ambitious parents: hence the name: but I am not actually…"

I turned to him, something in his voice making me wonder. "Is it possible you don't know?"

"Edward", said Merlin impatiently, "this is ridiculous. You may have gods watching over you but Apollo isn't taking a particularly active role and he has never given men his powers anyway."

I turned and looked at him. "Not Apollo." I said flatly. "My prophetic gift comes from Artemis."

Merlin took a deep breath. He looked almost as surprised as he looked pleased. "So the chaste goddess of the moon finally begins to accept the need of all things: the need to change." He looked at me, and for a moment he was smiling. "Yes very good, very good."

"It is nice having the gift of foresight." I said lightly, "It is much less fun seeing what the future holds."

Merlin met my gaze levelly. "And what exactly does the future hold Edward?"

And for a moment all I could see was red hair and green eyes, and for a moment I could once again taste the sweat on my sister's skin as I kissed her. I wanted to say. "I start fucking my younger sister and in the resulting revulsion the world goes to hell in a handcart." Our relationship the most beautiful form of poison that the world has ever seen.

But instead I met Merlin's eyes and said. "Jessica loses faith that you love her because you don't give her children. She comes to believe that the only thing you want her for is to raise Danielle as a substitute mother. I don't have the full details into exactly how one event leads to another but she ends up taking her own life. That leaves Danielle emotionally in, let's just say, a bit of a state."

Merlin looked at me, and his eyes were very still. "Jessica's… condition means that being pregnant would be extremely risky for her, especially in childbirth. If I give her children she could well die." He paused, and his voice shook. "As my first wife did. And she wasn't in a wheelchair."

Merlin took a deep breath, "Did your vision suggest anything about the risks of childbirth to Jessica's life?" He asked softy.

I looked him straight in the eye, and felt the brown magic moving under Merlin's subtle command as he quietly examined my words and body language for the slightest hint of deception, like a magical lie detector. But I was prepared for this, and my grey magic subtly faded the tell-tale signs of a lie away from my words.

"Nothing." I said. "Only that she will die by her own hand if she does not have children of her own. And Danielle will blame herself as the reason that her mummy is dead."

I held Merlin's gaze and he stood deep in thought for a long time, then he looked at me, and while he was not smiling neither was his face grim. "Okay," he said, "It is clear then what road I must now take." He paused then looked at me searchingly. "I do not believe I am that Merlin of Legend Edward but if you are so sure…I have always felt like there was a part of me missing, like my power and knowledge were somehow shorn into different pieces. There are days when I wake up in the morning, and I can almost taste what it is I am missing. It is like the smell of wood smoke on an autumn's day, mixed in with the sudden flash of red, sharp pain.

As for me finding a king to put on a throne... you don't need me to tell you that there is far more to my role than I am prepared to share with you. And that is the way it will remain. Just as you would never reveal all your secrets to me."

He looked at me. "Edward I know that if I let you live and that if no one else takes you down I know what you will become. A dark lord. A dark lord like no other. One driven not by hate, but by love. And that makes you more dangerous than anyone motivated just by anger alone could ever be. You will go out into the world and you will do great and terrible things. But I, who can see all this, cannot see how I could ever make my daughter happy again if I lift up my hand against you. And I will not sacrifice her, not for anything in this world. Danielle now almost never stops smiling, and for that it seems I will risk the lives of thousands of strangers. What does that say about me I wonder?

You don't know the path you are on Edward, the things that you will do if you live. Your road from here is bleak. And should you live every footstep you take will be trodden in blood."

There was a short, tense silence.

"Well I do know some things." I said at last, trying to lighten the mood. "Like the fact that if we even try to start fighting the night before your and Jessica's engagement party Jessica will kill us both. Come, let's go and see how my sisters and your daughter are doing."

"Yes," said Merlin quietly, "and let us hope the future doesn't end with us fighting to the death."

Chapter 14

The thing about grey magic is that, when you really have to walk this world unseen, it is very, very easy. No one notices your movements, or, and perhaps more importantly, even your absence.

It was less than two hours since I had finished my conversation with Merlin, and now I stood on a rock ledge on the Old Man of Prestham: very near to the summit of the hill. Above me was only one final rock slope which would need to be climbed rather than walked, then the summit of windblown grass, and above that nothing but the endless miles of empty sky. Below me fell the bare sandstone of the rock face, then the trees of the lower slopes, then finally the lights of the houses of Prestham, gathered neatly at the foot of the hill. Out from the town on the lower slopes the lights of Merlin's cottage shone through the trees with a warmth that was entirely lacking from the rest of the world. From here you couldn't see the slopes on the other side of the hill on which my parents' house was built.

Around me trees had grown naturally in a rough circle surrounding a rugged outcrop of stone. I had two bad cuts on my shoulder: one just below the base of my neck: and a deep puncture wound on my left leg where it had been hit hard by an animal horn. I had sealed the ounds shut with magic fire, which prevented further bleeding, but meant that I could feel where my flesh was both torn and burned.

I had been hurt but I had triumphed: and that was all that in the end mattered. In my hands I held the weakly twitching form of a serpobat. It had the wings and body of a great black bat, but the venomous fangs and tail of a serpent, the scales razor sharp. The lashings of the tail explained the cuts on my shoulder. I stood before the outcrop of stone, my makeshift altar, and raised the serpobat high into the air. I began my prayer.

"Artemis, mistress of the animals, protector of the innocent, guardian of women in the throes of childbirth; or by whatever name you currently wish to be called. Whether you stand today as Artemis the Friendly or Artemis the Terrible I call upon you," - even as I said those words I really hoped that Artemis was in a good mood at this moment - "invoking all that which we have shared. You have sent me moonlight, and visions, and have helped me to save my older sister from darkness. To you I offer the lifeblood of this creature of magic, to you will I tear apart its flesh; that in return you may shelter any child that grows within Jessica's body and deliver it to health and life: and not to death and darkness."

I seized the serpobat in my hand and took its head in my mouth, tearing with my teeth. They cut through bone and flesh and the creature spasmed in death inside my mouth. I turned and, fighting not to gag on the black blood, spat the head onto the altar. Fire of all colours and of none roared on the stone, and I knew that my offering had been accepted. The gods of Greece and Rome had always hungered for red meat. I held the bat's corpse over the flames, till its flesh smouldered and cooked and its blood burned. Then I devoured the flesh. And for every bite I took another was taken from the other side, as I shared in the feasting with my goddess. Then the offering was over, and the flames on the altar died. The strangest thing was that, even though the fire had cooked the meat, its flames had burned cold not hot: bringing an unsettling chill into the air: not warming it. But this was not the end: my prayers of worship were far from done.

Then I turned to where the dinofox lay whimpering, its mind's ability to focus and concentrate faded in a whirl of grey magic. The dinofox had the body of a fox but the horns and crest of a triceratops and the spiked long tail of a stegosaurus. I staggered under its weight as I dragged it to the altar. It was so heavy to lift that I almost felt like I was hurling it on to the top of the altar: not lifting it. I raised my knife high into the air. For a moment as I did so the dinofox looked up at me, and in the panic in its eyes I felt a pain burn suddenly inside my heart, a gnawing emptiness.

But this was nature, the law of blood and claw. And only the strongest would survive.

"To the virgin huntress," I screamed, "to the cold light of the ever-shining moon!" And I cut out the dinofox's heart, took one bite to honour my communion with my goddess, and then hurled the bleeding organ into the night air. Flames leapt and roared in mid-air and it was consumed.

In ancient sacrifice I knew what the Greeks and Romans had done. They had burnt the useless offal of their animal sacrifice on the altars of the gods and had saved the best meat for themselves. Was it any wonder that in the end their gods had turned from them, that in the end Rome had fallen to the blood and fire of the barbarian? Instead I cut out the offal, the worst part, the intestines of the dinofox, and raised it to my lips. I took a savage bite, and the next moment I was having to fight the urge to gag, to throw up, but I made myself swallow through the rancid taste. I would not offer the bad cuts of meat to the goddess, not for a sacrifice this important. "Huntress, to you I dedicate the life of this predator, that you may shelter my sister Jessica through pregnancy, and see her safely delivered of her child; and not cast down into death as she struggles to bring new life into this world."

"Enough Edward," said a voice, strong and beautiful. "I don't want you making yourself ill. And that is what will happen if you keep eating raw offal. And a goddess should take all of life in her offerings, the best along with the worst." Flames leapt up along the altar, and the dinofox began to cook. Its flesh ran with juices as it cooked and turned from red to brown. Its bones cracked, the marrow melted, and its skin and fur were consumed entirely by flame. Then the fire died away and was gone, and on the other side of the altar stood a small woman, breathtakingly beautiful: a woman who shone with all the power of the divine. She glowed with luminescence, moonlight made flesh, born up on colourful feathered wings.

She sat down before the altar and I joined her. "I accept your offerings and invoke my blessing for your sister." Artemis said lightly. "You have sacrificed to me monsters that prey on the innocents of mankind and I accept the offerings of their lives gladly. Plus dinofox is like really delicious! It's like pretty much my favourite take away ever!"

We both ate in silence for a while, until the flesh was gone.

"So Jessica's safe now?" I said hopefully, "She won't die in childbirth?"

Artemis turned to me and looked a little guilty. "Well kind of," she offered at last, "like sort of fifty-fifty?"

My tones turned to ice. "And what exactly is that meant to mean goddess? She either is safe or she isn't. And didn't you just say that you accepted my offerings?"

Artemis flushed guiltily, and squeezed my shoulder. Her hands were so ice cold it made me shiver even though I had already adjusted to the late evening chill. "Well you know there are two sides to me right? There's me, Artemis the Friendly, who looks after the innocent and kills monsters and I'm defo up for helping out. You were dead brave in your hunting and I'm really happy with what you just did. If your sister is pregers on my watch then she's in no danger at all!"

"And if it's the other part of you that is around when my sister is with child?" I asked coldly, "or when she is due?"

Artemis couldn't meet my gaze and looked at the floor. "The sacrifices you have just offered to me would mean nothing to her. I want to protect the innocent and see monsters die. She wants to... well just to hurt two types of men. Nothing else matters to her: nothing else at all!"

I thought about this for a moment. Then "What kind of men?" I asked flatly. "What blood offerings would she accept?"

Artemis raised her eyes and they were trembling. "She accepts any kind but there's two types she prefers above all. Men who hurt women and men who are innocent. Softly spoken men. Those who are kind and who treat other people well."

I thought about that for a long while. "Would she accept any other kind of offering but blood?" I asked at last. "Saving women from distress perhaps, burning chick lit books, or offerings of manly food like beer and steak. Anything else at all?"

"No," said Artemis miserably, "she wants only one thing: the blood of men!"

I looked at her with implacable cold. "Do you hate us so much Huntress? Are we as a gender so abhorrent to you?"

Artemis looked at me in astonishment. "I am not her!" She almost squealed. Her voice went ragged and for a moment she sounded almost desperate. "I hate Artemis the Terrible! I am Artemis the Friendly! I like men and women, it's just men make me... well nervous. Sex and what it does has always scared me."

Even though you're the god of childbirth? I thought distantly. The more I know about this goddess the less I understand. You seem to be a mix of completely incompatible elements. But then again isn't that obvious from the start? Of all the different candidates the gods had for a candidate of perpetual virginity, why on earth die they pick an astonishingly beautiful and nubile young woman?

I looked at Artemis. "What are the chances of it being you who is around when my sister needs you and what are the chances of it being... Her?" Artemis shrugged, licking her lips nervously. "What way will the wind and weather blow a year from today Edward? I have more idea of that than I do of how my own nature will ebb and flow."

I sighed and put my arm around her shoulders. I was beginning to grow quite attached to my patron goddess, this side of her anyway. I made myself ignore the searing cold that blasted my flesh the moment I touched her. "Thanks Artemis." I said. "You've been a great help actually. You've told me everything that I need to know."

"Well your sacrifice was cool!" said Artemis gently, "Plus it means I don't have to think about cooking dinner now. Next time though I'd love some squirrels too, red if you've got any."

Just over an hour and a half later I was back on Chester's streets. I had steeled myself on the train journey and was now ready to do what had to be done. It was dark, shops closed, bars open. It was that time of night when the bars and clubs were full but the streets were quiet. Revellers were now at their intended destination, and, apart from beggars with nowhere else to go, no one else was any longer outside. I walked invisible, clad in grey. I had to be careful, if I was caught using grey magic as an offensive weapon that would be death. I saw where a beggar sat huddled in the darkness, and drew my dagger very calmly. I walked up besides him, then settled myself down to wait. I thought about what I was about to do, and felt quite ill: but the vision had made it quite clear what the consequences of inaction would be. I waited while a few groups came past, and a few couples. I watched them carefully, waiting for my chance. But there were either too many people together for it to be sensible for me to make my move, or something about the people passing made me hesitate: a lack of any obvious cruelty. But then a couple came down the street, at a time when it was completely deserted except for the beggar, who had fallen to sleep. I knew almost instantly that I had found exactly what I had been looking for. The girl could barely walk and was trying to disjointedly stagger every which way, yet she smelt only lightly of alcohol. It took very little observation to be almost certain that her drink had been spiked. The man supporting her had a cruel smile of anticipation on his face.

But then he didn't expect the next event in his life to be me slitting his throat with one swift movement, letting the intangibility around my blade drop so that it rematerialised to cut his throat in one swift and smooth motion.

"To Artemis the Terrible." I hissed in the man's ear as he died, "Take this offering you cold bitch and protect my sister through her childbirth, always." A great fire, white and furiously hot rose up, consuming all of the dying man: even the flecks of blood on my blade. The beggar looked up with a start, awoken suddenly out of sleep by the burst of terrible heat that had consumed the dying man so completely. The fire's heat was so intense I could feel myself sweat.

The girl blinked, far too out of it to be sure of what had happened, then, without anyone now to support her, fell sharply. I caught her as she fell, before she could hit the tiles and possibly really hurt herself, then lowered her gently and safely to the floor. The beggar looked up, then came over to help. Gently we placed her into the recovery position, and as we succeeded we smiled at each other. He was middle aged, with a long brown beard, slightly dirty and matted, and a trench coat that had clearly seen better days.

The only blessing was that he died swiftly as I cut his throat from ear to ear, whispering Artemis the Terrible's name. But I am still haunted by the look in his eyes as he died. By the realisation that I saw in his face that a world that he had thought could not hurt him anymore had found one last new way to betray him. Then the strange white fire consumed the innocent man utterly, and he was gone in mere moments as though he had never been. That Jessica's child may be born alive and well had been my second prayer. Each goddess had now been offered two sacrifices, one for each prayer. I knew distantly that I had won, that the future had now been changed, but the thought of what I had just done drifted inside me like a blank emptiness, eating away at my core.

Merlin's voice echoed in my ears. "I know what you will become. A dark lord. A dark lord like no other. One driven not by hate, but by love. And that makes you more dangerous than anyone motivated just by anger alone could ever be. You will go out into the world and you will do great and terrible things."

I walked over to the drugged girl and then I paused, looking around uncertainly. I didn't like the thought of leaving an innocent girl completely unprotected in the centre of the street but I dared not do anything to help her. People would have seen her leave the club with the man I had killed, and if people knew someone had looked after her they would start asking questions as to who: and possibly start making the link between her helper and whoever had made her partner disappear.

I was safe from the law at the moment. There was no physical evidence of any crime at all, no bodies left to give me away and no witnesses at all. And the only grey magic used had been an almost impossible to detect and quite general intangibility spell, the type that might well be used by any grey wizard on Chester's streets. But if I was seen helping this girl then I would be linked to her, and through her to the first man's disappearance. And white wizards needed only the flimsiest of excuses to make grey wizards pay.

So I did the only thing I could think of. I prayed. I prayed to Artemis, but under the cold light of the moon those prayers found no answer. And I wondered what kind of goddess could hunger so much for the blood of men: but care not one iota for the suffering of her own gender. I found it hard to believe that Artemis the Terrible was a natural expression of divine power. Deep down, in a dark and buried corner of my mind I never let near the surface, I wondered about how natural Artemis the Friendly was too. My favourite goddess just didn't seem to make any real kind of overall sense.

So I prayed again, this time to my other god, to the wisdom of The Allfather. And I felt his power gather as he accepted my prayer. And the lord of slaughter and battle manifested his divine power and faded the almost unconscious girl away, so that she would not reappear until the morning: when she would rematerialise when the street was full of commuters walking to work and she was therefore quite safe. I smiled with relief, then turned and headed back towards the university accommodation where I was staying with Vicky the night before Jessica and Merlin's engagement party.

I had succeeded more easily than I had ever dared to hope but dark thoughts drifted through my head. Dark thoughts about the exact nature of the goddess that I had chosen to serve. The fact that Artemis the Terrible's fire burnt hot while Artemis the Friendly's burned cold almost terrified me. Everything I knew, everything, insisted it should be the other way round. It made me wonder whether any part of the foundations of my beliefs about what was happening was secure.

I had just reached the outskirts of the university library when the new vision hit me: hard. In a flash of terrible colours.

I stood on the mountain top, twenty seven years old; my seventeen year old sister in front of me. Not that I was supposed to think of her like that anymore. Somehow we had reached a state where the crime was not that we were fucking each other, but that Fate had made us brother and sister in the first place. It was Fate's fault for screwing us both over with an accident of birth, and not our sin for acting on our feelings of lust and love.

Above us the sky was dark with grey storm clouds, and the sky was filled with that cold drizzle that sucks all the life and warmth forever out of the day. I held up my hand and touched Vicky's face tenderly. "Is this definitely what you want?" I asked, "Once I cast this spell there is no turning back. You have made your choice."

Vicky leaned in, and kissed me on the lips: our tongues twisted around each other with a desperate need. She was sweet and tasted like fresh water after rain. The softness of her breasts against my chest was coiled agony even now: even after I had had her so many times. She was like sugar water, or the taste of spring. The more you had, the more you wanted. Were I to spend an ocean of my seed inside her still I would ache for her tightness once more. "This choice was made so long ago and I can't even imagine not choosing this." My sisterlover said: as firmly as she had told me a couple of weeks ago that in the "life plan" I was going to give her three kids then get a vasectomy so that no other woman ever had the slightest chance of flowering with my seed. "I would be with you though our love doomed the world and caused the skies and seas to run with blood." Vicky said, flatly and finally. She held up her left hand and clasped it in mine, her muscles strong and her skin soft and warm. "I will follow our love until whatever end. I wish and want no other life but this."

I took a deep breath, and committed myself fully to being the lover of my little sister. I called upon the power of the grey. And I was no longer a child, I was grown full into my power. Grown strong by a lifetime's endurance of abuse; and a lifetime of knowing that I had shared so many of my most precious moments with the person that I loved so much. My power blotted out all light and dark around me, and for a moment it was as though the whole world went monochrome: stripped of all colour and sound. And I FADED. So great was the flow of power that thunder tore across the heavens, and lightning fell as reality twisted in reaction to my spell.

But long had this been planned, and forged in secret, and the screams of reality could not prevent the great spell from being cast.

A moment later it was done, and colour and sound came back to the world. I swayed on my feet, drained by a sudden bleak weariness. I had never felt so tired or so empty: so utterly drained. But it was done; though the exhilaration of success alone kept me on my feet.

"It is done Vicky." I said softly. "No one save us two now remembers that we are...related." Vicky took me in her arms and kissed me passionately. "And if no one knows about it," she exclaimed triumphantly, "it doesn't matter! It's like it doesn't exist. We're just together now, just like any other couple in love. All objections and obstacles swept away." She smiled like the first light of the rising sun. "How does it feel being my boyfriend rather than my brother?" she asked. Then she nipped the end of my ear with her teeth. Her eyes went round like saucers as she asked innocently, "What on earth shall we get up to tonight to celebrate?"

I smiled as I embraced the girl that I loved more than life itself. But in my deepest heart of hearts I knew, even in that moment of passion, that everything that Vicky had just said was a lie. Taking her in my arms felt no cleaner or better than it had before I cast the spell. What we had was still just as dangerous and dark.

The next moment the vision was gone: and I was back in the present day standing alone outside the university library, feeling suddenly very cold in the dark.

And I wondered dully if what I had just done: if my double murder: had really changed anything. Or if the real reason that the world was going to plunge into fire and bloodshed within the next few years was nothing more than divine justice for what was going to happen between me and my little sister.

Chapter 15

I slept deeply, and without dreams.

But I woke not to the sun and the light of the morning but to the cold night air and the stillness of the early hours. He was sitting there, the old man in the cloak. The one-eyed god. Odin Allfather. A black raven was resting on each shoulder, and two wolves were curled around his feet. In his hand was a shaft of wood that formed both a walking stick of comfort and spear of incredible force: a weapon of death. I felt the power of the king of gods from where I was, a soft and subtle magical divinity that it took the closest studying to see how great and terrible it truly was: and even just to know that it was there at all. I walked slowly towards him. As I crossed the darkness I felt a cold light fall across me: sending shivers dancing up my spine: a whispered touch that was almost a caress. I looked behind me and saw that I was bathed in the touch of the chaste moonlight's kiss.

The one-eyed man's eye fixed me, and strange fires flickered in its unfathomable depths. His knowledge was so different from that of the all-knowing, omniscient in formal language, Christian God. The god of the Christians had all his knowledge freely given to him. He was like an endless encyclopaedia of knowledge; but presumably little used as the world was still full of evil.

Odin's knowledge was bought and paid for heavily. In many ways his life was a relentless search to acquire more and more understanding of the cosmos. His knowledge was that of the poet, artist and writer: and that of the military strategist and warlord. And his knowledge, in the same way as that contained in a powerful novel, was always used.

The Allfather spoke as I approached, his voice both clear and soft. "The goddess of the moon grows fond of you. She casts her eyes over you so that she may shelter you if my wrath should turn against you. Flickers of warmth that could become burning flames of passion beat in her cold heart. She draws herself to you ever more deeply, even knowing what will happen. Even knowing that the darkness inside her has so far prevented her from loving any man."

He raised up a goblet of hard carved wood and drank deep of a dark ale. "Is it not strange that almost all powerful men call civilisation the better, and barbarism simply a shameful remnant of the past? Yet had Artemis been born a Viking goddess she would have had a happy and well balanced life. But she was born into the Greek Pantheon, the religion of the civilised ancient Greeks; whose gods are all obsessed with sex and petty jealousies. And it was the ancient civilised world, to whom the gods had given so much, who renounced paganism seven hundred years before the conversion process overwhelmed the last pagan worshippers in Sweden. And it is in the barbarian world of the Viking that the knowledge seeker is the king of the gods, where as in the Greek Pantheon their knowledge seeker, Dionysius, is a permanently pissed alcoholic. Like most "students" in the civilised world he spends most of his time too pissed to stand up.

Artemis is in a complicated situation being the goddess of virginity in a pantheon like that. I am no Zeus,

Edward. King I may be but I do not seek to lie with any girl, mortal or immortal, that catches my eye. I do not seek to father the world with countless demi god bastard offspring, nor is my pantheon essentially made up only of my own squabbling children. And I do not force those who would not have me. When a girl lied to me and snuck from her bedchamber while I still hoped to make my amorous way in I did not pursue her until she flowered with my seed but simply let her go into what life she chose. About the only way to escape the unwanted attentions of an aroused male Greek god was to pray for another Greek god to turn you into a tree before the first god caught you. Much as being rejected plunged me into anguish turning the one who rejected me into a plant is not a course of action any Viking god would even contemplate. And yet this is the world in which Artemis must function as the guardian of female virginity. A world where the king of the gods and her own father in many ways stands for the fulfilment of male lust personified.''

''Does Zeus force girls?'' I asked uneasily. ''From what I have read he isn't just the pinnace of male lust; he is also the pinnacle of male attraction and power. He would take whatever form his soon to be lover most desired. By his very nature he would become whatever the girl he wished to seduce desired in her innermost heart. Whether that is foul and twisted, becoming a great black swan, or even just all too tellingly simply, a shower of gold that caused Daphne to open up her lap and womb to him. Doesn't make it right, doesn't make it moral, but Zeus doesn't rape. He just seduces. Or overwhelms.''

Odin smiled. ''You think well, and your theory is strong. In most cases you would be correct. But there are a few, a very few, girls that Zeus could not seduce. If he wished to enjoy their delights and father their children force would be his only option.''

I turned a cold eye on him. "You on the other hand stand for the core of the Viking race. You worship knowledge, song, violence and poetry. Sex in a barbarian culture is just one satisfied instinct among many. It is only civilisation, which easily satisfies all other physical needs but that one, that starts to worship sex as an obsession. As king of the gods of the barbarians you can't turn into whatever form you wish when you want a girl. And you are a rapist."

The Allfather's voice went very flat. "Just the once. And not for lust. My child lay dead in my arms and prophecy foretold that only if I had a child of one certain woman could his death ever be avenged. I plied her with song and poetry but she would not have me."

His eye turned on me. "If someone took Jessica or Vicky from you, would you not follow the quest for vengeance wherever it took you, even until the darkest ends of the earth? If the only way to see them avenged was to father a child on a girl who would not give you her consent tell me: what would you do? Would you let the one who had murdered those most dear to you live?"

I sat down besides him. I faded the alcohol from the liquid in the wooden goblet in front of me. I needed my head to be clear: then I drank deeply. "I would do whatever it took to see their killer die." I said simply. "And I would hurt whoever got in the way, in whatever way that it was that I needed to."

Odin's eye gleamed with flame. "So we understand each other. But you have taken me far from my point. My point is I am not Zeus, the ever lustful, yet even I feel the wrongness in what Artemis has now become. Yet do not underestimate the strength of the fairy princess Edward. Beneath the dappiness lies a soul of pure steel. I pray for all our sakes that it will be strong enough to hold when the time comes. Even as she is Artemis the Friendly has done much that is good in this world."

And in his silence about Artemis the Terrible The Allfather said more about her than many words could have done.

Then Odin spoke again. "You played Artemis's vision well boy. And you have changed your fate. To what you shall soon see. But remember that to be anointed as our champion you must both change your fate and offer us both great sacrifice. And as you work on all that I also have a riddle for you: a riddle without whose answer all the sacrifice and visions sent by a beautiful fairy goddess will not aid you."

The Allfather smiled, and spread his hands. And suddenly the table before us was not empty, but filled with the figures of men and magic beasts, dwarfs and elves. Around it images of the gods danced and, far off on the other side, rose a pinnacle of black obsidian. The cruel order of The Mountain.

"Welcome to the way the gods see the world Edward." said Odin gently. "A world spread before us in all its beauty and magnificence. A world we can see, a world we can influence, a world we can care about; but not a world we are ever fully a part of. We are the players at the table, and the world is our pieces. We play the game constantly but we can never enter directly inside it. That is both our eternal curse and our eternal blessing."

I looked out across the figures of men and magical creatures, at the breath-taking beauty of seeing how all things were connected and how all the world fitted together into one surprisingly coherent whole. I understood in a moment how the gods' eye view was both simultaneously a thousand times more extensive then that of mortal men; and at the same time so hopelessly removed from it, devoid forever of how it felt to live through the reality of existing as mortal being in a vast physical universe.

I smiled a little. "In all the stories the gods are shown looking at the earth as though it was a chess game of black and white marble figures on a squared board. Not as real life figures in full colour and breath-taking detail."

Odin laughed. "Chess is a fine mechanical exercise but its abstract figures can do no justice to the world of life. And its mechanical rules, with no luck or chance and the consequences of all moves being formally and completely prescribed and predetermined, bear no real relationship to the real world of men: with its free will and luck and chance as well as skill and strategy. If you would fully experience the sport of the gods then wargaming, not chess or any other formal game of fixed and exact logic, is the true divine sport. When you model the figures with paint and love, as men did with statues in our temples in the ancient times, and when you play combat which is determined by statistics and probability and the raw chance of dice: then you truly understand how it is that the divine immortals experience and interact with the ever changing world of mortals."

I thought for a few moments. "Why do you gods play at all? You are forever, mortals are temporary. We age and die before your sight. The same way party poppers hold a mortal's attention for but a brief moment before the bang and rush of moving colour is gone forever. What attraction can we hold for you when we are so fleeting: and what interest are any brief temporary lives to those who are forever eternal?"

The Allfather smiled. "Often we claim boredom, we exist forever after all, or curiosity; to see what happens when we intervene, what ripples our changes make. We might claim competiveness to triumph over others, especially over other gods, or pity; to help those who are making a right mess of things through circumstances beyond their control. All these reasons have their place of course: but they are not the true reason. Not the real one. What not one of us will ever admit is that we intervene because we care, because the lights of your lives burn before our eyes so unimaginably bright and clear. We intervene because we love the intensity of those who live so briefly. Who blaze before our eyes like fireflies, an unbearably beautiful brightness to our eyes: that penetrates to the deepest corners of our forever hearts."

I stared across the pieces, across the forces of The Mountain's order that spread out bleakly across so much of the earth. "So how is the game going? How have your riddles and learning played out in practice?"

Odin shrugged. "Oh the game is over in this world Edward. The Mountain's order is everywhere and Artemis and I have only one card left to play. But once we anoint our hero with our final reserves all The Mountain's power will then move against him or her, and that will be the final stage of this game: which can then end only in The Mountain's complete, utter and final victory. The Age of Men will last forever: the Age of Magic forever beyond hope of restoration or renewal. Perhaps even now Artemis and I waste our time here. After all what is the true power of the Grey? There are a thousand, thousand other worlds than this. What care we if one world falls? Still in the vast void of emptiness of the universe a million, million other canvasses exist on which to play our games with the very brief but so very, very beautiful lives of mortals. If one flower withers and dies in a garden, cannot a thousand others still uncaring bloom?"

He smiled at me, and his grin was wolfish. I could feel in that moment The Allfather's eternal hunger for knowledge and blood. "You will not see me again Edward, not unless all the world is changed. And have I not just shown you how that is impossible? That the evil of the Mountain has already won the war for this world?"

I did not see Odin, The Wanderer and The Bringer of Death, depart. I never did. Just one moment he was there, with two great wolves lolling greedily at this feet, and the next he was gone: leaving me almost alone in the quiet emptiness of the night.

Artemis's moonlight still shone upon me, but that was so terribly cold: and the very chill of what I thought should surely be warm raised only dark thoughts in my heart. I realised silently that this time the riddle that had been set was far harder than my previous ones. My first task was to work out simply what it was.

Chapter 16

I was almost passed out at my desk in the university library when Vicky finally found me in the late afternoon of the following day. After The Allfather's visit I had faded into invisibility then made my way here in the middle of the night and started reading. But I had not yet even found a worthy text to read in depth, I was still just hopelessly scanning ancient texts of Greek, Norse and Arthurian lore: looking for something that would show me in which direction I should look to be concentrating my research. Again and again my gaze drifted now towards the forbidden section of the library. The part which you had to have permission from the powers of the state to access. I had previously quite easily faded out the defences of forbidden libraries to read the odd book or two that had really captured my curiosity. "The Real History of the Titanic" "The fall of Sparta: the Truth Behind the Legend", but taking the odd book out was one thing. Doing an undetected systematic search of the restricted and protected part of the university library would be quite another.

Vicky's arrival was like having a jolt of caffeine fired into my system, but I was still full of the same underlying weariness.

"Edward," she said crossly, "people arriving at Jessica and Merlin's party in couple of hours and you reading. Why you gone like Merlin?"

She looked at me suspiciously. She looked very pretty in her red dress and with the roses in her hair. White roses, to set off the bright crimson below. "I am reading," I thought distantly, "I am reading to try and find a way around the fact that my own god has just left me and told me I am trapped on the losing side." At least that's what Odin's words had literally said. I had a strong feeling that his real meaning had been something quite different.

But what I said out loud was, "Sorry sis, I got distracted. And is being like Merlin a bad thing?"

"No," said Vicky, "he does know loads. But he can afford to be scatty. Jessica is looking after him and no one I know want kill him. You need to be alert all the time to keep you safe. It okay Merlin scatty but it will get you killed dead!"

Vicky stopped, and seeing how tired I was suddenly looked at me closely. "You okay?"

"I'm fine." I said gently. "Just tired."

Vicky put her hands on her hips. "Why?" she demanded. "You been up all night?!"

I looked at her through eyes that were struggling to stay awake. "Yes Vicky. I couldn't sleep."

Vicky sighed. "Have to sleep silly. Staying up all night bad for you!" She was only four but she was still most definitely taking charge and telling me off.

Before I could stop her she reached out and touched my cheek, and a blast of white energy surged. The next moment I felt as fresh as if I had been asleep for twelve hours, and then had just been woken up by three strong cups of coffee.

I smiled at Vicky: touched: and now actually properly awake. "Thanks," I said, "but please be careful with doing that Vicky. You know it drains your energy to refresh other people.''

I fine!'' said Vicky determinedly: although she wasn't quite as bouncy as she had been just a few moments ago. ''I very sensible and had very good night's sleep. I not so tired I about to fall over!''

As we walked back towards where I would have to get changed for the engagement party we passed through a bar: pleasant and modern but closed to the general public as it had been booked for tonight's party; where a widescreen television was showing the results of a magic sporting event. The camera was glossing around to show the victor. He was a mass of muscle and sinew, his frame twice as wide and half again as tall as that of a normal man. He was aglow with the power of white magic, and was splattered in blood. Undefeated champion: the headlines were screaming: undefeated champion maintains his title. Master of all forms of combat whether armed, unarmed and even Pankration.

Vicky looked at me curiously. ''Edward what Pankration?''

I shuddered. ''There are many forms of magical contest in this world, each bound by its own rules. Pankration is the worst. It is a word which comes from Ancient Greek and it means fight to the death. Both contestants are sealed in by magical power and there are no rules. The combatants can fight with whatever weapons and magic they wish, but nothing can be passed through the wall of power surrounding them until the conflict is over; not though the Wizard of Many Colours who rules all Britain was trying to break down the magical barrier around the fight.''

Vicky muttered something under her breath to herself and tried hard not to look too excited. She'd spoken softly enough that I couldn't hear her exact words. But I knew her well enough to know pretty much what she'd just said. "No Vicky that is not something that even you are ever going to be able to do, that is a record that even you are never going to be able to break." I told her levelly. "You could keep going until you were so tired that you did fall over and you would still achieve nothing against the barriers of a Pankration fight. So forget you ever had that thought of being the first person ever to break down one of those barriers."

"Won't know until try." said Vicky sulkily. Then she brightened up again. "But that not what makes Pankration interesting! Most magical combats have protection around to stop other people so why Pankration so special?"

"I'm not sure special is the word I would use." I muttered, "But the other forms of combat have rules that determine when they end. It might be you being knocked out, or a certain point's level being reached: decided either by prefixed rules or by external judges. But Pankration only ends when one person accepts the unconditional surrender of the other, or when one of the two combatants is dead."

I looked at the pictures of Gawain, flashing on the television screen. He looked more like a berserker than a Christian knight, a wild terrible savagery raging though him as he lifted up his blood streaked arms soaked in victory before a baying crowd. The camera caught his eyes, wild and red-rimmed with rage and hate.

Vicky looked curiously at him. "Why Gawain so popular Edward?"

I looked at my little sister sadly. "He's a few weeks short of his sixteenth birthday and he's already beaten every champion in each of the major individual events. Only medals he hasn't won so far are for the doubles: and that's because when the berserk rage comes on him he can't distinguish between friend and foe. He just tears his way through absolutely everyone around him: lashing out at friend and foe without distinction. It's not pretty. He's also a killer. He's dragged down three major champions in Pankration combats and literally pummelled them to death while they lay helpless at his feet. Their cries for mercy just seemed to excite him more. In the ring he's a killer without remorse or pity: and the crowds love him for it. Sir Bleoberis de Ganis, Sir Hectimere and Sir Persant, each he's left so little of there wasn't even enough left for burial."

Vicky's fingers flickered, and white magic flashed. "He should let them give up and live." She said flatly, "It was mean kill them when he'd won! Someone needs stop him."

I turned to her sharply. "Yes someone probably does and…"

Vicky reached out and squeezed my hand. "It will be me then. I stopped Mike and Jess. I good at stopping bad guys."

The vision flashed. This time the colours were more beautiful than ever: so bright in their thousand different shades of light that they hurt my eyes.

I was staring into the eyes of my girlfriend, the green fire in them currently even sharper and brighter than the red fire of her hair. It still felt weird calling her my girl, still made me feel that I was lying to myself. Part of me distantly wondered what would happen if we did ever break up. Would Vicky just go back from being my full on girlfriend to a more normal relationship as just my little sister? Part of me smiled absently: although without any real humour. "Are you still in contact with your ex? Yes she's my sister and you'll see her at Christmas when we go round to meet my parents. She's dying to meet you and I'm sure you'll get on great. Don't think it's very likely we'll ever get back together romantically but hey, you never know about these things do you?"

But I could only smile about it because I knew that whatever the future held we weren't going to break up: not ever. I couldn't picture a life without Vicky in it. Much as my girlfriend believed it was the skilful use of her curves that had overwhelmed my resistance to incest, her most powerful weapon had simply been my fear of not remaining as the main person in her life; not having her around with me each day if I said no to her advances. Not that her curves were entirely insignificant in the picture of course...

And Vicky, she'd told me frequently that she didn't want any other man. That they would just compete with her, not complement her naturally the way that I did. The thought of any other guy touching her made her turn cold at night: and wake up shaking in a sweat. I was the only man she had ever met who didn't engage her competitive instinct. "If I wasn't with you," Vicky had told me once, in one her very, very rare reflective moments, "I think I'd probably be a lesbian. And I wouldn't date a hot girl. I'd go for one of those bookish, anorak style ones who looks like they spend all their days buried in libraries. She'd have to be pagan of course, but even then it wouldn't be the same as it is with you now." And she'd reached out to hold my cheek. "You are the only person I have ever met who is so completely opposite to me: but who also enjoys killing just as much as I do."

The roar around me swept my thoughts of the past away. "Vicky," I said thickly, "I don't want you to do this. Not Pankration, not against him."

My eighteen year old girlfriend smiled at me, and ruffled my hair. "I know." She said sweetly. "You're worried about me and that's cute. But don't worry cuddlebear. I've got this."

I looked at her flatly. "Gawain has never lost a match: ever: and he's killed twenty one people. Even you are going to struggle against a thirty year old with this much white magic power. I know you want to fight him but not Pan…''

My sisterlover leaned across and kissed me. ''Love you but you still don't get it. I don't lose. I won't ever lose.''

She turned and leapt over the ropes into the boxing ring. The crowd roared and Vicky flushed with pleasure. A year ago almost everyone had seen her only as a hot girl to get up the crowd's adrenalin before the real fighting started. Now she was seen as one of the finest fighters in the western world: and one who had left a string of battered and broken bodies, and even several corpses, behind her. After Gawain Vicky was the most brutal fighter in the ring. She'd even whispered in my ear that nothing made her adrenaline flow like being bathed in her opponent's blood. There were now a couple of times we'd made love - who was I kidding - fucked hard and desperate, while she was still covered in another man's red gore.

Vicky bowed and waved to the crowd, basking in the applause. She'd always loved being the centre of the limelight. The attention of others was like a drug to her. After I'd cast the great fading spell I'd been completely unsure where our new love life was going in the first few, very new and strange, days. The sheer weirdness of being with Vicky openly in public instead of in constant private moments had been disorientating: and even quite odd. I'd never really realised what is was like to be dating someone who was just so loud and active all the time: life a constant blur of colour and busyness. And whereas before I had always been the centre of her attention on secret, close, personal dates I was now just one person among many supposed to be competing for her attention in the bright whirl of her social circle. I had wondered if going public and official had taken all the thrill out of our relationship for Vicky. A bleak part of me had questioned whether it had been, subconsciously at least, the forbidden pleasure of incest that Vicky had wanted rather than actually me. After all she could have had almost any other man on the planet easily, was it really coincidence that she'd gone for the one man she wasn't allowed to be with? Had our love life been based on little more than the tension of being caught sharpening our sexual pleasure unbearably?

Then I'd read the magazines that Vicky loved, only now with photos of me and Vicky all over the covers. I'd started with a dull expectation of dread, expecting to read about nothing more than low levels of chemistry and problems already brewing. Instead I'd read, in shock, about how happy Vicky was, how excited she was in her new relationship and how she was already in love. The heart of the girl who cared for nothing but fighting had finally melted: everyone agreed. Opinion articles I'd expected to speculate in dismal terms about just how little time this relationship had left to stagger on for instead sparkled with just how long it would be before I popped the question to Vicky. Some even speculated on just how many kids Vicky wanted to have with me. One magazine had even shown photos of us compared to people Vicky had been with previously: all of them some of the most successful men in Britain. All of them brief flings for show, none of which had ever progressed into anything physical.

I stared at the contrast between photos of her previous relationships, and the new photographs of us as a couple. In the old photos of the previous, failed, relationships Vicky's emotions ranged from bored to moody. With me they didn't range, she just glowed with happiness.

I was still reading the magazines when a strong pair of arms came around my waist and a soft body pressed itself very firmly against my back. I could feel the teasing weight of Vicky's boobs playing below my shoulder blades, but I could also sense the hard muscles in her body, lying underneath her soft curves. The vision of red-haired beauty above the body of a killer. Her touch was a deliberate shot of adrenalin and lust delivered directly to the bloodstream, and I found my thoughts turning fast towards the desperate release of a quickie.

"You reading up on us?" Vicky murmured in my ear, her breath caressing the sensitive skin inside it. "They are really happy with us aren't they?" She leaned her head to one side of my neck so that her gaze was on my face. On the surface it was soft, loving; but underneath you could see the cold steel: the constant determination to get exactly what she wanted. "So when are you going to ask me to marry you exactly? We've known each other eighteen years after all. A girl could get the wrong idea."

I swallowed, being very careful with my words. "I really didn't think you were happy with me since we went official. I thought since the thrill of incest went out you'd found the reality of being with someone who is reflective, someone who is more introverted then the normal chatterboxes you have previously gone out…"

"What are you going on about Edward?" asked Vicky dangerously, the steel in her voice suddenly very sharp. "I hated being with socially astute men. They tried saying things when I was talking! You sit and listen and work out what's going on so I can be the centre of attention and still know everything that's happening, because you tell me later. We rock!

Why?" and her voice was suddenly very quiet: and very dangerous. "Is being official not working out for you? Were you quiet happy sticking it into me in secret as your sister, but being openly with me as my boyfriend isn't what you want? Missing the thrill of incest?"

I ruffled her hair gently, "You are so daft sometimes… babe." I had almost said sis. "Of course this is better it's just… I'm sharing a part of your life I never did before. I'm more used to the shadows than the limelight. Apart from anything else a few years ago a union of grey and white wizard would have been unthinkable anyway."

The tension drained out of Vicky. You could almost physically feel her change of mood. "Yeah well that's the War isn't it? Changed everything. Grey and white wizards dating is still not exactly common but it's no big deal anymore. Turns out you need grey wizards to do well at wars so everything changes. Few years ago a grey and a white wizard together as a couple would have been a no-go area. Now things are much more sensible. And no one had better bloody well try and change things back to how they used to be if and when the fighting is ever done! Then I would get really mad!"

I sat down and she sank into my lap, and rested her head against my shoulder. "When are you going to ask me to marry you?" she asked, "soon? We can't start on having a family until I'm properly married you know, wouldn't be right."

I took a deep breath. "At Christmas? That's six months so it won't look too much like a whirlwind…"

Vicky kissed me on the mouth. She tasted of love and laughter. "Mmmm don't care about that. Make it three months at most."

"Don't know," I teased "don't know if you'll say yes."

Vicky laughed at that, then she broke down giggling. "I've already shown you the ring I want."- The most beautiful and expensive one in the shop. You could buy a small house for less. - "Propose to me with that, properly and you know I'll say yes." She smiled at me, and ran her hand through her hair. Then she leaned in close. "Even if you asked me today?"

"I can't afford…" I began, but Vicky just shrugged. "I'll give you the money. I earn enough from my prize fighting alone, and that's before you put in my modelling and page three appearances."

Suddenly her arms tightened around me, and a tone crept into her voice that I had only ever heard once or twice before. A tone when Vicky's seemingly unsurmountable confidence suddenly grew very small, and at times seemed to even vanish entirely. "You do want to marry me don't you?" She asked fretfully, her voice suddenly shaky with distress. "You do love me and want to spend the rest of your life with me don't you?"

I pushed aside the doubts of the last few days and kissed her on the lips, remembering all that we had shared across all the years that we had been close. "Of course I do… babe x" It still felt so strange talking to her using openly sexual terms of endearment. "I love you and I want to marry you."

Vicky's arms tightened, almost convulsively. "Please Edward," she said, tears in her eyes, "propose soon!"

"Okay." I said softly. "I'll get the ring later today." Seeing Vicky in so much pain and uncertainty was like a knife cutting into my chest. "Although you have kind of spoilt the surprise for yourself."

Vicky snuggled her head as close into me as she could. "Don't care about the surprise." She said thickly. "Just want you to give me a ring so I can say yes."

My sisterlover took a deep breath, and suddenly the steel was back in her voice. Sharper even than when she stood in the arena, sharper than even when she bloodily battered men to death in magical combat. Vicky rose so that the green fire of her eyes burned directly into my grey ones and she gripped my arm so hard that her fingernails cut jagged blood across my skin. "You are mine Edward you got that? Look at another woman and I might, just might, let that go. Kiss or touch one and I'll hurt her badly. Dare to even think about fucking someone else and," she took a deep breath, "I'll kill her

205

and then I'll beat you bloody." Her voice was filled with love, possession, and need: raw and terrible.

I took her in my arms and held her to me. "Calm down babe." I told her gently. "I don't want to be with anyone but you. Relax. The only other girl I've ever been with besides you is Laura and that was years ago, before we got…"

I hesitated suddenly. I sickly remembered how Laura had disappeared overnight and without warning from our school less than a month after Vicky and I had made love for the first time. "Vicky," I said hesitantly, "with Laura you didn't…" my voice trailed away.

"Why?" snapped Vicky, fire burning suddenly terribly in her eyes. "Why does it matter? Do you still want to be with her? Do you still want to fuck her? Did you like her more than you do…"

"No miss over possessive much." I sighed, "I just don't think she should have been hurt for being with me before we got together. You know I dumped her the morning after we first slept together."

Vicky scowled at me, then sighed. "She's in the United States, in the New World. I told her that if she wanted to be safe from me she needed to be on the other side of the planet." For a moment she looked a little guilty. She started playing with her hair. "Do you think I overreacted?"

"Yes." and "Completely." were the honest answers to her question, but they wouldn't help anything. I looked my girlfriend in the eye and said simply "Depends."

"Depends on what?" said Vicky, half moodily, half nervous.

"On whether Laura really is in the United States, or whether she is just dead and buried in a ditch."

Vicky sighed with relief. "No I didn't hurt her. I hate her because she was with you but you are right cuddlebear. She was with you before we got together so,

206

as she ran away when I confronted her, I don't have any right to do anything. Last I knew Laura was fine.''

Vicky twirled a piece of her red hair in the sunlight: it danced a thousand motes of bright crimson. ''You're not to contact her though. I don't want you talking to someone you've slept with.''

I kissed my little sister gently. Until we got together officially after the fading spell had been cast I had never seen just how much her insecurity about me tore apart her heart. ''I haven't thought about Laura in years.'' I said gently. ''Now just forget about all this. You've no reason to be jealous, so stop sulking just because you haven't yet got a ring.''

Memory of the girl I loved, of the girl I wouldn't be allowed to break up from even if I wanted to, fled as the speakers boomed at the entrance of the world champion to the title match. ''Gawain, undefeated champion takes to the ring once more! He's crushed sorcerers from all nations and all continents. He is an unstoppable beast both physically and with white magic. The most powerful of all The Knights of the Table Round.''

''And I'm not going to be stopped,'' bellowed a huge voice, 'by one jumped up pretty, little girl. Especially a jumped up little, pagan girl!''

Vicky was sitting one of the ring posts and she blew a bubble at him. The lights of the arena danced across the priceless jewels of her engagement ring. She'd got the ring she really wanted now: the same way that in the end she always got exactly what it was that she wanted. ''I'm not pretty,'' my girlfriend yelled, ''I'm beautiful.'' The crowd roared.

''Enjoy it while it lasts.'' snarled Gawain. ''I'm about to beat it out of you.'' The crowd roared again: even louder.

''How?'' mocked Vicky, ''with the aid of your one dead carpenter god? Bringing the Prince of Peace to a

Pankration match is like bringing a spoon to a sword or axe fight. What's the matter, not man enough to worship the real gods?

Athene, bringer of victory, champion of civilisation, daughter of Zeus and sexiest lesbian there has ever been: by all the victories I have dedicated to you I now remind you of all that has passed between us: including some very sexy dreams."

Some of the crowd hooted, some roared, some glared silent. Religion was a massive deal nowadays: involving us all. An issue people lived and died for. "I implore your aid in this fight Athene. Grant me victory that we may see the champion of the false god humbled, and that the crowds may once more scream out in the arena for the triumph of the pagan religion. For Faith" Vicky screamed, and lightning burned around her in the air.

Gawain roared back, He had been terrible enough at sixteen, at thirty he was now a vast hulk of muscle and strength.

He wore nothing save a loin cloth round his waist and a simple cross of silver around his neck. "For The Faith" he thundered, and half the crowd screamed for him, while half were silent. Then the champion came bounding into the ring with a roar.

Vicky leapt down upon him as he entered the ring, blazing like lightning. She met him with an explosion of power and blazing energy that echoed throughout the arena. Light flashed painfully sharp, and the world spun. Everything around me went whirly and bright. When I forced my vision back, just moments later, Vicky was standing at the centre of the ring, looking shaky. Then she turned and spat blood onto the ring floor: in many ways that was shocking. It was rare indeed that anyone had the power to actually hurt her. But Gawain was a broken mass of burned flesh at her feet. His spine had been shattered in multiple places, and his head lolled to one side in death. Large parts of his body were burned black. Vicky reached down and tore the world championship belt from him, and held it up into the air. Half the crowd went wild in victory: half just sat in stunned silence. Vicky basked in the applause, then turned and slipped out from the ropes and took me in her arms.

"It's so cute watching you worry over me cuddlebear." She whispered in my ear. "But you don't need to sweetie. I never lose. I won't ever lose." She kissed me passionately, and I tasted the blood in her mouth, hot and salty. Then she turned and raised up the championship belt once more with a scream of victory that was echoed in the howling of the crowds.

Then she turned back to me and kissed me again: even harder. "Let's get out of here fast sweetie. I want to fuck you in celebration right now so badly that it hurts."

Then the vision was gone, and I was back in the bar with a four year old with red hair holding my hand innocently.

I stared at my little sister, too many images and visions crowding my mind for me to make thoughts coherent. But Vicky was already focusing, white magic burning around her. There came a sudden hiss and a fizz as strong magic snapped before her power like a twig.

The manager at the bar looked up at her, and his face was suddenly angry.

"What did you do?" I asked Vicky, my voice haggard and desperate.

Vicky looked at me in surprise. "I broke kiddy lock on the big tv, otherwise not be able watch the fight!"

Angry staff members were beginning to converge towards us and Vicky looked at me, confused, and a little uncertain and distressed. "Why don't you cast grey magic to cover it up Edward? That's what you always do when I break things! I don't want to be in trouble!!!"

209

And that same voice echoed in my ears from a possible future, echoing through my thoughts. "If you dare to fuck another girl I will kill her then beat you bloody." And then a scream of triumph as she descended down from the ringside ropes to take Gawain's life: backlit by the terrible glow of her own white magic.

I forced my thoughts down and reached for the grey, feeling sick. I faded the memories of all the angry strangers, and all tension was instantly gone from the room.

"Oh look," said Vicky, "mummy over there. I can watch fighting while you get ready for party. Could you go get Danielle and then I see boxing while Danielle uses blue magic to make mummy think we just watching a cartoon?"

"Okay," I said, still feeling light headed, "I'll go and get her now." I walked towards the entrance as Vicky walked over to our mum and sat down with her in front of the big bar television. I crossed out of sight behind an interior wall, then made myself stop to listen.

"No Vicky." said my mum's voice tiredly. "Four is far too young to be watching the fighting. Why don't we watch a nice cartoon about a dinosaur instead?"

"Yes Vicky I know that your fight at the swimming pool was more bloody but you know you are supposed to feel very sorry about that, you hurt a lot of people."

"Well I know you saved your brother but you hurt a lot of other people too."

"Vicky you can't hurt people just because they don't get out of the way. And you said you were really sorry about everything that happened. It is in the report."

"So Vicky if you were not sorry about anything then you did why did you say it?"

"So Vicky, Edward told you that if you opened your eyes as big as saucers and pinched the inside of your knee hard enough to make yourself cry then people would think that you were sorry and you wouldn't get in any trouble even though you weren't really sorry at all?"

"Is there anything about The Pool of Fire and Blood that you are actually sorry about?"

"You are sorry about what happened to Mike, Jessica's ex-boyfriend? Well that's good because you…"

"So you're not sorry that you killed Mike?"

"You are sorry that they took Mike's body away when he was a baddy? Why, what were you going to do with Mike's body?"

"I see. So the only thing you are sorry about from the whole thing is that you didn't get Mike's body after he was dead. And that's because you wanted to feed him to the fish because he tried to drown your brother in the fishpond?"

"So Vicky is that how you are going to deal with every problem in your life? Just hit it as hard as you can? What are you going to do if that doesn't work?"

"HIT IT AGAIN EVEN HARDER?!!!"

I turned away from the bar feeling ill. What was my relationship with my younger sister turning Vicky into?

Chapter 17

I felt as though I was falling down an inexorably steep slope towards a sheer fatal drop: while all the while white noise played tunelessly in my ears. At first what the visions of the future were trying to tell me had seemed so plain and straightforward. Vicky dies in the future because Jessica either doesn't have kids and ends up killing herself in despair, or my elder sister does try to start a family but she and her child die in childbirth: sending Merlin mad. Either way my little sister ends up dying at King Arthur's hand.

So back in the present I make sure Merlin and Jessica will have children, closing down future one; and sacrifice to Artemis to gain her protection for Jessica during any future pregnancy: closing down future two. While I wait for a divine sign to see if I have succeeded I also have the opportunity to work on a great sacrifice to both of my gods, - or with Artemis the Terrible is that three? -, so that they give me power as their champion. That would secure the continuation of my divine riddles and visions and would give me a much better chance of facing the future going forwards.

But when I get divine confirmation that I have closed down both of these dark future possibilities where Jessica dies, instead of life getting easier and giving me a clear and straightforward path to follow the gods instead overwhelm me with divine riddles and visions. The future becomes a hopeless kaleidoscope of dancing confusion which it's almost impossible for me to read. Then Odin says that the war for this world is lost because the moment he and Artemis use their last reserves to give me power the Mountain will instantly see what is happening and simply strike me down.

But while these are the literal words of The Allfather he also quietly tells me that there is hope by setting me a riddle. Something that he would not waste time with if there genuinely was no chance at all of success. He just doesn't tell me what that riddle is. And then Artemis shows me visions of the future which show what a love of violence is growing fast inside my little sister; who it also seems will grow up to be the love of my life. "If you dare to think about fucking someone else I will kill them and beat you bloody." The fact it was a girl saying that hid its true horror. To comprehend how bleak and hopeless those words really were you just had to imagine how it would have felt if it had been me saying them to Vicky.

I forced down those thoughts, and forced away the new vision to the back of my mind. Better a life with a troubled Vicky it in it, than a future in it with no Vicky at all. "And why should she feel sorry about The Pool of Fire and Blood?" I thought, suddenly angry. It was the terror of what had happened then that meant that no one now dared to lay a finger on me. Without the fear that the bloodshed of the slaughter had unleashed I had no doubt at all that someone would have very quickly taken Jess and Mike's place. Why should Vicky be ashamed or sorry that bystanders had been caught in the crossfire, bystanders who would not have raised a finger to help while chlorine flooded my lungs? Bystanders who would have walked on by while I died by breathing in deep far too much chlorinated swimming water. Vicky hadn't targeted any innocents deliberately, she simply hadn't hesitated if they became between me and her. The same way I wouldn't hesitate if I was protecting her. Same way I hadn't hesitated to take life to protect Jessica.

I fastened the last of the buttons on my shirt, and walked out into the hall of the university formal reception rooms where the guests were gathered for Jessica and Merlin's engagement party. My father was there, animatedly chatting to Merlin. His wife: my mum: standing looking pretty on his arm. That was the function my father expected her to serve at social gatherings. Merlin was standing by Jessica, his arms resting on her shoulders. He looked like the happiest man in the world and Jessica was glowing on their special night. He wore a smart brown suit that Jessica had clearly chosen for him, and for one of the first times in Merlin's life at important social occasions all his clothes actually fit. Jessica was wearing a blue dress and there were fresh flowers in her hair. Vicky and Danielle were standing by Jessica's feet looking very pretty in red and green. Zuggles was close by Danielle. His coat had had a wash and a brush and he had a pretty red collar that Danielle had drawn beautiful blue flowers on.

On the table were glasses of champagne spread over a white table cloth, and plates of canapés. "Did you enjoy the fight?" I asked Vicky, and she shrugged. "Not watch fight. Danielle not like fights so we watch cartoons instead and Danielle help teach me to draw pictures. Was fun!" Hope leapt a little in my chest and I smiled and ruffled her hair.

I approached Merlin and Jessica, and felt the raw magical power of my father. It had been so long since he had shown any interest in me that I had almost forgotten how strong he actually was. The power of his presence was overbearing. When he looked at you with those brown eyes you felt he was looking into your soul, engaging with you at the deepest level. His words were soft but enthusiastic, and filled you with a strange excitement as they bent you to his will. He made you feel that doing exactly what he wanted was the only possible course of action any reasonable man could take. The worst part about it was how much he mirrored me. The same gestures of affection, the same ruffling of hair or squeezing of a shoulder. But while I fought for people to follow their own path, however closely or dissimilar it was to mine, my father only ever fought to get people to do what would make his life easier and better.

''You know,'' he was saying to Merlin, ''I think Jessica and you are really going to be such a good match. I bet my daughter stood out so brightly in that library, *surrounded by all the dead wood of the others who hang around there*, catching your eye straight away.''

I faded away as much of the white magic power behind my father's sentence as I could, with all its damning connotations for those who were Jessica's work colleagues and friends, before it could burn its suggestive power into Jessica and Merlin. The fading took so much power that blood started to seep down my back. But I managed to fade out everything from ''surrounded'' to ''there''.

''You know Merlin these rooms you've picked out are so fantastic. *I would never have dreamed that this so called University of Chester could have a hidden spot like this. Really Merlin you are wasted here, Oxbridge is the only place that you should really be studying.* I'm sure this engagement party will be a wonderful prelude to your wedding. You really should try the new hotel that's opened at the top of Prestham Hill. It has the best facilities for a really large wedding.''

I slid down to a sitting positon, unable to hold onto the power of the grey. I had managed to fade away all the white magic behind everything from "I" to "studying". I would have faded my father's last sentence as well if I could. Merlin and Jessica wanted a small wedding and had already picked out a small old hotel, full of history and character and with a stunningly beautiful garden, for a few select guests. But everything was swept away before the force of a white wizard's command. But my collapse did something that was good. It drew my father's attention. He turned to me, and away from Merlin and Jessica.

"You look an absolute state." My father said, staring down at where I lay gasping in blood and sweat. "Not that it, like anything else you do, actually really matters. I very much doubt that I will ever be standing as a proud parent at your marriage ceremony." Then he turned and walked away. I stared coldly at his back, a pain that I had had from early childhood brought sharply back up to the surface once more. In a world that was against me my father could have done the brave thing and stood up for me. Instead he had taken the easy route, as he always did with everything in his life, and chosen to be even more ashamed of me than the rest of the world.

Jessica wheeled herself over towards me, concerned, but I barely noticed her at that moment. I simply sat in a great deal of pain, little of it physical. I wondered for a moment why Vicky hadn't come running over to me. She was always the first to heal me when I got hurt, the first to stand up against any who stood against me. Then I saw her laughing in my father's arms, howling with delight, and I felt as though someone had torn me open from the inside. The pain of my father's rejection was a pinprick compared to this: an ocean of unending pain and emptiness. And I wondered, suddenly and sickly, if my father had been paying my little sister a bit more attention on the day of The Pool of Fire and Blood whether Vicky would have still saved me, or whether my father would have distracted her completely and she would not even have noticed as I died.

And I knew in that moment that I would not attempt to alter the future. I did not care if my future was incest, or even if my relationship with Vicky became abusive. I would take a kiss with a fist from her over not being the main person in her life. Over not being her husband: the father of her children. I swore to myself that when we grew up she would never look on any other man the way she would look on me.

"You know there was a time I thought our father was the most powerful and influential man alive." said Jessica, not even trying to disguise her coldness. "A time when I would have done almost anything to win his approval. A time when I thought he had more influence over the minds of men than any other wizard." Her words helped me to refocus on the present and I forced my grey magic to kick in.

My blood and sweat faded and I forced myself to my feet. "And now?" I said, grimly looking at where my father held my younger sister's undivided attention: engrossing her in some story about what a clever man he was. Besides her Danielle stood uncertain: unsure why she had suddenly been completely forgotten by her normally utterly loyal playmate. My father's wife, my mum, stood alone by the champagne table, currently forgotten: like an ornament. Simply put back on the shelf for the time being.

Jessica laid her hand on my arm. Her words were soft but strong. Deep and from the heart. "I would have said his power is nothing besides that of yours."

I laughed raggedly. "His power in white magic is so great that he can compel you to do what he wants with just a few words. Just a smile and a flash of magic and the sale job's made. What is the power of the grey against that? It took everything I had to fade away just a couple of his suggestions into nothing."

Jessica smiled. "The power to get a girl lying in a room with no life up and back out again. The power of a wizard who can help her get a life, a job and a real family. No force of white magic could have instilled in me that deep a command. You are stronger than him. He yelled that I was an embarrassment to him and all his family stood for. Yet here we are, with him now proudly celebrating my success, as he sees it, and wanting to claim as much credit from it for himself as possible."

"I wasn't stronger than him today." I said bleakly. "I tried to stop his magic and…"

"Well my conversation with my father seems to be over and I neither hate my work colleagues nor am I splitting Danielle and Vicky up by moving half way across the country so Merlin can work at Oxbridge. It would be gutting if Vicky and Danielle ended up living too far apart to play together: gutting for both of them." My older sister smiled and squeezed my hand. "Plus I'd kind of miss having you around as well you know? I do seem to be having a large wedding, which will be difficult for me and Merlin to afford. And I was hoping to use a small wedding to see if Danielle could end up making some more friends her own age, but…"

"I could try and fade that large wedding suggestion from your mind…" I began, but Jessica shook her head. "We'll just have a small party later. Let my embarrassment of a father, let John, think he's won. If there isn't a big event he'll know something has gone wrong with the compulsion sales magic he just used on us. And I'd rather he stayed happily blissful of the fact that he's not convinced us to move to Oxbridge."

I glanced at where my father was now entertaining his wife, Vicky and Danielle with some big story. It was so much easier just to talk at people about how good you were rather than to get to know stuff about them and talk with them. We are trained to talk from the moment we are born, but most of us in the west never have so much as a single moment's training in listening. I wondered idly which of my father's stories he was telling now. He didn't have that big a repertoire. There were lots of hand gestures and mock angry voices, and silly voices to indicate stupid company bosses he'd outsmarted. That suggested that it was the story about setting up his own businesses on the side, using all his advantages as a civil servant to ensure that no one dared to compete with him. Either that, or it was the story about how he'd taken the ideas of poor academics and commercialised them, then twisted the legal system to make sure the researchers no longer had any commercial rights at all to their own ideas. My father was, of course, just making sure that all credit and financial reward went where it was truly due.

Not that my father had ever bothered to tell me any of his normal stories. I only knew them because I'd overheard him telling them to others so many times. All I ever got was short intense bursts about how shit I was and how you had lads from working class communities, like himself, who'd been given nothing and achieved everything. While I on the other hand had been given the world on a silver spoon and all I was doing was just throwing everything away.

"It took me months to get you up again." I said. "Had our father given you a spoken command…"

Jessica shrugged. "Had he commanded me he could have got me out on the drive at the front of our house to exercise. He could have forced me into a job, maybe even into a bitter life of sorts. But he could not have made me want to live again, as you did. And you, not he, are the man I now think of as my real father."

I turned and stared at her. "But that's … We're basically the same age!" I began: and Jessica laughed

219

loudly. "Grey wizards grow up fast Edward, or they don't get to grow up at all. And if everything went wrong who do you think I would turn to? I love Merlin and he is brilliant at what he does but there are times I can't even trust him to tie up his own shoelaces. You faced down the Voice of the Mountain for me. You are my light in dark places, the light for me when all other lights went out. You are the magic that gave birth to the new world that I now live in: a thousand times better than the old one I was born into. You know I am sure Merlin has a far more learned reason for why The Voice of The Mountain, the godlike ruler of this world, hates grey wizards so much. But to me it is very simple. Grey wizards bring the one emotion that is always the most dangerous to any state of order and inertia. They bring hope. Everything I have in my life now is because of you. You gave me my happiness and as much independence as I now have. If that's not the definition of good parenting then what is?"

I looked at Jessica, "You're older than I am!" I protested. Jessica laughed again. "What does that matter? Am I Danielle's biological parent Edward? Doesn't stop her calling me mummy! Why do you think it is any different for adults? Is there anytime, anyplace, anywhere, that if I got into trouble you wouldn't look out for me?"

I held Jessica's eyes for a long moment. "Unless you turn back into Jess I will always be there for you." I said simply. Then I took the knife from the table besides me and cut our two hands across the middle. Then I held our cuts together so our mixing blood powered a very strong form of magic.

"By blood I mingle
And by blood I bind.
Think of me in your distress
And my aid you shall find.

Should one threaten your life to spill
Call on me, and know that I will kill.

I sealed the protection spell between us with fire: sealing our wounds closed. "Be careful tonight." I warned. "You know people may say many cruel things about you because you are so young and pretty and because you are marrying a man so much older than you. And you know people will also say cruel things because you are in a wheelchair. They can't say them directly because that isn't accepted in high society anymore. So they will find other ways to attack you and express that underlying dislike and the fact that they look down upon your disability." Jessica rolled her eyes. "That is all such a dadsy thing to say." She said, less than half teasing.

I turned and walked into the party, using grey magic so that barely anyone noticed that I was there. It was easier for everyone that way. The party took an hour or so to get going, while people arrived gradually, but then it became very busy and lively: which would make my older sister very happy. Jessica was very popular in the library and had made a lot of effort with the invitations to both her and Merlin's friends. Jess and Jessica were as different as night and day in many ways but they both loved being the cool kid on the block. What had changed most was my older sister's attitude towards people who weren't part of the in-crowd.

And John had also made sure that his eldest daughter's engagement party to the most prestigious academic in the west was very well attended: now there was a chance to boost his pride he wanted in on the action. I walked the party silently, watching and listening for things involving my daughter- my elder sister I tried to correct myself but the thought did not stick. Elder sister conjured up only images of Jess, faded and lacking in energy and colour: the distant memory of someone long dead.

Some of what I heard about Jessica was nice. Her friends at the library were thrilled that she had found someone stable and kind: someone who would bring out her kindness rather than her party girl side. And someone who wouldn't resent the time needed to help her get dressed and bathed each day. Merlin was so amazed and happy to have found his soulmate and a loving mummy for his daughter that I don't think he even remembered that Jessica was in a wheelchair most of the time. And even when he did remember he found the matter of little interest. It was one of the things that Jessica loved the most about him. There were concerns about whether Merlin was more interested in having a wife or a mother for his child, and most of her friends hoped that Jessica would be expecting a child of her own soon. That would make the transition for her much easier, they all agreed. Plus who wouldn't want to have Danielle as a big sister: and that also meant that Danielle wouldn't be an only child any more.

The university professors' comments were more mixed. Most approved of how Jessica had really helped organise Merlin, so that now he turned up to work looking presentable, and didn't have terrible trouble at lunchtime because he'd forgotten either to make his sandwiches or remember where he'd put them. Before Jessica had become involved in his life Merlin couldn't even get food at the work canteen because he'd forgotten his wallet so often that his credit was exhausted. But most of the senior management staff couldn't bring themselves to be entirely nice about the fact that a man in his forties was dating an exceptionally pretty teenager of only moderate magical power. There were a lot of comments about what exactly was it that Jessica brought to the table apart from the enticing tightness between her legs. None of governors on the university board of trustees seemed capable of considering the match from Jessica's point of view, or ever thinking about what being in a wheelchair might mean for her. And certainly none of them could consider that Jessica, as a wizard of far less power and intelligence than themselves, could possibly have any skills to bring to the table of her own: apart from sex and her ability to bear Merlin children. They made many jokes about whether his pretty new wife would distract him from his research long enough for another researcher to take the number one spot. Not one of them seemed to have noticed or cared that before Jessica met Merlin and Danielle both daddy and daughter had been desperately unhappy. None of the management staff also, despite being responsible for managing his performance, seemed to have a clue how daft their jokes were as Merlin, now he was with Jessica, was as a result less likely than ever before to lose his number one researcher spot on the international research tables list. Not only did Jessica's influence mean that he didn't spend nearly half his research time searching for his notes, but the thought of Danielle was no longer a constant darkness of pain and guilt: but now a source of pleasure and comfort.

The people who my father had brought with him were the worst. They were the epitome of the rich upper middle class. Business owners, civil servants, the heads of law and banking firms. They were dressed and made up stunningly, and considered themselves as existing at the highest level of all culture. The only possible thing they could imagine that Jessica, as the stupid girl whose idiocy had caused The Pool of Fire and Blood, was bringing to the marriage was her body, her cunt, and her womb. And most of them were muttering to themselves about how some men would go for anything that looked fit; and it really didn't matter about the girl's level of

223

education at all. Worst, in hearing a lot of filth about my daughter - my elder sister! - , that basically made me realise that most of these people saw her as nothing other than a fit vagina, were the comments about how paralysis was supposed to sharpen your remaining senses: meaning that girls in wheelchairs had particularly sensitive cunts. My father's friends thought beautiful clothes and a certain way of speaking made them cultured, but there was not a single thing that they discussed which would not have been out of place in the gutter.

I wandered, invisible, through the mass of supposedly cultured people who ran this area of our country, and wondered how on earth they had got into this positon. They had an odd and distasteful combination of completely arrogant certainty and a complete lack of understanding of anything at all that actually was going on. I knew that in my heart I was a creature of the wild: one who would always naturally prefer savage barbarian vigour to the soft beauty of civilisation. Yet I hesitated to give fully into hate. If you removed Vicky, Jessica, and Artemis from my life then all colour would be gone from my world: and the little of anything that would be left would not come close to making life worth living. And yet they were all creatures of civilisation too. But there had to be a better way than what I saw around me tonight. There had to be a more effective way of getting the right sort of people into positions of authority than this.

And always I fought with the white magic powered suggestions of my father. Always he moved around the party, glorifying in what a good marriage his daughter was making. Uncaring that everywhere he went he reinforced the image that Jessica had caught her man through youth and beauty alone. Constantly he boasted of how proud a father he was: welcoming someone like

Merlin into the family. Everywhere he went his words reinforced the image of Jessica as nothing more than a hot womb on wheels: now ripe for breeding prestigious grandchildren with a very powerful wizard: thus bringing new glory and power to John's family. My father boasted of Jessica's success in ensnaring Merlin into marriage with the same energy with which he had once wanted her confined to her room and out of everyone's sight and view after The Pool of Fire and Blood: back when he thought that she was making him look very bad in all the most important circles of dinner party guests. Had my father been asked about how he had treated Jessica during that time I doubted he would have even remembered being cruel to her. That memory didn't now fit his current self-image.

My grey magic whirled, and wherever he went I followed, fading away as much of his words as I could. But tonight his power was greater than mine, much greater. In this relaxed social setting it took so much more power to fade away a white magic command then to plant it implacably deep in someone's mind. As a white wizard my father was in his element tonight, at a relaxed social gathering for all the most important people. I was a geek grey wizard at a party. It didn't get much worse than that. It was as bad as the coolest kid in the school being forced to play in a fantasy wargaming tournament. And I had to maintain invisibility as well. But I fought to protect the way people saw my sisterdaughter with every fibre of my being. And, in utter invisibility and unseen by all: even my father: I fought for the first time in a major way directly against my father's power. The power of grey magic against the power of the white. I did not know it at the time but it had been many centuries since such a battle between those two sources of power had been fought in the West.

But it was in the midst of all this that The Allfather's riddle came to me. The sentence he had stuck in the middle of his speech about the fall of the world that bore no real relationship to anything else that he had said at that point. "What is the true power of the grey?" A question just placed disconnectedly in the middle of his words, hidden by being placed in my direct line of sight. In many ways the best way of all to hide anything of true importance.

And the power of the grey is to fade: no its true power is to disappear. And I suddenly understood Odin's plan, the broad outlines of it at least. When he and Artemis marked a champion, when their last reserves were spent, The Voice would simply use his power to strike that champion down. That was what Odin had said. But what if in the moment of being chosen that champion used the power of the grey to fade all memory of himself from the world: even from the minds of Artemis and Odin: and even from that of The Mountain itself? Then The Mountain would see his conquest of the world as finished, seeing all the reserves of his opponents spent, and would no doubt savour the complacency of stretching out what would now seem inevitable victory. Like the tormenting, with the slow drawing out of the final stages in chess or wargaming, of an opponent you have already beaten. A course of action the sadism of The Mountain would surely be unable to resist. And while he wasted his power and time the champion of the gods could walk invisible to wherever his power was most needed. And then I could strike, unseen and unnoticed, directly at The Mountain's heart.

And that quickly I had a solution to the riddle of The Allfather: a foundation upon which to stand. But to secure the favour of my gods as their champion I still needed to offer up either two or three great sacrifices:

depending on whether I interpreted Artemis as one goddess or two.

But though I had solved the riddle of The Allfather I still could not match my power against that of my father's with any true hope of victory. His strength was like a beacon of false light which burned away the darkness of my grey. Easy answers are always so much more attractive than the complexity of true knowledge.

I soon abandoned the upper middle class to my father, they would have nothing to do with Jessica anyway, play no real part in her life. I faded the few suggestions that my father made to Jessica's friends, the odd occasions he degenerated himself to mixing with them, away into nothing: destroying the poison he would have spread throughout their minds. Among Merlin's academic work colleagues we warred incessantly, him all unknowing. I stopped I think, perhaps half, before exhaustion drove me to my knees. I tried to mark those of Merlin's colleagues whom I failed to prevent from suggestion, those who I had failed to stop seeing my sisterdaughter as anything other than a slut, but, in the whirl of pain and utter exhaustion I had no energy to see, and everything blurred.

I sank downwards towards the floor, wearied beyond point of grief. I watched, utterly spent, as my father moved among the academics around Merlin, his every word a poison I was powerless to stop. But, even through my pain and weariness, I noticed how the spells flashed oddly around Nimue, around that beautiful manager of Merlin's whose eyes still wandered towards my daughter's fiancée with naked hunger in them. The white magic simply flickered around her then was gone, with an audible crack that sounded almost like chewing. "What was she?" I wondered through the exhaustion, but I was too weary for the thought to carry any real weight. I found myself contemplating distantly if I had spent all my strength that night against the wrong opponent: if I had fallen into some clever and carefully laid trap of The Voice's own design.

Where was Vicky I wondered exhaustedly? Where was my protector, and my source of strength? And then I remembered bitterly that she had been happily sent to bed hours before by my father. Of course, I thought bleakly. In what world could I ever dare and try to compete with him? Pain surged up and I felt my strength, worn down by my hopeless struggle against John, finally break. I managed to crawl behind a settee in the room, then I was so weary I actually felt myself pass out.

Chapter 18

I lay in a darkness deeper than thought and memory. It was the first time in my life I had matched my power directly against that of another wizard: and tasted only the ashes of defeat. It would not be the last time.

I was lost in the uttermost layers of unconsciousness, when I felt the burning cold bringing me back to the surface. As light formed out of the darkness and shapes out of the shadows I heard her voice calling my name. It was both soft and clear, strong and intimate. But above all I just felt the searing cold of her hand on my chest, the delicious pressure of her nails hard against my skin, and when full senses returned to my eyes they were almost seared by the blinding blue of her eyes: as my heart was touched by the wide concern in her so bright blue gaze. I felt something catch life in me, something I had never felt for real before. Something I had only previously experienced in distant visions of possible futures: and only then for another, very different, girl. In that raw moment of awareness, before the mental structures that rule our waking lives and are built up from infancy could kick in, I felt a terrible intense need. And realised that I liked Artemis: and not as a friend or even as a goddess. Just as a girl.

"Great," I thought distantly, "the women I desire are the eternal virgin and, will be in time, my younger sister. The part of my subconscious mind controlling who I fall in love with really lets me make excellent choices." I called up grey magic to fade the call of my blood. There was little more dangerous in this world than having an erection before the chaste maiden of the moon. According to myth only two mortal men were known to have been aroused by her. The punishment for one had been to be turned into a stag and instantly ripped apart by his own hunting dogs. The other had been turned permanently into a girl and forced to spend the rest of her life praying fervently to Artemis in the hope that the goddess didn't decide just one day to have her killed after all.

Even though my desire faded fast before my grey magic Artemis still felt the change in me. She drew back suddenly and went very still. "Edward," she said carefully, "if you're starting to feel that way about me then that changes everything. I am the goddess of female virginity. For a man to get too close to me can bring nothing but blood and horror. I guess we'll have to…"

"You've never been close to a grey wizard though have you?" I said mildly. "First guy Jessica fancied after The Pool of Fire and Blood was one of those bad boys that bring out all the worst in her. Yet a bit of grey magic and she can't even really remember him: and last night got very happily engaged to a scatty and eccentric middle-aged wizard in his forties. Fading out desire is far from the least of the grey magic's powers."

I took her hand in mine and, seizing the grey magic with everything I had, placed her soft palm gently between my legs. My nose started to bleed from the effort of my magic but the only physical reaction I had was to shiver at the midnight chill of her touch. Moments later I moved her hand away. I didn't want that cold to damage me: it would be nice to have the option to have children later in life.

"See?" I said, "No arousal. With the help of grey magic we can stay as goddess and worshipper, nothing more and nothing less." I raised an eyebrow. "Unless maybe we sort of become friends?"

Artemis looked at me uncertainly, still tense and poised at any moment for flight. "But in the end almost all the men I end up spending time with end up wanting me as far more than a friend-even when I don't flirt with them at all!- and that can only lead to…" she began.

"Not if your male friend is bright enough to realise exactly what you are." I cut in firmly. "Look at you Artemis. You're friendly, stunningly beautiful and very likeable: at least the side of you that I have met so far is. You are quite literally a friendly fairy princess of the gods: you should have suitors hanging out the door. But you don't: you are completely untouched. The only way that makes any sense is if you are a venus fly trap."

Artemis looked at me in confusion. "Edward I am the goddess of many things but I have never thought of myself as a plant that eats flies before. What are you going on about?"

I smiled grimly. "The venus fly trap looks lovely and enticing to flies from the outside. So they fly in and then the other, brutal, side of the plant is revealed as it devours them. Without the nice side the nasty side would have nothing to eat. Same with you I think. How many men has lovely Artemis the Friendly brought to Artemis the Terrible's door?"

Artemis opened her mouth, her eyes wide with horror. "I'm Artemis the Terrible's bait!" she squealed in horror and surprise. "She uses the fact I'm friendly and chatty to help her trap and kill men!"

"Yes." I replied mildly. "This man can see that if he ends up fancying the lovely beautiful goddess he ends

231

up like the poor flies in the trap. And I don't want to be turned into either a stag or a girl Artemis, thanks all the same. But your visions and your friendship," I smiled at her, "that's worth something. Hey you're the one who keeps showing me visions of the future where the only girl I end up fancying is my little sister." My voice hardened for a moment, suddenly very bleak. "Maybe the reason I end up turning to incest is that I am all too successful in using grey magic to suppress my feelings for you: and the frustration generated finds its way out by a most unnatural course."

"Hmmm…" said Artemis, "you are right, we don't get together in any of the visions I've sent you. Plus you did stop your elder sister getting with that bad boy. Didn't stop Artemis the Terrible from ripping him into two; simply because the fact he wanted to fuck Jessica just so he could say that he'd had a girl in a wheelchair annoyed her. But Jessica was already going steady with Merlin and she wasn't in contact with that bastard when he died so that is kind of irrelevant. Really sad and shows just how much of a bitch my other side is: but doesn't change what you did with your grey magic when feelings of lust got in the way of what needed to happen."

Yes I thought. Really sad as that man you killed for next to no reason leaves a very young daughter behind. And while he didn't seem to be much of a dad to her he was probably better than nothing. But then Artemis the Terrible doesn't care about little details like that does she: not when there is the chance to hurt a man experiencing arousal.

Artemis squeezed my shoulder. The cold burned. "Let's try friends. After all, you are right. If you do start thinking about the fact I'm hot you can always just use your grey magic to sort it out."

"The same way that a fly is fine just skimming around the safe edges of the Venus fly trap," I thought warily, "but the longer it stays there the more that it will want to go in." But I smiled and squeezed her hand back. "Friends." I said simply. Without Artemis's visions I would be lost in any case. And there was another reason. I liked Artemis, and I was a worshipper of The Allfather. And Artemis's virginity was a riddle wrapped inside an enigma. The most difficult of all riddles, and the one with the sweetest reward of all. And just because no one had ever solved it before didn't mean that no one ever could. I told myself that wasn't just the fly trap talking.

As the tension faded I realised suddenly that I was exhausted, and in a great deal of pain. I had, after all, collapsed last night after being defeated in a magic battle. Even just the sight of afternoon sunlight through the glass windows hurt my eyes. As I held up one arm to shield them Artemis handed me a small glass of something. I took it numbly and drank. It looked like nothing more than tap water, but it tasted like honey nectar and the sugar of giant bees.

I had taken no more than a sip when Artemis snapped it back firmly. I looked at her confused. "You just offered that to..."

Artemis mock punched me on the arm. I had to seize grey magic instantly as my body tried to react, my cock tried to harden. Artemis rolled her eyes and laughed. "Typical boy." She smiled. "But remember that I'm really just a nasty plant looking to eat up all those careless flies!" She was laughing: but there was a very real warning behind her words. I shuddered, then asked. "Why did you snatch that back so quick, you just offered me that glass!"

Artemis smiled, fully relaxed once more. "Yes greedy, but only one sip! This is the nectar of the gods! Ambrosia!

It's not normally meant for humans. The fact we are giving it to you shows you how happy Odin and I are."

I looked at her curiously. "Am I the first person ever to taste it?"

Artemis smiled and crossed her legs. "No we let favoured mortals have a sip from time to time. That's from me and The Allfather. Odin wants you to have it because he's pleased you solved some of his riddles and I want you to have it because I'm pleased you used my vision to change your fate. Plus I'm dead happy that we can now get past the fact that you fancy me-eugh!- and still be friends. I can't show you more visions of what will happen to the world next right now because the future is still in flux; but you have already changed it away from what you saw in your first visions of death and failure. And I think you've probably had more than enough visions about the future of your personal life for a good long while!"

I looked at Artemis closely, pushing thoughts of my private life aside for now. "Changed to something better or to something worse?" I asked carefully. Artemis's eyes on mine were unreadable: the blue as clear and sharp as the early morning sky. Her brown hair fell down around the soft skin of her small neck and she was so breathtakingly beautiful that in that moment just looking at her hurt. I seized grey magic so deeply that my ears started to bleed. Artemis deliberately ignored my reaction although, and it was the strangest thing, for a moment light danced in her eyes like the birth of stars and it looked like it was taking all that she had not to smile. But her words were calm. "Impossible to tell right now, you have cast the future into confusion and chaos when you shut down the two dark routes that originally faced you. I will send you a new vision as soon as I know more."

I looked at her cautiously. "So long as it is you of course. So long as you don't get grumpy and become…"

Artemis reached out to touch my face. "That won't happen at this point Edward. Not right now. Things are too important and running far too close to call for me to risk becoming Artemis the Terrible anytime soon." She paused. "Well as long as you can keep your new silly feelings under control at least. Then we will be just fine."

"If I've done so well," I said suspiciously, "How come you were so careful with how much Ambrosia I could drink. It was like you didn't trust me to take any more than a…"

"We have to be careful with our gifts of the gods to mortals." said Artemis. "We gave a king the gift of unlimited ambrosia once and he went mad. Fed the flesh of his own children to the gods at a banquet. He resides now in the darkest corner of Tartarus, what the Christians mistakenly call hell. He stands in a river up to his neck that flows away each time he lowers his mouth to drink from it, and bunches of grapes hang above him that disappear when he stretches out his hands to seize them. Our power can overwhelm the minds and bodies of mortals."

"Didn't one of your prophets go so insane that she was unable to explain any of the visions she saw?" I asked, "She saw the ruin of her city and people and no one believed her as her sanity cracked. The fact that she was right about everything, but not believed because of the way she presented her material, was grimly ironic."

Artemis's mouth twisted. "Cassandra of Troy, that really worked out badly. Foreseeing the ruin of her own people and her own murder after being carried off as a spoil of war, and having no one believe a word she said. My brother Apollo has always been far too free with his gifts of the power to see the future. Another of his prophets, of his sibyls, granted both immortality and the gift of prophecy begs and prays now eternally for death, a prayer that is forever unanswered. And her foresight now shows her nothing more than that her suffering is eternal. You can always tell when my brother is thinking with his little head rather than his big head. Whenever there's a guy or girl he fancies his decision making goes completely to pot. He's a dead good brother though, really protective and loyal."

I shuddered as I remembered a particularly horrid story. Artemis smiled at me sympathetically. "You're thinking of a really nasty example of gods and mortals interacting aren't you?"

"Tithonus," I said, and shuddered. "To whom the goddess of the dawn asked Zeus to grant immortality, but forgot to ask for eternal youth. He couldn't die, however much he aged, and after unending sickness and weariness the goddess locked him alone into her bedroom, where he turned in to a cicada beetle, and begs in a whispered voice for a death that can never come."

Artemis looked awkward. "That would never have happened under the light of the moon." She said, "I am not that careless, nor that callous and cruel."

"Still," I replied wryly, "you're not exactly selling the powers of the gods here, by telling me what broken ruins they have made out of people when they went wrong."

Artemis looked at me. "Many trained priests and thespods of the pagan times did just fine with our gifts thank you. And I'm sure you'll be able to handle the gifts of prophecy as well as any of our oracles. Just make sure you never start thinking about how to get my pants off and you'll do just fine! Hey," she said smiling, "you've done great so far!!! And these next visions should be easier to handle anyway," she said, getting down to business. "Because they are about the past, fixed, certain and set in stone. Not about the future, with all its countless thousand different dancing paths and streams.

The vision flared before my eyes: the colours that announced its beginning, as always, indescribably bright and dazzling.

It was a week ago in a small and very magical cottage in a deep dark wood: where the creatures of magic who roamed beneath the leaves of the summer trees were not half so magical as the people living in the warm and snug cottage in the middle of the natural wilderness.

Danielle was sitting quietly in the hall, trying to decide which of her birthday presents she liked best. There was the big play sword Vicky had given her, with magical flashing lights and blasts of thunder. Vicky obviously thought it was an amazing present but Danielle didn't really like fighting and was wondering if she could get away with giving it back to Vicky on her birthday without anyone noticing. Deep down she just thought that hitting people with things wasn't a very nice game. But it had been fun having a friend round on her birthday. It had never happened before, it had always been just her and daddy. And although daddy had tried very hard he'd never been very good with presents. He'd got her socks and flowers, or big books that were too heavy to lift and too big to read and that she didn't understand. They didn't even have any pictures!

But this year, even though the presents said from both mummy and daddy, Danielle knew who had really chosen them. Of course daddy would have helped but he wouldn't have been allowed to do anything important: that would be a disaster! Danielle had new colouring pencils, all shiny and new with a lovely bright green sharpener. She had new colouring books of animals, particularly dogs and birds and magical creatures. She also had two new story books full of pictures. It was more presents then she knew had existed in the whole world. She was still trying to decide which was her favourite present when mummy came into the hall.

Mummy came slowly because she was in a wheelchair and she couldn't walk. Mummy used to be able to walk daddy said. And it hadn't been that long since she couldn't. Danielle had heard the mean things some people said about her mummy as they passed by. Horrible things that were spiteful and mean. Danielle hated fighting but if she could have got away with it she would have boxed their ears, then twisted them until they said sorry. No one should be mean about her mummy! And if she ever found who had hurt her mummy in the first place, who had made it so that she couldn't walk and had to go everywhere in a wheelchair... There was no one to see, except me in the flashback, but if there had been they would have suddenly seen how terrible it is when the normally calm eyes of an almost tranquil child grow suddenly so terribly cold. If she ever found who hurt her mummy Danielle was going to hurt them too: badly.

Mummy wheeled herself close and Danielle scrambled up into her lap, where she gave mummy a hug. Mummy was wearing that dress that was brown with fluffy teddies on it. Danielle knew that mummy didn't really like that dress, she thought it made her look middle aged and frumpy, but she knew Danielle liked the bears.

And that was the present she had liked the best Danielle decided suddenly. The stuffed toy she had been given by mummy as a surprise, after she thought she had already had all her presents. The stuffed animal in the shape of a dog with great eagle wings.

"You must be tired." said mummy gently, "You got up really early and then you had your presents and then Vicky came to play. I bet you want to go to sleep soon!"

"No!" Danielle protested, horrified. "Not want to go to bed yet! Still my birthday!"

"Is it?" said mummy mischievously, "And is there anything in all the excitement which you think you might have forgotten. Anything at all?"

Danielle blushed and looked shyly at the ground. She was afraid to ask for more after she had already been given the best presents ever, and had a friend round to play on her birthday.

"Not had my tea," Danielle said shyly, "or,", and she peered up at mummy hopefully, "or a story?"

"Tea and a story?" said mummy, "That is a lot isn't it! But then, it is a very special day. You do only turn five once don't you? So shall we see what we can do?" Her smile became extra mischievous, even naughty. "I told daddy to make you tea today, shall we go and see what he's done?"

"No!!!" cried Danielle, overtaken by horror before she could stop herself. "Not soggy cereal and daddy's sandwiches! Not on birthday!" then she realised what she had said and stared at the ground, bright red and mortified. She hadn't wanted to be mean about daddy.

"Oh I quite agree!" said mummy with a giggle. "No one wants daddy making sandwiches unless they are about to starve to death. But shall we go and see? Maybe daddy has done something really special and surprised you!?"

"Maybe." said Danielle, trying to be polite. But it was a very reluctant flat-footed girl, with a very disappointed face, who followed mummy round towards the table in the garden. She loved daddy very much but he was not up to making a birthday tea.

As she rounded the corner she stopped and gave a scream. "Chocolate cones, little hot dogs and raspberry popcorn!" She hurled up her arms and ran screaming towards her daddy and the table.

Then she stopped and turned around and looked at mummy suspiciously. "Daddy not know how to make

239

nice food. When he try it taste funny and I get bad belly ache." Danielle looked suspiciously both at mummy behind her and at daddy sat at the table.

"Daddy not make this." She said, without even a hint of a question. "Mummy make this."

"Yes." said Merlin softly. "You have a very special mummy now. One who is amazing at taking care of you and loves you very much."

Danielle looked at Merlin sternly. "Taking care of us both daddy." she reminded him firmly. "Before mummy came you eating soggy cereal all the time and none of your clothes fit." She shook her head sadly. "And your hat keep falling down over your eyes so you not see where you going and you keep bumping into things. Now mummy has given you a lovely hat which stays on your head and not fall down at all!"

Mummy giggled, her cheeks red. "Daddy did try you know love. He tried very hard today. He did help with your birthday tea you know."

Danielle suddenly went very tense and stared at the meal as if it was about to explode. "Why?" she asked fearfully, "What did daddy do?"

"I set the table." said daddy proudly, stroking his beard.

Danielle hmmed sceptically. Then, still tense, she got down on her knees to have a good look at something. She summoned blue magic to make the pot plants lighter, and used brown to reinforce the natural energy of the wind as she lifted them all up.

"Danielle, love, what are you…" mummy began confused, but Danielle was already lowering the pot plants back down carefully into their positions, a relieved expression on her face. She handled her combination of blue and brown magic with such skill that even the keenest eye would have struggled to see any difference to the positons of the plants at all.

"Daddy did set the table." she confirmed happily "Daddy broke a plate and hid it under a pot plant so he not get in trouble."

Daddy looked sheepishly at mummy but she just rolled her eyes and laughed. "Honey how are you so brilliant in so many ways and just so completely useless at others?"

Danielle was already moving to the table, her eyes fixed on the food. There followed a silent period of intense eating when Danielle thought she had never eaten anything so delicious in all her life. She ate until she was full to burst. Not that that stopped her managing a piece of pudding when mummy told her that she had baked her a birthday cake. A special cake, with a picture of a dog with great wings made from lovely icing, then five candles on top. "Tuggles." said Danielle sadly for a moment when she saw it. And luckily neither Merlin nor Danielle saw that for a moment Jessica's face went stark white. Then the dangerous moment passed unseen and Danielle blew out the candles and wished that mummy and daddy would be safe always.

After the cake daddy carried Danielle to bed while mummy followed more slowly in her wheelchair. Then, once Danielle was snuggled up in bed, daddy read her a story about an adventurous shark, and mummy did scary and funny faces. And then, because it was Danielle's birthday, they read her a second story, with mummy doing the reading and daddy doing the faces. And after they were done Danielle got kissed and hugged goodnight by both of them. Danielle liked that daddy wasn't shaky and awkward with his hugs anymore: like he felt very bad about something. And she liked even more that daddy didn't cry anymore when he thought she couldn't see: that made her very happy indeed. Then mummy and daddy left her in her room:

telling her that they loved her very much: and shut the door gently.

The moment they were gone Danielle got up. She knew that even on her birthday it was really important that she was a good girl, and that she didn't forget her prayers. She knelt down by her bed, in front of the three statues that she used to help her focus on the three gods that she had chosen to worship.

She thought of all the good things that her mummy had done. Danielle thought about how she had nice new pyjamas and how when she came to choose her clothes in the morning she now had several to choose from instead of trying to work out if any would fit. She thought about how mummy had got her a nice summer quilt, so she didn't have to choose between sweltering under her winter quilt or lying cold without any quilt at all. She thought about how often she had prayed for the gods to find her a mummy. And she had never dreamed that she would be found a mummy this good, or who she loved so much.

She held out a piece of birthday cake she had smuggled from the table and offered it up to Artemis her first goddess, who was after all, among many other things, the goddess of little girls. A strange fire burned, and then the cake was gone. Danielle nodded to herself, she knew that Artemis liked tasty treats just as much as she did.

Then Danielle thought about the goddess of hearth and home, about the goddess Hestia. The goddess who she had prayed would give her a lovely garden for her and Zuggles to play in. And she held out her favourite new colouring crayon, unused, and watched as it was consumed by fire.

Then she started praying to her last god. A Viking god this time. Tyr, the god of promises and kept oaths. The god who had had his hand torn off by the wolf Fenrir to show the terrible consequences of not keeping your word. She cut a strand of her hair from her new stuffed animal teddy bear, just one single one, carefully selected to be the best possible, and held it up as an offering to the god. It also burned with strange fire and was consumed. And she thought about the promises she had made to the gods. The promises that if they sent her a mummy to look after both her and lovely scatty daddy she would make sure she always kept that mummy safe.

Danielle had heard enough to know mummy was not powerful with magic, but she also knew enough to know that she herself was very powerful. She was not as strong as Vicky of course, but she wondered if she might one day be as powerful as Edward. And it wasn't all about power: that was one reason why she didn't like the play swords Vicky loved so much. She was blue and brown, she wasn't going to fight with pure power like a white wizard. She would use skill and illusion, and the strength of nature. Magic was like drawing a picture, you didn't use strength to make drawings pretty or nice: or nasty.

And Danielle remembered, remembered the truth that The Voice that she really hadn't liked, whose very tones had caused her skin to shiver and made her want to run crying to mummy or daddy; she remembered what he had promised her. That if she got powerful enough: one day: she would be able to use the blue and brown so skilfully she would be able to fix mummy's back: and make her walk again.

Danielle fell asleep, warm and snuggly beneath her quilt, dreaming of being the one to make her mummy better. Then mummy could go swimming at Water World too.

The vision ended, but before I could even begin to catch my breath the second one started to blaze before my eyes: The colours that announced it: as always: almost blindingly bright.

It was yesterday night after the engagement party had finally finished. Jessica and Merlin were in a guest bedroom of the university halls. Both of them were naked. She was sat on Merlin's lap with her hands behind his back, and as they gasped and moved with powerful, ever faster, thrusts together, she had, just briefly, no thought of being disabled, no thoughts of having a broken body. She was in that moment just a young woman in love, riding and being ridden by the man she loved. They came together with a cry, and Jessica fell forward against Merlin's chest, where she snuggled while he held her firmly against him with his arms.

There was a silence when they just held each other, her blond hair streaming down his chest. "You know," whispered Jessica after a awhile, "according to a lot of your work colleagues this is all I bring to the table. According to quite a lot of them all we do every day is have sex. Oh and I look after your child for you. That's it apparently."

She leaned even closer to him and smiled, but beneath it you could tell she was hurting a little, "You know I don't believe they have even given me credit for me showing you how to make sandwiches."

Merlin's hands were soft on her back, but there was in them a tenderness and a raw possession. A man who cared almost nothing for any earthly goods, held her with a rawness and a need that was like a man on fire. And the quiet words he spoke burned with a need to heal even this level of pain in the young woman that he loved. "Despite the fact that they are clever in so many ways tonight too many of my work colleagues showed that they understand nothing about us as a couple. You and Danielle –my two girls- mean everything to me." He held up a hand and cupped her face. "I can't really remember what my life was like before I met you. What was waking up like when you weren't in my arms? How did my house cope without your laughter in it? How did I cope without you to help me organise myself? I can't now even imagine my life without you in it. And I don't want to."

Jessica ran her hands down his back gently, his words soothing her pain, and kissed the tip of his ear. She smiled sweetly as she felt him harden inside her. "Again?" she asked cutely, wide eyed and innocent. It happened three times again.

"You know." said Jessica, afterwards. Flushed with sweat and the afterglow of repeated intense orgasm. "You never really talk about the sex part of our relationship. For most men in their for..." she blushed and looked guiltily. She corrected herself. "For most middle aged men having a pretty teenage girlfriend..."

"Fiancée" said Merlin his voice quiet but utterly implacable in what was going to happen next. "Soon to be my wife."

Jessica glowed for a moment at the absolute and almost ruthless certainty in those words. Then she turned to Merlin, curiosity dancing in her eyes. "Is it not kind of like a dream come true though? Being with a beautiful teenager?" She raised an eyebrow archly, "Now trying for a kid with her? Of course," she said, mock solemnly, "we're only doing all this for Danielle's sake. So that she can have a little brother or sister. Whether reproduction is fun or not is entirely besides the point isn't it?" And then she giggled, chewing mischievously on a piece of her golden hair. It made her look unbelievably hot and she knew it.

"Being with you is a dream." said Merlin quietly, "I have nightmares sometimes that I never met you, that you were never real. Just a fancy born from my imagination. There is some difference in our ages, but I don't ever really think about it now. It bothered me in the beginning, but I love you and you love me back, so what else is there to think about? I want the rest of my life to be with you. I have never loved anyone the way I love you, not even," he paused and looked very guilty, "not even my first wife."

There was a long silence in which neither of them said anything. Then Jessica reached in and just kissed Merlin, with tears in her eyes. She didn't say anything, but in that moment her heart was melting. You would normally have said in a circumstance like this that the woman suddenly felt sweet sixteen again but, secretly, Jessica was only sixteen in the first place. But she felt in that moment beyond blessed, beyond special.

After a long while during which they just held each other Jessica realised she had to do something. Otherwise she was so happy she would probably just start crying. She took a deep breath. "I love you too. And you, you and Danielle, you both bring out the best in me. Without you two I'd just be another drunk party girl high on drugs most of the time." She reached out her hand and let her fingers play with Merlin's chest hair. "Want to try and give Danielle a little brother or sister one more time?"

He did.

The vision faded and I sat there glaring at Artemis. "Is there any reason that I have just been made to watch my sister's love life?"- calling her my daughter, even if that was now the reality of our psychological and emotional relationship, was just too weird- "I would have been quite happy with you just showing me that she was happy. At least that sorts out my being attracted to you problem, Artemis." I said wryly, "After being forced to watch that it's going to be at least a week before I can even begin to think about sex without feeling ill."

"No," said Artemis, "you wouldn't have been happy with me just telling you that Jessica is very happy with Merlin. No more than if I had just said oh Danielle is very happy with her new mummy. You needed to see the actual reality to fully understand what your saving of Jessica has done. And you will need to know that you have done good soon. You will need things to hold onto when the storm hits, when…''

She stopped, and trailed off sadly.

''When?'' I asked, my voice somehow both gentle and sharp at the same time.

Artemis looked at me and her gaze was sad. ''When you see what the future holds.'' And half a tear crept out from under her eye. I held out my hand and wiped it from her. The cold of her skin was like whiplash on my hand.

''Hey.'' I said lightly. I had faced a dark future for as long as I could remember, long before I ever saw my first vision of what might be to come. After a while constant tension stops feeling like anything, you just go numb. ''It can't be all bad though can it? Last two guys who fancied you that I know about; one ended up being eaten alive by his own dogs and the other went through an unwanted sex change. This time you're just crying for me even though nothing bad has happened yet!''

Artemis swallowed. ''I am a fly trap Edward, and you must never act or think on this again. But the difference is this time the fact a man fancies me doesn't scare me. If it wasn't for Artemis the Terrible I'd be your girl right now: cause I fancy you right back. But this conversation can't ever lead anywhere Edward.'' And she looked at me through eyes that were suddenly torn with fear. ''Because if it does you're going to die horribly at my hand. And I'm going to have to live with the memory of killing you for all eternity. And you know what the worst part of all this is?

Artemis the Terrible will find that memory fun.''

Chapter 19

I was sitting at the table nursing a hot cup of coffee and a bacon sandwich. I supposed I should be trying to work out what to do next, but all I could think about was the fact that the girl I liked liked me back. That, I kept telling myself, was the hard part. With any other girl that would have been right. But, deep down, I knew that was not the case with Artemis. Men were supposed to like her. To like her and to get no closer to being with her than their seed could get to impregnating the cold dust and stone of the moon. Then I was momentarily distracted as someone I barely ever thought about, but did pop up idly in my life from time to time, came into the university guest quarter's kitchen.

"Brother." I said, disinterestedly.

Jacob was smart, in his super fashionable brown suit. Unlike most academics smartness had always come naturally to him, although only when he cared about it. Today was obviously one of those days.

"Didn't expect to see you here." I said flatly. "You've wanted nothing to do with Jessica since she was left half paralysed Jacob. You just left her to rot alone in her room: and now that she's made something of her life you suddenly want to be here to bask in all the credit. Like a fouled bluebottle feeding on carrion."

Jacob looked at me, and raised an ironic eyebrow. I was shocked: for him that was as expressive of emotion as Vicky having a shouting fit. He had always been the master of exerting himself as absolutely little as possible. Raising an eyebrow like that would have sometimes counted for him as his full day's work.

"Oh brother," he said, almost sadly, "so idealistic, so with your head up in the clouds. So dreaming of a better world. Hasn't the way you've been treated taught you anything? What do you think makes someone rich or elite? It's not producing anything. The very clothes that a successful man wears, the suit, are a demonstration that he doesn't do anything useful: or else his clothes would get all mucked up. The clothes a labourer wears, the ones that do get mucked up, show both that he is productive and useful: and how low his status is as a result. The productive parts of the economy are always done by people who are more or less slaves Edward. People get rich by feeding off others' successes, not by producing anything useful themselves. Look at England itself. Built up from 796 to 1066 to defend against the Viking invasions, and then look what happens. They crush the last Viking invasion successfully in 1066 and what is the result? Less than a month later the English are crushed, most of their leaders are dead and England is open to centuries of exploitation by the Normans. Hundreds of years of them collecting tax revenues from a state they did nothing to build, but instead just took over in one single day of bloody battle: hurting an awful lot of people in the process. That's what it means to be successful Edward. Being productive yourself just means that the elite are going to turn up to take what you have got and claim it for themselves."

I closed my eyes. "Not always." I said softly. "In the beginning to be part of the elite meant to lead from the front: to wear armour, not posh clothes. For power and privilege to be earned by the strength of your sword and the stoutness of your heart. Look at a state like Sparta, where privilege had to be constantly earned and re-earned by enduring danger and bloodshed. In the great times of history, the birth of nations, the elites truly do earn their place in history: and don't just feed like parasites on the productive parts of our economy."

Jacob shuddered. "And who but a mad man would want to live in a world that looked anything at all like that? That sounds like a lot of hard work. Much nicer now, living in a slow complacent nation enduring an unending period of managed decline. I get to cream off all the good stuff and not do any hard work. Why would anyone want to change that?"

I shrugged but felt a little uncomfortable. Whenever I did find myself having to talk to my older brother I always found the experience rather unsettling. In a world where most people actively hated me for being a grey wizard utter indifference to me was something I found quite disconcerting. But I managed to make a polite enough reply to my older brother. "Maybe because exploiting others is wrong. Maybe out of a sense of decency and morality? Or maybe just out of a practical sense of what are you going to do when the rotten state finally falls?"

Jacob moved over to make a cup of coffee, laughing to himself. "Morality. That would be the braying of pointless noise about BIG ISSUES that we all make at student debates right? Fun but come on, it's not like anyone takes stuff like that seriously is it? I mean once the hangovers settled down and you are actually up in the morning what really matters is the money you're making, the possessions you have, and the tightness of the cunt you're enjoying. Oh and as for what I will do if the rotting state and order of things collapses during my lifetime, well just fuck off somewhere else and find some other people to exploit. Not exactly going to hang around if all the shit's starting to hit the fan now am I?''

I tightened my hand so hard that my cup of coffee shook. ''My father will be so proud of you. You're cut from so similar a shade of cloth.''

Jacob smiled. ''Not really. I mean I appreciate all the money and privilege he's given me but dad's all about image and looking good at parties. Me, I'm more about just enjoying life and privilege. I like boozing with the lads, chasing hot women, and knowing I've got a dead prestigious and important job. I don't need to hog the limelight all the time like John does. To be honest Edward I think our father's a bit of a cunt but, you know, got to keep him happy as he's got one hell of an inheritance to leave to someone one day. And it is a bit tricky because there are, you know, four of us.'' He shot me a dismissive glance. ''Although, let's be honest about this, there are basically three of us. Let's face it, you only embrace morality because you've got no other choice. The world has given you nothing: so you've just had to make your own fun. I mean I do kind of actually admire how far you've got as a grey wizard, fuck you must have like the highest value added: the most progress made given your dismal starting point: of any wizard in this whole country. And yes morality is better than nothing I guess. Probably a lot better. But let's face it Edward, given the choice you would be me.''

I turned to look out of the window. I watched the morning sunlight dancing over the stone face of the Old Man of Prestham, and felt very sick. ''I would never be you.'' I said, ''I would never make those choices that…''

The Voice drifted as it spoke in my ears. ''We can't know that Edward, not you, not even I. There is no temptation in this world that I can offer you that you would want, and no part that I desire for you to play in my plan except for you to die and be forgotten as soon as

251

possible. But if I could offer you say, the love of Artemis, would you not at least be tempted?"

I thought for a while, my thoughts drifting in the dancing sun beams. Then I smiled, I was a worshipper of The Allfather: I knew when I had been set a false question. "It's like Artemis said, it's the choices I chose to make in following what seemed to me the natural development of grey magic that have shaped who I am. The reason I want Artemis's love: rather than that of a mortal girl my own age: is that I have to win it for myself. I don't want to end up with a girl who only wants me because she sees me as rich and successful. It's the route that I have chosen that means The Voice has nothing to offer me, not some random twist of luck or fate."

I turned back towards where Jacob was frying bacon, the oil sizzling as he made his breakfast.

"People are not all like you you know." I said coldly. "Jessica isn't any more. Offered the choice between a helpful life or one as a spoilt parasite she made the right choice."

Jacob laughed softly. "You're saying Jessica isn't like me because she's adapted herself well to her new environment? You do realise that going with the flow is kind of my whole philosophy on life right? You don't tend to think about things in these terms, so obsessed with what's right and wrong rather than how other people see things, that I don't think you get just how prestigious bagging Merlin is do you?! It turns out I really underestimated what my sister was capable of after she got herself half paralysed. She never was much good at magic or studying: but let's face it she really doesn't need to be when she's got so much good stuff on the outside. But I never thought that even when she could walk she'd be able to bag Merlin. Fucking hell do you know how many women have tried to get his interest over the years? And the closest most of them have got to any action is getting to listen to a rambling lecture on the reproductive capacity of Merlin's favourite vegetables. Or how to breed giant bees which make especially delicious honey.

But my little sis, she sees what she wants and she just fucking takes it. Who knew? She had just what it took to get the man she really wanted. It was so funny seeing everyone at the party last night thinking Merlin was just going for sis's big boobs and tight teenage cunt. Not one of them seemed to be able to reflect on just how many girls have tried using their physical charms on him and got nowhere. And by all the gods they sounded so stupid when they started banging on about how gutted they bet she is that Merlin comes with a kid! The fact that she genuinely loves his kid and is so good at making her happy is the key to Merlin's heart!

Ironic isn't it? Jess dies at The Pool of Fire and Blood, but if she could see what Jessica would achieve afterwards I think she would have died willingly and with a smile on her face. None of the boys she used to hang out with could have given her a patch of the reputation she will enjoy as Merlin's wife. And the way he needs Jessica will get her so much more respect in the long term than the way Mike and her other boyfriends wanted her. Being hot and pretty on a prestigious man's arm will get you noticed, but as much negatively as positively. But being the reason Merlin's kid is happy, and from the way Jessica's actual friends were talking last night Danielle is not going to be an only child for very much longer at all, and the reason that he turns up to work looking smart and not a dishevelled mess, and the reason his house now looks neat? Overtime Jessica's going to get herself a very good reputation indeed.

Funny really, you've put so much effort so successfully into making Jessica's life so much better when she treated you so badly for so long. I do kind of wonder whether you'll get your fair share back though. For all the hard, unseen work you've done quietly and very effectively on her behalf."

Jacob's words made me feel very uncomfortable indeed. "Jessica and Jess are nothing at all alike." I began. "Just because you change your colour each time the wind blows in a new direction doesn't mean she…"

Jacob raised both his hands as though weighing something up. "Yes," he murmured, "and No. The answer lies somewhere in-between. Jessica offers very different things to what Jess did when she came to the marriage market: but they both want the same thing. Or can you look me in the eye and tell me that Jessica would be just as happy to marry a penniless PHD student just starting out as she is to marry the very well established and respected magical researcher Merlin? In your own way you are as deluded about who your elder sister is as everyone else was at that party last night. Isn't that why you have to think about her as two separate people, Jess and Jessica? Because deep down renaming her allows you not to think about the fact that at the end of the day you are just talking about the same girl?"

I had no answer, only a sudden uncertainty and pain. I just suddenly wanted rid of my elder brother, my elder brother who had an answer for everything and everyone: and who always knew exactly what to do to make sure that he was okay. Instead of clever words all I had to spit at Jacob were simple words of defiance.

"Jessica's a lovely girl now: and a great sister. I love her very much."

Jacob laughed softly. "If Jessica really loved you Edward, the last thing she would have done is to date another brown wizard. You do remember how much her last boyfriend Mike hated you right? And he was only half brown. You do know what the speciality of brown wizards is don't you Edward? Or did all the dunkings you went through drive that right out of your head? Gods it was so funny to see you splashing around so completely helplessly and wondering if this time you'd actually drown. I really miss watching those. Once you've seen something like that in the flesh even the best action flick pales in comparison."

"Brown is the magic of nature and growing things." I said, ignoring Jacob's distasteful trip down memory lane. Unpleasant as he was Jacob had always been far fonder of bluster and bluff than he was of actually doing anything. Not because deep down he was some kind of nice guy: just because underneath all the layers of unpleasantness his most defining trait was that he was completely lazy. "And each brown wizard has his or her own specialist knowledge area." I continued. "Merlin's is medicinal plants and history: you know I've never been sure exactly which period. He seems to range all over the ancient world: and he has a phenomenal knowledge of old myths and religions. You're brown. What do you specialise in again? Pulling women isn't it? One thousand and one ways to make a doofus seem attractive? You really would need to be studying that full-time to get any woman to jump into bed with you."

"Weapons of war," said Jacob dreamily, "and loose women. I spend my days devising ever more effective ways to kill people, and my nights getting ever better at finding my way into more women's pants. Gods I love Oxbridge." He turned and looked up at the ceiling dreamily. "Heavens knows why Merlin chooses this dump at Chester to study in when he could be honoured even at the great university itself. Still," he said, cheering up a little, "dad will get that all sorted. He's so good at pulling strings."

"You mean his powers of persuasion." I said flatly. "The way he influences people through what is basically mind control?"

Jacob shrugged his shoulders. "Wealth, magical power, informal influence. What does it matter how dad gets his money and power so long as he does? I'm the kid of a rich and successful businessman: what do I care about how he makes his millions? I'm just happy spending them.

Anyway my point is all brown wizards have a special responsibility for making sure no grey wizard becomes too powerful. And who is the most powerful brown wizard of them all, why that's right Merlin! And Jessica has got him watching right over you: just where he can see your every move. I don't think she did it deliberately, but equally I'm pretty sure she doesn't care all that much either. You might well wish Mike had drowned you in that fishpond by the time Merlin's done with you. With all his power I'm pretty sure he'll be able to come up with a much better way of killing you than just drowning."

"Okay brother," I said, "but to be honest bearing in mind that this is a dump and not worthy of your time I'm obviously too stupid to understand what you're saying. To me it just sounds like your babbling nonsense. Why don't you just head on back to Oxbridge where your talents will really be appreciated."

Jacob laughed. "Hey I'm brown too you know. And maybe, if just maybe you are right and Jessica is more changed then I realised; and is actually using her very considerable influence over Merlin to keep you safe; well someone needs to keep an eye on you then don't they?"

I looked at my older brother coolly. "Us spending more time together is not going to turn out very well: not for you anyway." I turned my eyes on his and smiled. "Wouldn't want my contempt for you to become dislike now would we Jacob? You might find having me as your enemy quite an uncomfortable experience. Now," I said, "I've got things to do. I'd appreciate it if once you've finished eating you just buggered off as fast as possible.

But either way we're done now until we next get to exchange insults at Christmas. Hope your life sucks till then."

Jacob stopped for a moment, his mouth twisting: an odd expression fell across his face. "You can't just walk out on me you know. We're brothers and…" I stared at him for a moment in surprise, Jacob was more than bright enough to have recognised the seriousness of my warning shot and yet he had just blatantly ignored it for no clear reason: and I had no idea why. I looked into his eyes, really looked into them for probably the first time in my entire life, and in the fear in them I suddenly saw an answer that scared me. Jacob didn't do fear: he was too laconic and it took up far too much energy that could be spent feeling good about himself and his station in life. But right now he was terrified.

Suddenly everything went very cold. "You are stalling me brown wizard." I said flatly. "This isn't a real conversation: you are just trying all you can to tie up all my time and attention for as long as possible.

Why?"

"Stalling you," laughed Jacob, "why that's…"

But my grey magic was already searching for an answer. "You have reinforced my arm with natural strength," I whispered, "but why?" Then I looked at the cuts on my hand, the unnatural cuts reinforced with grey to let me know if either of my sisters were in dire peril. And the reinforced healing had healed one of them: silently rendering my warning system useless.

I turned eyes on Jacob that were colder than midnight ice.

"Brother, why are you stopping my protection spell for one of my sisters from working?"

"Edward," Jacob began, his eyes round and starting to panic. "let's be reasonable."

"Release the spell that binds me to Jessica brother or I will kill you where you stand."

"Fuck you Edward!" Jacob shouted, suddenly angry. Fear suddenly even stronger than his natural inertia. "You think I'm afraid of you? I could take you any day of the week. I'm properly educated: my brown powers would make mincemeat out of your unsophisticated grey. But if we fight you think I don't know you'll set Vicky on me, that you'll get your tame little blood hound to kill me? Gods only know what freak of nature gave that girl such unbelievable power. But I'm sure we can be sensible, and reason our way out of this without fighting. I'll tell you what's going on if you let me go. Just promise that once I'm finished I leave unharmed and the going is good."

But he had not released the spell which rendered my warning system useless and so the time for words was now well past. It was the time for blades and blood. I struck with all the power of the grey, fading all the muscle of Jacob's heart into nothing half way through its beat. I could almost feel the sudden terrible pressure inside Jacob's body as in one moment it found itself fighting desperately for life. But Jacob was a brown wizard, and life magic was natural to him. He drank deep and desperate as the dying man he now was from his source of power: and the tide of brown magic unleashed literally forced his heart back into being. I could not have stood before that flood of brown power any more than a twig drifting on the surface of the water could have held against a strong current. But nor did I try to. I was not an idiot. And I had a lifetime's experience of having to fight fast. Even as Jacob's heart rematerialized to beat again I struck with grey magic once more: this time fading the stone beneath his feet out of existence. He roared, and swung his power wildly, suddenly panicked, but I was faster. I had spent a lifetime having to be fast:

to fade away the strikes of the tormentors that would have killed me. I was already moving. I seized a knife laid out on the dining table for breakfast, and faded its dull edge with grey magic into a blade razor sharp and fatally lethal. Jacob used his brown power to reinforce his arms to give him the strength to haul himself back up through the floor, which he then reknit under his feet. But it took him time as stone is natural but it is not alive, and therefore not quite as amenable to brown magic as is any substance of life. He no doubt thought that he was securing his area, when in reality all that he was doing was wasting precious time.

Jacob started to gather brown magic to raise up his defences around himself, but, in one smooth motion before he could prepare himself, I cut his throat. One of his hands moved towards his throat to heal himself, but even as it did I drove my knife back, seized his head with one hand, and used grey magic to tear a hole in his magic defences. His throat had just finished healing and reknitting when I slammed my knife into his left eye so hard that it came out the other side of his head. I tore the blade free with a silent snarl, and dropped down to follow his falling body, driving my knife again and again into his heart. Then I twisted the blade savagely, tearing apart the struggling organ as it still fought desperately to beat. l stabbed him about twelve more times, then left the knife driven straight through his heart and out his back: the blade standing proud in the middle of the sorry remains of the once mighty organ. I bit my lip as I fought down the urge to fade away the last of Jacob's soul and life with the power of the grey. The brown had phenomenal powers of magical healing. But I dared not use the grey as an offensive magical weapon: that would lead only to my stark and brutal execution. I had used it at the start of the magical conflict, but Jacob's own successful defence against me fading away his heart should have destroyed all the evidence. But to use grey magic now? I might as well use the knife in my hand to take my own life.

But there were no rules and regulations about the use of fire magic as an offensive weapon of war. I thought of all the times that Jacob had, quite disinterestedly, tortured me as a child: and the power of flame came easily. My older brother's body went up like tinderflame. I turned away grimly, even a brown wizard would need to be not that far short of Merlin's level of power and skill to survive that; and then to successfully rebuild his body.

The brown magic strengthening my arm- "Stupid move that," I thought distantly, "to strengthen a grey wizard's knife hand."- faded and was gone: its power broken. But the result of that brought no relief, only sudden horror rushing through me. One of the wounds on my hand was suddenly screaming. I seized the power of the grey, and tried to teleport myself to my sister's side. Nothing happened. I stopped, shaken. That was impossible. That couldn't…

But it had. So I started running.

Chapter 20

I had never moved so fast, yet by the time I reached Jessica's room I knew that her chances were looking very bleak. The ache of my protection spell had faded as I ran until I could feel almost nothing. Now the pain was so intangible that it was hardly there at all. If I had not been actively focusing on it, all my thoughts bent on it, I would have never even noticed the slight occasional twinges. But desperate as I was I did not run headlong into my sister's room like an idiot, to be cut down by whatever awaited me. Experience had long taught me that losing control of your emotions and giving way to stupidity aids no one. Instead I was clad in invisibility as I stepped through the walls of Merlin and Jessica's bedroom in the university accommodation. Needing to move fast does not mean doing something that will just get you killed.

But once inside the bedroom I saw nothing but Jessica wheeling herself round on her wheelchair, a slightly impatient and therefore uncharacteristic look on her face. On the other side of the room Merlin was trimming his beard. There was nothing on first sight that seemed wrong or dangerous at all. Absolutely nothing. I had walked in on nothing but an ordinary and everyday domestic scene. But the cut on my hand was still stinging: even if only so very faintly. And my laconic coward of a brother had not bestirred himself for nothing.

So I settled myself in a chair out of the way and for a long time I just waited: and I watched. I watched with all the power and subtleness of the grey. I studied each interaction between the engaged couple. For the first few minutes, apart from a slight sense of oddness, I thought I must be going mad. That the protection spell had simply gone faulty. But over and over I compared the interactions of the two against the memories of the visions in my mind: of the memory of Jessica and Merlin together the previous night. And as watched I finally started to see all the little things that didn't actually add up. The thousand tiny and seemingly insignificant details that only the searching eye of the microscope would ever find.

Merlin was still Merlin, but Jessica was not Jessica. She looked and sounded almost the same, but only at first glance. Once you started looking for it closely the differences between whoever this person really was and my older sister were all too visible and real. There was an impatience hidden just below the surface in this imposter, a restlessness that had not been any part of Jessica's new life. Something I might have almost called a hunger.

And whoever this new woman was she was also possessed of a very real cruelty. She made slightly barbed comments about Merlin's appearance that Jessica would have never passed. And she was too sexual, too flirty with her body, in a way my older sister had never been since The Pool of Fire and Blood. And this imposter was far too in love with her own beauty to be the real Jessica.

And she was also too frustrated with the fact that she was in a wheelchair. Now Jessica had Merlin and

Danielle in her life I think she herself often forgot that she was disabled. But for this new person being in a wheelchair was clearly a new and unpleasant experience.

After a while Merlin and whoever this other person was went out, but not before my invisible hands had slipped the imposter's phone from her pocket. Breaking through the security code, even with magical defences, was child's play to a grey wizard. I flicked through the contacts until I found the name I was looking for. Then I called him.

"Hello?" answered Jacob sounding terrified. So the bastard was still alive. If only grey magic was a legal weapon of war. "I held him up like you wanted but he twigged that something was wrong at the end. Still I kept my promise to you by keeping Edward out of the way during the critical period so I'm okay and we're done yes?"

I hung up. I knew almost everything I needed to know. Almost.

I slipped from the bedroom and walked down to the university reception. There was nobody there except the university administrative staff. Good, that meant there was far more chance that what I was about to do would go unnoticed. "Excuse me?" I said mildly, "I need to speak to the head of History and Experimental Biology. An odd combination but you know! I believe her name is Nimue?"

The receptionist looked at me like I was talking in Ancient Greek. A language that, since I had started to read about the Greek Gods, I was beginning to learn. "What are you talking about?" he asked me in complete confusion. "Neither of those departments have had a proper manager since the two people who did manage them disappeared overnight a couple of years ago. All they found of them were a few cracked bones chewed down to the marrow. Since then the two departments

263

have notionally been managed by Merlin: which means of course that they haven't been managed at all and… "

"Thank you." I said bleakly: and met the receptionist's eyes. "We never had this conversation." And I hit his memory of it with all the power of the grey. Then I turned and walked from the reception: my thoughts bleak.

I had read enough about Merlin and Nimue to know they weren't just wizards of phenomenal power: whose blue magic could create the most powerful and believably enticing illusions in the minds of men. They were also shape changers.

Chapter 21

You could feel the quiet peace of deep learning rising from the spires of Oxbridge: Britain's oldest university. The great seat of learning rose dreamily over gentle rolling country fields and a river ran calmly and smoothly through the centre of the town which proudly held the world-renowned institution of higher learning. Oxbridge was stunningly beautiful, particularly with the sun setting in a golden glow behind the ancient town: bathing the walls and buildings in a soft warm red.

I loved it. The juxtaposition with what I was about to do pleased me. The peaceful setting made the perfect contrast for the scene of blood and vengeance. And of course the beauty of Oxbridge only made me hate it more. After all anyone who loved learning and knowledge and was academically gifted enough was welcome here: except grey wizards of course. Couldn't have scum like that studying at university. I was a worshipper of The Allfather, the barbarian god of knowledge, and yet was banned from all the seats of higher learning in the civilised world. In a weird way: that kind of figured.

"Like ghosts," I said to the small child at my side, who was still shaking with anger, "let us walk invisible through these streets. There are enough wizards of sufficient power here that if they chose they could bring even you down. Wizards of all colours, all backgrounds, all creeds and nationalities. Except grey of course.'' My voice hardened. ''We grey trash of course aren't welcome in a lovely and civilised place like this.''

I looked at Vicky, and I had never seen her so quiet. I didn't know if it was concern for Jessica, a child's murderous rage at the horrendous notion of kidnapping, or just fury that she hadn't been able to break through the spell of shape changing that Nimue had wrought. I think it was probably the first time in her life that Vicky had ever failed at anything. My little sister had the power to be able to break the spell, of that there was no doubt, but Nimue's shimmering coils of brown and blue magic simply didn't give Vicky's power anything to latch onto. She had spent five minutes blasting light magic pointlessly into empty air: trying to uselessly chase down the elusive essence of illusion itself.

I had thought about telling Merlin what had happened, but of all people the net of deceit was most hopelessly entertwinned around his mind, a net long in the making. And if it came to my word against the person he believed was Jessica… I shook my head grimly. That could not lead anywhere good. And from everything I had read about Arthurian myth Nimue was Merlin's natural antidote: a power specifically designed to cripple his. After all his strength was so vast that without an antidote what would stop him from having the power to do pretty much whatever he wished all the time? I found myself looking at Vicky, the only wizard I had ever met who was even more powerful than Merlin. I found myself praying to all the gods I knew that she didn't have an antidote out there. Just the thought made my blood run cold.

We moved quickly though the fading light. The shops and cafes were closed but, the bars were starting to wake up: the true essence of student life far more than any library. We moved on, uncaring. Vicky didn't so much as glance at the lights and loud music, even though she normally loved anything that looked like a party.

We came to the college quickly, less than ten minutes' walk from the railway station. We passed through one of the student entrances, across the attractive lawns, and into one of the distinguished old buildings which served as a student residential hall. It was really nice. The sort of place reserved for those who were going to be the future of this country. People who mattered. Not a place for people like me. There was a keycard lock reinforced with powerful white magic. I was a grey wizard livid with power and fury: it wasn't even a contest. I reached out again with my magic and felt the infinitesimally small fragment of pain that reminded me that Jessica still lived; somewhere. That gave me a hope so desperate it was almost pain.

I climbed the stairways of the student halls: which were a combination of grand classical architecture and the everyday mess of a student residence. We came to the third floor corridor and the door I wanted was ahead of me. It was shielded by powerful brown magic, magic strong enough to make me hesitate, magic built up over several weeks of desperate incantations to make the room almost impenetrable to a grey wizard. Even in the cold depths of my anger I took a moment to admire what Jacob had done. It was a very impressive piece of defensive magic: a room its owner thought was well prepared against magical attack.

Then Vicky just blew the door down: while I faded away all the noise and sound from the impact with grey magic. Impressive defensive magic: and pointless. But then pretty much everything was against the power of my little sister.

Jacob started up from where he was in the middle of a room that, even for him, was more of a dishevelled mess than usual. He was in the middle of throwing clothes into a suitcase: he'd been preparing to run, a clever move.

He froze when he saw us, and in the precious few seconds that cost him, a blast of light magic from Vicky had him pinned against the wall, his legs and arms outspread helplessly. Her power blocked Jacob from reaching for his brown magic. Vicky stalked into the room with fury screwing up her face.

I followed her, very calmly stepping over the threshold. "Excellent Vicky, but just make sure you keep him alive. We need him to talk."

I raised my eyes to look into my older brother's coldly. "You look great for a dead man. But a word of advice brother. If you are going to try and run for your life either pack the previous day or, you know, pack quicker. That's twice in one day your lack of reflexes have left you helpless. Beaten by two of your siblings in magical combat within twenty four hours: quite pathetic really."

"You only won last time because you went for me first." snarled Jacob. "In a fair fight you'd never take me." I raised an eyebrow. Our fight this morning hadn't been fair? What exactly did Jacob consider a fair fight I wondered? Presumably, like any educated person, only one that he won. Jacob ranted on, "Otherwise you'd have never brought your little bloodhound to fight your battles with you. Sheltering behind a four year old's…"

"Edward," said Vicky confused, "where is bloodhound? Can I see it? I like dogs." My eyes never left Jacob's face. "There is no bloodhound sis. He's just calling you my pet dog."

There was a silence, then Vicky snarled. There was a flash of blazing light, and Jacob's head cracked back like from a whip. When he raised it again two of his teeth were missing and his mouth was bleeding. I ruffled

Vicky's hair. "Nice shot. I like the blood part though, your hair is red like blood pouring from an open wound. Maybe you're a bloodwolf? You're certainly fierce and independent enough."

Vicky smiled at that. "A bloodwolf. Big and tough!!!"

I turned my eyes back to Jacob. "Enough foreplay. Time for you to talk. Where is Jessica and I want to hear everything you know about Nimue."

Jacob laughed, "Or what Edward? You're going to get Vicky to blow me to bits? Fine go ahead and do it. I don't want to die but well done you caught me! Enjoy your little moment. But if you think anything you can do can compare with what she would do if…"

"She won't know Jacob," I said icily, "you have two choices. Let me explain them to you. One, is we kill you. Properly this time, and Vicky uses white magic to make sure there isn't one bit of life left anywhere in you. No grey magic will be used and your remains will never be found. We'll be fine. There won't seem to be any crime to accuse us of and you'll just get listed as a missing person. You'll be dead. Kind of like forever. All your friends forget you and your girlfriend goes on to marry someone else. She'll end up fucking another man and ultimately go on to have his children: not yours. Ten years' time and you'll be lucky to be so much as a photo on someone else's social media feed.

Or you talk and I use grey magic so powerful that everyone forgets who you ever were, including Nimue. Only Vicky and I will remember. You don't get to keep the life you have here, all your privileges and wealth and grades and possessions are the price you pay for selling out your own sister: but you get to live. A light punishment for what you've done to Jessica. To be honest I'm really uneasy that with this route you get to survive: feels like leaving a very uncomfortable loose end completely untied."

269

"He let Jess live too," said Vicky enthusiastically, "when I want kill her dead. And that was very good. Now I have a sister called Jessica who is much better than Jess, who was just rubbish and always mean to me. Called me horrible names! Just talk and we let you live too. I not even put you in a wheelchair!"

For a moment Jacob's face was pained with indecision. I realised that he really, really, wanted to live. For a moment I was sure he was going to talk. But then the dark terror of Nimue fell across him, and I saw the indecision die in his eyes. Jacob swallowed drily, fear making him struggle to find even the breath for words. "If Nimue ever found out that I talked, if she did to me what she's doing to Jessica, or what she will do to Merlin and in time Danielle…"

"Why what she doing?!" demanded Vicky. "It sound nasty!"

"Just kill me." whispered Jacob. "There's nothing you could do that could scare me more than her. She is the darkest power I have ever met."

There was a short silence, and then the room filled with the sound of a cold, dark laughter: my own. It sounded strange even in my ears. I turned round and looked at Vicky. "Vicky," I said gently, "could you put your fingers in your ears and close your eyes please. Keep the spell up on Jacob but I don't want you to hear or see this next bit." I didn't want her to experience anything that might further her bloodlust.

The four year old shook her head firmly. "No Edward not shutting eyes. Need to see if you get in trouble. Not like Jacob. And we a team."

"Okay." I said quietly, not letting a sudden doubt haunt me. I had to save Jessica, the risk of Vicky's rising bloodlust would just have to be a problem for another day. I turned back to Jacob.

270

"Is it possible?" I marvelled. "You grew up with me all those years and yet you never knew? You never knew what your and everyone elses' cruelty created? I knew that you were never that interested in me but you really didn't think much about me at all as we grew up did you? Obviously not, not if you now think that I will just kill you if you don't tell me what I need to know. You're very bright yet I genuinely believe that you have no real idea of the consequences that your actions towards me have unleashed." I moved close to him. "Do you remember laughing as you pissed all over me after one of Jess's boyfriends had knocked me so bloody that I thought he had broken almost all of my ribs? Do you remember using your brown magic to make yourself strong enough to hold me and control my thrashing when my arm was trapped in an oven at one hundred and ninety degrees, and laughing while my flesh burned so badly it actually started to cook? Do you remember the hours of agony while I just lay there screaming with the seared well done flesh on my arm bleeding like a particularly well prepared beef steak: before Vicky came back home from playgroup and fixed me. And the worst thing was you didn't even do it because you hated me. It was just the way things were going and you found it fun. And now you think I can't hurt you worse than Nimue can?"

Jacob shifted, suddenly unsettled and uneasy. "Edward," he said weakly, "you were so kind as a child. We had to peel you off people you were that clingy. You always used to put love on the birthday cards you wrote, even to total strangers, and kisses. You wouldn't…"

"I was brutalised by this world." I said simply, "You and everyone else laughed at my kindness so the dark twisted it into something else. Something that now drives every move I make. I choose those I care about, and nothing else matters to me. Not rules, not others' morality. I serve only love and the will of the gods, and I believe at the core that they are the same thing. Welcome to the results of your own handiwork Jacob. You are now at the mercy of that same monster your own careless actions helped to create."

I spoke softly to Jacob, my voice suddenly very cold. "Out of pain and divine intervention Jessica was born: as surely as any new child is born from its mother's womb. Born again: by the will of The Allfather of the world and the huntress of the moon. Pray to them if you wish, perhaps they will intercede for you as they did for her. But I doubt it. Though her actions towards me were far darker than yours she was driven by pain and frustration of her own as Jess. But what excuse can be made for you? This world has pretty much bent over backwards to give you everything you want, and yet you have never raised so much as a single finger to help anyone besides yourself. You would help or torture anyone or anything without the slightest hesitation or flicker of doubt, depending entirely upon whichever fitted your own purposes best."

"Edward..." began Jacob, croakingly, but all the colour and sound drained from him beneath my implacable stare.

I walked forward and placed my hands between his legs. Then I grasped his cock. "You've always been so proud of this haven't you?" I said softly. "Both how big you get when you are hard and how many girls you've stuck it into to. Tell me Jacob, have you ever heard of the woman's death?"

Jacob went white but he shook his head mutely. I grinned, bleakly and soullessly. "It's a terrible title. Perhaps you can think of a nice new modern one while I'm inflicting it on you. First it's factually stupid as you can't do it to a woman; and second it's just downright sexist. Castrating a man does not turn him into a woman. But you know? Letting you die from bleeding to death from your castration, well yes that will kill you, so the title does have some redemptive features I guess. Maybe one star out of five?"

I turned to Vicky. "Pass me the knife."

"Don't need knife." said Vicky sweetly. "All have do is swish my hand and cut Jacob's willy off with white magic. Just tell me when ready." I closed my eyes in pain for a moment. How quickly and surely her bloodlust was growing: and all because of her relationship with me.

I turned and looked deep into Jacob's eyes. "What are you?" my older brother whispered. "What have you become?"

I thought for a moment. "A pagan sorcerer? Perhaps I'm even starting to become a dark lord? Now choose brother, talk and live, or stay silent and wish for death long before you have finished bleeding out to die."

He talked of course. What man on earth wouldn't? I thought for a long time afterwards about just killing him. Not out of anger or rage: just out of the very cold and practical calculation that letting him live could prove dangerous to me and my family. Jacob had so little underlying consistency of personality that the idea of breaking my promise not to kill him if he talked bothered me very little. But when I took up the knife to end his life all I could hear was the memory of what The Voice had said to me, that seemed so long ago, but was actually only this morning. When my first real conversation with Jacob for months had just been really getting going, when The Voice had spoken in my ear to compare my starting lot in life to that of my older brother's. "If I could offer you say, the love of Artemis, would you not at least be tempted?" The Voice of The Mountain had whispered in my mind. And the truth was that, whatever I had said at the time, deep down I did not really know. If I had been born in Jacob's position, if I had had everything I wanted handed me on a plate, would I not have become like

273

Jacob myself? If Artemis had been mine easily how much attention or care would I have ever paid to anything going on in the outside world? Or would I have just spent my days designing more and more effective weapons for her to kill with, and my nights working on more and more ways to get inside her pants? If I could be so tempted by that lifestyle, how could I blame Jacob for just accepting his lot when it had given him almost everything he wanted so easily? Why should he even think about helping me to fight my battles? I had never once thought about helping him to fight his. And so whether it was guilt or confusion something stayed my hand, and I did not take Jacob's life.

Instead I cast a great grey magic, and the man who had once been the pride of Oxbridge became, in a few terrible instants, a homeless penniless wretch. I took even his memories of himself so that he remembered nothing, not even his own name. We took him with us back on the train, unconscious; hidden from visibility by the power of my grey magic. Then, when we had travelled far and changed trains a couple of times, my older brother was hurled, naked and with no possessions, into the most remote piece of countryside I could find: a couple of counties and hundreds of miles away from Oxbridge. Grey magic faded the wall of the train in front of us and Vicky used the raw force of white magic to throw aside Jacob's unconscious body. As he was cast into the foulest piece of mud and shit in a farmer's field that I had ever seen I wondered whether he would build a new life after this, or whether he would just crawl through years of ill health and madness.

I couldn't have cared less. There would be no forgiveness for any of those who chose to hurt my family. Something which I now defined by love and not by blood.

But in what was to come I would pay a heavy price indeed for having let my elder brother live. All my life I had thought I was forever beyond The Voice's power. And yet the day when I let Jacob live turned out to be one of the eternal tempter's greatest victories of all.

Chapter 22

The late night train cut through the darkness, speeding me and Vicky north from where we had left the broken man who had once been my brother in some nameless field to the south. My little sister looked at me across the table, chewing on some of her hair absently. Finally she looked at me intently and asked, "Edward what pagan?"

I looked at her surprised. "What, why?"

"When Jacob asked what you were you say pagan sorcerer," said Vicky, "and Danielle say she a pagan and she been showing me little statues of gods. But you worship some different ones and some the same. She doesn't pray to Odin. You don't pray to Try or Hestia. But you both pray to Artemis. I not understand."

"A sorcerer is," I began, and Vicky waved her hand impatiently. "I know what sorcerer is silly. I a child, not a BABY! A sorcerer someone who can cast magic. I want know what pagan is." I paused for a moment, it was a very complex topic to try to explain to a young child.

"It all began a long time ago." I said. "Once upon a time, in this very land we are in now, once all the world was pagan. People believed in whatever gods they wished, gods who visited them in dreams and for whom they built temples, painted pictures and built statues.

Pagans sang songs for the gods and danced in their honour at festivals. They told great stories about them. And all was always in change and flux, all things constantly evolving. New gods arose, new paintings and new versions and interpretations of the old gods. And not only did each person choose their own gods so did each culture. The Romans chose one set of gods, the Vikings another, the Egyptians a different set yet again. But which set you worshipped was all up to you: and even if you wanted to mix it all up by worshipping lots of gods from different pantheons that was good too. It was a time of Faith, when you had to think about what you believed and make important moral decisions for yourself. The higher powers would help but never tell you directly what to do. And when they did communicate with their worshippers it was through dreams and visions, which rarely meant exactly what they seemed. The gods walked among mortals in this world and men and women offered them prayers and sacrifice for their favours. If men grew wicked the gods chose prophets, frequently the wife of a man who would become a hero, to send visions to. The great Gaulish rebellion and the great rebellion of Spartacus against the Roman Empire were examples of the gods at work to right wickedness in the lands of men. It was a golden age."

Vicky licked her lips. "What happen next Edward? What go wrong? Why we not still all pagan now? It sound really nice."

I laughed softly. "In a faraway land on the other side of the world: nothing. In the East the great prophets such as Krishna and the Buddha fused their new divine knowledge with existing teachings: and though their religions became known by other names they still have the truth of paganism at their heart. They still remember and teach that the right way is different for all, and that the right path for each man and woman is for him and her to find and walk alone. There is no one set way to the truth that all must follow. They don't call it paganism anymore. They call it Buddhism, or Hinduism, or one of several other names: but in all essentials their spiritual heritage has evolved unbroken since the dawning of the world. There have been no sharp breaks with the past: no false prophets to lead us all astray. In China the tomb of their first emperor still stands unopened, not because the people there can't open it, but because they still believe in the same gods as all those thousands of years ago: and so they still honour the ancients' sacred places of rest."

"Here?" asked Vicky anxiously, "what happen in West?"

I thought a while before I continued with the story. It started in the light but ended in a very dark place: the exact opposite to the way that the flow of time was supposed to run. "A great pagan empire was built, an empire which kept a balance in the world. The pagan barbarian worshippers of Odin to the north, the pagans of civilisation under Zeus, called by his Latin name of Jupiter, holding up the Roman Empire to the South. Then one man came, one man who said that Faith was wrong, that the old gods were demons. That there was no Faith, only THE FAITH. And that all that was true was forever written in one holy book. And in time, somehow in a way that I don't fully understand, this person who said there was only One God and One Way destroyed the followings of all the other gods, and is the father of our modern world: where we now believe only in one right way and forget the many ways to the truth the true gods taught us ever existed. They call those who follow the greatest of the false prophets Christians. There are two other main false prophets, Moses who founded Judaism and Muhammed who founded Islam. But for the West it

278

is Christianity which is almost exclusively responsible for the destruction of the true pagan religion.

And nowadays even those in the West who don't believe in Christ or the one true god, the secularists, still follow in the fundamentals of Christ's false tradition. In some way the secularists are merely the next evolution in the stage of the Christian heresy. Christianity began with the denial of the vast majority of gods. It is merely the next logical stage in its development for secularism to come in and deny the existence of all gods including the one true god, while simultaneously claiming the one true right way of secularism is the only way that is right and is the way that everyone must follow. Then secularists take philosophies about the world, like right or left wing, and treat them as the only right way, as their God. It gives them a great feeling of certainty and purpose: and means that they never have to actually think about anything or pay any real attention to what's actually going on around them: their one true factual way does all of their thinking for them. In the end without any magic or creativity in their lives secularists are left worshiping a detached intellectual set of theories which bare no relationship to reality at all. And to think they claim that to believe in any gods is silly because it is unrealistic, while even the smallest look in a mirror would show the secularists that they are clinging to ideas that are completely contradictory and any real experience of real life quickly demonstrates are utterly nonsensical."

Vicky thought about it for a moment. Then she said. "I believer in Faith. I pagan. I not bloodhound to be told what to do. I bloodwolf that make own choices. I not scared to think about hard things. I want grow up to be big and tough!"

She turned and rummaged in her backpack and pulled out a colouring book. "Look Edward! Book of all the gods! Danielle give it me. I look and choose own gods!" She started to rummage through it excitedly. Then she stopped and looked at me disgusted. "You and Danielle worship silly little goddess of girls and who like riding cute animals. That is stupid! She look so boring! She very silly little goddess. Not going to worship her." Disappointed, she started flicking through the book again.

"Odin looks good." Vicky smiled at me. "He has dark cloak and big sharp spear and he make me think of you. He look very sensible god." She wrinkled her nose in disgust. "But I bet I find other gods much better than silly Artemis." She flicked through the book hopefully. "Oh look Edward here a very good goddess. She has spear like Odin and flying bird like him. But she also has big suit of armour and really big shield. She must be one of the best gods there is!"

"Athene." I said, "Goddess of war, wisdom and civilisation. Last bit means she doesn't do very much for me but I think you and her will get along nicely." I smiled. "Did you know that she and Artemis are both goddesses of war? In a fight between them though Artemis would win hands down, she's got a bow and Athene only has a spear. Death from a distance."

Vicky looked at me in pure disgust. "No silly. Artemis shoot arrow but Athene stop it with big shield, then stab silly little goddess of silly little girls with big spear. And that THAT. You want to worship her then you and Danielle be silly together. I going to look for some more sensible gods: but I know that Athene is the best goddess ever! She girl god of fighting!" Vicky bent her head as she turned back to the book and started to study it intently, chewing her lip as she examined each illustration carefully and occasionally turned the pages. I had never seen her so intent on anything in all her life.

But I was tired and my attention drifted: and wasn't the whole point of paganism that Vicky would chose her own beliefs and gods without anyone's help? I still wasn't quite sure how I'd ended up having such a close relationship with Artemis. Odin was an obvious choice for me but Artemis? The fact Danielle worshipped her at her age was entirely logical: the fact that I wanted to worship her sometimes felt strange even to me.

I turned to stare out the train window, though the night's darkness meant that I could see nothing of the fields and woods we passed. It was cloudy and overcast, so the cold light of the huntress did not currently watch from the moon out over the world of men. Then the wind blew up, streaking the drops of rainwater against the train window. I frowned, feeling something stirring. Then I started suddenly as I felt the sudden power of the moon's light bathing the cold dark earth: the feeling of power flowing around me was so strong I almost gasped. I saw that the clouds had blown away leaving the full moon shining down from the heavens naked onto the earth. I wondered why I could now feel the presence and power of the moonlight, even before I ever saw it.

A woman's voice murmured in my ear. The voice of someone that I had feelings for that I should not, the voice of a goddess my little sister thought was nothing more than a silly little goddess of girls. "Because the more a god and a worshipper work together the more entwined they become. The more we work together the more our power will become one." And I could almost feel Artemis gathering her power for the vision before she unleashed it. And I could taste that it was a possible future. They tasted sweet, but fragile, their existence fleeting and easily broken. Visions of the fixed past tasted different, dark and rich. Those visions were clear set implacably in stone. But whatever the type of vision, they always burned with all the thousand different colours of the rainbow.

This new vision tasted like a future I had already seen, but now altered already by choices made since my first glimpse of what could be to come. Some streams were now running in very different courses; but others in exactly the same. But, I wondered, did the new future flow ultimately to any better an end?

The sun beat down from the centre of the sky and all around us the land was bathed in a shining heat haze. You could see, here and there if you looked closely, the small areas of dead dirt and dust that were starting to spread even in the heart of this: one of the healthiest wildernesses: spreading as the order of The Mountain spread around the world. There was a time, even a couple of years ago, that we would have rested from the heat. A time that I would have used grey magic to shelter us from the remorseless drain of the implacable sun. The sun which drained my magical strength, even as it boosted the power of our opponents' sorcery. But that time was before the midday sun hung in the centre of the sky for five hours at a time each day: before the days grew ever longer and the nights ever shorter. Before a Christian knight of England drew a sword from a stone, and became King Arthur. Before the new monarch's rule spread over all the British Isles and then Europe. He had established his new regime primarily by military conquest: but almost everywhere he had been heavily supported by the local pre-existing elites.

Order and secularism ruled everywhere now: backed up by the Knights of the Table Round and by other Christian sorcerer fanatics. The wild had fallen, the elves and the free dwarfs were dead or scattered: even creatures of magic had been hunted to extinction or rounded up into zoos. Once beautiful animals of wild power were now nothing more than stuffed exhibits in museums; or forced into zoos to put on tawdry shows for young school children. The Mountain's rule was now everywhere, absolute, unchallenged. Any who dared oppose it found themselves confronted by the might and power of one of the new Knights of the Table Round. Should any enemy of The Mountain somehow manage to overwhelm these champions of white magic and steel then very shortly an army would arrive to ram the message: the message of unending order and the end of change: home in fire and blood.

Vicky and I moved under the tree cover, further up the mountain. Not The Mountain on the other side of the world: just an ordinary everyday peak. Even here the trees were sickening from the constant sun, from the power of order grown too strong. Vicky was twenty now, in the full flush of beauty, with long red hair and curves that drew any man's eye. In a dying world she was a defiant flush of health and life. She enjoyed the attention, but she would never do more than laugh or mildly flirt. She actually recoiled from any attempt to touch. She had given herself to one man, and gave herself to him alone. She wore chainmail armour, even she could not run in plate day after day, and carried two sharp blades across her back, swords that could cut through almost any metal or armour in the world. She alone could easily pierce and cut through even the armour of the Knights of the Table Round: King Arthur's protection alone lying beyond her skill.

Our world has seen breath-taking technological change over the centuries. Computers, banking systems, motorised transport, airplanes; yet since the fifteenth century military technology has remained absolutely fixed, the axe and sword, the pike and crossbow, still the defining weapons of war. Researchers tried unsuccessfully to develop weapons based on gunpowder for a couple of centuries, but magic in this world is too powerful to ever let science and technology become a threat to it. Science fiction novels vividly describe imagined worlds in which gunpowder was made to power devices which fired fast little bits of metal (which they called guns and bullets), airplanes were used to drop things which caused explosions (which they called bombs) and strange armoured cars existed (which they called tanks). All simply speculative escapism, nothing like that could ever exist in this world.

I was thirty. I had a couple of daggers attached to my waist and carried a spear on my back, in honour of my god The Allfather. The huntress Artemis had abandoned me long ago. The absence still felt like a hole in my power: and my heart. Thinking about the divine maiden of the moon turned my thoughts towards despair and I found myself wondering bleakly how many pagans were now left in this world after the mass persecutions that King Arthur had ruthlessly enforced. We had been slaughtered before of course, but under his regime the forced conversion and the slaughter of pagans had run on an industrialised scale: until there hadn't been enough of us left for his regime to keep on killing.

We came through the woods to where the trees overhung a gently ascending path, the main route through the mountains. Then I dropped down to the floor, gasping from the heat. Vicky sat down next to me and passed me the water bottle. I drank deep: water as delicious as sparkling fruit juice in my thirst.

Vicky smiled at me, then laid her head upon my shoulder, and tilted her head up so that her eyes looked up into my face. She was so beautiful. Even after four years together I still found her proximity breath-taking. ''You find the heat so difficult don't you?'' my wife said, as she leaned over and kissed me on the lips, not quickly. I could taste her tongue and our sweat mingling in my mouth. It was sweeter and more addictive than any drug. I kissed her back.

Then I lay back against the rock behind me and Vicky sank into my arms. We lay there for a while, until the sun gradually faded from the sky, and the shadows of dusk started to creep across the sky.

"We're not going to make it are we Edward?" Vicky asked at last. There was no grief in her voice, no bitterness. She was simply stating something as obvious as that the sun would rise tomorrow.

I took her hand in mine and squeezed it tightly. We were together at least: at the end of everything. "No," I said, "we have the chance to do one last good thing before we fall, but no: there is no hope left for us. This is our last day alive."

"Do you think we ever had a chance?" Vicky asked distantly, only half curious, "Do you think it was mistakes that we made that blew it: or were we just fucked from the beginning?" She flicked her red hair from where strands of it had fallen over her eyes. "Did we muck everything up Edward or were we basically just up against Fate itself?" she asked idly.

I stroked her hair and held her close. I wanted to feel her warmth, the shape of her body, one last time. To have the woman I loved in my arms for just a little longer before we both went forever into the dark. It was so hard to believe that tomorrow she would be dead and cold: her features which were now so expressive forever fixed and still. Her bright voice, even in these dark days still mostly so full of hope and fire, finally silenced forever. This time tomorrow we would both be starting to rot. I forced my thoughts back from despair and back to the all too brief present. "I think the main mistake was…" I began.

And this time there was no crackle like there was sudden interference. No two different versions of the future fighting to be the road taken in the end. This time only one bleak route stretched forward.

"… the way we failed to stop Nimue when we still might have had a chance. She rose up like a dark demon out of legend and just devoured all those that we cared about, leaving just a few broken bones which had been cracked open so that she could consume even the marrow." I shrugged, the road that had led the world into this hell was all too painfully clear: unravelling it took no real analysis. "Nimue took Jessica's shape and used that to get close to Merlin, whom she ate alive: piece by slow piece, on his wedding day. His own marriage oaths held him helpless against her as the age old pattern repeated, and she devoured him alive." I stopped, my thoughts bleak. But it wasn't Merlin's broken bones I was thinking about, but Danielle's screams as she fought to avenge her father, and was then devoured alive, eaten from the feet up so she could see and feel herself being consumed alive. Black juices breaking down her body to strip it down into nothing but raw nutrients. The other memory of the beginning of Nimue's rise which still haunted me was that of Jessica's desiccated body. She had been kept alive while Nimue drew power from her to maintain the shape change, but once Merlin was gone that was no longer needed, and my sister had been left as a desiccated corpse with the skin drawn tight over her bones. Nimue hadn't considered her important enough or powerful enough to be worth devouring. My elder sister had been, completely indifferently, just left to die. With the power Nimue gained from Merlin who was there then to stop her from placing her puppet Arthur on the throne, and using him to enact the persecutions to destroy any who she felt might be able to challenge her? Pagans and Christians burned alike in the fires of her wrath, and she built altars to herself on which she consumed men and women alive, seeing herself, a living creature, as a goddess herself. The only concept pagans have of blasphemy. Gods and mortals, however much we may mix, are always separated by an unfathomable and unbreachable divide.

I hesitated. "The only other thing I sometimes wonder is if…" I trailed away awkwardly.

Vicky's voice went very flat. "Edward this had better not be the line of all this bad stuff is happening because you and I are in an incestuous relationship. I hated it the first time you came up with it and the fact that you repeat it every now and then doesn't make it any less rubbish. I have told you, a thousand times, we love each other. There is nothing else to it. As children we loved each other as brother and sister. When we became older that love just evolved into something else. Who cares if everyone else thinks it's abomination? *And you honestly believe that us being together triggered Nimue's rise? For the gods' sake we were children back then Edward, thoughts of sex hadn't even crossed our minds. And you think that bitch would not have inflicted misery on as much of mankind as she could if we weren't together? Get real Edward.* Would you rather that I was with someone else? That I whispered, "I love you." in another man's ear? That I came against a more suitable lover's cock in the middle of the night with that cry of pleasure that only you know?"

I closed my eyes. "It would be less painful to have my heart cut alive from my chest." But: just because the thought of not having Vicky as my lover was agony: that did not mean I was wrong about our incest having played a key role in bringing all this suffering into the world. I wondered quietly almost everyday if all the misery around us was the divine punishment of the gods for the forbidden closeness which we two shared. But at the end of all things it is too late to start reviewing whether the choices we made so long ago were right or wrong. We had sown a whirlwind with our love: we must now ride it until whatever end.

And, while in some deep sense I did believe that my relationship with Vicky was a curse that ate like a cancer into the very substance of our world, I did not believe it had anything to do with Nimue's rise. Her cruelty and her hunger for power did not come from any interaction with us. In every legend I had ever read she always consumed Merlin and took his power. Whatever the general significance of my forbidden relationship with Vicky: it mattered little to the cruelty and ambition of the abomination called Nimue. I wondered if there had ever been a chance to find any kind of power that could have broken the dark story of Merlin and Nimue: and turned the tide of history and myth. In not one of the old legends and stories was there even a hint that Merlin could ever hope to triumph over Nimue: not one flicker or glimmer of hope. Not one ray of bright moonlight to shine out against the onrushing terror of Nimue's bright and terrible new day.

We waited, waited until the sun sank low in the sky, and the shadows crept across the mountains. Then finally we heard the *horse and the rider pull up.*

The rider was all too familiar, even though neither of us had seen her in that exact physical form before. But Nimue has always appeared in the shape of a very attractive woman. She was currently in the form of a beautiful young woman with brown hair in her twenties: and in the full flush of her womanhood. But both my sisterlover and I knew who Nimue really was. The great devourer. A creature of nothing but malice and unending cruelty.

I leapt down from the rock, naked spear in my hand: clad in all the power of the grey. Behind me I heard my sister's shriek as she descended down from the heavens like a lightning bolt, her sword glowing in her hand with light and flame. No enemy had ever stood before her and lived, and she was the reason why nearly half the spaces at the Table Round now sat empty. And I had killed so many now that I had long since lost count of the amount of wizards who had fallen to my power. It would not have surprised me to learn that it was the best part of a thousand.

But Nimue had now devoured so many that her power was beyond all limits. Her magical strength of brown and blue whirled, and suddenly the natural force of my momentum was sped up by the brown even as the blue turned all my vision to illusion. My head hit hard against a rock and I barely even felt the flash of red pain before darkness took me.

I was surprised to open my eyes many hours later: I had not expected to wake. My head hurt and every time I moved my vision was shaky: shapes jagged and unclear. But above me Vicky stood, her red hair flowing in the sun. She held out her hand and helped me up. I went through the motions numbly, not really able to think through my shock. "You… you won?" I managed, in stunned disbelief, hope and something that could have been the beginning of joy starting to blossom in my chest.

Then I felt Vicky's sword cut through my chest, felt the steel rip its way through my flesh to come out the other side. I looked up, feeling myself start to die, into the laughing eyes of the shape changer. "No Edward," said a mocking voice, "your wife didn't. But even in a world that satisfies my every desire and appetite, she was the most delicious of all I have ever tasted, and the most powerful. I will always remember how she tasted even better than she screamed."

I sank down to my knees, death reaching for me, and very close to taking me into its cold and eternal embrace. "You know?" mocked Vicky's voice, filled with a cruel laughter that had never been hers in life, rang in my ears, "I so rarely get to just sit and watch men die. I normally get hungry and can't stop myself from snacking. Did you think all your plotting and scheming would aid you wizard? All your planning to alter the future all those years ago achieved was to make The Voice angry, and make him anoint me as his champion, dooming the world to a far darker fate than if it had just fallen to a mad Merlin and his King Arthur. I owe you so much: without your struggles The Voice would never have given me half so much of his power: and I wouldn't have gotten to eat half so many interesting things. You know watching someone die without trying to consume their power is an odd feeling, but you greys just taste disgusting: and your powers are so difficult to digest. In the end it's just not worth the effort of bothering to eat you. And I have to say watching you die like this, knowing that you've just lost absolutely everything, is just so much more fun. The way I'm getting to enjoy your death is a real novelty for me."

Death and darkness came: almost as a relief.

Interference: extreme crackling. A new and different vision of a new and different possible future.

It was the next day after I had faded out most of Jacob's mind. I was still fourteen, Vicky four. The dagger was in my hand, its blade razor sharp. Just the touch of it was sharp enough to cut your skin and draw blood. Besides what Vicky had in her hand though, it looked as dangerous as a child's plastic toy. Her play sword was now stainless steel, ringed with flame.

"Repeat what I told you." I said to Vicky. Vicky looked at me and took a deep breath. "I have win quickly, before Nimue use blue illusions to confuse me and brown magic to force me use all my energy quickly while I can't even see her to hit her with my white magic. But I more powerful with magic than she is overall. I need to cross the room and cut her head off with one swing before she react and do something to stop me, while you stop Merlin and Danielle from noticing anything with grey fading magic. Then we run and use grey magic to hide from Merlin until we can find where Jessica really is and explain everything that happened."

I ruffled her hair. "I love you sister. Now go and make sure we get this right."

I seized the power of the grey. Vicky took a deep breath, then threw open the unlocked door of Jessica and Merlin's bedroom. I faded Vicky and I from visibility and detection with everything I had. It took more out of me than concealing anything ever had before. Merlin and Danielle were both desperately powerful and anything to do with Jessica mattered to them more than words could ever say. But they were not expecting anything dangerous at all to happen: least of all for their own friends to suddenly attack them out of nowhere. But even with their complete lack of suspicion the effort of maintaining my spell screamed and blood poured from behind my fingernails: but the grey fading magic held. Nimue, wearing Jessica's shape, could call illusions to her in seconds, but she was thrown completely by a sudden blast of light from Vicky. Surprise made Nimue waste precious time she didn't have. And, as The Pool of Fire and Blood had shown, once she was pissed off Vicky didn't waste any time. She crossed the room and struck a truly terrible blow with her magical sword.

The lightning of Zeus in the days of old had not more power than that blade as it fell: burning like the light at the centre of the sun. The desperate defences of blue and brown Nimue gathered as that terrible blow fell could no more have stopped that sword's fall than a piece of grass could have stood tall against a lawnmower. The sword stroke severed Nimue's head from her neck: killing her instantly. And, for all Nimue's power, there was no question of brown regeneration: not from against the power that was behind that stroke.

And then everything went wrong very quickly indeed.

The protection spell on my arm flashed with a sudden, terrible pain: and then fell away into dust. In one instant it went from still active to forever silent: not even leaving behind the slightest trace of the scar that there had once been. And I knew in that moment that Jessica was dead, that Nimue and Jessica must have become linked in some way: and that the bond had meant that Vicky's sword stroke had just unintentionally slain them both. I felt all my motivation fall away in pain and grief, and the grey magic fading what was happening from Merlin and Danielle's sight was, in one instant, simply gone.

Vicky spun in victory with a yell of savage triumph. Then she stopped in sudden terrible shock as she saw both Danielle and Merlin staring in utter disbelief at what they believed to be Jessica's headless corpse. Vicky looked at me in horror and panic, but pain and despair had done what nothing else in this life had ever done: broken my will to fight. I reached for the motivation, for the strength to move and act, and for the first time felt absolutely nothing. A few stunned, silent, horrible seconds passed: during which our last chance to slip away faded and was gone. All I could see was Jessica's dead face, staring up at me. I had been so proud of how clever I was, of how the way I thought and my insights had kept me alive against all the odds. And now my "cleverness" had just killed one of the people that I loved most in all the world.

Then Merlin's attack came: driven by pure fury and rage. He hit Vicky with a surge of brown magic so powerful she would have died as every internal organ in her body ruptured in an unnatural growth spurt. I gathered myself enough to throw the power of the grey against the attack. It was fortunate he had targeted Vicky not me: had he struck at me I think I would probably not have been able to summon up the will to protect myself at all: and would probably have just let myself die. As it was, for a few moments I managed to hold off the power of the brown from affecting Vicky. Then my power, matched in raw strength against Merlin's, failed and my body literally faded itself into death. My heart disappearing as I consumed the last of my resources to fuel my grey magic defences of Vicky: to try and stop Merlin's magic as it sought her life. What little there was left of me to hit the floor was nothing more than a very dead bundle of lifeless blood and flesh. Not that it mattered: by this time Vicky was dead anyway.

She had stood watching me and Merlin, utterly unsure what to do as her friends and family were suddenly fighting each other with the intent to kill. And then she looked down in shock at the dark sword blade suddenly sticking through her chest. Danielle was holding the once play sword that Vicky herself had given Danielle for her birthday. Changed now by Danielle's blue and brown magic into a weapon of sharpened obsidian black stone. Even as Vicky stood staring at her once friend, Danielle calmly drew the blade back and stabbed my little sister in the heart once again, her brown eyes completely cold. There would be no forgiveness ever for anyone who hurt her mummy.

The visions faded and I was back on the train. Across from me Vicky was curled up on her chair in sleep. On the table in front of me sat a very beautiful and increasingly familiar fairy princess.

I hurt and all my senses were numb but my heart still tried to skip a beat when I saw her: but I was luckily in too much pain for that to succeed.

Artemis reached out and touched my cheek. The cold was searing, but I still barely felt it through my pain. "I know those visions must have hurt so much Edward, and I am sorry. Last time I showed you a vision of Danielle, Merlin and Jessica you thought I had done nothing but show you inappropriate personal details: yet it was those that enabled you to detect Nimue as a shape changer when nothing else would have done. The ways of the gods are often shrouded in mystery.

Visions aren't just about giving you dry knowledge Edward. They are about making you feel knowledge. And that is the only true form of learning that there is. Jacob told you Nimue was beyond your power, but that wouldn't have stopped you trying something stupid if things got desperate. What you have just seen: hopefully that will."

I closed my eyes. "From your visions and the interrogation of Jacob I have got a really good idea of everything that's wrong. I know that Nimue wants to devour the magical strength of others and is power crazy.

293

I know that she is linked, in the early stages of having changed shape, to the person whose form she is now wearing, and that to kill Nimue without breaking the link first would also kill my elder sister. I know the illusion on Danielle and Merlin is so strong that they cannot be turned to our side." I opened my eyes and looked at Artemis distantly. "Does my favourite goddess have any good news to add: or is it all just really that grim?"

Artemis smiled for a moment, a fleeting moment that was less than a second in eternity, but it was still there. "Only that I will be at your side supporting you until the end. I can never be your girl but I am your goddess: and I will be with you until all this is done: one way or another. You have three months until the wedding when Nimue will devour Merlin alive and Jessica will die as Nimue abandons that form like a snake shedding a now useless skin."

She took a deep breath. "Oh and Edward? Please remember that being clever is the only advantage you have at the moment. Doing anything that is stupid will be the end of everything for us all."

It took me a moment to realise that Artemis was talking about both my conflict with Nimue and my relationship with a certain female goddess of virginity that I liked in the wrong way far, far too much.

Chapter 23

The library was empty as I walked along through the quiet aisles, past where the silent tidy desks and the packed and creaking bookshelves sat waiting. It was late now, the early hours of the morning. Vicky slept safe and sound in her bed at home. But my work had only just begun. I crossed the floors of the Chester University library and walked towards the dark entrance to the restricted section. My grey power faded out the spells meant to detect unauthorised access, but the effort meant my hands started to shake within just moments of making my presence undetectable. My thoughts started to grow grim. Using grey magic to cover me as I removed the odd tome from here for reading at home, that was one thing. I had done that easily enough plenty of times before. But to resist the detection spells constantly while reading, that would take a lot of power. Enough to slow any progress I might make to a crawl. And that was before you factored in that there was no light to read by, unless I switched on an electric light, clearly displaying my presence to any who cared to look. If I used fire magic to make a light that would be even more suspicious, not to mention the more magic I used in the restricted section out of hours the more grey magic I would need to stop me setting off pretty much every alarm in the entire building.

The clouds shifted above me, and a few moonbeams fell through the window to bathe me in their light. Instantly all the pressure of the detection spells fell away, and I could see as clearly as in the daylight. But it felt so cold. But what did you expect from the embrace of the chaste virgin of the moon?

''Hey!'' said a familiar voice. I looked up to see Artemis sitting on a desk in the restricted area ahead of me. She was so beautiful that my heart leapt. She waved at me smiling. ''The power of my moonlight can weaken magic hostile to me or my purposes, cutting out the protection spells for you. Plus it gives you light to read by without having to switch on the lights, which would be like dead suspicious in the middle of the night wouldn't it? People would work out you were up here reading books you shouldn't be and would come up to stop you!''

I thought about it. ''It works great for the protection spells, yes, and moonlight is not suspicious in the way that electric light is but if someone looks closely enough they're still going to see my shadow: framed against your moonlight. What you've done is a really good start but I'm still going to need to use grey magic to…''

Artemis was smiling, her cheeks flushed red with pleasure. ''What shadow Edward? Have you noticed how little light is currently shining through the windows? There's barely a flicker of moonlight. No one can see anything.''

I started to frown, surely with this much light and illumination the moon must be basically shining full through the window behind me and my shadow must… Then I stopped and stared at Artemis. The moon was dim in the sky and slanted far away, so barely any of its light fell into the library. Artemis was right, I would cast no shadow. But moonlight illuminated the whole room around me in full colour as clearly as if it was the middle of the day. "But that's, that's impossible…" I began, "there shouldn't be enough moonlight falling into this room for me to see anything: and even the brightest moonlight only ever lets you see things in black and white…"

Artemis smiled. "In my friendly divine form my power is of many colours. And the closer we get the more power you will take from the moonlight. The deeper you fall in love with me the more powerful the bond will become." She giggled and her face flushed the brightest shade of scarlet I had ever seen. "If you can really see in full colour then you're further gone than I realised Edward. You must have one hell of a crush."

I took a deep breath. I stared at the beautiful girl of colour and life who was becoming all my dreams made true. Loving, lively, and just fun. And who in the full colour of her moonlight was more eerie than anything I had ever seen, more terrible than all the power of The Voice of The Mountain. This girl was an eternal virgin, a fly trap for men. My love for her could lead only to my death. The friendly flirtiness led only to a darkness deeper than any of The Allfather's riddles. Artemis was nothing like the Holy Virgin of the Christians, The Virgin Mary, simple and sweet. In her own way Artemis was more of a sex goddess than the goddess of love herself: Aphrodite: could ever be.

"Just please don't act on your feelings towards me Edward." said Artemis quietly. "I have the blood of far too many men on my hands already. It would break my heart if I ended up being the death of you: worse still if I ended up killing you myself."

I took a deep breath. "I'm here to try and gain the power and knowledge to be able to challenge Nimue and thus save my elder sister's life. That's more than

297

motivating enough for me not to be thinking about how to get into your pants. Let's just focus on the research and try and forget how we feel about each other.''

I turned my attention back to the restricted section and settled down into reading the books: dark works of forbidden lore: learned tomes on the shadowy and secret aspects of history. I searched the library collection through the search engine first, and created a pile of the books and journal articles that I wanted to read. I started with the ones in modern English. Over the past few months I had been teaching myself Old Norse and Ancient Greek, the language of my gods. But I was still rudimentary. I'd been trying to pick up on Latin too: as so many of the later works on my gods had been written in that language.

A couple of hours later I was interrupted by a hand on my shoulder, a cold that now felt beautiful, which told me that it was the fingers of the girl I loved that were resting on my skin. ''Hey,'' said Artemis looking over my shoulder hopefully, ''how're you doing? You seem to have done almost a hundred pages since you started! That looks a lot but is it? I am the goddess of many things but not of books and studying. I like knowing things but I've always found talking much more interesting than reading!'' She smiled and shrugged: I made myself not think about the way that made her small breasts move. Before I met Artemis I would never have believed that A cups would become my favourite size. Now I thought slim curves were far more beautiful than large.

''It just depends on what I'm reading.'' I said. ''Just judging by page number is false. You can read hundreds of pages quickly because you're not really learning anything, a few pages really slowly but learn loads. But I've made a good enough start I'd say. Nothing groundbreaking yet but I'm starting to get a feel for which areas I should be focusing on!''

Artemis smiled, and held up a dead squirrel on a stick. "Reading's like hunting then. Sometimes you like hunt forever and you still don't get anything to eat. Other times you can't walk two paces without shooting lots of good things that will be really tasty."

I looked at the food and smiled. "χάριν οἶδα σοι" I said.

Artemis looked at me in astonishment as if I had just started speaking, well, Ancient Greek. Which I had, and as it was her first language she should know that.

"Edward what was that?" giggled Artemis.

I shuffled uncertainly. "It was supposed to be thank you in Ancient Greek. Wasn't it?"

Artemis shook her head, struggling to hold in her sweet laughter. "No!" she said "Doesn't sound anything like that at all!" She said what I had tried to say, only properly. It sounded very different.

"See!" she giggled. "That will teach you for showing off to me!"

"I wasn't showing off." I said, "It's just Ancient Greek is your first language and I guessed it would be your favourite, so I thought..."

"Oh," said Artemis softly, and her voice was suddenly quite different. As soft and gentle as the running water of a stream. "That's the first time that a mortal has spoken to me in that language in over a thousand years. That's so sweet. Even if it did sound utterly ridiculous!"

There was a long, silent moment: when I could feel in every fibre of my body just how much I wanted this girl. Through a stillness it felt like my conscious mind had lost all control to my desire as I leaned to her so close that I could feel the soft breath of her mouth, rising so cold over the hairs on my cheeks. Artemis's mouth opened, and I saw the small red tip of her tongue resting on the corner of her lips. She opened her mouth as a girl waiting and wanting to be kissed. An inviting softness ringed in that eerie blue of her lips: an invitation to certain death.

There was a long moment before I made the hardest decision I have ever taken in my life. I reached in and kissed her: on the cheek. The absolute borderline of what a friend might do: but not one step across. Even knowing I might die I couldn't bring myself in that moment not to touch her at all. Artemis made a sort of involuntary cry in the back of her throat, an instinctive call of pain. Because I hadn't kissed her properly or because she didn't now get to kill me I wondered dazedly.

As I pulled away there was a lengthy pause: and then Artemis shook herself like she was coming out of a daze. She looked at me for a while. Then she took a deep breath. "Being the goddess of virginity absolutely sucks when you find a guy you really like. It makes being in love just really horrible!" She sighed, and there were tears in her eyes. Then the emotion passed and the goddess was all business again. She sat down next to me, and we both tried to brush the moment aside, both of us fighting not to take and hold the other's hand.

"You want to share my squirrel?" asked Artemis.

I smiled at her. "You mean like when you ate the serpobat I sacrificed to you?"

Artemis blushed. She was doing a lot of that around me lately I realised. She didn't just blush red either I realised suddenly, now she was so close to me. When she blushed all the colours of the rainbow danced gently in her cheeks. "No Edward not as an act of worship. Just as like... well not as worshipper and god."

"Okay," I said gently. We ate from both ends of the stick, our eyes drinking in each other as the meat melted in our mouths and hot juices bathed our taste buds.

"This is lovely." I said as we finished: talking both about food and just about getting to eat with her: with Artemis. "Who knew squirrels could be so tasty?"

"Not all squirrels are." said Artemis. "But red squirrels are delicious. Problem is I've eaten and hunted so many of them over the centuries that they are now almost an endangered species. People say the reason they are struggling to survive is the grey squirrel but actually it is mostly me: if red squirrels weren't so much more tasty than grey squirrels then they'd still be doing absolutely fine. I got greedy and for centuries didn't keep track of just how many I was eating! So now I ration myself and only eat grey most of the time. So this is a special treat Edward! Don't get used to this!"

I smiled at her. "Doesn't that mean that you're going to end up endangering the grey squirrels too?" I asked. Artemis giggled, and brushed my face with her cold hand. Her nails were as sharply blue as her lips. "No silly! I've learned my lesson: I'm a clever girl." Her face fell. "Just not a clever girl with studying and books and things."

"There are other forms of cleverness you know Artemis." I said lightly. "I doubt I'd be very good with hunting and shooting arrows and stuff. And you're much better at being chatty and talkative than I am." I reached out and squeezed her hand. I said thanks in Ancient Greek again, and almost got it right this time: although the corners of Artemis's mouth still twitched at my pronunciation. And then the dark tomes of the library were calling once more. I turned back to them and was soon once again engrossed in the secrets of magic, in unearthing the hidden shadows of the past.

I had three months before Nimue would consume Merlin on their wedding day: and my elder sister would then die as Nimue carelessly shed her no longer needed form. Day followed day, night followed night. I stumbled through school like a zombie, not that anyone really noticed or cared. In some ways school was actually more pleasant being exhausted. I didn't feel the scorn of the others and the boredom of a curriculum that taught us how good the modern world was and basked in self-congratulation from morning until night. Then I was sharp again for the few hours when Vicky was back from school and was still awake and wanted to play with me. My little sister's laughter and smiles were, along with the time I spent with Artemis, the only relief from the dark timetable my life had become trapped in. After Vicky was worn out and put to bed I seized a few hours' sleep myself, having some time before Chester University library shut to students at midnight: and it became safe for me to enter the restricted section.

It took me a few nights of confused reading and analysis to understand what Artemis had been showing me in the visions. The clues had been hidden carefully and I began to realise that there was no formula or fixed set of rules for interpreting the dreams and visions of the gods, each must be understood and worked on separately. The visions had been showing me how Nimue could be defeated: and that was by the power of grey magic.

In the first vision of the future Nimue had targeted me first, not Vicky: despite Vicky's magical power being so much stronger than mine that it was basically on another level. An even greater clue had been that having mortally wounded me Nimue, the great devourer herself, had made no attempt to consume my power but had just let me die. Her only given reason had been pathetic excuses about difficult digestion. In the second vision my use of grey magic to hide mine and Vicky's presence had prevented two people, Merlin and Danielle, from coming to help Nimue until it was too late and she was already dead. This was despite the fact that both Merlin and Danielle were under the power of the most advanced brown and blue magical illusions that Nimue had.

But while grey magic was theoretically an excellent weapon with which to combat Nimue the visions also gave me no illusions that I was currently in any position to challenge Nimue in a direct contest of magical strength. It had taken all my power to hide mine and Vicky's presence from Danielle and Merlin for just a few moments. I had no chance of permanently destroying the illusions Nimue had placed upon them with my current strength in magic. And if I couldn't break through her illusions then I had no hope of finding where Nimue had hidden Jessica, and to challenge Nimue without knowing that would be death to my elder sister as sure as stabbing her directly in the heart.

But even if killing Nimue wouldn't currently also kill Jessica there was still no way I could face the legendary enchantress at the moment with any real hope of success. Nimue's power, due to a very long lifetime of experience indeed, was naturally far above mine. And that was before The Mountain had chosen her as his champion, investing her with his dark strength. On my side Artemis was excellent at making moon eyes at me: quite literally!: and Odin specialised in setting me challenging dark riddles. But neither was yet prepared to commit a true portion of their divine strength to me. Either I found a way to make them commit, or discovered another source of power altogether, or I was going to die: and Jessica was going to die.

I could still feel my body fading into a lifeless corpse: as I fought and lost against the vast reservoir of Merlin's full unleashed power in the second vision on the train. That defeat and death still haunted my dreams.

The dark clock ticked in my mind and I worked hard at giving myself and my elder sister a fighting chance. I learned many things, and my magical power grew. I learnt of the holy wars of the Viking age when they swept the lands of the Christians in fire and blood for the best

303

part of three centuries, of the fall of the Roman Empire before the flames of Attila the Hun which left half of Europe in ash, of the constitution of the great warrior state of Sparta and its wars against both foreign invaders and other Greek states. I read of more recent events too, the destruction of much of the United States army by the Chinese troops in the North Korean mountains, when one of the least civilised nations of the world routed one of the most advanced with cold steel and the power of magic. And then I read of how a similar pattern repeated itself again in Vietnam barely more than a decade later: the civilised world unable to absorb a fraction of the losses that the Vietnamese took as they fought their way onto victory. I learned of Merlin, who came and went seemingly as he pleased throughout history. Playing the game of gods and kings towards an aim only he could see: the great shaper and weaver of history: until each time Nimue caught him fast and made an end to his story. It wasn't just Arthur he set on the throne either, but also his father Uther Pendragon, and before him Arthur's uncle, who was called Pendragon himself and who gave his name to the whole line that followed. In many ways Merlin was closer to Uther then he ever was to the other two: even Arthur. And I learned the secrets of the gods, Norse and Greek, and even started to be able to more and more confidently read their myths in the original tongues in which they were written. I hoped that my interest in Ancient Greek was not too driven by my desire to be able to converse in her original tongue with the girl that I loved. And all the time I worked Artemis bathed me in the loving light of her cold moon. Her showing up with snacks from what she had been hunting sustained me in a way that nothing else could have done. We always ate together on the opposite sides of the same spit, our eyes feasting on each other as surely as we feasted on the bloody flesh of her kills.

But though I learnt many things and grew greatly in power nowhere could I find what I most needed. Steady consistent progress over the three months: no matter how impressive: would not give me any real chance of defeating Nimue at the end. I needed to find something that would completely change the rules of the game: but here I felt like all my efforts were getting me nowhere. A month of desperate study and hard work trickled like blood through my struggling fingers: while my real objective seemed more out of sight than ever. I pushed myself ever harder, driving myself on with adrenaline and far too much strong coffee, struggling to keep reading even when the texts before my eyes became nothing but a meaningless blur, words and letters losing all meaning and becoming nothing more than black ink printed on a white page.

I didn't even know or feel when I finally pushed myself so hard, with so little left, that I just passed out where I was at work in the library.

I woke up hopelessly disorientated, my head a distant mass of pain. "What happened?" I gasped, my throat parched and desperate for water. "Where am I?"

"Safe." Said a soft voice that I had grown to find so beautiful: like moonlight dancing on a silver spring. "Well as long as you don't make a pass at me and make my grumpy side come out! Then you won't be safe at all!" she giggled. And, although I still felt a mass of pain, all the tension drained out of me at the sound of the girl I loved. I managed to turn my head through my weariness, and saw a bright fire just across from me, smoke rising up into the air before ascending up a nearby chimney.

"I felt you pass out through my moonlight." said Artemis. "You were working yourself so hard that you fell to sleep right where you were sitting!"

I tried to rise, and instantly felt sick. I fell back, the world swaying uncertainly. The price my bleak schedule had demanded was now catching up to me with a vengeance. Artemis flew over and landed next to me. She tucked me firmly back down under what I realised was the cover of a bed. "You are going nowhere until you feel better!" She told me sternly. "I'm cooking us some rabbit I caught and if you're well enough to eat it…"

Even with her next to me the adrenaline surge I felt wasn't enough to stop me passing out again: my exhaustion was total.

The next time I was woken by the warm breath of the sun gently teasing my face. I opened my eyes and realised that I felt much better than I had in days. I wasn't quite back to my usual self, but things felt a thousand times more normal than they had the last time I woke: when just the thought of moving had made me feel sick. I looked around and realised with surprise that I was inside a tree. The entrance and exit was not a door, but through a swelling that might have been a natural opening in the bark. It was covered by a curtain of naturally growing moss and ivy that kept out the wind and rain. Inside the trunk the walls were rich with tree rings on them, showing the tree's age. Each ring standing for a year of living growth.

Inside the dwelling the furnishings were simple. There was a wooden table of living wood grown right out of the floor, half for preparing food and half for eating it. There was a carefully tended fire pit in the centre, for cooking and warmth, and positioned so the smoke would flow directly up out of the naturally formed chimney in the living bark. There were flowers in ceramic jars covered with paintings of the gods, and a bookshelf, lined with books on animals, and soppy romances, and popular history. There were a lot about Ancient Greece of course, where Artemis's worship had been at its height. I smiled, we all like reading and learning about ourselves after all.

There was an arm chair in one corner of the room and another wooden table of living oak next to it, where Artemis read or worked on her laptop. She had also positioned her television and games console so that she could play them from her chair. There was no electricity supply: obviously: through the tree but it would have been simple enough for the goddess to use magic to connect all her relevant appliances to the electricity mains. In one corner of the tree were sets of simple board games, the sort of fun quiz games that you might play at Christmas. They looked like they had almost never been used: some of them were still in their plastic wrapping. I wondered why. Living tendrils of ivy and vine grew from the ceiling. I lay in one corner of the room on a great bed of carven oak covered in fresh sheets and leaves.

I pulled myself up in the bed and noticed that Artemis had made me sandwiches out of the rabbit she had been cooking for us both last night. She had put some kind of ketchup on them. It gave a delicious meat that tasted like chicken a real bite. I ate the sandwiches slowly, and then drank from the bottle of sparkling water she had left besides them. It tasted of lemon and fruit. It sparkled on my tongue. After I had eaten and drunk I felt better than I had in days.

I placed the plate and empty bottle back by the bed and started to...

"Don't you dare get up." said Artemis grimly, her fingers suddenly poking me firmly in the chest. I had no idea where she had suddenly appeared from. "You still look quite poorly, and the moment you are back up you will be running off back to the library to work yourself so hard that you become ill again: silly! So you're staying here until you're totally better, clear!" The look in her blue eyes allowed no argument at all. She was making

307

sure I had some time off: whether I wanted it or not. She looked stunning, clad in bright red garments that offset the soft blue of her eyes and lips.

Artemis saw the look in my eyes and smiled lightly. "You must be feeling better if you are noticing that I am hot again. When I first brought you in I could have been dancing around completely naked and you still would have just passed out."

I lay back, she was right. I still didn't feel like I had any real credits in the bank and the moment I was up I would be back to studying in the library. The way I felt at the moment that would burn me out fast: probably in just a matter of hours.

"Where am I?" I asked quietly. "It looks lovely."

Artemis smiled at that. And squeezed my shoulder. "It's where I live. My home. I try to take good care of it. I'm dead house proud even though hardly anyone ever comes to see it." She looked at me and blushed. "You know you're the first mortal in a thousand years to see it, apart from animals of course." That explained the unopened board games I thought sadly.

She smiled, then pulled herself under the covers too. I could feel her lying almost next to me, feel the way she made the bed sheets twist and move. A sudden surge of desire and alarm ran through me: so strong that I had to catch my breath.

"Artemis," I said warningly, "isn't this dang…"

"Oh please," said Artemis, "Like you're remotely up to doing anything in a bed at the moment besides sleeping and getting better. Even if you rolled right on top of me you wouldn't have the energy to do anything interesting at the moment." That had definitely been true last night, I was far less sure that was true now. "Plus like after all I've done to look after you are you going to kick me out of my own bed?" she asked cheekily, "That would be like well mean! While you're too poorly to be thinking naughty thoughts about me: and so we're quite safe: why don't we just talk and stuff? Be really cool to just have a bit of us time…"

"But I can almost feel the time to save Jessica slipping away like sand through my fingers..." I protested strongly. "I've spent a month researching and so far I've got nothing to show for it at all and…"

Artemis raised an eyebrow. "You've got nothing to show for it Edward? Really? I can feel the power you've gained this last month coming off you in waves. And I bet you've learned all kinds of interesting stuff. Probably even how to say thank you in Ancient Greek properly!

Also when I brought you in you looked like death warmed up. I've seen corpses with more colour in their cheeks! You working yourself into exhaustion isn't going to help anyone Edward, least of all your elder sister. You're taking this weekend off and they'll be no more work till Monday. So unless you don't want to, there's no reason at all not to just chill and hang around with me. Vicky can't expect you to be there for her twenty four hours of every single day: that's not healthy for either of you."

She was right of course. But the problem wasn't that I didn't want to chill and hang around with her: it was that I wanted to chill and hang around with her far too much.

"I'm not getting any better at speaking Ancient Greek," I said, "because you don't need to be able to say it to do research, you just need to be able to read it…"

Artemis raised an eyebrow at that, her face vehement with disagreement. She sang a couple of lines of Ancient Greek. I have always struggled to appreciate music but even I could tell that her singing voice was superb. Not really a surprise I guessed: her twin brother Apollo was the god of music after all. She turned and raised an eyebrow and looked at me sceptically. "That was the first couple of lines of the Odyssey." she said, "One of the five great epic poems written in Ancient Greek. How can you fully understand it if you don't get how it sounds? It would be like reading one of your modern pop songs and not hearing it played. You wouldn't really get the point of it at all!!!"

I didn't really have an answer to that. And I didn't really have time to even learn how to read Ancient Greek at the moment let alone learn how to speak it. "You know," I said, slightly awkwardly, "you don't come across that well in the great epics. Your one reference in either of them consists of you having a stroppy speech, dropping your arrows everywhere and running off to your mum in a teenage style tantrum."

"Well," said Artemis sulkily, "it's not my fault if only two of the five great epics survive is it? I'm not the goddess of libraries and record keeping am I?"

"There wasn't a god or goddess of Ancient Greek library and record keeping was there?" I asked.

"NO!!!" said Artemeis annoyed, "three divinities of war but not one god of books and libraries! No wonder three of the five epics got lost during the course of history. It's all my father Zeus's fault for not delegating properly." She stopped and looked a little guilty. "Well technically my brother Apollo is god of music so he should really have stored the five epic poems somewhere safe. But he's a dead good brother and I don't want to say it is his fault: even though it kind of so totally is! He's far too into singing his music, and sometimes forgets the importance of writing enough of it down to keep it safe for the future! Always thinking about making a good enough impression on those around him and never enough about what's going to happen next. He's dead nice to me though, taught me loads about singing and dancing and even about sport.

I'm still mad he forgot where he put the last copy of the epic of Hercules though. I was like Hercules's best friend and everything. When he became a god it was me he always used to check up on to see if I was killing enough monsters when I went out hunting. If I came back in my silver hunting chariot loaded with just rabbits and dead squirrels he'd say "Now that isn't very good is it Artemis? That's not keeping anyone that safe now is it? Go back out and do your job properly."

"Did you?" I asked cheekily.

Artemis squeezed my cheek. The cold brush of her blue fingers sent lust burning like lightning through my veins.

"Most of the time." She admitted guiltily. "Unless there was dancing and singing on Mount Olympus. Then I would just go partying instead." She shrugged her shoulders, and though we were not touching I could feel how every part of her body moved.

"Were you attracted to Hercules?" I asked, my frustration at not being able to just take Artemis into my arms and start tearing off her clothes turning suddenly into a surge of painful jealously.

Artemis rolled her eyes, but she was smiling. "Hello over possessive much, goddess of virginity here! Plus like he's my half-brother- eugh! And anyway the big muscled action hero guy isn't my type, we'd just end up competing with each other! I want to be with someone who knows lots of interesting things to tell me, because I'm never going to sit down and read big heavy books and find them out for myself: not when I could be hunting, fighting monsters or dancing!"

"It's a shame that so few stories of you survive when you're feeling friendly," I said, feeling almost embarrassed about the relief that had flooded through me when she had told me that she wasn't attracted to Hercules. "Because when you read any book of myths there are no shortage of stories of you…"

"Slaughtering the innocent?" said Artemis flatly, her voice suddenly cold. "Killing women who call out to me in the pains of childbirth, slaughtering kings of men who I almost randomly decide haven't offered me appropriate sacrifices, murdering the children of those who compare their fertility with my lack of children? Having an image at an altar in Sparta that demands more and more male blood if it isn't fed every year; with brutal flogging of young boys: sometimes to the death? Yes my terrible side does get more of the publicity. I focus on helping people and killing monsters. I don't really mind that much of what I do gets forgotten so long as I know I've helped people- although I'm still well pissed that my only surviving direct appearance in epic Greek poetry depicts me only as a stroppy ineffective teenager arrg!- but Artemis the Terrible? She wants people to feel it as she lays each cold corpse on the ground. She wants everyone to know just how much of a bitch she is."

Artemis took a deep breath. "I'm not being fair to you Edward. I'm fighting with all I have to show you only the best version of myself. And one day that's going to lead to one us making a move on the other: and getting you killed. I don't want to show you Artemis the Terrible: because I am so happy that you are in love with me. I am so scared that when you see her that will change. But I need to be fair to you. You need to know what you've got yourself into by becoming involved with me. You need to know what any man risks by becoming involved with Artemis in any real way. You need to know who I really am: my terrible side is as much a part of me as my friendly. Perhaps more so in some ways because…" she cut off sharply, not letting herself finish. For a moment she looked scared that she had said too much.

"Anyway," she continued after an awkward pause. "I'm going to show you what happened to the last man I dared to let myself feel anything for. I'm going to take you back about two and a half thousand years into the heart of Ancient Greece. And Edward, this isn't a nice story. It is nothing but darkness with an end that is unbearably bleak.

Just please," Artemis held out one cold hand to clasp my shoulder, her voice trembling, "please even if you can't love me as you do now after this: please don't start hating me when you see what my other side is really like. And please remember that my love for you is as real as HER hatred for all men."

There was a short, tense silence: in which neither of us had anything to say. Then Artemis gathered herself, drawing deep on her divine power. She called out in a great voice: one which rang with all the power and magic of the divine. She was speaking as the goddess once more: not as the sweet girl that loved me.

"Now behold Edward. Behold the truth of Artemis the Terrible! Behold the truth of…HER."

Chapter 24

The music of the lyre sang from the temple grove, and among the empty boughs and dead leaves of the trees the girl was dancing. It was a beautiful formal and decorous dance: matched exactly to the carefully planned form and structured rhythm of the elaborate music. She danced slowly: peacefully: the troubles normally on her mind for a moment forgotten and put aside. Lost in the music, in these precious moments of escapism, her thoughts no more or less than keeping step to the complex beat. The music crescendoed, and she whirled in the harsh light of the winter's sun, blue eyes shining and brown hair swinging in the wind, and landed deftly on her feet: her grace and sense of rhythm almost perfect.

''Well done Artemis!'' said her brother Apollo proudly. ''As always you surpass all the other goddesses in skill and beauty. Even the goddess of love herself would struggle to compete with you!''

''Careful Apollo!'' teased Artemis the Friendly gently, ''You don't want Aphrodite to hear you! You know the only reason she won't have an affair with you, like she has had with pretty much all the other male Greek Gods, is that you're close to me: and as goddess of sex and love personified she thinks having a goddess of female virginity is just dead weird. She hates me: and on the odd occasion that a man starts worshipping me very seriously she just can't stand it!''

Apollo shrugged his shoulders, and did a very bad impression of nonchalance. "Who wants a girl whose been with everyone? I feel myself lucky to be above her sawdry attentions. I wouldn't want her if she offered herself to me on a plate!''

Artemis giggled, and gave her brother a hug. "I don't have to be your twin sister to know that's a lie! Aphrodite becomes whatever the man she's after most wants. What guy would ever say no to that?'' She sat down next to Apollo and leaned her head on his shoulder. "And, while you're a great brother, if I wasn't your sister I really don't think we'd get on. I don't think you've met a pretty girl who you've either not been interested in or who you've not lost interest in after a passionate love affair where you've babsed them up!'' She laughed softly. "As your sister I'm about the only girl you have, apart from our mother of course, ever treated well.''

Apollo's form was that of a young man, devastatingly handsome. His form rippled with muscle and his long hair hung down below his shoulders: uncut as he had never married. Like his elder twin sister he was the divine representative of unmarried members of his sex. But unlike his unhappily virginal sister he had had more than his fair share of action between the sheets. And as the bed of the divine is always fruitful his seed had flowered in many places: many both immortal nymphs and human women had found themselves carrying his children. He had even sired one of the great gods, the healer Asclepius, out of wedlock. Such was the difference in the moral code for properly behaved young men and young women: the one supposed to have as much fun as humanly possible before settling down, the other supposed to keep a firm "Keep Out" sign between their legs until marriage. Not that Apollo restricted his sexual desire to women. He had penetrated many young men who took his fancy too: restraint of any kind was almost unknown to any of the gods of Ancient Greece. But not Artemis: who knew pretty much nothing else but.

Apollo looked at her carefully, concern in his eyes. ''I'm not here today to talk about my love life Artemis. I'm quite happy with all the action I'm getting thanks very much. I'm here to talk about developments in your love life: that aspect of your life which is so complicated and tragic.''

Artemis's friendly embrace suddenly went taut and cold: she turned away moodily from her brother. ''I haven't got a love life remember? The closest I ever get to any action is a chaste kiss on the cheek, no more intimate or sexy than the ones I give my mother. As far as any romantic relationships and me are concerned it's just the same old, same old single Artemis. Back when I was just three I asked my dad Zeus for eternal virginity didn't I? Seemed like a good idea at the time but now, as pretty much the only god or goddess who can't ever have a family of her own, it pretty much sucks. And not only am I stuck with it but I've got a younger twin brother who takes the vow far more seriously than I do.''

Artemis threw up her arms in sudden exasperation. ''How can you be so bloody protective of me losing my maidenhood when you have slept with so many girls yourself: many of them virgins beforehand! I mean, by all the gods, you've slept with more men than I have. The way you are about me getting with a guy: any guy: it's like the definition of hypocrisy! Name me one other person whose life is restricted just by the fact she said something completely stupid when she was just three!''

A shadow passed over Apollo's face. And for a long moment the god of sun and prophecy, who in his own love life sowed his seed freely without doubt or fear of consequence, looked very bleak: as though a sudden darkness had arisen to eclipse all his light. When he spoke next it was almost in a whisper.

"Sometimes I feel it is almost like the cover story we invented to protect your reputation has twisted in your mind into becoming the actual truth. You did ask for eternal virginity when you were three but no one ever really took that seriously: it was just an unusual remark by a friendly and fun child. And while no brother ever feels completely relaxed about his sister dating, gods look at the way I treat other women just to see why! I really wish you could find a proper young Greek god to marry and make you happy. But I'd take even one of those grey wizards, even though they are so far below your station and class that they should think themselves lucky just to look at you let alone date you, over what has come to happen to you. It's not your bloody maidenhood I care about Artemis it's you! And we both know that what…" Apollo stopped, and swallowed drily, almost gagging on his words as he choked on a memory almost unbelievably vile and foul. "We both know what happened to you…" he finally managed with great difficultly, "left you too broken to ever love a man or woman as anything more than a friend. We both know what… what gave birth to HER."

Artemis drew into herself, her body smaller than ever in the shadows of the setting winter sun. The heat was bleeding out of the air, the wind was rising: and she suddenly felt very cold. "Why what happened to me? I know that SHE wasn't always with me but I don't know why she… If something dreadful was done to me then surely I would remember? Why would I forget?"

Apollo looked at her. Then he reached out and squeezed her hand: his affection for his sister clear in how tight he clasped her. "If you have truly forgotten what happened: what was done to you," he whispered, "then we are truly blessed. That would be a joy beyond any I have ever dared to hope for."

Artemis looked at Apollo, her blue eyes pleading. "Can we talk about something else brother? Please? I can feel...HER... stirring as we talk. And I hate HER so much. And now I think about it I can feel that I am missing something: something very important. It's like a black hole burning right inside my memory. And just touching its outskirts, I can feel HER growing angry: feel HER awakening. And I don't want to change. I never want to change: but I really don't want to change when you're here to see me. I hate it when people I care about have to mix with...HER."

She glanced around desperately, trying to think of something, anything, to take her mind far away. "I know! Let's talk about that song I just danced too. It was dead complicated and sophisticated! It must have taken you absolutely ages to write!"

"Nearly a year and a half." said Apollo proudly. "Like any true artist I would never dream of putting less than my full care and craft into each and every one of my compositions. Proper music has form and structure. It is practiced and performed at ceremonies. It builds on itself, always looking at all the good practice which went before. Like proper dancing, evolving within the traditional structured and regimented forms. Anything that is not composed with such due diligence, care and attention is nothing more than the music of savages smashing sticks together and goggling in astonishment at the loud noise they are making. Truly primitive."

"That is cool." said Artemis. "Formal dancing makes me feel really sophisticated." She stopped and looked at Apollo guiltily. "But sometimes it would be nice to just dance free flow. You know, just to go with the moment and get lost in what's happening. Sometimes part of the fun can be that you have no idea what will happen next!"

Apollo scowled. "You know for such a sophisticated and proper girl Artemis you do have a few areas where you act practically common. Goodness knows where you get it from. Sometimes your taste is so terrible I'm relieved that I don't have to sit and watch the type of men you might bring home if you could. I'd set you up with the richest white wizards in the country, with the best manners and the smartest clothes and shoes, and I bet you'd still go flying after some grey wizard with blood on his dagger and his head stuck in a book. For a princess of the gods you don't half have some funny ideas about what you want in life.

"*Just to go with the moment and get lost in what's happening. Sometimes part of the fun can be that you have no idea what will happen next!*" You sounded less like a properly brought up young lady and more like one of Dionysus's loose girls. And you're a different class to them Artemis: a totally different league."

"I think Dionysus is dead interesting," said Artemis. "He has the most exciting sounding parties and raves right into the early hours of the morning. I love the formal and structured stuff Apollo, but nowadays that's all I ever kind of get to do. What's wrong with wanting to meet some new people and just chat now and then? Even a princess can get lonely you know? Plus like I don't know what you've got against grey wizards. Every time I chat with a white wizard the whole conversation is them talking at me until I'm convinced that they're really clever and I'm just dead stupid, and they spend an awful lot of time trying to look down my bra. I talk to a grey wizard and I get to learn loads of interesting stuff and I feel like the cleverest girl in the world. Plus I have to flirt dead hard to get them to even notice that I'm a girl: it's like a well good challenge!" Artemis paused for a moment, looking a bit shamefaced. "Not that I would ever flirt with anyone that I didn't fancy myself!'' she added quickly, ''That would be like well mean!''

Apollo sighed, there was a time that they would have been arguing passionately about this: to the extent that it would put a strain on their relationship. Nowadays: as long as SHE existed: the argument was almost comforting, an attempt by both of them to fool themselves that one day there would only be Artemis the Friendly again. ''Sister there is no way I'd let you near Dionysus. First he's a disgusting old man in a cloak who's way too old for you. Second he's a drunken alcoholic who staggers around from one place to another. The only things he does is start very bloody wars and get extremely pissed, usually at exactly the same time. The man may be a god but he barely belongs in our pantheon at all. The lout can scarcely be considered at all civilised.''

''Wins wars,'' muttered Artemis under her breath, ''except occasionally when he really has had a silly amount to drink even for him. But I'm sure someone sensible like me could help him with that.'' But she deliberately spoke too quietly for her brother to really hear.

''Of course he'd love to have the pretty virgin princess of the gods at one of his parties: not that you'd stay that way there for long.'' muttered Apollo darkly. ''Oh I'm sure he'd love to have you as one of his maenads: one of his raving women that dance in orgiastic dances, and who then tear innocent victims to pieces with their hands. Then to finish off they have casual sex with anyone around them, even as they're too intoxicated and drunk to even stand up straight. It's like a mockery of the civilisation of the rest of the gods.''

''I would not get drunk and end up sleeping with just anyone just because I was allowed to go to a naughty party.'' Said Artemis, stung and quite hurt. ''I am a nice girl. I know when and where I shouldn't put out.'' She sighed sadly. "Even in my case when that answer seems to be like: never. But even if it wasn't I'd only ever sleep with a man who I was dating and who loved me very much. Just because I'm curious about what goes on in life outside my tree doesn't make me a whore! I can look after myself you know!"

"Yeah that's what Aphrodite said." muttered Apollo sharply, "And as goddess of love and sex I think she had just a little bit more idea what she was getting herself into with Dionysus than you do. *"Oh don't complain so much Apollo! I'm not going to fall for any of that dirty old man's tricks. Oh stop being so silly! I am the goddess of love and sex itself: you think he can pull any trick to get into my pants that I haven't seen a thousand times before? I'm just going to go and have a couple of drinks and a good time. Let's face it how many of your parties have I been to, and all your music and dancing and wine hasn't helped you get into my pants has it? Not even once. I've heard you've even spent years writing sad songs about a beautiful girl who doesn't love you back. They're beautiful but they're still not going to get you any action with me. Don't get me wrong I don't dislike you, but I'm not going to end up having a kid that's anything like that weird virginal twin sister of yours."* And then what happens?

She goes to one of Dionysus's raves, has a few tastes of his "special brew" and the next thing you know she's intoxicated and he's on top of her. Few months time she's walking round with a bulging baby belly. Then she gives birth to the ugliest child with the most enormous genitals, the most disgusting child she's ever borne. How can you want to risk going to a party like that Artemis? Can you imagine what it would be like having to nurse and mother an ugly child!" Apollo gave a visible shudder at the very thought.

Artemis put her hands on her hips indignantly. "First of all you must think I am like well shallow! I would be a dead good mother. Even if my child was as ugly as sin I would defiantly love him-or her!- anyway. Second I am not Aphrodite! She is a total slut: give me a time when she hasn't come back from a party with a pregnant belly. If I wasn't your sister, and she didn't hate me so much, you two would have had like a dozen kids by now. But I'm a good girl! I would not get laid just because I was allowed to go singing and dancing! I would never have kids with a man I did not love with all my heart and soul! It's not like I think it's impressive Dionysus can't handle his drink! He'd be a much more impressive god if he could. Might not lose any battles at all then!"

Apollo sighed. "Yes I forgot the god you really want to meet is Odin. Of course, why go for an alcoholic god of war who can't handle his drink and stand up straight when you can have an alcoholic god of war who can handle his drink and stand up straight: so that there's nothing to stop him from spreading war freely across the continent. Nothing to stop his power casting down any who dare stand in his way. And anyone who fights him or his people dies. You do know Odin isn't available don't you Artemis? He's married to Freya. A party girl whose love life is so extreme it makes Aphrodite's sex life look as interesting as yours. Aphrodite hasn't worked her way around absolutely every male god in the Greek pantheon after all: just you know, most of them. But there's not a Viking god, male or female, who doesn't know Freya's loving embrace."

Artemis looked very indignant. "I just think that Odin's dead interesting! I would never have an affair with a married man! And I'd love to meet a grey wizard who was single. Doesn't mean I fancy Odin!" she paused, then blushed a little. "Well maybe a bit?" she ventured nervously, "but isn't knowing new stuff like really interesting? Why can't I get to know a grey wizard who will tell me loads of stuff and make me feel dead clever?

And I'm sure they'd like me because I'm so good at hunting and fighting. We'd be like a perfect team!"

"It isn't actually one of your worst ideas." Admitted Apollo reluctantly. "Although I would be a bit more interested if you had ever actually managed to work up the courage to speak to a grey wizard: instead of turning a bright shade of beetroot and flying for cover in the nearest grove of trees almost every time one actually appears."

Artemis looked awkward. "I want to go up and speak to them, but I get so nervous. I just know I'll say something stupid and they'll think I'm just a silly little girl. I can't offer them sex and love: and I can't understand the big books they read so I don't know what they'll get from talking to me. Just some huntress chatting about how much she likes eating squirrel: I bet grey wizards would find me really boring."

Apollo reached out and ruffled her hair. "You're not silly Artemis. A little naive sometimes, but you're a clever, brave and very determined girl. Sometimes you're actually too stubborn for your own good! Anyone who thought you were dull would merely be showing their own lack of sophistication and understanding." He scowled suddenly. "And if I found out about it, well then they would have to worry about a lot more than just bad sunburn."

Then he sighed, and for a moment looked just very tired. "But it's not your relationship with a grey wizard that's currently causing me concern." He looked up to where the winter sun was starting to set in the sky. "Come," he said gently, "let's go inside. There is much of importance about what is now happening in your love life that we urgently need to discuss."

Chapter 25

The sun was setting and the air was growing cold with the winter night as the divine twins approached the blessed grove where Artemis lived. The last light of the setting sun bathed her home in rugged beauty. She lived in a wild grove of trees high up on a grassy mountainside: and at the centre of the copse a bright spring ran out into a stream giving life and water. The grove teemed with animal life but Artemis rarely hunted there: it would be too easy and no real challenge. Unless it was the weekend and she was feeling lazy. Then as mistress of the animals and divine huntress all she had to do was pretty much fall out of bed to find her food. There was a stone altar next to the spring, where people came from far and wide to make their offerings in fire to the goddess. Artemis, even though she was always slim and muscular, was especially fond of being offered food: the first fruits of the harvest especially: and she also had a very soft spot for small stone or clay statues of herself. Artemis would never admit it but she liked small painted idols of herself even more than her mirror. Although the sun still shone in the sky the moon could already be seen clearly, the celestial twins of the heavens as unified in the vast reaches of space and sky as the divine twins were down on the everyday earth.

A couple of grey shapes raced across the darkening ground towards them: in every movement the sleek action of the predator. Their howling would have frozen the blood in most mortals' veins. Apollo was largely indifferent, as a cultured and civilised god animals were of little interest to him at all: but he smiled to see the joy on Artemis's face. One of the strongest emotions in his life was that he loved his twin sister very much.

Artemis picked up her pace and ran to meet them, laughing as the first great grey shape bounded into her arms, while the second yelped excitedly, running round and round her heels. In that moment the lonely girl who wanted to go dancing at naughty parties was gone as though she had never been; and there was simply the divine huntress in her element: as much a part of nature as any other wild beast. For in the heart of Artemis there is a savagery that can never be truly tamed: nor should it be. She is a goddess of civilisation, yet her true love is the wild. It was the most natural of all things that she should show so little interest in white wizards, who would want to keep her indoors, and should want to be instead with the grey wizards of barbarian kind, who would lead her deeper into the wilderness. And yet for all her love of nature she was not a goddess of the barbarians: at her core she was a civilised goddess of the hunt. She was fascinated by and sexually attracted to barbarians; but she was not one of them, nor did she have any wish to be so: she was well proud of being a fully civilised and properly educated princess. She wanted a barbarian in her arms and in her bed not because she wanted to be a barbarian herself: but because she wanted all her civilised friends to whisper to themselves about what a brave and daring little fairy princess Artemis was: taking such risks in going for dangerous and unpredictable men like that. She was the heart and cunt that would bind the fire of the wild to civilisation, for through her love barbarian vitality would all be channelled into the future growth of the civilisation Artemis loved. For what barbarian would try and take the beauty or wealth of the civilised world by force so long as Artemis was there to offer him her bed and love freely? Even the most brutal of all extremism would be tamed by the warmth of her heart and the tight embrace of her womb and cunt.

Artemis held the wolf up in her arms so close that he could lick her face. She was so small that you would expect her to struggle to hold up a fully grown grey wolf, but she could do it very easily. It was dangerous to be fooled too much by Artemis's sexual femininity. Her slimness was steel, her muscles had the strength of stars, her gaze was sharp enough to see the wind whisper though the grass many miles away. Her slim appearance was deceptive. Hundreds of years of living in the wilderness had given her sinews of muscle and the flexibility of the leaping mountain goat, or the striking viper. She laughed as the first wolf licked her face, and the second nipped at her heels anxiously, whining desperately for the goddess to pay her some attention.

"Hey Grey Death," she smiled at the wolf in her arms, "nice to see you too!" She shifted, and was suddenly effortlessly holding the wolf one armed, stroking the head of the wolf running round her heels with her now free hand. The she-wolf calmed at the goddess's touch, almost purring in happiness. "Hey you too Swift Wind!" she said "I haven't forgotten you just because Grey Death wants to be so cuddly!". Swift Wind had previously ripped the hands from men to devour them raw, but she whined and knelt at the goddess's embrace, as docile and happy as a new born kitten. Grey Death rested his head against Artemis's cheek and his yellow eyes stared into his goddess's adoringly. Artemis ran her hands across the wolf's teeth, then sighed in intense frustration. "We've been eating rabbits again haven't we Grey

Death?'' she said sternly, though any human voice would have heard nothing but a strange series of howls as she spoke in wolf tongue: haunting and eerie on the wind. For Artemis knows the spoken tongues of all beasts and birds as surely as she knows how to speak Ancient Greek or, nowadays, modern English. She may only have been moderately fond of reading and writing but as a natural chatterbox speaking and listening to new languages had always come naturally to her.

''I know rabbits are both tasty and delicious but you must eat red meat too: hunt stag and deer and fill your mouths with rich blood and red flesh. You need to be strong to hunt and look after your young.'' The goddess said very firmly. The wolves' heads dropped as their goddess gave them a right telling off. Grey Death howled mournfully and Swift Wind whimpered in shame. Artemis looked very sternly at them for a moment then, convinced that they had indeed learned their lesson, laughed gently. Her voice the sound of moonlight on stream water. Her face relaxed. ''Go hunt now you two, and the light of my moon will guide you through the night. I know how tasty treats can be but I couldn't just spend all my time eating red squirrels now could I? I'd end up in a right funny place. Now go, eat well: and no more rabbits for a week or there'll be trouble! As new parents you need to eat properly to keep your strength up!'' She gave one last great howl, which rose up wild and terrible against the moon, and the next moment the two wolves were running into the forest, their grey cloaks sleek in the shining white light. They ran to fulfil their goddess's command.

Apollo laughed, and ruffled his sister's hair. ''Nice pets, but I've never got you and animals. I've never met a wild animal that doesn't love you with all their heart, gentle mistress of the animals. But you are also the maiden of the hunt, who brings death with spear and arrow. Who sheds their lifeblood with a triumphant scream while bathing in the cold baleful light of your own moon."

Artemis turned to her brother, and her eyes shone with a strange joyful light: she looked eerie, strange, far more goddess now than girl. "They are not my pets brother: I have no pets. To me all animals are wild and free. And though I am a civilised princess and am not in any way a creature of nature myself: the wild means more to me than all the gold on Mount Olympus. You see a child watching animals and they always cheer if the hunted escapes death, but that shows how so many cultured people quickly understand so little. For if the hunter always failed would not then my beloved wolves and bears all starve to death? One of the most horrible ways to die that I can think of! Far more cruel then simply dying in a brief flash of blood and fur!

I hunt often for my own food, though I will not deny the thrill of the chase is more sweet to me than the sound of any pleasure ever brought to Aphrodite by man, but I shed the blood of predators freely as well. And when my animals struggle in the cold winter often they do not weaken through hunger, but fall instead upon fresh red meat in the most unlikely places: with merely the trace marks of a silver arrow wound to mark my gift to them.

Othertimes I protect the squirrels and rabbits, and deal death to the creatures that hunt them. Then I attach the heads and skins of their predators to my wall as trophies of my victory. But though I love the hunt with all my soul I never hunt just for fun and sport. I hunt as the demands of my creatures dictate. I follow the needs of the wild itself and bring death merely to service the great cycle of life, that nature may thrive and life spring. For is not the blood of fresh meat the true heart and soul of nature: its true essence seen best in the redness of tooth and claw: or well shot silver arrow?"

328

Artemis took Apollo's hand. ''Come brother. You wish to talk but I can feel the moon rise. I will not say you no but I would not be without the thrill of the chase this night, not when the full moon rules in the heavens and my heart sings for lifeblood. And unless you have somehow learned to shoot that decorative set of arrows you carry everywhere, or throw that ornamental spear you are so proud of, you are not hunting with me. You are very good at singing songs: not so good in the thrill of action when blood is flowing!''

They came to the entrance of the place Artemis called home. No house for her, no hut or cottage: nor any dwelling ever built by the hand of man. She lived inside a great oak tree, many fathoms of living wood high. Its branches full of life and vitality as they grew up into the sky. Artemis looked up into the canopy of her tree, and squeezed her brother's hand with excitement and pride. ''You know Apollo how many birds of the forest have come to live in the branches of my tree? They see it as a great honour to live so close by me, and no animal will harm or prey upon another beneath its sacred boughs. I've got ravens and owls and even a pair of great golden eagles!!'' She spoke with the same excitement that a proud home owner has when showing off a newly built patio or extension, but with a fierce joy in her voice which comes from the love of living things and has no equal in any of the works of men or elves: or even the unsurpassed craftsmanship of the dwarves in forging treasures far beneath the earth from gold and priceless jewels.

She whispered in her brother's ear gleefully. ''The animals cheat though. They think I don't see but I do Apollo, I do! The owls drag mice out of the shadows and kill them just the other side of the shade. The eagles are even more discrete about it. They pick up hares and rabbits and then they carry them to the other side of the forest and eat them there."

Apollo frowned, his eyes suddenly hard. "Isn't that blasphemy against your worship? You are my sister and no one should show you disrespect and live. You should strike them with the cutting edge of your star metal spear, or cut them down with cruel arrow shafts. Or I could send a plague to remind them that they need to show you…"

"Oh come on brother," said Artemis her eyes shining. "They are not doing anything wrong! They are not breaking any of the rules. They are just being themselves: they are creatures of the wild: never meant to be tame! Let them be."

She turned and led him into her house. Even Apollo, who was in love with all things of civilisation and that are manmade, smiled as he entered where Artemis lived. It looked pretty much the same as it did three thousand years later, only the tree was younger and its rings not so pronounced: and obviously the television, games station and magazines weren't there. The books, while similar, were different too. They weren't for show, Artemis did read in her leisure time, so she needed to keep updating her collection.

Apollo's eyes took in everything he saw in the room, and then narrowed tightly. "Why is there only one bed huntress?" he asked sharply. "Where does the hunter sleep? It had better be far from anywhere that might entice him towards your bed."

"In a tent out the back." said Artemis lightly. "He comes in to eat with me sometimes and share my fire but he won't ever stay the night. I offered to grow him a nice room in the wall for privacy but he declined, even when I said I would cover it with flowers and rich tendrils of flowing ivy. He said it would be blasphemous to get too close to his goddess: that he respected the eternal boundary between the gods and men."

"Sounds like he's being far more sensible about all this than you." said Apollo coolly. He was still looking at her closely. "And why exactly does the goddess of virginity need a bed big enough for a Dionysian orgy? You always sleep alone. You don't need enough space for four or five of you."

Artemis folded her arms and suddenly looked very grumpy. "Oh give it a rest brother. Orion isn't interested in me in that way. He swore himself to death twelve months ago. His heart is with his dead wife, and in slaying as many dark monsters as he can in her honour before he falls."

Apollo's eyes were still determined. "Why the big bed if everything is so innocent?"

Artemis blushed and looked embarrassed. "You know how I have always liked having teddy bears? Even though everyone kind of thought I would grow out of it when I stopped being a little girl."

"Yes." said Apollo, confused by the unexpected turn the conversation had taken. "You've got hundreds of the things back on Mount Olympus. When a young girl reaches adulthood and marriage they usually turn from your worship to that of Aphrodite as they pass into a new stage of their lives. They sacrifice many of the most precious things of their childhood to you at that point, hoping for your blessing as they leave your service. You already had far too many teddy bears cluttering up the place: even before you went on a century and a half of requesting your priests to ask your worshippers for "MORE TEDDY BEARS!!!". For that entire period every time anyone wanted to know what to sacrifice to you when they left childhood you ended up getting another stuffed bear. You know mentally there are parts of you that I think have never really grown out of being the thought processes of a very little girl."

Artemis blushed. Her cheeks shone for a moment with all the colours of the rainbow. "Yes, well, it turns out the only thing better thing than sleeping with a teddy bear is sleeping with a real life bear! Particularly a big brown grizzly one. It's just like having a cosy teddy bear, except they growl and snarl and have big sharp claws and everything, its's ace! Polar bears are awesome too, but you don't get them in this part of the world. Too hot for them: they get ill." She concluded sadly.

Artemis stopped for a moment, frowning in thought. "Of course it does mean you need a large enough bed for the bear to sleep comfortably. On my birthday I sometimes dress them up and put ribbons in their hair, and give them little bells that tinkle everywhere they walk... Of course I take it all off afterwards, I wouldn't leave them like that, that would be cruel!!! They wouldn't be able to hunt anything like that, their bells would jingle all the time and all the other animals would know that they were coming!"

"Artemis" said Apollo, feeling suddenly quite queasy. "You do know that bears are carnivorous don't you? That one day your real life teddy bear is going to wake up and decide to have the little fairy asleep next to it for breakfast?"

"That has happened." admitted Artemis thoughtfully, "but only twice. I'm immortal though, so while it hurt I did get over it. In fact I think the bear was more upset about eating the goddess he worshipped than..."

She stopped, suddenly indignantly putting her hands on her hips, because Apollo was creased up where he sat, every muscle in his body hurting as he desperately tried to stop himself from laughing. Who knows where the conversation would have headed next, from the sudden dangerous glint in Artemis's eyes probably to quite a tricky place for Apollo, when at that moment Orion, the greatest hunter this world has ever seen, came quietly into the house inside the living tree. He barely made a sound as he slipped through the living tendrils of ivy and moss that covered the entrance.

In an instant Apollo was gone, so fast that a hunter with senses less sharp than Orion would probably have never even known that he was ever there. But while the god of sun and prophecy was no longer there in a physical sense he was still watching his sister, and now the hunter; watching very intently indeed.

Orion walked across to Artemis carefully, his face impassive, and knelt at her feet: but then raised his head to meet her eyes. It was the compromise that they had agreed on. Orion refused flatly to talk to Artemis directly at eye level: which he said would be disrespectful to her divinity: but she insisted that he talk to her properly like a friend: not just keep praying to her like a goddess all the time.

Apollo's first impressions of what he saw were indeterminate, he didn't know whether to be pleased or worried about the interactions between the two people that he watched. Orion's face was drawn, haggard, lined with grief. His head and arms were crossed with so many scars that, particularly with the one that ran across his whole face and brutally disfigured his left cheek and jaw, he could no longer be considered even remotely handsome. The fanaticism that had burned in his eyes since his wife's death still shone in his eyes yet, almost despite himself, as he looked up at Artemis his gaze drank in her beauty, which even six months ago he would have noticed no more than the muscles of a man. And Apollo also saw that, while his sister's face did not glow with the force of true love, and while the passion she had shown for being the mistress of animals was

333

greater than the sexual excitement she showed for this man, her cheeks still burned a brighter shade of various beautiful colours as she noticed Orion's attention. His sister was not in love: but she genuinely liked this man. And for a girl as lonely for company as his twin sister that was a dangerous combination: very dangerous.

"You hunting for me tonight Orion?" Artemis asked, her voice slightly breathless. "It's the full moon, so you'd better catch me something good. I'll be well cross otherwise!" One of her hands played absently with his hair, the other came down so her fingers rested gently at the base of his neck. "So don't you dare come back without a nice big monster head and a huge bag of tasty red squirrels!"

Orion's face was bleak with constant grief, yet her flirting touched something in him. Something that made him smile. He had little left to give in his dead heart to any woman, but that little the sweetness of Artemis the Friendly was slowly and surely breathing into life. His words were calm as he replied gently to her. "I always hunt for your honour and glory: and always strive to honour the trust you have shown in me by anointing me as your champion. But tonight, under the light of your full moon, I shall either bathe in the darkest of blood for your honour; or shall instead shed my own as a sacrifice. Either the life of the foulest monster I can find or my own heart's blood shall be yours this night. It is no less than you, on this most holy of your nights, truly deserve."

Artemis knelt down before Orion, and kissed him on the lips. It was not quite an act of romance, not quite explicitly sexual instead of implicitly. Both Orion's and Artemis's tongues stayed firmly in their mouths. The kiss teased at the very edge of what might or might not be love and lust: but though it teetered on a pinhead it did not cross the line, not quite. Less than a millimetre of a hair's width short.

"I don't want your blood." Said Artemis softly, her very breath almost a caress. "I would miss you far too much if you were gone. If whatever monster or beast you find tonight is beyond your strength just leave it: I would far rather have you alive than a hundred stuffed monster heads mounted on my wall."

Orion looked at her, and even in the unending ache of pain and grief for his dead wife that was almost all his life had now become, I saw how Artemis's affection touched some part of the hunter that was not quite as dead as he had believed.

"I swore an oath to avenge my wife Artemis," said Orion uncertainly. "I swore to fight to avenge her death until I had slain a thousand, thousand foul monsters like the one that took her life. I swore not to stop until either the whole world was rid of evil or I was dead: knowing that ridding the world of darkness was something I could never achieve. Knowing that I was binding myself to just a morally acceptable form of suicide. I cannot now go back on that oath. I…"

Artemis smiled, and her voice went almost dreamy. "I swore an oath when I was three you know! Said I was going to be a virgin forever. Doesn't mean I always have to keep it." She looked directly into Orion's eyes "What I want now as a young woman is very different to what I wanted as a small child. Circumstances change. And sometimes the best oaths in the world are not meant to be kept forever." Her meaning could not have been clearer if she had danced naked in front of him.

There was a very long silence, a pause in the heart of the world: in which you could have heard a pin drop at the peak of a mountain. Then Artemis kissed Orion again. And this time: as their tongues entwined: there was no doubt that she was crossing the line that she was now never meant to cross. This time there could be no mistaking her intent or exactly what it was that she wanted. Caught by surprise for a moment raw desire and instinct kicked in, and Orion kissed her back: passionately: firmly embracing her in his strong arms as he held her tightly against his chest.

But then he remembered his dead wife: and who and what Artemis really was. And that there was far more to her then just the friendliness and beauty of the sweet fairy princess of the gods. He pulled away, the strange fanaticism in his eyes once more much stronger than love or lust. He reached out and squeezed Artemis's shoulder with real affection: but not with the passion of true love. He did not have that left in him to give.

When he spoke it was soft and sad, concerned for Artemis's happiness and wellbeing. "Divine Huntress: chaste maiden of the moon: of all the gods and goddesses I have ever worshipped you mean the most to me. For you do not shelter yourself on the summit of Mount Olympus in bliss and comfort but live in the mortal world: to share in the pain and grief that is the lot of mortals. And I pray that one day you will find someone who can love you as you deserve: with all their heart and soul. You deserve the comfort and passion of love as much as any girl that I have ever met. But, though it grieves my soul to hurt you, that person cannot be me. My heart beats for my dead wife alone. I love you as a worshipper loves his goddess; but not as a man loves a woman. Were it not weakness and sin I would take my own life simply to end my grief and to be with my dead wife either in the underworld, or when we are spun out again in reincarnation to meet again in the world of the living.

As a goddess you have given me the strength to be a hero: to let my end be a thing of beauty and triumph. Because of you I have rid the world of much darkness, and have not wasted my strength in suicide but have instead spared many others from my wife Merope's fate:

murder and death at the hands of a monster. You have been the foundation of my strength and of any joy that I have managed to find in these closing stages of my life: but I will always be in love with Merope. You deserve a man, Artemis, who can love you with all his heart and soul as the first woman in his life. But my heart is dead huntress and, though my body still lives and breathes, I am, maiden of the moon, nothing more than a ghost. I am just the sorry remnants of a man who died a year ago, in a vampire's dungeon on an island surrounded by the sea.

But I will honour this holy night for you with monster blood. And if I fall instead I ask simply this, let my death be remembered not with grief, but just as a worthy offering to the glory of your divinity."

Orion rose, slowly but surely, and squeezed the goddess's hand tightly. Partly in affection, partly in apology. Then he turned, his spear clenched tightly in one hand: white with stress. The next moment he was gone into the night. His heart sought little now but that the last stage of his life be a story of triumph and not waste and pity.

There was a long silence after he was gone, when very little moved in the room at the heart of a living tree. Then a very, if almost guilty, relieved Apollo reappeared in the room, besides a very still and shaken young woman. For a time neither of them knew quite what to say. Apollo turned and walked around the room, admiring the stuffed animal heads on the walls. For though he felt his sister's pain he could not hide how the tension had drained out of him when Orion had turned her down. "How many of these are the hunter's gifts to you?" he asked at last, almost gently. "If more than a few then his worship to your honour is great indeed."

Artemis was sitting by the table, staring blankly at the tree wall. She seemed to be gazing at the tree's ring patterns on her walls but she, whose eyes normally rejoiced in any natural life, currently saw nothing at all: her world shaken and suddenly full of a very unexpected type of pain. Naive and sweet, with no real experience of love or men, it had simply never occurred to her that she could grow to care for a man who would not care for her, anymore then she would have ever wanted a man to care for her who she could not love back in return.

"Most of them." She said at last, thickly, her voice choked. "There are three that I am dead proud of, they came from monsters so fierce. The harpy's head, the head of a bronze sentinel of Hephaestus, and that great big minotaur head over there. That last one I'm so happy with. I was so proud of Orion when he survived that fight: I was so scared that his wounds would kill him. It's where he got that nasty scar which means most women don't find him nice to look at any more. I don't mind it: I just think it shows how brave he is."

There was a sudden unexpected sound in the rafters of the tree above them, and Apollo looked up. "You have birds living with you inside your tree?" He asked gently, amused. "As well as outside?"

"Yes." said Artemis weakly. "I have a couple of nesting owls that always make me think of wisdom. And I have a flock of ravens that I'm helping look after. They've just had young recently." Normally her voice would have rung with pride and enthusiasm as she buzzed about all this: right now the pain as her words shook showed she was struggling to so much as care.

Apollo's voice was gentle. "Why raven's sister, what do they mean…" Then he stopped as realisation suddenly set in. "Ah yes of course, Odin's birds." He stood looking at his sister for a long time. "You know," he said at last, "just because you can't have lovers doesn't mean you shouldn't be able to make friends. If you really want to meet Odin you have my blessing, so long as I am there to supervise the meeting. I don't think either of you would get carried away, but it's safer just not to take any chances isn't it? You know Odin isn't half as bad as Dionysus. And for all that the Viking gods are primitives, they aren't half as obsessed with sex as we the civilised are. Much as I love civilisation if you want to look at its downsides just compare our grey wizard god, Dionysus: a drunken, murderous, alcoholic inspiring beautiful women to tear apart and devour the flesh of their own sons: to the Viking's grey wizard god Odin. Their king and knowledge seeker, who has endured the greatest personal sacrifices to satisfy his never ending hunger for knowledge. He even sacrificed his own eye in his quest to understand the deepest secrets of the cosmos! Much as he's an uncouth barbarian with no culture whatsoever you've got to admire his sheer determination in seeking out new understanding of the universe. That; and his razor sharp mind. That truly has no equal in all the heavens or earth. If he was civilised I'd almost be tempted to say he was one of the greatest gods in existence. And when a woman rejects him he even accepts it and moves on. In that way he's a thousand times better than our father, whose slept with everyone and everything that he can get his hands on whether they want it or…"

Apollo suddenly realised exactly what it was that he was saying, and stopped instantly: his face suddenly white. But he had been lucky. Artemis was still hurting too much to have been paying him any real attention beyond the bare minimum of what was polite. She had missed a great deal of what her twin brother had just said: very luckily.

"What would I write to Odin?" Artemis asked distantly, despairingly. "I'm a pretty little girl, but that's just annoying and distracting really because you can't ever so much as even touch me: and although I love knowing stuff I'm not really all that clever so I've not got much to tell you back unless you happen to be interested in the different ways that different kinds of squirrel taste. Which let's face it: no one is. But please Odin, tell me lots of interesting things for nothing in return, I don't know why? Maybe you just feel sorry for me? Let's face it there's not much other reason to get to know me is there?

Apollo why would the king of the Viking gods be interested in me? Why would anyone: boy or girl? The way I am... because of HER... no one will ever really want to get to know me. SHE means that, let's face it, even as a friend I'm a pretty lousy proposition. So why would the great king of the Norse gods Odin, who no doubt has lots of interesting things to do and interesting people to fill his time with, want to come and spend some of his time with the silly little fairy who has to live all by herself in a forest so she can't hurt anyone? He wouldn't would he? No one sensible would.''

''He will be interested in you.'' said Apollo, firmly. ''Maybe you can be like a sister to him. You've been a great one to me. I have slept with many women, but no woman I've been with do I trust or rely on half so much as you. I will write to him straight away tomorrow morning; no damn it; I'll write to him tonight! Why waste any time?!''

He turned and walked over to the arm chair where Artemis normally sat to read: full of sudden purpose and energy. That was all very good; except that it meant that he didn't see his twin sister's form suddenly shimmer and change, as the hunter's kiss called the darker side of his sister forth: and the Friendly's pain and despair meant that she lacked her usual willpower of steel to resist. Blissfully oblivious to the terrible change that had come over his elder twin sister Apollo sat down fervently to write. ''Why I'll have a message sent by raven to Odin within...'' he began excitedly.

Then his vision went up in a thousand shards of broken light as he was hit hard: straight across his face and on his head with all the force of a lightning bolt. He could feel his skull vibrate and his teeth tearing free from his flesh. But the pain was so intense that even the mind of a god could endure it for barely seconds. He fell through the pain into unseeing, unfeeling darkness: unconsciousness seeming in that moment of agony nothing but a blessed relief.

But he would shed many tears in later years that he had passed out: and so not been able to rally the gods to stop what Artemis the Terrible did next. It would have spared many, gods and mortals, much pain. Perhaps Artemis the Friendly most of all. And throughout his long immortal life, most of Apollo's tears have always been for her.

Chapter 26

Apollo walked up the mountains of Chios, and the sky was lit red and gold with the approach of the god of the sun.

It was a winter's day but the sun now burned as hot as at the height of summer. The sun had not been strong for a long while. For a year the days had been short and the sun cold. Even the middle of summer had felt like the depths of winter. The sun god had been terribly wounded by his twin sister: and all his strength had been pouring into his recovery. Which had meant poor harvests, less food, and much death in the increased cold for the sick and weak.

And that had meant the deaths of many men, and so Artemis the Terrible had laughed with joy and screamed with victory as she had felt each man die.

But all that was done now. Her brother was a god, and he had godlike powers of recovery. Now even in winter the sun burned with the power of his renewed divine strength: and his determination and rage. He had come for revenge: and to reclaim the one side of Artemis that he considered to be his true sister.

Below him and far away the waves lapped the base of the island of Chios, and even up here in the mountains you could still taste the salt spray carried on the wind.

Below struggling fields of crops and cattle stretched desperately across a troubled land, competing with dark oak forests haunted by monsters of terror and legend. The soil of the island was rich and deep and the weather pleasant and well suited to the spread of life. But the darkness of the goddess who ruled this island meant that all life lived here in fear of her shadow and the incessant price of blood that she demanded: the incessant price of male blood. The island was not dead, no not even dying. It was very sick, but not the type of sickness that would prove fatal. The type instead that would linger on forever, condemning all those who endured it not to death: but to a terrible half-life of bare existence.

Apollo walked up the cold grey stone of the mountain. All around him sheer precipices fell away with dazzling suddenness, and the dark trees that lined the paths around him struggled ever more for life, became ever more stunted and twisted. They bore a bleak harvest. From the moment you started your walk up the mountain slopes all the trees were hung with the decaying and decomposing bodies of men. Some were fresh, barely starting to rot, others were little more than decayed skeletons and bone.

The god's mouth twisted, but the pace of his ascent did not slacken. After many grim hours he crossed the final ridge and came to the bleak lake at the summit of the mountain. Across at its centre a distant building could be seen. A grand boat awaited, a glorious ship, fitted for the high seas: fated now only to move back and forth across a simple lake. The crew were skeletons of men, some nailed to their posts. The captain was strapped to the tiller with chains. Apollo shuddered. At least those hanging from the trees earlier had been simply dead. Here were those who had done so much to anger the dark huntress that taking their lives had not been enough to sate her dark hunger. He climbed the gangplank to the ship, and moved to stand next to the dead captain at the tiller. The dead man's head moved silently for a moment, to watch him with dead empty eye sockets that somehow were still laughing. "Do you think that you can bring The Friendly back?" they seemed to mock him. "Do you think your love for her will mean anything here: at the heart of HER domain?" The dead man could not speak but Apollo could hear the hissing air passing meaninglessly through the space where his vocal cords had once been.

The god of the sun shuddered as around him the broken remnants of the huntress's anger moved to work, their dead bone moving through the empty routine as the ship moved silently from its moorings out onto the lake. The worst of it all was that it was a galley fit for kings, carved of the finest wood, its sails embroidered in gold. Artemis the Terrible had always loved being a princess.

Apollo stood by the mast, and stared hard at the temple rising up before him. He tried not to breathe too hard, below him the water of the lake glistened in the sun. It was completely beautiful, completely clear. It looked like nothing more than normal mountain water, and it tasted the same as any other. But it was so deadly that a thimble full of it could kill a man. No life moved in the water, no plants grew, no fish swam, yet at the bottom of the lake all you could see was rotting and death. Even in this dark form Artemis was still the mistress of the animals, and even here they were drawn to serve her. Fish swam upstream to reach the lake of poison, before it filled their gills and they sank dying to the bottom. Animals climbed from the forest and tried to swim the lake before the poison claimed their fleeting lives. Birds flew overhead, but the sun's heat sent water vapour into the air so deadly they fell from the sky into the water below. "Artemis's Tears" her terrified worshippers called the lake, and when she was angered the huntress would let some of her water flow down into the lands below, to bring untold death and misery. The title was an obscenity in itself, Artemis the Terrible did not cry: she did not know the taste of grief.

Apollo was immortal, forever beyond death, but even holding his breath the vapour in the air made him feel ill. He was after all god of the sun, and his very presence made the toxic lake water below heat and steam, filled with all the poison of all the rotted wasted animal life in its depths.

But the galley drew up on the island at the centre of the lake unopposed, and the sun god descended back onto land, grimly. Behind him the galley pulled silently away back across the lake, its purpose done. Once it reached the other side its dead crew would resume their patient waiting. That might be merely moments, or it might be all eternity itself. Either way they would wait simply for the next person who wished to cross the lake.

Apollo stood before a grand temple of the purest white marble, rising from an island of pure gold. He walked forward cautiously, pleased to have left the horror of the lake and ship behind him: but knowing that he now drew into the very heart of Artemis the Terrible's most sacred place. The temple was vast, and open to the air. Through its great empty halls of white marble the winds blew and echoed coldly. Apollo walked through empty hall after empty hall, and the only thing that accompanied him was death. For each room had a severed penis mounted in pride of place on the wall, framed and stuffed so that it soared erect over the entire room, and below each one was the skeleton of the castrated male it had come from, nailed to the wall below it with bolts of solid steel. Beneath each skeleton dark bloodstains on the wall showed exactly how they had died. The woman's death: castrated and made to bleed out to death while their very severed member was stuffed and mounted on the wall above them, mocking their now impotency as they died. Killed for nothing but the crime of being attracted to female beauty, of daring to think that Artemis the Terrible was desirable in the way that a man loves a woman.

Apollo lost count of how many rooms he walked through, each the same as the next. Each dedicated to the death of a single castrated male member of his species. Yet he knew when finally he had come to the very centre of the temple, to the one room that was different to the others. It was smaller than the rest, and had a stone altar at its heart, one covered in fresh red blood. And still covered in soot from a recent fire. Behind it stood a statue so lifelike that for a moment Apollo thought it was Artemis the Terrible herself. But the form did not move, simply stood as still as a graven image in stone, utterly indifferent to all that lived and moved around it. On the other side of the altar, nailed to the wall upside down with steel struts, was the body of Orion. It was brutally clear from the cut and empty jaggedness between his legs and the dark red stains on the marble wall how he had died, although of his missing cock there was no sign. Apollo looked at Orion's corpse, still very fresh, and then turned and vomited hard, gagging at what Artemis had done to her own champion. Then he stood and walked to the altar. How many men had she castrated here he wondered bleakly. Before dragging them out to die nailed to the inside walls of her temple. How many scenes of untold horror and darkness had these four walls witnessed?

He looked at the altar, with was covered with razor sharp jagged shards of steel, formed to spell out Aeon, Ancient Greek for the word eternity. He stepped to the altar and looked down at them. ''The shattered shards of Artemis the Terrible's heart,'' he said softly, ''and was it not said long ago, in words of prophecy and song, that only the power of love and blood has any chance of delivering the huntress from unending darkness."

He held out his hand without flinching, and so sharp was the steel it cut blood from his fingers before they had even touched the bleak metal. Male divine blood flowed out upon the altar.

"Artemis the Terrible, twin sister of mine, by the hate I bear you, and all the pain that you have ever done to me and my true sister, I call you forth by the blood I now shed upon this altar that my true sister may be restored to me: and you: foul abomination: may be cast forever out into the deepest darkness."

There was a long silence, and then what had seemed to be a statue slowly turned its head to fix Apollo with her bleak eyes.

"For a man to call upon me in prayer can show only the darkest madness of the mind, so I find those words of yours most suited to calling me forth, my pampered little prince of a brother."

Her voice could not have been more different from the friendly, lively, everyday chatter of Artemis the Friendly. The Terrible's voice was languid, cultured, the very definition of "posh". She was royal blood, and you would know it. Physically they were even more distinct even though, at the deepest instinctive level, even a blind man would have recognised them as being fundamentally the same girl.

Artemis the Friendly was short, barely half the height of an average man. Artemis the Terrible was more than a head and half taller than any man I had ever seen. But both had the same lithe form and deadly strong muscles, both could move like the wind and strike with devastating physical force.

Artemis the Friendly was a goddess of many colours, Artemis the Terrible of just one. White magic rolled off her in unending waves of power. While Artemis the

Friendly wore a variety of garments, in several colours but often in bright red and frequently either quite revealing or tight in suggestive places, Artemis the Terrible wore a single loose tunic of the finest silk, with gold edges, that fell down skirt like below her waist. It left her arms free and ended at the base of her neck, but apart from that it hinted at and revealed nothing. Where Artemis the Friendly liked cheap and cheerful jewellery and any sort of touristy nick knacks Artemis the Terrible had a belt and arm bands of the purest gold.

Their choice of weapons was similar, both used a bow and dagger. Artemis the Terrible had a larger bow as befitted her size and the bow was white yew with gold working; not brown oak with leather workings; and the Terrible's dagger handle was gold as opposed to wood: but in combat both would have been equally deadly. Both shot the same ice cold arrows of deadly moonlight.

They had broadly the same facial features but the overall appearance was strikingly different. Artemis the Friendly had bright blue eyes and soft deep dark brown hair. Artemis the Terrible had eyes of terribly bleak and piercing green, and red hair that flowed like fire down her shoulders. In a weird way she looked a little like Vicky would do when she was grown, if all the love and concern in Vicky was turned to nothing but madness and hate. While Artemis the Friendly had uniquely charming blue lips and finger nails Artemis the Terrible had the normal red lips and nails of a fully grown young woman, but her fingernails had lengthened and ossified over the years into jagged and dangerous claws: razor sharp.

Where Artemis the Friendly was pale and covered in green tattoos Artemis the Terrible's skin was flush with health but was completely plain and unadorned. And where Artemis the Friendly had small and sweet little human teeth the Terrible had instead a pair of glistening fangs, as sharp and brutal as the steel shards on her stone altar.

But perhaps the most striking difference was their wings. Artemis the Friendly had gentle almost gossamer wings: green bones with the flesh pink that were almost transparent in bright light. Artemis the Terrible had the great outstretched wings of a large and ferocious eagle, covered in brown feathers and her wingspan three times that of her other self.

But whether she appeared as either the fairy or the vampire princess Artemis was always stunningly beautiful: a vision of loveliness and delight that made the darkness in her soul even more horrifying. Had her evil warped her features she would have been far easier to endure.

"Tell me, prince of the gods who shared my mother's womb with me, why is it that you so prefer the common little preferences of my Sappy side, who lives in a tree caring for animals like an ill-bred peasant, to the princess who sits in a marble palace on an island of gold, surrounded by the offerings of men who have given up all they are to her? Is it that seeing me reduced to so little makes you feel better about the worthless way you spend your own pointless days? Like all men you prey on women, you want Sappy back simply because seeing me sad makes you feel all good about yourself: seeing me as I am now in my full majesty simply shows how far from the true nature of the divine all the male gods of our pantheon have fallen."

Apollo's eyes flashed with anger. "Artemis the Friendly is the true princess. She is kind and sweet and all who see her love her. I would have her sat in a palace of gold, eating grapes from summer dishes and drinking only the sweetest wines. I would have her marry a prince of the gods and be the mother to a thousand divine dynasties. And you dare to blame her for living like a peasant? You dare to blame her for having the courage to live alone, surrounded by those so far below her divine: let alone her royal: station? You are the reason, you cold bitch, that she has sacrificed herself! For she knows that only by hiding herself away from all the things that she wants most in this world may you be contained. And you think this is a palace of glory?! You think this a fine temple?! This is a mockery of all that the gods are Artemis! You are not really worshipped as a goddess here: the people on this island do not kneel to your divine right! You are but a demon of horror: who rules through force alone! You have no more right to your claim to power here than the lowest thug or bandit does to the possessions he takes at sword or knife point. If the people in this island could they would torch this place! This place which is no real temple but merely a charnel house to death: and by all the gods I'd help them do it! Demons have no place in the heavens!''

Artemis laughed, cold and cruel. ''Can you not feel the new age coming brother? A new divine age dawns, an age when all the gods shall be destroyed, or be seen as nothing but demons. I merely prepare myself for what is to come. For it is I, The Terrible, and Hecate, goddess of witchcraft, and Loki the foul Viking trickster, who shall thrive in this new age: as the demons we truly are. While all your claims to divinity, and all the other gods like you who dare to claim they are the righteous lords of the heavens, will be swept aside by a man who is nothing more than a carpenter. All is ending Apollo, and Sappy's power will fade in this new age like all the rest.''

Apollo laughed coldly. ''Paganism has reigned since the beginning of time. Now Zeus rules the south, Odin rules the north: what power could bring that down to its knees?''

''Why nothing, my most simple and hopeless brother, nothing so long as the gods in it remain true. But even

350

The Allfather cannot stand alone if the gods of civilisation fall. And Zeus? Why my all-powerful father, ruler of the heavens and earth; he cannot even save me from myself now can he? If he cannot do that do you honestly think the pantheon of paganism can still endure what is to come? Honestly think it can endure the seismic shock that is to come in the life, death and resurrection of The Christ?''

Apollo swayed on his feet, suddenly uncertain. He looked suddenly grey and old, and you could feel the coldness as the sun weakened in the heavens. He laid his hand across his brow, and grey clouds overcast the sky, taking the heat and light from the air. ''I can never forgive my father for failing you so badly.'' said Apollo harshly, ''And he should never be forgiven for it: not so long as all the worlds last, and not so long as ever eternity reigns. But no more can I forgive you: The Terrible. What you do now has brought more grief and darkness into the world than all his thunderbolts could have ever done. Give me back The Friendly, demon. For whether you be right about the future or not I know that today I will take back with me the sister that I love.'' There was a silence, and then Apollo raised his head and his eyes were fire, burning with the same impossible temperatures that rage in the centre of the sun. ''And know this,'' he cried, as the words of prophecy burned within him with terror and fury, and the sun's light and heat once more filled the sky. The daylight was so suddenly so bright it was searing.

''Know that maybe the gods shall fall, and a new age, the age of Christ and the death of magic shall come. But know also this. Not all that age shall have a power that can break the strength of ''Sappy's'' heart. Not unless the age that shall come after the age of Christ shall die ere it can be truly born: not unless the age of the carpenter shall truly last forever. And know that in ''Sappy'' you have an enemy who may prove to be beyond even the power of your darkness; and know that the love in her may one day prove stronger than all your rage and hate. For her love one day a man may try and win even your heart, dark virgin, and all your terror shall not break the love he feels for the smile in The Friendly's eyes, or the softness he feels melt inside him as he longs to take her hand in his.''

The sun burned bright as it fell upon the cold centre of Artemis's power, upon a temple that in those days had not the words to describe its pure unadulterated evil but would nowadays be called the living representation of hell on earth. The dark goddess of the moon did not move, though she was bathed in the fierce glow of the burning sun star. She stood as still as the graven image of stone she had seemed to be when Apollo had first entered her temple.

''Your words do not move me brother. And you think that I, who plan the breaking of all my father's kingdom and all the kingdoms of the divine and men, you think that I cannot break your milkweed of a sister? You think that The Friendly, that milksop and plaything of men, who loves her brother and wants nothing more than to have a gentle husband to love her and make her feel happy: you think I cannot break her? Behold today Apollo, how even now the wheels of her destruction move. Of all the opponents that I have it burns my blood the most with fury that any should dare to think that The Friendly could dare to stand against me. For I am the one true Artemis, and she is nothing but the shattered memory of a girl who died long ago: the memory of a girl too weak to remember what really happened to her. Too weak even to remember the evil that gave birth to ME. Why do you think that she is so cold Apollo? Why do you think that her lips and eyes and fingers are blue? She is nothing more than a walking corpse my most deluded brother: while my flesh beats warm and alive. My body sustains all the healthy functions of life, her weak semblance of life is sustained only by the will that drives her dying body, holding herself in stasis as she fights uselessly against the encroaching end."

Apollo folded his arms. "And how do you plan to break the willpower of the strongest girl I know? You say she is too weak to remember; I say she is strong enough to forget and move on with the life she had before. You are the one who is too weak to put the past behind you, and the one who lets it rule your every thought and deed."

"I will break her by destroying all those she cares about." Hissed Artemis the Terrible, baring her fangs with a snarl against the power of the sun.

Apollo did not move but you could feel the power gathering in him, the sudden surge of heat and light. Artemis the Terrible stared back at him, her green eyes cold. You could feel the light magic suddenly coming off her in waves: the sheer air around her vibrating with its force.

Then Artemis laughed cruelly, and the tension fell away. "I have already hurt you recently brother: and fighting you today I would achieve little. The pagan age still reigns, and I might actually lose. Besides neither of us can die, and there are so many better ways for me to make The Sappy cry her tears of dead black blood than to waste my power in a pointless contest of strength with you. After all you are immortal, if I hurt you, you will, in the end, still just get better." She turned and smiled at where Orion's lifeless, castrated corpse was nailed with steel spikes to the inside marble wall of her altar room.

"He on the other hand is much less fortunate. Properly sacrificed he will stay decently dead. Another beautiful ornament to go with all the others on my walls. Truly their lives ended the way all men's always should.

What you see before you today is the way all the males of the species should end their miserable lives."

"Will you have his penis stuffed on the wall as well?" asked Apollo sarcastically. "Just another part of your demonstration of how you have truly mastered your dealings with the members of my sex? He was your champion you know, he gave twelve months of his life to you. Foolish as he was to kiss you, he deserved a far better end than this."

Artemis smiled tightly. "Oh no brother, he had to pay worse than all the others. He actually dared to kiss me, to interact with me as though I was a sexual object purely there for his pleasure. He had to be appropriately punished Apollo: he had to pay properly for what he did. I made him witness every moment as I led monsters to devastate each region he had saved, as I killed and slaughtered all those he had spent the last twelve months trying to protect. And when I was done with that, when every place he had saved was nothing more than a lifeless wasteland of fire and ash we came back here, to the island he had cleared from monsters to win his wife Merope's hand. And I made him watch as I and my monsters killed almost every person on this island, and then repopulated it with monsters a thousand times worse than before he came: a lovely scorpion woman chief among them. She did such a good job that she is now one of my champions. Then, when he saw that he had failed in everything, failed as a lover, failed as an avenging champion, I took Orion to this altar at the heart of my temple and gave him the woman's death he so richly deserved."

Apollo shuddered. "The scorpion woman is a foul creature worthy of as dark a mistress as you. Tell me, why not then just kill all the islanders you bitch? Don't try and pretend there is any compassion at all inside your heart. There is nothing in you but madness and hate: you

354

are not worthy of the title of goddess in any way: not one at all."

"But of course I let some of them live brother," laughed Artemis, "for if I had killed them all would there not then have been an end to their suffering? Now a frightened remnant is cursed to live forever in my shadow, forever more this island will now be a rich provider of the suffering of men. And soon my power as a "demon", as you put it, shall outlast those of the gods who will not turn to darkness and evil in the coming reign of Christ."

Apollo shuddered at her words, then turned to look at Orion. He clearly did not take her threats about the coming of a new religious age very seriously. "I do not hesitate to shed the blood of the unworthy at my altars, no true pagan god does, but how can even you think he deserved a punishment like that?" he muttered dazedly, bleakly. "All Orion did was kiss you, at your instigation, once and all so briefly. He even said he wasn't going to take things any further."

Artemis snarled, her teeth showing suddenly red. "He dared to touch me sexually. No man, or woman, shall ever do that and live: understand! He was punished exactly as he deserved. You want to know where his cock is? I ate it brother. I devoured the bleeding flesh in front of him, made him watch as I first cooked it and then ate it in front of him. You know it was quite delicious, the only truly good relationship a woman can have with a man's willy."

Apollo fell to his knees, gagging, and was very sick. That was twice now since he had entered this room at the centre of her bleak temple.

"You didn't ask about the firewood though, the remnants of the fire you can see, even now, on my altar." said Artemis, softly and almost thoughtfully. "That fire was the last thing Orion ever saw, after I had castrated

355

him and made him watch as I devoured his penis in front of him. It's best cooked medium to well done by the way: in case you ever want to try: brings out all the flavour." Apollo vomited again.

"Anyway the reason Orion's nailed upside down to that rock is to ensure that he would bleed slowly and therefore die slowly. My lovely meal wasn't quite his last punishment. I used the firewood from the oak tree he planted above where he buried his wife to make the fire on which I cooked his severed cock, and then I burned the rest of the tree just because I could. I wanted him to know as he died that he had achieved absolutely nothing with his life, not even managing to give the woman he loved a proper resting place."

There was a long sick silence, in which two people who absolutely hated each other decided on their next move. Deep down both of them were beginning to hope and hunger for violence. But instead in the end Artemis the Terrible simply laughed, her cruelty and sadism echoing from every corner of the marble and gold. A cruel smile danced across her eyes. "You know what, my useless excuse of a brother? I think you've been punished enough for letting me be kissed: you've suffered agony for nearly a year after all: as your wounds oh so slowly kit themselves back together. But Sappy hasn't paid at all yet: and that is a situation that I find most unsatisfactory: and in urgent need of addressing. So I'll tell you what. I'll give you what you think you want: I'll give you Sappy back, right here and right now." Her eyes danced with cruel mirth. "She will remember everything I- we- have just done, so you might want to hold her tight brother. Because by all the gods in a moment she is going to scream. Quite loudly I think: and for a long time. She will be in a very great deal of pain indeed. Who knows? This might even be the shattering of the last straw she has that keeps her clinging onto life. Won't it be a relief for us all when The Friendly finally stops struggling and admits that she's dead? That she died centuries ago. A day for the richest chocolate and champagne I should think."

There was a shuddering, a flicker of power, and suddenly where a sadistic vampire had stood there was only a little fairy, knelt on the ground in grief.

Apollo stumbled towards her, but he was too late. Not that he could have done anything at that point. Not that anyone really could. In moments The Friendly had torn Orion's body from where it was nailed brutally to the wall and was clutching it to her chest, and her screams tore the air with her agony. "No." screamed Artemis the Friendly as it felt like her heart was suddenly being ripped apart into a thousand splinters: a more terrible cry than any that had ever been heard even when the world was young and born in fire and blood and melting ice.

"No." she howled. "Orion please, please don't be dead: and not dead like this! Not because of me!" She arched her back towards the heavens: her whole body wracked by screaming. "Why did the gods let this happen? Why do you let HER exist? I would die myself if it would end her with me! I would offer anything to be rid of her: anything at all!"

Only the sky stared down, in grey unending silence. Artemis screamed again, more terrible than any flash of lightning or thunderclap in the mountains. "Please somebody help me." She howled like a dying animal. She cried out in desperate pain and grief: But it was all hopeless: utterly hopeless. "Please. Please." She wept, her face streaked with tears of blood. As a living corpse she had not water in her eye ducts to cry, just the dead black blood in her veins. Her spine convulsed as her chest shook with sobs and her tears seemed not to slow or stop, though her tunic was soaked in the lifeless poison her heart still struggled to beat through her veins. But the skies stayed grey and cold. Her father was king of the gods, divine lord of the heavens, yet for some reason the cries of his favourite daughter had no answer: not from him nor any other power. Even if they were watching, they remained silent and still: and did nothing. The pagan age was already sick and dying: just waiting to fall.

From the bleak island of Artemis the Terrible Artemis the Friendly found no answer to her cries. She was, she realised, in this war completely alone. The war between fairy princess and vampire princess could ultimately be decided only by the strength of the two combatants alone. For who was the true Artemis, and who just the imposter that wore her face and name?

Only one thing did Artemis the Friendly know for sure. She was undead, a corpse sustained by will power alone. An undead girl that would not die. Sustained only be her desperate desire: above all things: to be a good girl. To be true and gentle and kind.

And though that day Artemis the Friendly bled freely at the hand of Artemis the Terrible, and though she felt the pain of what had happened to Orion in every part of her mind and soul, she did not give in and just let things end as The Terrible wanted. Against all the power of the hells that the Terrible could throw at her the little that was left of Artemis the Friendly buckled.

But she did not break.

Chapter 27

One day later.

There is nothing in this life like the intensity of total war.

Whatever Artemis the Terrible had planned when she unleashed all the powers of hell upon The Friendly it had not been this. There's a saying that you can't kill a dead fly. It also seems that it is very hard to kill a dead woman. And now the fairy princess intended to hit back. After all, Artemis the Friendly was as absolutely convinced that she was the one true Artemis, as The Terrible was convinced that is was the dark side of the virgin that was the only real chaste goddess of the moon.

Artemis the Friendly stood at the roots of Mount Olympus, and around her burned the forges of the gods: the room rang with the deafening sound of fire and flame. Artemis launched herself up into the air. "Take a good look you Stupid Bitch." She shouted- her name for Artemis the Terrible- "How's the collapse of the pagan age working out for you? From here looks like paganism is working out just great to me. And these people who you want to get rid of," she yelled furiously, "they're our family and friends. If there's a problem we sit down together and work out how to get rid of the problem, don't we? We don't get rid of the people!!! But hey –

you're too stupid to understand that aren't you - you stupid self-centred bitch!''

Artemis flew straight and landed at the centre of the workshop, right on top of the great anvil of Hephaestus himself: the crippled god of smiths who both managed and led the working of the great smithies below Mount Olympus. The fall of hammers banging on sheet metal filled Artemis's ears and the sound of the forges roared with flame. Her eyes glowed in the light of the fire. It felt like every beat of life and strength around her filled her with power and energy. She ran her fingers lovingly over the cold steel beneath her touch: the anvil of Hephaestus. It was a divine construction of terrible power, years of Hephaestus's life poured into its crafting. The one item in all creation where the interlocked bolts and rings of steel were strong enough to endure the forging of pure magic into the thunderbolts of Zeus. The most terrible weapons in the world. Hephaestus had forged many deadly weapons, from the club of Hercules to the sword of Achilles. His great hammer had pounded metal into the spear, sword and axe. But none of those weapons, for all the blood they had shed, came close to the power of the thunderbolts. They were the essence of Zeus's power, the foundation of his rule. So long as his thunderbolts reigned in the sky so the age of pagan magic would endure. Should they fall then the age of man and Christ had come.

The crippled god of the smithies knew the harm and bloodshed his weapons were going out into the world to do. He knew how much of the gold of Olympus flowed from the brutal arms trade, how war tore always across the scattered Greek city states which were the birthplace of what could become civilisation. But though his weapons, which had once sheltered Greece in the Persian wars, now merely helped Sparta and Athens turn their forces upon each other, still he obeyed the commands of almighty Zeus. He hated the father of the gods with all he had, the God who had rejected him twice. Once as a child for being ugly, Zeus had hurled Hephaestus out from the summit of Mount Olympus. The smith god had luckily landed in the sea water unharmed, and had been adopted by a goddess of the sea. Then, after his skill in forging weapons of war and ornaments of jewellery and gold as an adult had won his way back to the summit of Mount Olympus, he had been hurled from that great peak a second time: this time for the crime of daring to stand up to his great father and for the audacity of daring to have opinions of his own. And this time he had not been so lucky as to land in the water: and his impact on striking the land had broken his legs beyond all repair. Yet Hephaestus knelt still to the rule of the divine patriarch. The gods of Olympus were after all, still his family and friends: however much he disliked their overbearing absolutist king.

The god of the smithies had forged lightning and thunder from the stuff of raw magic unblinking. And yet today there were tears in his eyes, and his great hands: which could endure the heat at the centre of stars: shook as frail and infirm as an old man's whose strength is failing.

"Artemis I know The Terrible has just done something dreadful to you but…"

"But what Hephaestus?" asked Artemis, almost gently. "I should just hold her in and try to delay the end? Artemis the Terrible is wrong about almost everything in life: but she is right about one very important thing. Whatever happened to me that I can't remember no matter how hard I try Artemis the Terrible is the natural result. She is the true form of my divinity now. I am just a memory of how I used to be. Oh I look fine on the surface, but that's mostly because looking good has always mattered to me. I have to pour so much energy and strength into keeping this dead body alive. And even then you think I don't notice how much people shudder at my touch: at how cold the flesh of my corpse has become? And I was not born with eyes and lips that were rotting blue." She paused. "You know in the quiet moments of my life, in the whispering hours before I slip away into sleep, or those first few moments of confusion in the day when I wake, I can almost feel my body rotting. There are times when I am eating food and I lose concentration, and suddenly my tongue blackens and I can't taste anything, or a rotten tooth breaks from my suddenly decaying gums." She shuddered. "And there are times when the wind rises and my nose curdles at a smell a thousand times worse than souring milk: and then I realise it is only the stench of my own corpse carried back to me." Her eyes were bleak and hopeless. "If I just wait, wait and hope, then this just ends with my will breaking and HER becoming all that I am: and all that I will ever be for all the rest of eternity. And I would take any other fate than that. Any other fate than hurting the very people I love and care about. It's time to start taking risks."

"Sister." said a man urgently, and Apollo stepped forward to clasp his twin sister's hand desperately. "There is another way. There is a man, a sometimes worshipper of mine, who they say has powers of prophecy and knowledge of lore greater than that of any ever known by any man or even god. They say his knowledge rivals that of The Allfather himself. If you would just let me take you to him..."

"That's sweet brother," said Artemis softly, a tear of black blood leaking from one of her dead blue eyes. "But the time for words is now passed. It is the time for actions. If a deed of horror could change my form once, perhaps a deed of horror can change it again. You will not tell me what was done to me that rules my life and I can't remember what it was but…"

"Because telling you would be your death!" exclaimed Apollo. "Just look at what has happened to the part of you that does remember! The knowledge of the truth would break even your spirit. You would die forever, leaving that winged bitch to be all of you that there is!"

Artemis shrugged. "So be it then. I will not argue with you brother. Not now: not when I need all my strength for what is about to come. What I will do is inflict an instant of horror of my own. One that I can endure. One that fucking bitch will not. Let us see how she does with pain when it is her turn to drink deep of it. She is good enough at inflicting it on others."

Artemis took a deep breath, and then suddenly the fairy princess was almost unbelievably calm and implacably composed. A stillness settled over the forge as the truth of what was about to happen finally started to sink in. The horror at what was to come was almost palpable, you could taste it in the air.

To one side of Hephaestus's anvil the red coals glowed in a seemingly never ending line, but to no obvious purpose. No weapons in progress were being heated by them, nor would this have been a good way of creating heat to build up a forge fire: the heat loss into the open air was far too great. The fire that burned on these coals was divine. In places so hot that it burned white and blue, flames at temperatures and heats that were not meant for earth, but only for the innermost cores of the great stars: whose warm fires burn far from earth through fathoms unknown and not yet dreamt by men.

Only Artemis, the sweet little fairy princess, seemed untouched by the horror of what was about to come: but then the darkness had already taken so much of the light from her soul. What was one more attack upon the shattered broken remnants of her happiness? She lay down gently on the anvil and calmly stretched herself out across the cold steel. "I am ready." she said softly, "It is time."

"Sister." said Apollo, stepping forward urgently. "You don't have to do this! You don't have…"

"Yes." said Artemis the Friendly, in a tone that was somewhere the other side of the strength of steel. "Yes I do. What was it SHE called me again? Oh yes, that's right, Sappy. She claims that I died because I couldn't take the horror of what was done to me: well let's see how The Terrible copes with this. Whatever I become, if The Terrible dies, has to be better than what she- what I – am now." Her words were calm and clear, but another tear of dead black blood squeezed itself out of the corner of her left eye. If she had had any more left they would have flown freely but she was out. All she had done for the last day was cry.

"People died because SHE decided I can't cope with horror and pain. Silly little Artemis the Friendly: can't take anything that's uncomfortable. I might not be able to restore my own memory, and brother you still won't tell me what happened to me, but if Artemis the Friendly could die because of something bad that happened to her then the same can happen to Artemis the Terrible. I can remove all need for her to exist by enduring horror: creating memories that will crack her mind when she tries to become me once more. The sheer power of the magic about to be used should be enough to kill the bitch: it can't have taken this much to kill me in the first place can it? And isn't that what you do to a parasite: an infection: a cancer. You give it to the flames? Today I will create the memories that will see that bitch burn."

There was a long quiet in the carved halls of stone deep beneath the rock of Mount Olympus. Then Hephaestus walked forward to the altar like a sick old man: his steps shaky and faint. Apollo clung to a nearby pillar as though that was all that kept him up in this world. Artemis glanced at the Smith God curiously, as though he was doing no more than simply bringing her a cup of tea. Then she looked at herself. ''Start with my little toe.'' she said at last, ''Then break the rest of my toes then start on my fingers. If you start by breaking the big bones then I won't feel the pain of the little ones breaking: so make sure you follow the order of hammer strokes that will bring my body the most physical pain possible. I want that bitch to feel everything: I need her to die. Then you are to break every bone in my body Hephaestus: as we agreed. And you are not to stop when I start screaming. The louder I scream the better a job you are doing. Use my cries to spur you on, let their sound merely call you on to hit me harder. Let my screams of agony be just music dancing in your ears.''

''Little one,'' said Hephaestus sickly, ''there is no guarantee this will work and if it does not…''

''Yes.'' said Artemis, lightly, almost dreamily. ''I imagine that there is a very good chance that SHE will survive the first time. A parasite as vile and wretched as her will probably take a lot of killing. So if it doesn't work the first time you will just then have to do it again, and again.''

Hephaestus raised the hammer, then lowered it to his side again unused. ''Princess,'' he said quietly, ''I cannot do this.''

Artemis's eyes flashed fire. ''You just okay with being the crippled servant of your daddy are you? You have made all the lovely things that we enjoy on Mount Olympus, the women's jewellery, the golden goblets we drink from, even our weapons and Zeus's thunderbolts themselves: they all come from you. But does daddy ever show you any appreciation? Does he hell. He barely ever lets you go to the summit of Mount Olympus; and when he does he can't bring himself to even look at you: because he's ashamed you're a deformed cripple. The worst thing is that part of your ugliness is that he shattered your legs by hurling you from the top of Mount Olympus: just for having the nerve to answer back to him and to have opinions of your own. He can't bear to look at what he himself has done to you. After all, all you've ever had from him is scorn and blows.

But me? I'm beautiful and sweet and pretty much everything daddy wants in a daughter. Why when I was just three he gave me nine cities, and a nice bow and arrows, a lovely silver chariot and dominion over all the mountains and forests of the world. And who had to do all the hard work and make them all again? Oh yes that's right: you. I got all the good stuff, and you got just to do all the hard work that allowed me to be nothing more than just a pampered little princess. And here I am, daddy's precious little girl. You not man enough to take your vengeance?"

Hephaestus sighed. "That was a truly pathetic attempt to make me angry with you. Zeus yes, I despise my father, but you, you have never been anything but lightness and sweet. And you have always been kind to me. Reminding me how much I hate him isn't going to make me want to hurt you." He looked sickly at the anvil. "Especially not like this."

Artemis howled. "I was dead mean to you as a child. You made me my lovely chariot of silver and my beautiful bow and all I did in thanks was pull the hair out of your chest, so hard that it came up by the roots and you now have a bald patch. I…"

"You were a sweet little child." said Hephaestus softly, "I'm not going to hurt you because of that."

Artemis turned her gaze on him and her eyes were pleading. "Hephaestus if you love me you will do this. Please? What life do I have ahead of me if you do not?"

366

And the desperation in her voice would have broken the heart of a stone.

Hephaestus went white, but he picked up his hammer. He loved his half-sister very much. Hephaestus has stood at the smithies for days on end, laughing at the heat that would consume a mortal man in flames. For hours untold he has forged the great craftmanships of this world without rest or pause, yet today his strength failed: his resolve crumbled into dust. He could but deliver a few blows before he turned to a great cyclops and, weeping, placed the great hammer into his hands instead. And though no cyclops ever lets another share in his work, and jealousy guards all possession of it; and though they are so strong that sparks from the forge can fly harmlessly into their one great eye, utterly unblinking, yet today not one could deliver more than a few blows to Artemis before he too thrust the hammer aside to another and fled in tears.

Yet it was Hephaestus who returned, when the form on the anvil had been broken beyond form or recognition, for the torment of Artemis was not yet done. And he knew that however much he hurt her today only freedom from The Terrible gave Artemis any chance at all of future happiness. Hephaestus scooped up her shattered body in his hands and, almost gently, dragged it across the coals laid out for this purpose. And as he raked her body back and forth across the divine fires of the heart of stars the smithy filled with the burning stench of Artemis's charred flesh.

Three times she was broken on the anvil, and three times she was given to the flames. For the immortals can never die but always heal and in time are whole. And as long as her will endured even the undead goddess Artemis the Friendly, who should now no more cling to life than a skin that a snake has shed before growing another, was bound by those rules. And so strong was the steel in her soul that even her dead blue and rotting flesh regrew. And when all was done Artemis, her burns fading and her jagged bones reknitting, sat up and stared blankly at the wall: all her fire and energy gone. Apart from the blue in her eyes and in her fingernails there was again no clue, besides how cold she was, that she was even dead.

"It didn't work." she said flatly, with eyes as flat and lifeless as the empty debris of the stars. "I can still feel her, there inside me. These memories will hurt her, but her wounds are not fatal. She has won it seems. I can die but she cannot. I cannot win this war. Only darkness awaits me: a darkness that will never end. My immortality now hangs around my neck as nothing but a curse."

Apollo took her arm gently. "Artemis there is a man that can help you. He knows the lore of all things that live in this world. He will be able…"

"How can the lore of living help a dead girl?" asked the blue-eyed goddess brokenly. "It is done Apollo. And so am I."

"Because undead is not fully dead sister. Even the living dead are still part of the lore of life, even…"

"Apollo." said Artemis quietly. "I am very tired and I am very cold. I would like to go back home now please. Just go back to my lovely little tree house, and curl up in my warm bed under my quilt, and perhaps sleep forever."

A long time passed: a very long time indeed.

In all that time the Mistress of the Animals never once left her house. Often the animals, who remembered and loved her still, brought her food. The mice carried in berries, the squirrels brought her nuts, the wolves, whining as they missed her, brought her rabbits. The bats brought her insects and the birds drops of the morning dew. In the beginning birds came most mornings and left letters, but she never tried to read them. And, as the years and decades and then the centuries rolled by, though the animals never slackened in their devotion, the works of parchment and ink came less and less: until one day they no longer came at all.

Mostly during this time Artemis just lay there, listless and empty, drained of all energy and thought of life. If she had been human she would have ended her own life long ago: just to be rid of HER. But she was no mortal and so, knowing she could never die, she chose simply to exist as little as possible. To simply do nothing, and wait out all the ages of the world. For if she did nothing her will would not wear out would it not? Instead it would slide frictionless through the empty sands of time and never slacken or weaken in any way. And so SHE would never again be able to take her over and hurt anyone else: especially anyone that she cared about. The little fairy princess accepted that she could not now live as Artemis the Friendly in any real sense: but perhaps she could at least stop herself from becoming Artemis the Terrible ever again. And a thought crossed her mind as well. A small desperate glimmer of light that could almost have been called hope.

Artemis the Friendly was dead already so she would not age: her time as a goddess was already past. But Artemis the Terrible would have only a limited lifespan surely? For all gods and goddesses, while they do not age or die as mortals do, can evolve with the times into other forms. And the thought grew in the mind of The Mistress of Animals that if she simply waited, perhaps she could wait out the lifespan of the eagled-winged angel of death. She did not seek her own resurrection, or to become the living form of Artemis once more. She just simply didn't want all those innocent people and all of those that she loved to be hurt in the way that they would be if Artemis the Terrible was allowed to roam free: her cruelty and power unchecked by the slightest flicker of any compassion or mercy.

But after a long time, one morning with no difference that any external eye could see, The Mistress of Animals finally gave a little sigh, a sound of utter and complete defeat. As pained as any she had made when she had failed in the forges of fire. She was still weakening as the years passed, even if only a very little. For life itself is friction and movement and not even lying and trying to will yourself into nothingness can stop its flow entirely. But Artemis the Terrible was not weakening, she beat on. A bleak and dark constant in Artemis's mind exactly as terrible and just as strong as she had been all those years ago before Artemis lay down in her house to rest. As she had been before Artemis went into the fire forges of the gods themselves.

So in the end Artemis the Friendly found the strength to sit up and rub her eyes: she would not simply lie there just waiting until The Terrible became all that she was and all that she would ever be. She was not fresh or relieved by her long rest: but only even more exhausted. And the many years of empty nothing had only deepened the haunted bags under her eyes: her lips, fingernails and eyes were now even more blue.

But she was up and on her feet again, and she managed to get to the kitchen and get herself a cup of tea and a biscuit. And then, for the first time in centuries, she did feel a little better. She was sitting there, gathering herself, when the excited chirping of a squirrel drew her eyes. Her face lit up as she saw a red and a grey squirrel, chirping and running round and round her feet. They were actually shaking with excitement: rejoicing with all their hearts that their goddess had returned. Laughing Artemis picked them up and walked back towards the entrance to her tree house. "Come on." she said gently, "You should be nut gathering and preparing for winter:

not running around trying to play with me!'' She stepped out of her house for the first time in a very long while indeed, and for a moment there was an utter stillness in all the forests and wild places of the earth: as the chaste maiden of the moon stepped out once more into the sun's light, and all the animals of the world held their breath. Then the crash of birdsong: and all the other sounds of nature: under the midday sun was deafening, as all throughout the world every animal called out in joy to celebrate their goddess's return.

And for the first time since Orion's death many, many years ago: Artemis smiled. For just a few moments all the colours of the rainbow once more lit up the dead flesh of her cheeks. She felt new strength flow into her for the first time in a very long time: and she even remembered in that moment what it was like to feel glad. When she returned to inside her house she even felt well enough to make a start on reading her letters. She was still coming uncertainly back to activity and the flow of life after so long a period of inactivity, but she did notice straightaway that the paper of her letters was appalling quality, thin and faded. She wondered angrily why when she was going through her crisis her brother couldn't even be bothered to write to her on nice quality paper: she knew he had plenty.

Artemis was a bright girl in many ways but she'd never been one for reading old documents very closely. It's hardly her fault if she didn't realise that the paper the messages had been written on was actually excellent quality: it was just old. Really old.

Even ancient.

Chapter 28

There was a crash of smoke and soot as a little fairy crashed out of a very crooked chimney. Black dust and fumes went everywhere. With a great coughing and spluttering the young man at the writing desk sat up with a start.

"By all the great scotterings and confusings," he began, "what a right mess of a spluttering and wood smoke this is." He whirled a wand, not that he or any other wizard needed wands but he thought that they looked cool. Mostly this just showed that, while the wizard knew the names of the most complicated things in many of the most complex languages that have ever been written, he had absolutely no understanding of what the word cool could possibly mean. Not in any of them.

He was a young man, in his mid-thirties with a pointed hat decorated with pictures of the stars and the moon. He went to a nearby window, opened it, and waved his wand with a great energetic flourish. His magic; not the wand waving: the wizard was just doing that for fun and to put on a bit of a show: raised a wind from the mild and gentle whisper of a draft moving in the air: which then blew the cloud of wood dust and smoke out of the window. It was conceptually mostly a sound plan, the window letting in the draft was open and opened only onto a lawn so overgrown with grass and bushes and magical and strange plants that a good light splattering of the remnants from the fire was hardly here or there.

Of course the man was himself standing between the cloud of ash and the window. Some of it got past him and blew outside but the rest got hopelessly tangled in his hair and beard. It all resulted in a great deal of noise and confusion and banging around, while a poor confused little fairy stood up and dusted herself down. She would have come to help him out but she had a strong feeling that would only make matters worse.

After a while the wizard managed to get himself sorted. He hadn't managed to get rid of the wood dust he'd accidentally blown onto himself, he'd managed to get it absolutely everywhere in fact. But he had managed to level it out nicely, so that all his beard was now equally smudged black everywhere, and his brown robe now had a roughly even coating of ash.

He gave a great sigh, and then settled back at his writing desk. He was reading a great old book with a picture of one, no two beautiful women on the cover: inside a sphere with a line down the middle. The inside of one half was every colour imaginable: the other half was pure white. Artemis smiled as she recognised a picture of herself. Then her face grew bleak as she recognised the picture of The Terrible: the person who in all this world she hated the most.

There was a long pause, in which the man settled back into reading with a contented sigh, and the little fairy princess stood around unsure what to do. She looked around uncertainly, and waited politely for as long as she possibly could. She was proud of being a very well brought up young girl after all. She had climbed down through the most overgrown chimney, which somehow managed to have both a bats' nest and a birds' nest inside it at the same time: and lots and lots of spiders and cobwebs: to get into the most disorganised study room she could possible imagine. Books and models and even paintings were everywhere. She loved it though: it looked to her a very learned room indeed. She itched to go over to all those impressive looking hardbacks with beautiful pictures and the rich smell she always associated with books. It was moments like this that Artemis wished she could, sometimes anyway, be a bit more of a studious sort of girl. She would love to know what all these books could teach, but she knew that if she started reading them that after a short while her head would just hurt with all the long words and she wouldn't understand them at all. After a while she'd just be flicking through the book hopefully, looking for pretty pictures. Even when reading her letters she got fed up if they went on for too long: and they were never more than two or three pages!

"Hello?" said Artemis after a while, when it seemed like the young man behind the desk was just going to ignore her and keep on reading. He looked up at her and smiled, and waved vaguely. "Hello." he said friendly, not really listening, and then just went back to reading: as though no one had ever said anything at all.

Artemis looked around uncertainly. "I'm looking for Merlin." She said after a while, "I was told that he lives here. He wrote me some lovely letters and sent them to my tree house: my brother asked him to get in touch with me."

"I'm Merlin." said the young man. "So well done you've found me! And whoever told you that I lived here was right." He went back to reading.

There was an awkward silence. Then finally Artemis asked timidly, trying to be on her best behaviour and be very polite. "Could I have a cup of tea please? Lots of milk and two lovely sugars?"

Merlin looked at her very confused. "Why of course you can have a cup of tea! Who on earth is saying that you can't have a cup of tea?" He pointed over his shoulder. "The kitchen used to be that way, I think. I might have moved it." He frowned suddenly. "Is the milk still kept in the kitchen?" he wondered outloud. "I have a feeling I might have moved it but it didn't work out very well on the roof, kept falling off all the time. That wasn't a problem to start with but then it did start to smell really terrible after a while. No I'm sure I put the milk back in the kitchen. Anyway if you have a good rummage around I'm sure you'll find something." He pointed vaguely into the depths of a house that seemed even more confused than the disorganised chaos all around where he was currently sitting.

Artemis stood on tip toe and peered nervously into the depths of the house. She couldn't see anything that looked even remotely helpful. She had horrible visions of searching hopelessly for hours and not finding the milk until it had been sour for days. "Maybe you could make me a cup of tea Merlin?" she ventured finally. "I have come a long way to see you, all the way up from Greece to Iceland you know, and you did invite me especially. And I came up straight away even though compared to Greece, even in winter, Iceland is very, very cold!"

Merlin put his book down with a start. "Why of course I can make you a cup of tea! Why didn't you ask earlier? You poor thing! You should have asked me to make you a drink the moment you got here after a journey like that. And you must be so cold after Greece's hot weather as well! I'll see if I can dig you out a nice thick coat from somewhere. Now let's go and both get something to drink." He headed off confidently into the depths of the house and Artemeis flew cautiously after him just above the floor, hovering gently where she could just see over his shoulder. After about five minutes of Merlin rummaging around opening cupboards and shuffling aside piles of books that cluttered every work surface Artemis asked cautiously. "Merlin do you know where the milk and water are?"

Merlin looked at her sceptically. "Of course I know where the milk and water are my dear. I always know where everything is. All these people who bang on about me needing to be a bit more neat and tidy just don't understand my brilliance. I know where everything is, all the time."

Artemis looked at him, trying not to look sceptical and not succeeding very well. "Err good?" she questioned tentatively.

"Yes." said Merlin triumphantly. "It's quite simple, everything is always in the last place that you look." It was lucky that right then he didn't notice the look on Artemis's crestfallen face, it was really quite something. "And they do bang on so." He went on quite happily, utterly oblivious. "Oh Merlin you completed your four year thesis in one year and it was the most brilliant trainee thesis that has ever been done, but it would have been better if you hadn't spent the last three years of it desperately trying to find where you'd put your manuscript." He paused for a second. "It would have helped if I hadn't somehow left it in the middle of a bunch of books on cooking and how to make myself lunch. They are the only books that truly terrify me and that I don't understand." He shuddered terribly, "No I'm never going to go near any books like that!!!"

Fifteen or so minutes later they were sat back around Merlin's desk, drinking tea. Artemis had ended up making it, which meant that it was actually quite good.

After a while Merlin said sadly. "You seem a lovely little fairy and while I'm very certain I didn't invite you I would love you to stay to tea. Unfortunately it will have to be tomorrow, if you're free. I have a very important visitor tonight."

"Oh?" said Artemis, past the point of being surprised by anything. "Who is this important visitor?"

Merlin leaned in and whispered in her ear conspiratorially. "A very special person indeed. It's quite strange actually. I got a letter right out of the blue from her a couple of days ago and of course I invited her up here straight away. It is a good thing that wherever my magical house moves to, it always keeps the same address isn't it? Otherwise her first letter would never have arrived. You know she actually thought I lived in Greece next to Apollo's Temple! Do you know, this person I've invited to tea, she is actually…A GODDESS!!!"

Artemis giggled. "One called Artemis?" she laughed gently. Merlin looked at her in surprise. "How did you know? It's supposed to be a secret! I'm sure I didn't tell anyone: not even my wife!"

He turned and for a moment both their gazes fell upon a picture on his desk, a framed portrait of a beautiful young woman with blond hair, and around her neck a great green diamond. "The Lady of the Lake," murmured Merlin, "though she likes me to call her by her other name, her real name, Katrina. She is the love of my life. We've just had a child together you know. Lovely little girl, the most beautiful in all the world. She's called… well that's not that important is it? I couldn't be happier with my two girls, even if that new pretty young student Nimue keeps trying it on with me. It's disgusting, the way she keeps throwing herself at a man who is in love with someone else!" For a moment a darkness fell over his brows, and the normally scatty and dizzy features of brilliance were replaced by that of a young man who was genuinely deeply troubled. Then he shook his head, and his brows cleared and the storm was passed. "But I'm not here tonight to talk about my troubles am I?" he said gently. "Anyway I was just explaining that you are a lovely little fairy girl and I would love to have you round to tea tomorrow. But sadly you are going to have to have tea with someone else today because I'm having a top secret meeting with Artemis tonight!"

He leaned forward and told her confidentially. "You know I'm starting to get a little bit worried about her. Everything I've ever read says she's really punctual and early, but she's getting quite late now. She was due round about the same time that you fell out of the fireplace."

"Merlin." said the fairy princess, very clearly and slowly as though talking to a complete idiot: which given the circumstances was not entirely inappropriate, brilliant though the wizard was. "I am Artemis!"

Merlin looked at her in surprise, and a frown wrinkled his brow while he regarded her critically. "No I don't think so." he said sadly, after a long pause. "Her brother Apollo's writings are very clear, by the gods he goes on so much about it. Sometimes it feels like he simply won't stop going on at such great lengths about what a prim and proper girl Artemis is. She wouldn't go crawling through any chimneys let me tell you! Far too courteous a girl for any of that kind of nonsense you know. She would knock politely at the front door and wait for me to answer. Just like a prim and proper and well brought up young girl."

"I did go up to your front door!" said Artemis, in what was close to becoming a shriek of pure frustration. "Once it took me half an hour to get though that jungle of a forest that is growing in your front garden."

Merlin looked at her curiously. "Then why on earth didn't you knock at the door?"

"I did!" replied Artemis, practically yelling now. "I picked up that great big knocker on the front door and it bit me!" She pointed her hand indignantly at Merlin, where, even with her immortal healing powers, you could still see the blood on her knuckles. "It bit me!"

"Ah," said Merlin wisely, tapping his beard. "That's a special little spell of mine that I set specially. It's to scare off burglars."

The sound of pure frustration that exploded from Artemis's throat sounded like a cross between an express train coming out of a tunnel and a cat shredding new furniture. "Merlin!" she yelled, "Burglars are not going to knock on the front door are they?!"

"Oh," said Merlin, suddenly looking rather crestfallen. "I never thought of that did I? Seems a bit obvious now that you point it out."

Artemis took a deep breath and made herself start to calm down. "So I looked for a window to fly in but they were all locked and shut so the only thing left was to crawl in through your chimney. You know it was actually quite nice in there." She reflected, thinking of the bats and the birds and the spiders. "Lots of lovely animals for me to meet and talk to."

She turned to smile at Merlin, and stopped speechless. It was easy to forget, when you saw the scatiness and the absentmindedness, the raw power and knowledge of brown magic that his absence from the practical nature of everyday life let him achieve. He turned eyes on her that were now sharp and focused, and in whose depths shone knowledge that had never been seen in any of the ages of this world. The brown magic rose around him, and everything around him shone with life and strength, almost unbearably bright and intense, as the brown reinforced all the power of existence in its current form.

Every bond of life and atom in the room around them almost glowed with power.

"Hello Artemis." He said softly, "Do you know what time it is? Or even why you are really here?"

"My brother Apollo wrote to me and told me to come and see you to get help with…" Artemis began, but the brown wizard was already shaking his head sadly. "The man, that Merlin, that your brother wanted you so desperately to meet is long dead little fairy princess. Dead a thousand years and more: since the foul creature Nimue consumed his flesh and heart. I am not the next Merlin after him, nor even the one after that. It has been over one thousand and four hundred years since you lay down to sleep in your tree. You have woken into a new age. The age of the gods and paganism has fallen, the age of The," and here Merlin's mouth twisted in dark distaste, "One True God has come."

Artemis started, her face suddenly pale and shocked. For a moment it wasn't just her eyes, lips and fingernails; for a moment the veins all throughout her body showed dead and blue. "I thought when I was flying here from Greece that all our colourful temples seemed to have gone," she replied uncertainly, "and there seemed to be all these dull horrible buildings of grey stone that had replaced them everywhere…"

"Churches." said Merlin mildly.

"But I didn't really think much about it." Said Artemis shaken. "I just assumed that a new pagan cult was currently in vogue that liked a new type of building and…"

Merlin spoke softly. "Artemis do you know the story of Pandora's box?"

Artemis laughed, almost a giggle. "Of course Merlin. Every pagan does. How a box was opened which let out all the darkness and horror of evil into the world. But at the very bottom of it all, when all the powers of hate and madness had been let loose into the world, there came out the smallest butterfly: floating on tiny, almost transparent, wings. A butterfly that was in some ways the most powerful magic unleashed that day: stronger than all the forces of darkness. And that butterfly's name was hope.''

"Yes," said Merlin gently, "very good, very good. Now you see Artemis the story I am going to tell you, the true story of what happened while you lay dead to the world in the heart of your tree is like the story of Pandora's Box. It is horror after horror, but at the end there is light.''

He turned a sharp eye on her. "But before I tell you this story Artemis I must know that the horror of it will not break your spirit, and your will to live. For if Artemis the Friendly should fall and die now, then truly all hope is lost forever for us all. And I saw how blue death spread through your veins when I first spoke just now of the fall of the pagan age. Do you need space and time for a moment, or are you ready to begin our dark and bleak story of horror whose end for both gods and men so far contains little in it but the bitterest grief?''

Artemis put her back up straight and held her head up high and met Merlin's eyes proudly. "I'm a tough little fighter you know! I can stick with any story at all, so long as there's a happy ending to look forward to at the very end!" She flushed for a moment, all the colours of the rainbow: not the blue of death. "Sometimes when I'm reading a book and it gets too sad and tense I skip to the end to make sure it all ends up nice and happy. And if it doesn't I just put the book away and lock it in a cupboard!''

"There is a happy ending, or at least the possibility of one." said Merlin at last. "And that I hope will be enough for your heart and life to endure.

You fell "asleep" in what is now called the late fifth century BC, or five centuries before Christ came to give the date its full name. Even the times before he existed are nowadays given the name of their wretched, jealous god. For many years after you withdrew from the world it seemed on the surface as though all was going well: and that the pagan age would last forever. A great new pagan empire arose, the Empire of Rome. It was the greatest pagan state and institution the world had, and indeed has, ever seen and yet an emptiness lay at its heart.

For it should have been Greece that rose to bring in the greatest empire of the pagan age, but rather than uniting the great Greek city states of Sparta and Athens instead destroyed one another in perpetual warfare. And so instead of their twin institutions of a democratically elected parliament and a divinely anointed monarchy combining into the foundations of a new world both states, each exhausted and both refusing to compromise, were instead swept away by new and unforeseen rivals. And although the last of these new predators, Rome itself, borrowed the religion of Ancient Greece it is questionable that Rome ever put the true values of Greece at its heart: blinded as it was by its rush of sudden success and earthly power.

Then Caesar Augustus, the first true divine emperor of the whole Roman Empire, tried to build the world of civilisation not according to the true pagan principles of freedom of thought and individuality of belief, but to fix it shut instead with endless laws and decrees externally regulating how man should live. And the empire which he had founded soon did something that was an abomination by all moral and legal standards, both of that time and any other: and crucified an innocent man: Jesus Christ: the son of God. One of many innocents whose life the state's new approach now took, but never before or since has any state sanctioned murder had such drastic consequences.

It took nearly three hundred years until the ultimate blasphemy, until a Christian sat on the Roman Empire's throne: founded by the glory of the pagan gods themselves. But civilisation was already weak by that time, corrupted and undermined by a host of emperors who had tried to rule as though they were gods themselves, not merely divine servants whose role was simply to represent the will of the gods on earth. Mostly even those emperors who called themselves pagan did no better than the Christian usurpers after them: and so the whole strength of the empire was slowly undermined as all these would be tyrants wasted its lives and energy in incessant civil war. None of the great generals prepared to possibly concede that any of their rivals also had a right to individual thoughts and deeds.

Such corruption could not endure of course, for it went against the will of the gods of the wild and all the natural order of life. The barbarians of The Allfather swept through the rotting empire, breaking apart its rotten edifice in some of the most savage slaughter that the world has ever seen. But though the Roman Empire died in Attila the Hun's fires, though the corrupt state and empire fell in just punishment for its blasphemy in turning from the true gods, no amount of divine pagan fury could make up for the fall of civilised pagan gods: for the fall of half the pantheons of pagan time. Though the rotten edifice of Rome fell, and I sorrow greatly at the innocents who died, but for the institutions themselves none could but rejoice in the end at their fall, the fundamental corruption at the heart of paganism lived on, the weakness that had led Christ to rise in the first place. The gods of civilisation should have gathered in the fall of Rome and rebuilt the world anew in their image, building a new world that would have buried the religion of the dead carpenter forever. But they did not, and wave and wave of pagan invaders, though victorious in battle, time after time adopted the religion of their defeated peoples: the worship of one dead man.

For the gods of the barbarian, powerful though they are, are only half the story. They cannot stand alone, any more than the mind can live without the body. And the sickness at the core of the civilised pagan religion lingered on, meaning the whole pagan system was broken and could not function as it must. The health of one side could not compensate for the weakness of the whole. And as rebuilt civilisation spread from the ruins of Rome, built on the fire of the barbarian gods, it was nevertheless always Christian civilisation. And, as in time the barbarians gradually became civilised in this new day, the power of The Allfather faded too: not from any mystery of internal decline: simply because he was never meant or desired to be a god in the civilised lands. And Christianity demands that civilisation be spread everywhere, unlike Rome, which even at the height of its power, knew its natural limits.

We are now in the year 999 AD, and tomorrow Iceland will turn from pagan to Christian: and so the last wave of pagan warriors burning down the corruption of Christian civilisation will end. The Vikings, the last stand of The Allfather, will be done. Your family of the civilised gods are gone Artemis, gone near six hundred years and the isolated remnants of the barbarian gods shall soon fade. Soon you will be the only one left Artemis, the only pagan god that has not either become powerless or accepted their fate in the Christianised world of the one true God and chosen to exist as a demon, to be worshipped only as creature of pure evil. For in this new age all other sources of magic but Christ are evil and come from the devil, and no magical power but that of the Son of God can ever be good. But you, being both living dead and inactive, slipped through the cracks in the spread of Christianity's fingers. You have come back at the dawn of a dark age, the age of intolerance and the age of the one true religion. The godless age, and the age of man. For in time even the god part will begin to be forgotten in this new age, and people will simply worship their own opinions and believe that different thoughts and opinions are not vital and needed, but inherently corrupted and wrong. That what you yourself believe is the only one right path for everyone. This age will last a thousand years of man, and between two and three decades more." He raised an eyebrow. "Artemis the Terrible will love this age very much: should you ever lose your will to live and finally succumb to death."

"My family and friends," whispered Artemis the Friendly "are they…"

"Not dead." Said Merlin softly, "Not even the power of Christ can change the nature of the immortals." Artemis let out a long breath that she did not know that she had been holding. "But all powerless for so long as this age should last." Merlin continued. "Of all the gods who oppose the new divine regime soon only, apart from you: hidden by the fact that you're mostly dead: The Allfather will still stand against the new way of being. He has the power of the grey, he has always been good at hiding in the shadows. And he is the god of outlaws as much as the god of kings. He will not prosper in this age, but he will not struggle either. He will simply endure.

In the final year of this new Christian age The Allfather shall leave to, after choosing one final grey wizard to be the best chance to bring in the new pagan age. An age with the potential to build a new world based on the strength of the true gods, an age with the potential to fulfil all the first pagan age had a chance to do, and yet in the end failed so badly to achieve. Whether that wizard succeeds or fails shall determine whether the age of gods and magic shall return in just over a thousand years, or whether this new age of Christ shall last forever."

Merlin turned and looked at Artemis, who was pale and showing more dead blue veins and flesh then he liked. "I know it is hard for you." He said gently, "but you have to hold on Artemis. You have to be strong for us all."

"Why?" asked Artemis softly, despairingly. "Why do I even matter in any of this? We have The Allfather and the wizard he will choose, what's the point of having me around too? The Allfather is a far more powerful god than I could ever be, even if I wasn't dying and sick."

"Because," said Merlin quietly, "the force that will drive that champion, the force that will give him the strength to fight with everything he is and has to restore paganism: for the idea that magic is the most powerful and good force for change that there is and ever will be in this world: and that it springs not from one externally written book, forever written and fixed down, but is born new and constantly in the heart of every living thing. The force that will drive him to plunge the whole world into religious war to re-establish this ideal, the force that will drive him to recreate a world where the gods can be seen once more in every grove and stream, where the colour of temples, not the grey of churches, rules the landscape, that force will be his love for you. His feelings for you will be the colour that drives all his heart and deeds. For are you not, divine virgin princess of the gods, the deepest and most fundamental of all man's desires and dreams?"

Artemis blushed. "Am I?" she said nervously. "I think most men wouldn't want a woman who was half dead. Or who might get angry and castrate them and nail them to the wall while they bleed to death. And I think they might quite want to be able to have sex and children too."

Merlin laid his hand on her arm, gently. "Artemis most of the paths of your future are dark beyond any words that I have to tell. But there is a route that leads you to a place brighter than all the colours of the rainbow that have ever bloomed in your cheeks. A place with a future as happy as a girl as sweet as you truly deserves." There was a pause for a moment, a stillness while both of them collected their thoughts. Then Merlin spoke on, in a voice that was as soft as the gentle wind, but as hard and unyielding as steel.

"I know why you tried to purify yourself with fire Artemis," he said, "and I know that not star fire itself, nor even Hephaestus's hammer which forged the thunderbolts themselves could hurt HER. Not even at the heart of the power of the pagan age. I know why you lay in despair, seeing HER as a parasite, and hoping that if you did nothing she would starve from having nothing to feed on: starve and die. And I know you would have lain on your bed in that tree unmoving though it was a thousand, or a thousand thousand years. Though all the ages of the sun had been and past and a thousand civilisations had aged and died. Though a thousand new worlds had bloomed and then uncounted millennium later been buried in death still you would have waited in silence: alone: had you but felt the slightest weakening of The Terrible's power. But you rose because you felt the same as you did after you had been burned and broken, that not all your efforts had led to even the beginnings of what could be a fatal wound in the terror that haunted you. And so, with no answer in your mind but unwilling to just lie down, to give up and to die, you forced yourself back up into the world of the waking: fighting on even with so little hope."

Artemis's hands tightened on her empty cup. "Is there hope Merlin? You say there is a route to a brighter future for me: but I cannot see it. Of course I will fight on to

387

bring back my friends and family but even if a new pagan age should come again, even if I should give my heart to the man of my dreams and be loved back in return how can there be any end to the darkness which haunts me? I would love to get my family and friends back, but how will a new pagan age bring any more of an answer to The Terrible's power? She thrived even in the middle of the first pagan age before all the other gods lost all their power. Is there anything I can do to kill her Merlin: to kill her the way I died? I would do anything to be rid her: anything at all. I will do anything: I will walk all the reaches of heaven and earth, face any monster, endure any…''

Merlin's voice was cold, hard and flat as iron. ''Imagine a mountain made of steel, in a desert without wind or rain. Once every ten years a bird flies to its peak and drops a single drop of raw rainwater on its summit. No other force ever touches that mountain. When enough time has passed that the mountain itself has been washed away to nothing, know that the first second of eternity has not even begun.

So as is this, so is the vampire within you. She is as eternal as time, deathless as Zeus and Odin. Even if all you wish comes to pass, even if the war for the new age is won and your heart blooms with love, the winged vampire of death will always be a constant presence inside your mind and heart.''

The last light of hope in a little fairy's eyes glittered one last time, then faded and died. Blue veins showed though dying skin as she faded towards true death.

''BUT'', said Merlin, in that last moment before Artemis abandoned all her hope and simply lay down and died: so that at least her pain would be over: at least in death she would find some kind of peace. ''Know that one of my older selves, at your brother's request, went down deep to the deepest root of the holiest oracles. Far beneath the surface of the world I drank from the untouched water of the mountain spring that never touches the sunlit lands. I studied the writing carved in divine blood on the walls on the deepest caverns of the gods, where their statues stare from the cold rock carved into the very fabric of the earth, a light in their eyes that comes from no mortal flame, where the offerings of moral sacrifice pile at their feet uncounted. And they spoke of you."

Artemis looked up through eyes filled with tears. "What did they say?" she cried.

"They said take a message to the goddess, and speak not in riddles or dreams or confusion that she does not understand. Let her know but this. The pagan age will fall, and a new god shall come among men. But in time so the wheel will turn and a grey wizard will come, greater than any that were before: greater even than he that set all things in motion in the predawn of history, when the first beginnings of what would later be seen as the first seeds of the civilisations of this world began.

This new grey wizard will raise the pagan standard: and in a world ruled by the cross and secularism he will give all he has and is to restore the old gods, to restore the true religion. He will fight to raise back the old world: that the new age be swept away as though it had never been. He shall come in the power of the grey and by these signs shall you know him. He shall stand against his older sister, and shall show her such undeserving mercy and love that her soul shall be set free from the darkness. And when she is redeemed he shall love her so much that for her sake, and to save her life, he shall sacrifice in such a way that the rest of his life he will bear the image and form of The Allfather: darkest of all pagan gods. And he Artemis, he who shall stand alone against the Mountain and all the power of the age of men; on him rests your sole chance of happiness, and your sole hope that your two warring sides shall one day know peace. For he shall know the true power of the grey, the power that is beyond even its strength to fade all things that are into nothing. For its true power is that it can turn evil into good, and that even the black of the darkest night, through the grey, can become the sunlight of the new dawn.

But know that if he should fail then the fairy side of you shall fall: fall into despair so deep and dark that you shall be nothing but the cold vampire, that cruel hunter and castrator of men, and that as long as eternity lasts your life shall be nothing but unending pain and horror.''

So spoke Merlin, so spoke the pagan prophet of the gods, in words of prophecy that rang like thunder in my ears. Then all the vison fell away in a great blaze of colour, but I did not find myself where I had expected; sat back in the treehouse with Artemis the Friendly where my visions into the past had begun.

Instead I sat in the study, in front of this Merlin from long ago. A small circle of disorganised existence, surrounded only by impenetrable darkness. A moment: taken out of time.

Chapter 29

There were many questions that I had in that moment. Questions about what this was, how it was possible. It was not a vision anymore: that was certain. But, in those seconds that I struggled to work out what was suddenly going on around me, I realised that the visions I had just seen had given me an answer that was worth more than every single physical possession in the world, more than all the new and as yet unlearned knowledge in the cosmos.

"You smile Edward?", questioned Merlin carefully. 'Yet you have just seen horror after unrelenting horror. Do your lips twitch at the thought of Artemis the Terrible castrating you? Do you find the thought that Artemis the Friendly is nothing more than a living corpse amusing? Or did hearing of the fall of the pagan age bring you joy?"

My reply was simple. That is because it was honest. "I am happy because I know now that Artemis the Friendly really loves me. I was terrified that she was just one half of a darkly functioning whole, wanting me only to touch her so that The Terrible would have a reason to rise up from out of her to destroy me. Now I know the two halves are opposed to each other: and that the love The Friendly bears me is real. Artemis's two personalities work against each other: not together. Though all else I saw was darkness, that ray of light alone was worth it.''

Merlin's eyes smiled.

I turned and looked around me. "This is strange." I said, my thoughts moving quickly. A lifetime of having to react quickly to survive had been good training for always keeping myself moving, coping with what was happening now and thinking about the long term later. The visions I had just seen would need days of reviewing and analysis to fully comprehend: all I could do at the moment was make the best decisions I could in an environment where I had to think fast.

"This is not time travel. No such magic can exist for if it did all other powers would be as nothing: but you are not the Merlin of today. You are the Merlin of the tenth century: The Merlin witnessing the final end of the pagan age. How is such a thing possible?''

Merlin laughed gently. "You are master of the grey magic: the power to fade out existence from this world. But I am master of the brown: the power of life: and the blue: the power of change. Does it surprise you that you do not understand the full mysteries of a power so different to your own?''

"Clever way of saying you don't want me to know how you did this." I thought with a silent smile. "Once this is done that only makes sure I will do whatever it takes to find out.''

"You get three questions," said Merlin, "and what you ask will determine whether you gain the knowledge you need to have a chance.''

"And whether Artemis has a chance." I thought grimly.

I looked at Merlin for a long time and said nothing, watching him carefully. He simply sat watching me, a gentle smile on his face, a mischievous twinkle dancing in his eyes. A twinkle which never changed.

"So that's what Merlin had done!" I realised suddenly. I wasn't talking to a living breathing person here, it was like interacting with the help function on a computer. Merlin had poured his power and strength into a spell with a great deal of his knowledge and programmed it to respond in certain ways, but it was still essentially just a magical version of a robot or a computer, or an interactive database of information. The three questions must be the limit the construct could take before whatever its magical equivalent of batteries were exhausted.

I thought a lot about what I had seen. I needed to make sure that I asked the right questions. So no wasting resources on things I already knew like, "Is it possible to get rid of Artemis the Terrible?" I already knew the answer to that question, much as I disliked it.

I thought for a long time. If Artemis the Terrible could not be removed maybe she could be controlled in some way, maybe if Artemis the Friendly could compete with her on equal terms instead of when she was half dead then somehow the winged vampire could be made harmlessish…

But that was not the question I asked. I was a worshipper of The Allfather, so I asked the question whose answer I dreaded the most.

"Is there any power in the heavens and earth that can stop Artemis the Friendly from dying the true death?" I asked briefly.

"No," said Merlin quietly, "and she will die very soon."

The pain was so intense that I could barely breathe.

"Okay." I breathed at last. That answer, while dark, was exactly what I had expected.

Then I asked my second question, the one that if it went wrong I saw no end to the darkness.

"If The Friendly dies is there any power in the heavens and earth that could bring her back to life? Full life: as a goddess reborn in all her life and strength."

There was a long pause, as the twinkling in Merlin's eye flashed on and off and the magical computer of his knowledge worked out the complicated answer in the darkness. The pain in my chest was unbearable.

"Yes." Merlin finally said. "Artemis the Friendly is an immortal like all the gods. She can't really die at all. What will happen to her I explained with my mountain of steel and yearly rainwater analogy. The fundamental thought processes that make up The Friendly will always exist, buried deep inside Artemis. It's just that she will have no will or energy to bring that side of herself back, not though all eternity should pass. There is only one way she could be given a reason strong enough to call her back from death, strong enough for her to reignite her war with The Terrible, but this time on equal terms. And walking that way will be a trial that may be beyond even your strength Edward: certainly to endure it would take you to the very limits of dark enlightenment itself. But there are two things you must know.

First the rebirth of The Friendly in the fullness of her power would be the trigger for the most terrible war imaginable. For it would pit all the power of the one true God, all the power of Christianity and secularism, against all the power of paganism. And it would not be a war like the previous ones, which were terrible enough to reduce most of Europe to ash both under Attila the Hun and under the Vikings. This would be a war fought between a civilisation now based on all the power of the most popular religion in all the world, and the powers of both the barbarian and the civilised pagan gods. It would be a war unlike any other that has ever been seen, for last time the gods of the barbarians fought against the Christians alone. For the rebirth of The Friendly would

394

be the undoubted demonstration that the power of magic does not have to be Christian to be good, in a way the murky grey power of The Allfather alone could never be. And that demonstration would unleash both all the powers of paganism, as all the true gods began to return, and all the powers of Christianity. The true gods to restore the old order of things, the Christians to crush Artemis the Friendly back down into death and so end forever this last rebellion against their rule. The Christian faith could never allow a reborn Artemis the Friendly to live, for as long as she breathed in the fullness of life it would make a mockery of all the exclusive claims of their jealous religion that there is only one god that is good: and his name is Christ. The price of Artemis the Friendly's rebirth would be an ocean of blood: rivers of pain."

I was in love, and this world had done nothing for me. So far I couldn't have cared less.

"The second thing you should know is this. In this age of the world Artemis the Terrible will not permit anyone, not you or anyone else, to ever father a child on the virgin of the gods." I waited expectantly for that second part to go somewhere interesting. It's not like Merlin had just said anything remotely surprising as he concluded his second answer.

I guessed this age of Christ would last until Artemis the Friendly was resurrected from the dead. With Artemis the Friendly either dying or dead the fact that Artemis the Terrible would be able to stop her from having a child was no more news than that the sun would rise tomorrow. There was a whole temple of marble on an island of gold dedicated to the fact that Artemis the Terrible was really not interested in having children. So the fact that Merlin had highlighted something so obvious was in itself very interesting: but not something that I currently had any ideas about or any time to consider further.

I had but one question left. I thought about it for a long time. To many men my next question would have seemed strange: but already a clear path of what I was must do was beginning to form before my eyes.

"What would be the quickest and most effective way to kill Artemis the Friendly?" I asked brutally. "Even after all these years her spirit is steel and the strength of her soul is still strong."

The twinkle in Merlin's eye fluttered and started: and then began blinking on and off. For a moment I was terrified my magical computer was going to crash: it was clear that Merlin had never expected to be asked anything remotely like this question. But finally, though smoke was coming from out of Merlin's eyes and the edges of his robe and beard were on fire, the answer came.

"Tell her the truth of what happened to her so long ago: the time when she died. The horror of what The Terrible remembers, and The Friendly does not." Then my questions and answers were done: and only silence remained.

The next moment the colours of the room were fading and bleaching as the brown and blue magic of Merlin that had sustained them washed away. Colour, life and light faded from the room: then even the structure of the atoms themselves and the whole magical room and the construct of Merlin dissolved away into the darkness: almost as though they had never been.

And the next moment I was back in the treehouse with the fairy princess that I loved. Her hand was still on my shoulder, I was still in her bed: her fear was still in her eyes.

I smiled at her, and said softly. "Before you ask yes I do still love you. Now more than ever. You are the most amazing girl I have ever met. And I will do whatever it takes to ensure that I get to spend the rest of my life with you."

Artemis started crying.

"Hey," I said gently, "Artemis could you stop using your energy to keep your body looking alive for a moment. It's just there's something I want to do, and something I want to show you."

Artemis stared at me in shock. "But I like looking pretty." She said horrified. "I don't want anyone, least of all you, to see me like that. I'm rotting and I'm ugly and I smell foul."

"Please." I said. "Just trust me on this. We're going to need all the trust and love we can find for each other if we're going to get through this: and especially if we are somehow going to manage to come out of this as a couple: together."

Artemis looked at me for a moment, uncertain, then she sighed. "Okay." she said weakly. "But I don't get why you want me to do this. I'm just going to look horrible!"

And she let a lot of her power go.

The first thing that hit me was how she smelt. It was like yoghurt and milk that had been left in the heat of the sun for weeks, and then smeared up inside your nose and onto the roof of your mouth so that you could taste it on the back of your throat and feel it writhing all across your teeth and tongue. Artemis the Friendly had been dead for a very, very long time.

The next thing that hit me was her mostly empty eye sockets, where just a little goo of what had once been eyeballs remained: wriggling with fat worms who had feasted well upon her soft white tissue. Her fingers were blue and so swollen with rot that they looked obese. For a moment I almost thought she was pregnant, her gut was so fat and extended with all the wriggling maggots working their hungry way inside her. But it was just the decay of death that made her so bloated everywhere.

I would have taken a deep breath, but that would have only made me feel more sick as I drank in her rotting foulness. But I did find the strength to take the woman I loved fully into my arms.

"The Terrible will never let me hold you while you are warm." I said, trying not to breathe the suddenly rotten air around us, or feel the ways the maggots and worms writhed under Artemis's dead skin. "The arousal that would rise in me if I were to hold you like this while your body is more alive would awaken The Terrible at once. But like this, when all attraction is literally dead, I can hold you. I can have you in my arms. I can show you love, even if not lust."

I reached out a finger and wiped a tear of rotting black blood from below the sorry remains of one of Artemis's eyes. I reached out and placed it on the tip of my tongue.

"No," said Artemis frantically, "you'll poison yourself and…"

But though the taste was vile I had all the power of the grey. I channelled it into the rotting blood, until it bloomed once more fresh and red: and alive. I reached out and placed the precious blood drop gently on the third finger of her left hand: from where the veins led directly to the heart: the same place that an engagement ring would go on. The red tear rested delicately in the exact centre of the tip of her finger, where its bright living crimson blazed in defiance against the rotting features of her bloated corpse.

"Do you know why you now have hope?" I said softly, "Do you know why the grey can save you Artemis?"

The dead girl shook her head slowly, though she held up her hand to stare at the bright drop of red blood in utter astonishment: carefully as though she was holding a small living animal and was terrified that she might drop it: and the colours of the rainbow danced through her dead corpse as hope bloomed again inside her chest. She stared at the drop of her fresh divine blood in stunned disbelief: shaken beyond words to see new life come again from her long dead body.

"Because one of the greatest powers of the grey, of Odin Allfather, is necromancy." I said simply. "The power to raise the dead back to health and life."

Chapter 30

It was strange but the visions that Artemis had shown me of her life: the full horror unveiled: made things between us a thousand times easier, not more difficult. Before our relationship had been a confused fusion of love and lust: of desperately wanting to trust and touch, but not being able to do either. Now I trusted her as well as loved her. And now I knew that there was a path to her love, her arms and her bed, however long and hard it seemed, the feelings and attraction I had for her were more bearable. I could even touch her for comfort now, give her hugs and squeeze her hand. However much being with her and seeing her fanned the flames of desire under my skin: including the most sensitive parts of my skin of all: the moment we touched the dead coldness of her flesh brought back all the visions of the rotting corpse she was fighting hard not to become. And there is little better at killing all thoughts of arousal then the thought of dead, rotting flesh. And although things between us could not cross the line into physical intimacy: emotionally it felt like we were together now: as if we were a couple instead of two strangers tentatively flirting with each other and making moon eyes. Whether it was her coming with fresh bloody food for us to eat while I worked my way through the books in the restricted section of the library. Or whether, on the weekends where she made sure I had time to catch my breath and not work my way to exhaustion once more, she started to teach me how to hunt and shoot arrows, and made a great effort to make sure I spent some time out of doors: in her world. Sometimes we rolled down slopes, laughing as we tumbled down and the wind whistled through our hair. Let's face it, that was the only way either of us were going to get grass stains at the moment. And I saw what other men had died for just glimpsing accidentally: the goddess of virginity bathing naked in the water. We washed together in fast flowing, natural streams and pools that were perfectly clear. In the evenings I would explain what I had learned to her from my research, and she started to teach me to speak Ancient Greek, so we could talk together in the language she had grown up with as a child. And so, when we were together, we spoke a private language now understood almost only by each other. I called her αστέρι μου. In modern English that meant, "my star".

But though the light of my love for Artemis shone through my life, bringing me a type of happiness that I had never known, the bleak reality of my fight for my elder sister's and Merlin's life against Nimue remained. I had two months left of the three with which I had begun, and in that time I had to change the ending of a repeating story that seemed as old as time itself, a story which always ended with Merlin's death. Four more weeks passed, another month of my precious time slipping away even as I tried desperately to use it.

Four more weeks of pouring over dark works of lore and history and of Artemis lying in my bed each evening before the library closed: both of us naked but not daring to touch. Sometimes that was at her house, sometimes at mine. Four more weeks of trying not to think about the fact that my girlfriend, my star, was dying. And that

Merlin, who I was no closer to rescuing than before, was the only person I could think of who might be able to tell me what the magic was that would have the power to recall the woman I loved from the dead. I tried not to think about how at the heart of the pagan age even the great pagan prophet Orpheus hadn't been able to pull off bringing his wife back from the dead. If he, who had had the audacity to defy the power of Zeus himself at the height of his power, could not achieve it then how could I hope to achieve it now, so deep into the Christian age? It had been more than a thousand years since 999AD. A little over two decades since we passed that grim milestone: the millennium anniversary of the final end of the pagan age with the fall of Iceland.

But Artemis's visions had more than laid the foundation for my relationship with my new girlfriend. They had given me a vital glimpse into the pattern of Merlin's rise and fall. The first four weeks of my research before I had collapsed from exhaustion and overwork, while my knowledge and power had increased drastically, I had still felt like I was getting basically nowhere. But the harsh window into the past I had been shown had given me vital questions that needed answering: questions that could help me save Jessica and stop Nimue.

While all mortals were reborn again and again it was normally with no recollection or knowledge of their previous lives. And yet the more you looked throughout history the more you saw the repeating pattern of Merlin's life, over and over again he was reborn. And over and over the same Nimue, given immortality: or more accurately just immunity to death by aging: by the gods, consumed him alive. Why? Why was this cycle endlessly repeating itself? And why did the histories and legends keep on insisting that Merlin was trapped under rocks or sealed in magical prisons of air, when time and time again the cold fact of the historical record showed that Nimue simply killed him and devoured his power? I felt that the answer to this riddle of conflicting stories might well contain the clues to saving Merlin. And by saving him save also my elder sister and give me the knowledge to save the girl who now smiled at the centre of my heart. But nowhere in any of the tomes, even the most forbidden: written in human blood on parchments of sacrificial victims' skin: were there even the beginnings of any kind of real answer.

I was sat in the library late one afternoon. Vicky was playing with Danielle at my parents' house and I was taking the time I would have spent playing with my little sister to get in some extra reading. Not in the restricted section of course, not in the middle of the day, but there was plenty of what I needed to read that was in general circulation. Over the two months since Nimue had replaced Jessica great strain had been placed on mine and Vicky's relationships with Danielle and Merlin. Nimue had turned them against us with a thousand small words and phrases, a thousand emotional paper cuts. And their happiness deteriorated too as, without either Merlin or Danielle really knowing what was wrong: their minds still bound fast in Nimue's illusion: each of them struggled to make their relationship with what they thought was Jessica work. But it was a bleakly hopeless prospect and outlook for both of them: for the woman they both thought they loved was now nothing but a cunningly disguised parasite: whose soft phrases and words were all merely ultimately for her own benefit. Nimue could not offer Jessica' closest family a single real taste of my older sister's affection and love: which had from start to finish always been real. And on my hand the protection spell for Jessica burned less and less as time went on. I started to wake from nightmares screaming that the scar on my hand had faded to dust:

that the protection spell was finally fully broken as my elder sister was now dead.

But Vicky and Danielle's relationship still endured in this dark time, perhaps the foundation of it was too secure even for Nimue to break. Or perhaps it was just that leaving their friendship intact would simply make it easier for Nimue to eat me and Vicky later: when our time came.

As I worked my way through ancient and medieval history on that bright sunny afternoon, in the gentle calm before the dark storm that was gathering, I was thinking over what Artemis had said to me the previous evening. My girlfriend was starting to feel the stress now: after all she faced the darkest fate of us all if I should fail. The rest of us would merely die. She would suffer a very dark rebirth indeed.

"We're running out of time Edward." My αστέρι μου had said softly, laying her cold hand on my lower arm. For a moment all I had felt was the sudden desire to take her, there and then. To just lay her out on the base of my bed, the firm strength of my mattress pushing up her boobs and cunt, and to hades with all the consequences. It hadn't been helped by the fact that I knew there was a part of Artemis, a part she was also trying to repress, that wanted me to do exactly that. But the moment had passed. A few moments of desperate passionate pleasure were not worth letting the eagle-winged angel of death win.

Artemis's soft voice had spoken on, and I forced myself to focus on what she was saying: and not on how much I wanted to hear her soft voice gasping and moaning in pleasure as we both came together in uncontrolled sex and lust. Not how much I wanted her body thrusting both with and against mine until we both cried out together as we were racked helplessly by repeated orgasm.

404

"Maybe we just need to think about ways of getting you power: and fast." Artemis had said quietly. "I know it's not great and it's not what either of us want, but when you start running out of time sometimes you have to just cheat and take a shortcut. It's like if I went to your modern day schools. Apart from physical education and sports I think I'd muck around and gossip all the time, then just sleep with my boyfriend the night before the test so he'd give me his notes and explain them all to me. Then I'd do dead well on the test: maybe even better than him! You're trying to do your research all properly, which is ace and has made me dead impressed. But you can't find the answers you need right now. Maybe it's time to stop trying to work out what's happening with Merlin and just go for getting more and more magical power." She had drawn back from me so that there was a space between us. Normally when we lay together in the same bed you would have struggled to fit a hair's breadth of air between our two bodies: although we never allowed each other to touch.

Artemis had focused, and reached out into the centre of the moonlight we were both bathed in, her face wrapped in concentration. From the cold heart of the shining light she had drawn out a silver arrow shaft: its tip devastatingly sharp. A weapon forged out of the cold light of the moon itself. "If you became my champion you could use these arrows as a weapon Edward. And they are no common arrowheads." Artemis had said proudly, her voice lit up with animation. "They are forged from pure moonlight itself in virgin's blood. Sometimes from one of my high priestesses: the most deadly of all from mine. The slightest scratch is almost always death, for once these shafts draw blood the wounds they cause can never heal but will always bleed. In a matter of hours even the slightest of cuts on a little finger can lead to death by bleeding out. I am a dying god, but having my power with you while you fight would still be worth a great deal: just nowhere near as much as if I was healthy."

I looked at her and smiled sadly. "I'm sure they would be amazing Artemis but to be your champion Orion had to sacrifice monsters of great power to you. I'm guessing that to be your champion I'd have to do pretty much the same. So to get this extra power I would have to kill and sacrifice to you a monster nearly as powerful as Nimue. Something that would take almost as much time and energy: and almost as much risk: as just confronting Nimue directly right now. If I had more time Artemis it would be a great plan. But I don't even really have the time left for preparing for a direct confrontation with Nimue: let alone for preparing to fight another creature of great power as well."

Artemis's face had fallen and she had looked very flat. "We have so few options left Edward!" she had said desperately. "And we can't fuck this up: we have to win! It's the end for both of us if you fail here. If you have got any grey magic tricks left to pull out of the bag that would be awesome: and now would be the time to start using them!" She had squeezed my hand: to show me how much she cared about me: about all of this: and then she was gone. Leaving me to grasp a few hours of troubled sleep while she had hunted down monsters under the light of the moon. Whatever else happened, Artemis the Friendly was determined to be a helpful and a good goddess right until the end: whatever fate it was that awaited her.

There was a quick way of gaining power of course: there always had been. Not that it was one that would have ever been open to me. The easiest way for almost all wizards to gain power in this world was known to pretty much everyone: no need for in-depth research or hard individual work to walk the confused and often hidden path to the real truth of things. It was not a path which suited the strengths of grey wizards.

Far away, on the other side of the world, was a great desert: where the sun always shone. Beating down onto a wasteland empty of all life. Not the smallest cactus or the cruellest snake could live there, where the sun beat down, down always from the centre of the sky: always fixed at the exact height of midday. At the core of that expanding desert, which grew outward even as civilisation grew and flourished: death and order, marching together in their unbroken unity: was a tall mountain of black obsidian, whose peak rose so high that it disappeared into the reaches of the cloudless blue sky. The Mountain. Ascend to the dizzy heights of it's bleak stone peak and you would return with great power: with a ring of gold burned into your flesh. The higher you climbed before you returned, the greater the power. But the higher you climbed, the greater the risk. You came back in power and glory from the desert and The Mountain: or you did not come back at all.

But even if I had not been a grey wizard, there was no time left to walk the bleak path to The Mountain before Nimue planned to strike.

Artemis had shown me the power of her razor sharp arrows the previous evening. Now, on this deceptively gentle and sunny afternoon, I worked my way once more through Arthurian Legend: hoping desperately for any hint of a pattern or a key fragment of subtle knowledge that would help me unlock the secret of Merlin. But the seemingly endless array of text told me nothing that was really new.

A cawing outside the window roused me from dark thoughts: from the beginnings of despair. I looked up and saw two birds: two ravens circling outside the window. Ravens: birds of The Allfather. He had two I remembered, Huginn and Muninn. His dark winged messengers. He worried for both of them, but especially for Muninn. Concerned that they would struggle in their flights to gain knowledge for him.

The two ravens were behaving strangely, whirling round and round as though troubled. As their unusual behaviour distracted me I found myself playing with the idea that they were not just normal birds flying across the university, but were the actual messengers of The Allfather themselves, sent to give me a message. After all while he'd said he wasn't going to see me again until all the world was changed he'd never said anything about not sending me his pet birds in the meantime. But when I opened the window so that they could fly into the library if they chose the two ravens just ignored me. Instead they continued to circle aimlessly and with great difficulty, as though they were struggling badly to find something. There seemed to be something wrong with them.

Then far below them a figure walked out across the university paths, but with all power and focus gone from his gaze. He looked like a man in a deep unending sleep walk: a man walking listlessly towards an end of only horror. The two birds were excited by his presence. They careened wildly towards him, and circled him drunkenly overhead. He paid them no mind, no more care or attention than he paid to any of this surroundings: all of which seemed dead to him. But the two ravens flew above him urgently and desperately: as though they had suddenly found a treasure trove of the most priceless gold.

Then one of the birds turned and, with a great cry, started to fly away. But it did so in a crazy disjointed trajectory, weaving and wheeling all over the place, struggling desperately to follow a straight line. It looked either very drunk: or very seriously ill and confused. Above Merlin's head the second raven wasn't exactly a picture of straightforward reason and sanity. It stuck with following the wizard unlike its companion, but it also struggled to fly in a straight line: although its wavering was only erratic distortions from a straight line, not the strange completely distorted circles of its fellow bird: whose movement away from its original point was so laboured and slow that it was torturous just to watch. Although the second raven fluttered randomly from side to side I never had any real fear it would struggle so badly it would lose Merlin: while the first bird: now trying to fly away from him: would have to fight hard to reach even a close by destination.

If those were the messengers of The Allfather I thought amusedly, enjoying playing with idle possibilities after so many weeks of intense focused research, then it would be Huginn, the one who was less worried about by Odin, that was currently following Merlin, and Muninn, who greatly concerned The Allfather when he flew, that was currently struggling profoundly even to follow a straight line. And that would lead to the conclusion that…

And suddenly, like a flash of lightning, new knowledge that had not been there even half a moment before burst fully flowered into my mind: and I realised that The Allfather had sent me a message after all.

I seized the power of grey magic: and raced out of the library. Then I turned and was relieved, although not surprised bearing in mind how erratically it had been flying, to catch sight of the particularly struggling raven: of Muninn. I followed it, desperate not to lose the dark bird, even though its flightpath of incessant moving circles meant that was not terribly likely. Clad in the invisibility of grey power I followed the bird closely through fields and streams, through houses and gardens, even across roads where cars swept harmlessly through my intangible form and through woods where I frequently ran straight through the trees.

I walked from Chester for a good ten miles, though tension meant it felt like I had been walking for merely minutes, not for hours. Then the ground started to ascend as I found myself beginning to climb Prestham Hill, and the distance between me and the raven dropped away as I started to ascend upwards towards the sky. I climbed though the gentle trees and green woods that lined the lower slopes. Then I found myself half scrambling, half climbing, up the barren rock face. Up I went, over the steep gulleys and ridges of the rock face of the Old Man of Prestham: a name I now knew was more appropriate than I had ever dreamed. Upon the last ridge below the summit, where once I had sacrificed and shared meat with the divine huntress, in the days before just the sight of her had made my heart beat faster, I halted at last. It seemed this part of the journey was now at an end. The raven, Muninn, was before me, his beak pecking at the hard unyielding stone: giving me the clue to where the next part of my journey began. We were exactly between the eyes of the Old Man of Prestham. "I should have known," I thought distantly, "what I have been searching for for two months has been hidden right in front of me all the time."

The names of Odin's birds meant a great deal; wrapped in symbolism and dark lore. Huginn, who I did not doubt followed above the physical form of Merlin even as I stood here now, stood for thought: and where did the thought and consciousness of Merlin exist but in his physical body? But Muninn, Muninn who pecked at the rock face before me, he stood for memory. And what was it that Le Morte D'Arthur, the main reference point for the Arthurian myths in the modern world, had said? That Merlin was buried under a big rock. Not the most poetic of its phrases. But one that had turned out to be one of the most literally true. And I remembered Merlin's words to me in his university study as well, from what felt like so long ago. From before Nimue came.

"The Merlin of Legend has been sealed away inside hillside stone for over a millennium."

And: *"I do not believe I am that Merlin of Legend Edward but if you are so sure… I have always felt like there was a part of me missing, like my power and knowledge were somehow shorn into different pieces. There are days when I wake up in the morning, and I can almost taste what it is I am missing. It is like the smell of wood smoke on an autumn's day, mixed in with the sudden flash of red, sharp pain."*

I had finally found where Merlin's memories lay hidden. Buried under the rock beneath my feet.

Chapter 31

One moment I stood before a barren rock face of red sandstone. A difficult but well used route to the top of the hill taken by many, more daring, runners and walkers. Not exactly a tame part of the earth, but not fully part of the wilderness either. Beautiful and rugged, but aspects of it still close to being tamed.

The next second I took the power of the grey magic and, by simply walking through a barrier that dozen of people had climbed over never once dreaming that it was a wall, stepped through the red stone before me into one of the deepest and darkest secrets of magic that existed in this world. I moved easily through the red sandstone into a cool dry cavern of magic and power, hidden in plain sight from the eyes of man. As I crossed the threshold an old man's voice spoke in my ears. A voice that had told me once that hatred and love were the same emotion, just shaped differently by the light and dark. A voice that had told me that he would not see me again until all the world was changed. He had, I realised, said nothing about not hearing him. I had begun to realise that Odin Allfather chose all of his words as precisely and carefully as if they were written in his children's blood.

"Artemis is in love with you: and you with her: You both desire to begin the –ahem- mating dance. Even knowing that as a goddess any sexual contact she has means she must surely flower with child would I doubt stop either of you. And yet, even before you knew the truth about her, you knew enough to know that to lay so much as a finger on her was death. Think of that during this test. Think on it hard." I felt a cold shudder run down my spine. The myths of the gods were both very clever and very dangerous. When mortals mixed with gods and got it wrong they ended up more badly broken than words could ever describe.

Above me the ceiling seemed unbroken and smooth. Yet it had enough holes to let in fresh air: but almost no light. After Odin's words I suddenly wanted desperately to be able to see what lay before me: where the danger lay. I seized fire magic, and then kindled to life flame in my hands. What greeted me was seemingly very anticlimactic, which made me more uneasy than ever. The chamber was in the shape of a perfect small circle, carved long ago out of the sandstone. Carved: or formed by the raw power of magic. It was also full of dust, dust which never came from rock or any lifeless mineral. Dust which came from the flesh of the dead. Apart from at its exact centre the room was completely empty, save for its covering of grey dust: and the lifeless bones scattered all around the chamber as if someone had hurled them around the chamber in an incessant fury. On the chair in front of me sat the only remotely intact corpse, a fleshless skeleton: its bones white and cold. I reached out and touched it carefully, whoever he or she had been they had been dead a long time. But I could still feel the grey magic they had used to fade out their own heart. The hopelessness of suicide. Even in death its open jaw bone seemed to be screaming. That way of dying, while quick, was incredibly painful and bleak. In front of the chair

413

there was a desk, and these were the only furnishings in the room. They were plain, hard wood, and the walls around them were unmarked and plain. There was only one other thing in the room. Ahead of me on the desk sat the deepest object of my desire. Had I been asked to choose between this, and the tightness between Artemis's legs and the chance of her heart beating in tandem with my own, I would not have known how to answer. Every man has his own personal form of poison, as strong as the greatest callings of love and lust.

For most it is the ring of plain gold that The Voice of The Mountain offers: the power to take the best of all that this world already possesses. For most power and money, or some other form of possessions, are the deepest form of drug that can be offered to their soul. But grey wizards want something different, they want something that by definition can never exist in the world that is currently around us. That is why we alone are beyond The Voice's power to tempt, one of the reasons that he hates us all so much. We are not better than other people, no more immune to temptation, it is simply that he has nothing to offer us. For our poison is the bringing of the new into this world, or perhaps more accurately, the restoring of the very old that has been lost in the flow of "progress". For ancient values long dead take on a most beautiful and terrible power when they are reborn into a world and context far different to that in which they originally lived and died.

The book on the table before me was the stuff that all grey wizards' dreams are made of. For most people it would have seemed unappealing: uninviting and even dull. The book was tatty, tied together with bits of string. In places the typeface was clear and legible, in others it was written in handwriting so old and messy it was hard to even read let alone understand. At times it was typed in modern English in a modern style computer font.

Much of it was written by pen, but not in one but in a thousand different languages. Some: Greek, Latin and Old Norse: I recognised. Others I did not, although I suspected that at least one was Old English. There were parts where the book's paper was wet with the tears of those who had been reading it. Some pages were smudged with water, some with tears of blood. Sometimes the book was not parchment but human skin, and in those places often the ink was really blood. For real knowledge is not neat and tidy, produced in a text book with answers in the back that you just have to reach. To gain real understanding you must study the most difficult and confused materials imaginable, reaching for an answer that does not exist in the human comprehension of this world until you discover it.

I walked slowly across to the chair and gently removed the skeleton from it. I sat down and then looked at the book for a long while. I felt the burn to pick it up, to open it, to lose myself in its pages. But I stayed still, thinking. I didn't let myself read so much as a single word: no more than I would have let myself kiss Artemis fully on the lips. As I waited the book shimmered before my eyes, it colours changing. It wanted me to read it, it was trying to tempt to me. But I had lain night after night a hair's breadth from the naked virgin of the gods and never once touched her: all I had to do was to look around me at this chamber of death to tell that something was very wrong here. Whatever answer I would find here it would not be quick and easy. I sat on my hands so that they would not be tempted just to reach out and turn the pages. Before me the book danced on, calling for me to start reading it. Sometimes it was smart brown leather with pages forged from gold, at other times an old and peeling paperback almost falling apart before my eyes: at still others it glowed smoothly as a modern electronic reading device. But I ignored it and thought about the dead bones of the grey wizards that had come before me that now littered this place. I could feel the grey magic coming off what remained of them. So only greys had been able to find this place, that made sense, exploring the dark secrets of this world was our speciality.

But why had they all died down here? I presumed something must have trapped them, something which had let them in, but which wouldn't let them out. I had done my research, I knew what guarded Merlin's prison: a magical barrier made entirely of air. A barrier through which any could pass, but through which Merlin alone could not return through. So what had changed? What had meant that all these wizards had ended up dying so grimly down here in the dark? There was no obvious immediate answer, for none of the remains could be any of the Merlins who had ever existed throughout history. For, not in this lifetime or any other, had Merlin ever been even close to being a grey wizard.

I reached out with my senses, and felt the prison walls, all around the edge of this room, that magical barrier of air. It was there of course, and vastly powerful. In a lifetime I would not have had the slightest chance of breaking it. It was the work of a Great Spell, one of blue and brown magic One prepared over many, many years. And it was ancient as well. I could not prove this but I would have been very surprised if it had not been cast by the very first Merlin, all those thousands and thousands of years ago. And I had no doubt at all that it was linked implacably to his odd form of reincarnation, a process which had now been going on for so long it was now measured in centuries the way other world events were measured in years.

In the end I turned my gaze back to the book. It, apart from the magical shield, was the only thing of power and significance hidden here beneath the earth. The dead bones still hung with the fading grey magic that the wizards had used in despair to end their own lives, but that could no longer tell me anything new. The only answers lay in this book before me.

But I still didn't read it.

I looked at it closely, studying it hard. Not its words and what it said: just its composition and what it was. I could feel the power in it, greater than any mortal power I had ever felt before. Strong enough to put even the phenomenal strength of my little sister straight into the shade. And finally, as I watched it carefully, I worked out what the book must be. This was the tangible form of Merlin's memories, all the memories of all his past selves: separated from his current and conscious form which even now, I doubted not, was being circled by one of The Allfather's ravens.

The legends were wrong, I realised suddenly. Merlin hadn't been trapped by Nimue. I felt suddenly very cold. Merlin was a great prophet, he had seen that his doom was coming and known he could not escape it. But he did not wish his power and learning to pass to another, at least not one so foul and dark as Nimue. So he had cast a great spell, a spell that split him into two. Time and time again Nimue reached out to devour his mind and power, but each time the great spell killed Merlin before she could, tearing him apart and storing all his memories here. But the spell had distorted the natural reincarnation process, meaning Merlin kept being reborn as the same person. And each time the process repeated: as history flowed on the memories of Merlin built upon each other lifetime after lifetime. And now before me was stood the incredible result of those thousands of years of struggle. Lifetime after lifetime, memory after memory, bound into the form of the most powerful book of magic ever imaginable.

Merlin had initiated an incredibly risky game of poker I realised sickly: with higher stakes then even he initially had ever dared to guess. One day the cycle would either end with Nimue dying or Merlin being fully consumed, memories and all. And whichever happened, the one of the two left standing would be the most powerful sorcerer on this earth, and very possibly any other.

Of course I could end it all by taking this power for myself, I thought suddenly. A few moments to absorb all this power and my strength would be at the very boundaries of mortal limits. The hunger burned inside me so intense it was pain.

But I did nothing. No more than I would have reached out a hand to caress Artemis's breasts.

Instead I turned from the book and walked away, walked away from the cavern that was ultimately nothing more than a death trap for grey wizards. I felt a dull horror as I approached the magical shield of air, wondering sickly if it would bind into this place to die like it had so many others before me. I knew for a few hopeless moments that if the air held me in then everything in my life was over.

But the magical barrier let me pass unresisted, and I faded my way back out through the red sandstone: back to the safety of the rock face and the cool night air. I lay back against the cold stone, thinking carefully. After a short while I realised what had happened, and shuddered at just the thought. The grey wizards who had died in there had started to read the book, and in so doing absorbed some of the memories and knowledge of Merlin. Enough for the guardian spell to recognise them as though they were the brown-blue wizard himself, and so to then trap them hopelessly to die inside its foul web. Merlin was protecting his secrets well.

It would have been like the depths of hades to be trapped in there I thought bleakly. All the knowledge a grey wizard could ever possibly desire: and absolutely no way to use any of it to help anyone. The only use for your new understanding would be in devising the least painful possible method of suicide. And you would die alone in the dark, knowing that you would never again see any other human face.

I started shaking, even where I sat totally safe on the rock face: a route I had climbed for fun so many times. All the time passing centimetres from a place where despairing men had ended their own lives in the darkness. Just behind me lay all the power and knowledge I would ever need to defeat Nimue and save Jessica: yet I dared not read so much as a word of it. It was like the old saying of sailors stranded on the ocean, dying of thirst while surrounded all the time by sea water. "Water, water everywhere and not a drop to drink." All that impossible ocean did was make you feel even more inadequate and useless than if there had been no water there at all. Knowing the knowledge and power to save my elder sister lay right before me, but that I could not touch it, that hurt more than I had ever dared believe.

I wondered briefly if I should even be trying to save Merlin. If I removed his only known antidote, Nimue, and he ever regained the power that lay behind me I would be utterly helpless against him: even if he decided Vicky was too much of a threat and decided to remove her from the scene. Although the death trap behind me seemed unbreakable, I was as certain as I was that the sun would rise tomorrow, that Merlin would be able to walk back out with all his new memories and power intact. He had, after all, been the one that designed the trap in the first place.

And in so doing signed the death warrant of who knew how many grey wizards.

I had escaped a very bleak form of death. But though I had found the answer to the riddle of Merlin and Nimue it, like the answer to the riddle of Artemis, gave me nothing that would help me defeat Nimue or that would help me to save Jessica. With only a month to go I didn't now even have any questions left to which I was still searching for answers. Merlin probably did know how to tap this source of power, but unless I could defeat Nimue first all I would do by telling him about this would be to feed my enemy a thousand times more power when she finally devoured Merlin, and with his knowledge restored I had no doubt that would then be the final end of this cycle of distorted resurrections.

I found myself laughing harshly, despairingly. After two months I now had excellent long term plans for both Merlin and Artemis: I just needed to defeat Nimue first for either of them to be of any relevance at all. And that outcome was still further away from me than the stars: and I was very fast running out of time.

I found myself wondering why Odin had even sent me here, to something so useless that could so easily have just proven my end. And then I suddenly had a very sick feeling in my stomach. I had walked away from a death trap because Odin had described it as being like trying to have a sexual relationship with Artemis.

Was Odin simply trying to tell me that I was deceived in believing that I could ever win the love of the virgin of the gods? Was trying to be with her utterly delusional, ultimately no more possible than trying to square a circle? An exercise that starts off as a fun intellectual challenge, but as soon as any real time is put into it, becomes nothing more than a complete waste of the time that is given to you in this life.

Despite the fact that Artemis the Friendly wanted a boyfriend so much she had still, in thousands of years, never given herself to any man.

Why should I be arrogant enough to think that with me her story would have a different kind of ending?

Chapter 32

I had no questions left to answer any more, and the remaining four weeks before Merlin and Jessica's wedding seemed to vanish as surely as if I had faded them with grey magic myself. I gained in lore and knowledge and magical power, but found no new questions to ask, let alone answers. Whatever the answer was, it remained beyond my sight. And the last of my time was disappearing and then was gone. All I had left was to wonder whether the tears in the huntress's eyes were because I was failing or because, like all men who had dreamed of her before me, she had always known that I would fail.

It was the final night before the wedding. The day when Nimue would consume Merlin and all hope would be lost: for both him and for my elder sister. Tomorrow Merlin's own marriage vows would render him unable to protect himself against the parasite that intended to devour him: as it had so many fateful times before. I felt myself going through the motions for one last late night library session. But I knew, even as I prepared myself, that it was mostly just because keeping busy would be better for keeping my mind off what was about to happen tomorrow than would be doing nothing.

Vicky came to me and sat on my lap. She was scared and so nervous that I knew that she wouldn't sleep. "Edward," she said, almost guiltily, as though she found it hard to admit that she thought that I had failed, "you always been dead good at seeing what to do but now I think you stuck. So if you not think of something clever and good by tomorrow I go fight Nimue myself, in Pankration. I am not going just give up!"

I looked at her tiredly. It made as much sense as anything else right now. Die at Nimue's hands in a Panktration battle or die at Nimue's hands an hour or so later after she was finished with Merlin and had devoured his power, what was the difference?

"What makes you think she'll agree to fight you one on one?" I asked tiredly. "Especially in a circle of power that stops anyone else getting involved in your battle to the death? She isn't going to want to go toe to toe with you and take a chance when she can just say no and eat Merlin. From her point of view it makes much more sense to kill and eat you later, when she has already consumed Merlin and has all his power at her command. I'm guessing that each time she eats Merlin she must get some of his power, some of his memories before they can escape. Otherwise she wouldn't keep doing this." And even though what I had seen inside Prestham Hill had convinced me that the vast majority of Merlin's memories escaped each time, I had also little doubt that even the little that was left would still be a great feast of power. Otherwise why would Nimue permit this cycle to just continue across the centuries?

Vicky shook her head. Her face had that stubborn look which I knew from long experience meant that she had made up her mind and nothing anyone did or said would ever change it. And that was that. "It on TV Edward. Pankration not like other magic fights. The other side not need say yes. If you very similar in magic power you can force Panktration. If other wizard is lot more powerful or lot more weaker then they do need say yes. Too much more powerful you can't force Pankration on them, too much weaker and their magical presence is too small, they just keep slipping away! But I not much stronger than Nimue, not now that she so old and she eaten so many people! I can force her into Pankration and tomorrow I will."

"Fight Nimue and you will die." I said simply "You're stronger than her but she won't let your magic touch her through her magical illusions of blue and brown magic. Soon you will be exhausted from all your white magic attacks, none of which she will let hit anything, and then Nimue will eat you alive. You are the most powerful wizard I know, but Nimue has thousands of years of dark experience to put behind her magical deceptions. It would be like going to a sword fight with just a spoon."

Vicky shrugged. "Rather die fighting with spoon than give up! Zeus and Athene not give up, and Odin not give up either! They would fight!"

She was right, but then they were immortal after all. I worshipped the gods, but they could lose every battle, every mortal that they loved, and in a thousand, thousand years what would it matter? Still they would exist: still they would live on. We mortals only had the one life. And once we lost it that was it: forever.

"Vicky..." I said quietly, but not even really sure myself what I was about to say.

"Edward," said Vicky, "I not just let my big sister and my best friend die and the baddies win. I go fight. I am bloodwolf, not your bloodhound. You not want me to fight, come up with a better plan! You always had good plans before!" She stopped and looked at me sternly. "I think the problem is that you now pray to a little goddess of silly girls: and that has melted your brain. You not have any of these problems if you choose to worship some sensible gods like me. How is a goddess that likes fluffy stuffed animals going to help in a fight?" and Vicky shook her head in disbelief that anyone could be so stupid as to worship Artemis. Even at that age Vicky already had a pronounced dislike for what she saw as nothing more than a goddess of stupid little girls.

"You not want me to fight," continued Vicky firmly, "then come up with something sensible tonight. Otherwise when they say "anyone not want these two married" that is when I start the fight." She patted me on the shoulder. "Good luck!" she said helpfully: and still slightly hopefully.

But when I sat down in the restricted section of the university library less than an hour later all my hope had gone. I had lost many battles in my life, it was part of what made me powerful, but never before had I lost a war. And to lose battles is one thing, that can be recovered from. To lose wars, that is quite another. I no longer even had the energy to read properly, my eyes just scanned the same lines of text over and over, the pages of the books in my hands no longer turned. I felt my chance to find any meaningful answers was long past. I prayed to my gods, desperate prayers to the cold huntress and the seer warlord that I knew would not be answered: they had already given me all the help that they were prepared to give. In the emptiness, devoid of purpose and passion, my drive gone, I didn't even notice sleep sneak up on me.

I woke in the early hours of the morning, the last of my precious time to try and find some answers: any answers: all gone. Before me the sun was now beginning to creep over the edge of the horizon, bringing in the red dawn of this fateful day. It was done: the war was over and I had lost. I turned to stand up, not even sure where I was going or what I was going to do. Just, like the chaste virgin of the moon over a thousand years ago as she lay alone in her treehouse bed, determined I would not simply wait helplessly for the end.

I got the biggest shock of my life.

Merlin stood by me, his gaunt frame outlined in the glow of the rising dawn. I don't know how long he had been standing there, but he had not been there when I fell into deep sleep. I seized my power in panic, convinced in that instant that Nimue had sent him to make an end of me. Sent Merlin to destroy the grey wizard whose power she could not eat.

But Merlin was no threat to me now. Although he stood outlined in the dazzling bright glow of the rising sun his eyes were distant and faraway. "I know that I have been taught to hate you these last three months." he said, as calmly and relaxed as if we were strangers simply discussing the day's weather. "I know that the creature wearing Jessica's face has turned me against you with a thousand small words and acts, a thousand small cuts and gashes a million times more dangerous than any single strike. I know that my doom is coming, the doom that always finds me no matter how hard I fight and run: and I can feel myself start to fall once again as the legends foretell. And I know that, inevitably, Nimue has won again."

Then he looked at me, and there was a sudden absolute terror in his gaze, and at the same time a desperate hope. A hope strong enough to pierce the foundation of this world, powerful enough to burn the bright streams red with blood. His eyes were a bright and magical fire, despair and elation burning together in a desperate mix. "I know that I am once more bound in Nimue's spell, in her web of subtle magic and dark illusion. Beneath the mask I see her cruelty and evil come out in every word that now passes through her mouth. Words that are in the voice of the woman I love, but words that Jessica would never even want to say.

425

And then I felt your struggles Edward, the strivings you have made, driven by both your gods, as you battle in a hopeless struggle against Nimue's web. But, even though it is pointless, even though your struggling simply draws the web ever tighter around us all, even though there is no way that you can win, still you fight on. I felt it first when a raven flew above me and would not leave, and I saw you travel to my death trap in the mountain. And I thought as you descended into it, and as I just watched on helplessly, that never again would I see your face living in the sunlit lands.

And yet you came back, back to the world of the living. Back, having turned down like no other grey wizard before you, one of the two deepest temptations of your heart. The other you resist each night, when you lie down next to the naked virgin of the gods who loves you: but the two of you never touch: even though you both long to do so with all your hearts. And your struggles brought me back to myself, just a little. Just enough to remember how much I love Danielle and Jessica, and that love was enough to make me do a desperate thing. I have broken the great spell I cast so long ago Edward: back when the earth was much younger. I have taken all that power back into me, so that I would have the strength to come to you tonight, to show you the one way that there is hope.

But know now that if you fail it is all now truly over, my gamble was desperate indeed. With the great spell broken so ends my unusual cycle of resurrection, and if I die Nimue will consume all that I ever was: and her power and victory shall be so great that it is hard to see an end to it for many thousands of years, possibly not so long as this age and this earth lasts. So with both elation and despair dancing in my heart, I bring you now the only hope that you have left.''

He laid down a piece of plain white paper on the table. It was completely blank. I could feel my heart turning in my mouth. "Turn it over only when I am gone." Said Merlin quietly. "And it is also best that I do not remember this conversation or this meeting: or else I would betray what I have just done to Nimue, and this last ray of hope would die ere it could be fully cast."

Dazily, as though in a dream, l placed my hand gently on Merlin's lower arm and called forth the power of the grey to fade away his thoughts and memories of this meeting. There was no resistance, and the grey magic did its work swiftly. The next moment Merlin was just looking at me with confusion and dislike in his eyes: his true personality all faded once more under the terrible power of Nimue's spell. He turned and staggered away, uncaring and unnoticing of his surroundings. Looking nothing more than a scatty, disorganised man falling apart, who was so confused and disorientated he might very easily be seriously unwell.

Even if Merlin had noticed me in those confused moments straight after I had stopped fading his memories; all I had been doing was sitting in front of a pile of books, looking exhausted, with a single sheet of plain A4 paper in front of me, without a single note on it. Nothing that Nimue would care about, or see as a threat if she did for some reason fish that image out of his mind. Once I was sure that Merlin was truly gone, and I was once more definitely completely alone in the library, I turned the paper desperately. My heart beating with an eagerness in my chest that went beyond any physical pain.

It was not what I expected. The paper had on it no writing, and no coloured ink. Just a simple drawing, done in pencil. It wasn't even shaded.

Just the image of a great single eye: wreathed in flame.

It took me only a few moments to work out what Merlin was telling me. And what, if I wanted to save my elder sister and to defeat Nimue, I must now do. But all I could feel was cold horror. Odin had not been lying when he said that to bind my power to him as his champion he would demand the greatest sacrifice.

There was a flash of coloured light beside me, all the colours of the rainbow by my side; and I knew that Artemis was there. I found myself wondering whether I was insane to even worship her, let alone regard her as my girlfriend: my girl.

"Did you know?" I asked quietly, "All these long hours that we spent together. The times I read to you the most interesting things my research had discovered, the times you taught me how to say your name in Ancient Greek. The times you taught me how to shoot, or the countless evenings we lay in bed together: talking for hours about absolutely everything, and about absolutely nothing at all. All those times you could have just told me what I needed to do. You would have known this was an answer all along. Yet you did not tell me. Why? You say you love me, you have said it a thousand times and yet you did not tell me this."

"Of course I knew," said Artemis, "but I could not tell you my love: though my heart ached and tears ran from my dead eyes. The gods are bound by ancient laws Edward. Were we to intervene in violation of those laws our power would be too great for reality to withstand. Entire worlds have died because gods became too embroiled in conflict with each other, neither willing to back down. By the end they were fighting over nothing more than the possession of lifeless rock and ash: where once life had bloomed everywhere. I helped spur you on as much as I could. I tried to be your comfort and your source of strength. To, like The Allfather's interventions,

428

keep you going so your struggle would finally wake up Merlin so he could give you this chance."

"After this how do I know that anything you have ever said or done is real?" I said tiredly, feeling my heart poised on the point of breaking. "Least of all the love you claim that you have for me?"

"All of it was real." Said Artemis softly, the light in her eyes like the coloured lights of the gentlest stars. She squeezed my upper arm softly with her cold hand. "Especially my love for you. When The Allfather showed you the truth of Merlin and you thought he might be warning you off me the pain of you thinking that I might not really love you nearly tore me in two. It hurt worse than a thousand hangovers and more than dancing over a river of shattered glass." She took a deep breath, and blew out her cheeks. "I don't know if I should tell you this, because I don't understand it at all. The Allfather told me to tell you that you can never take the virginity of the maiden of the gods but that there are futures when her love for you leads to her bearing your children." She smiled at me sadly. "I don't understand how the two parts of that story go together at all Edward, but I do know that I love you, and that the second part of that story sounds really nice."

Then she was gone, a thousand colours melting into the dawn sun. And I had no time to think further about my impossible love life.

And I had a terrible choice to make. How much was I prepared to sacrifice to save the life of my older sister? The sister who had spent most of her life trying very hard to make sure that I was dead.

Chapter 33

I understood as never before why man had turned to the easy answers of Christianity, it offered a release from the torture of sacrifice to the gods. The pain of what I had done was indescribable. I could feel the burn of my charred flesh shifting every time I moved: it made nausea sway sickly in my stomach. I could feel the acid biting in the back of my throat as I fought not to gag. But even through the price I had paid I could feel the new power flowing in my veins. What I had been magically was just a pale shadow of what I now was.

"Vicky do you have a play sword you could turn into a real magical blade for me?" I called through her bedroom door. I managed, just about, to keep my voice normal; although the effort meant that I had to place one hand on the wall to steady myself. Everything around me swayed sickly.

"Why Edward?" Said Vicky suspiciously, obviously worried I had spent last night coming up with some complicated plan to stop her fighting Nimue. "I need my sword to fight Nimue. You not stop me! And I gave other good one to Danielle."

"That's fine." I said lightly. Vicky's plans were now completely irrelevant. Unless I managed to get everything wrong. "Any kind of magic sword will do, so long as you make the edge sharp."

"Got old rubbish one." said Vicky, "It heavy and uncomfortable so I not use it." She opened the door and channelled her magic into the blade to reawaken its power, like charging a flat mobile phone. There was a flash of light and I felt the sword flare with magic. Then Vicky channelled her magic again and the dull edge that made the sword safe to play with fell away to razor sharp steel. I opened the bag I had wrapped in grey magic.

"Why you want white magic sword anyway?" Vicky asked crossly. She was tense and scared I realised: small wonder. Not only were her friends and family in danger but this was the first time I had ever really failed her. She was finding that hard I realised. "Wizards only use magic items of their own colour. You use this sword and you be hurt badly!"

"Just open the door and drop it in the bag." I said gently, "Grey magic will protect me while I carry it, and I don't intend to use it."

Vicky held out the sword carefully. I placed the bag beneath her and she dropped the blade into it. She looked up at me. "Have you got a new plan Edward?" she asked hopefully. "Something good for us to do?" I smiled. That set off the pain ringing in my skull and sent sharp flashing lights jagging across my vision, but I still managed it. "Just make sure that Nimue's attention is all on you today." I said "Make her think you are going to fight her soon, but don't let the fight get started before the wedding vows, then everything will be sorted I promise. So long as the plan works."

Vicky looked hopeful, but not sure I wasn't making the whole thing up. She looked at me closely, then asked confused. "Edward why you hiding in long cloak with hood drawn down? I can't see all your face..."

The pain was a constant, a bedrock of hammers beating against my skull. The nausea was worse, it came and went in a series of incessant never-ending waves. At the pressure of Vicky's question I felt a tide of filth rise at the very base of my throat where the skin was most soft and sensitive, the taste of acid at the back of my mouth. I was suddenly very sick. Vicky looked at me in horror as I faded the debris away with grey magic. No wonder Christianity sounded cool all those hundreds of years ago I thought. The sacrifice happened to someone else a long time ago. Christ got hurt once so now no one else ever has to. Yeah! But even in the depths of my agony I knew that philosophy was ridiculous. And besides why should someone else be the one who paid for my sake? I had been hurt by my sacrifice, but I had also gained a level of power beyond my wildest dreams.

"Edward you okay?" asked Vicky anxiously. "You look poorly. Maybe we get you some Calpol and…"

"I'm fine." I said. "It will pass. Keep your focus on your big sister and your best friend. They need you more today than I do."

I tried to smile at her to calm the situation down, but the pain that moving my jaw caused as the muscle actions rippled across my face caused my fingers to tear through the plaster on the house wall as I desperately tried to clutch onto something: onto anything. Vicky stared at me in shock. "Edward what wrong: what…" Then her voice changed. "Edward you feel different! You feel…." She stopped stunned. "More powerful! Lot more powerful. Nearly as powerful as me! How that happen?"

"I sacrificed to the darkest god." I said grimly. "I made a sacrifice to Odin Allfather in return for the power of him anointing me as his champion. The pain I feel now will pass: the power will not." I reached out and squeezed her on the shoulder. "I told you I had a plan and that it was working."

Then I turned and walked away. Time was of an essence for what I intended to do to work, and already I could feel it threatening to slip away through my fingers.

I walked invisible, clad in grey magic, to Merlin's cottage. It was an easy couple of miles downhill walk I had done a hundred times before. But never before when a misplaced step on a branch or a sharp piece of ground made fresh bolts of pain explode through my skull. I lost count of the number of times that I was sick. But tension and need pulled my steps on, making me fight my way on to the cottage: even though the inside of my head wanted to split and tear itself apart.

Finally I crossed to the edge of the dark woods and came out by the end of Merlin's garden. It looked very different now to three months ago: a parasite will always leave the host on which it feeds a foul and ill mess. When Jessica had been there she had controlled the chaos of Merlin but not crushed it, letting life in his garden bloom. The gardens had been ordered and most of the grass well mown, but the flower beds had been full of colour and life. Parts of the lawn had even been left deliberately to grow wild with meadow flowers. Now all was neatly cut lawns and red roses, their petals red as blood. It was clean, stark, cold. And gravel had replaced the meadow flowers and most of the grass. Parasites have no interest in encouraging the growth of living things. All they know how to do is take. Zuggles, Danielle's beloved dog, had annoyed Nimue, and long since been sent to the house of some distant friend far away.

The sun was shining, but the wind blew cold. The brightness made my vision sharp and jagged and the wind made the fireball of pain in my face ache. But I already hurt so much some part of me was almost now past caring. The door to the house opened and out came three figures, Merlin, Danielle and Merlin's best friend: a halfling I didn't really know called Renly. Nimue disguised as Jessica had spent the night apart at my father's house as tradition demanded so she was nowhere nearby to stop me. I had arrived in time before the three left for social drinks with friends before the wedding, with the actual ceremony due to take place in the early afternoon. My plan, hastily drawn up last night through a headache that threatened to tear my skull apart and pain that I never even knew existed, might be shaky: but for now it held. Merlin walked onwards in a smart black suit, like a sick man in a dazed dream. His clothes were both immaculate and the height of current fashion, but they were ones Jessica would never have chosen for him. She knew that he loved brown the best. I realised sickly as I watched that Merlin's wedding suit had been arranged by Nimue to make it look as though he was attending his own funeral today: which is exactly what she intended. Renly, dressed smartly, moved by Merlin's side as his best man: and whatever thoughts and emotions moved behind his face it was impossible to tell. I did not know him well enough to risk trusting him today.

Behind them walked Danielle in a plain white dress. She looked pretty as a picture, but not one which would have held anyone's attention long. She looked completely empty of any sort of life. Even her walk was listless with no trace of childish energy or enthusiasm. And if her mind had been her own she would never have chosen white as a colour to wear on a special day. Both her and Merlin moved listlessly with Renly towards the smart black car that had pulled up outside the front gate to take them to the pre-wedding pub: and would later take them to the wedding itself. It was effectively a black hearse ferrying them to death. I stepped behind them clad in grey and took Danielle's hand. I faded her not only from sight but also from the memory that she was there from the minds of all around us. I placed one hand over Danielle's mouth, to stop her making a sound that might betray me, then washed her current state of mind with grey: leaving her completely placid and energy less. She was already so under the power of illusion there was little strength left in her mind to resist me. I stood with her while Merlin and Renly got into the taxi and drove away. Soon they were gone, and I was there with a little girl in my arms whose mind was so vacant she was closer to sleep than consciousness even though she was technically awake. Then I did what I could not have done before last night, and let some of my new power loose.

The illusion planted in Danielle's mind by Nimue was strong but its roots did not go deep. It was like a filmy miasma of cobwebs drawn around the surface, suppressing rather than damaging the fundamental mental processes deeper down. Against what I had been before this illusion would have been unbreakable. Against the new powers at my command the illusion simply flickered: and then went out of existence. Danielle started, and then shook her head slowly as though she was starting to come out of very, very deep sleep. But the power of the cobwebs' illusion was not fully gone, not yet. If I just left Danielle now and did no more in time it would remerge. But time was what Nimue didn't now have. Time was, for the moment at least, finally on my side.

I took Danielle by the hand and led her into the interior of the cottage she called home. She followed easily, not resisting. It was like leading a slowly waking sleep walker. You could see the changes that Nimue's poison had started to work here too. Whereas before the small cottage had, apart from Danielle's bedroom, been just one big room: It was now crisscrossed with harsh interior walls splitting everything into relentlessly separate areas. They were cold things of brick and plaster that had no place in the warmth of the tumbledown

435

cottage. They chocked its eternal warmth with the sick aspect of modernity. And they concealed a very dark secret of their own. I turned to the one between Nimue and Merlin's bedroom and the lounge, and then walked up to it. I rested my hands against it, checking with my magic, but I already knew what I would find. Odin's power is that of the all-seeing eye. Once I had become his champion Nimue stood no more chance of still being able to hide what she had done to Jessica from me, than the night did of hiding away successfully from the rise of the morning sun.

I faded the side of the wall that faced me away into nothing. There was a dark space inside it in which something lay resting: something which I had fought for three months to find. I reached into the wall and took out the pale white thing that in rough outline resembled a human body and laid it with the greatest gentleness I had on the couch in the lounge. The holes in the wall to let air through were so small that they were almost impossible to see: even if you were focusing on looking for them.

The form had the basic outline of a non-descript human body, but it appeared in no way like a living person. It was completely white and unbearably thin. Its features were stretched tight across its bones. It had no nails, no hair, no facial features. Even the muscles were wasted and washed away. That is why the body had survived on no food and water for three months. It had almost nothing left to do, was barely processing even the most rudimentary chemical and neurological reactions. Its chest hardly even moved as it very occasionally rose and fell a little to draw in a very small breath. Three months ago this had been the laughing healthy form of my elder sister on her engagement night. Three months of hard parasitic feeding had left her drained almost beyond recognition. Almost: but not quite: not from the eyes of a child who loved her mummy with everything she had: and oh so very much.

Danielle gave a startled cry. At some deep instinctive level, beyond conscious thought and deed, every cell inside her screamed as she recognised both her mummy: and that she was very sick. It is always quiet tranquil children that are the most dangerous when they finally flip. The storm that had torn apart so many lives at The Pool of Fire and Blood, so long ago, was a faint echo of the tempest of fury which now engulfed this little girl: her whole form shaking with the rage and fear that now tore inside her. "Mummy!" she screamed, "Mummy!". And Nimue's illusion burned from her eyes; Danielle's soul and mind rising back up from the depths in a whirlwind of power and fury. The cobwebs which had once lain across her mind were scattered and destroyed as though they had never been. "Mummy!" Jessica's daughter screamed, running forward towards her desperately, tears pouring down from her eyes.

I had to seize Danielle with both arms to hold her back, and for a moment I thought she might still tear free from my grasp, so hard did she fight against me like a wild thing. And for one terrible moment I wondered if everything would be lost because Danielle actually loved Jessica too much. "Danielle." I yelled desperately. "Danielle you can't touch mummy at the moment! Your mummy is very sick. Even giving her a hug might kill her."

Danielle screamed, a howl like a thousand moments of agony turned into one. "Mummy not die. No No N0!" She thrashed and raged in my arms like an animal. In that moment there could be no doubt that she would have torn apart anyone and anything to make her mummy safe again.

"Well." I said coldly, hating what I had to do but needing Danielle to calm down, needing her to listen. Or everything was indeed truly lost. "That is up to you. Mummy might live or mummy might die. It all depends on whether or not you can save her." I stopped, hating myself, then went on. "But this isn't the first time you have tried to save someone is it Danielle? Do you remember what happened the last time?"

Danielle jolted in my arms with painful memories, but it stilled her fury, made her listen. Her face went white and sick. "Tuggles," she said sickly, "and I not save him. My lovely dog died." The dark memory stilled the passion of her fury, turned it into a terrible calm.

Part of me knew the horror of what I must do, but I had not spared myself. Nor would I spare others: not even children. Jessica would live, and Nimue would die, and my family would live. Let everything else burn.

"Well you could have saved your dog," I said cruelly, "but you didn't. You could have been quieter and quicker in getting away. Or you could have screamed for your daddy earlier, when there was still a chance he could have healed Tuggles; or even stopped him from being hurt in the first place. But you made too many mistakes. You lost and Tuggles died. Tell me Danielle how many times have your prayed to the gods to have another chance? How many countless times have you begged and begged to have another go, to have another chance to save him?"

Danielle stared at me through eyes that were misty with her tears. "Thousands of times. Sometimes hundred times a night, or hundred times a day."

"Then understand Danielle, that though not even the gods themselves can unwind time and undo the fixed stone of history, that your prayers, that our prayers, have been answered today. You have been given this one chance to save mummy: but knowing from last time with Tuggles just how important it is to get this right first time. This is the one chance you will ever get to see your mummy again, the chance that if you fail you will have a hundred thousand times to pray and beg hopelessly to be here, in this spot, with this opportunity again. But knowing that you never will: and that mummy is gone for good. That your mummy is dead.

Or you get it right and win, and you get mummy back forever.

So it's up to you Danielle. Is mummy going to live or is mummy going to die?''

Danielle looked at me, and her big brown eyes had suddenly become as grim as black obsidian itself. Midnight stone on The Mountain had not that level of utterly implacable resolve. ''Mummy is going to live.'' Danielle said simply. ''Tell me what do: quickly please!''

''Good.'' I said. ''Then you need to do what I cannot. Jessica has been drained of life and energy by Nimue, by the person pretending to be your mummy. I can't just kill Nimue at the moment, as long as the two are linked that would kill them both.''

''We break link!'' said Danielle. ''We get Vicky and she swing sword of white light and…''

I shook my head. That made the pain in it explode and for a moment everything went black with nausea. Distracted from the pain by the speed events around me were taking the sudden terrible reminder of my agony nearly made me pass out where I stood. For a moment, despite all my efforts, I was convinced that the world was just going to fall away into unconscious darkness. But, somehow, from somewhere, I found the strength to hang on: even if it was just by the edge of my fingernails. Danielle's face widened in alarm as what she could see of my face through my hood went in one instant from pale and clammy to almost grey. I bit my lip and tasted the blood. The salt and sting called me back, rooting me firmly in the remorseless clarity of consciousness no matter how much the pain of my sacrifice hurt. I could not afford to fall, not now: not while Nimue still breathed.

"That is a good plan Danielle, but we need Vicky to distract Nimue so she doesn't see what we're about to do. We can't break the link just yet. Look at how little is left of mummy: at the moment the only thing keeping her alive is the link. Nimue is using her power to keep Jessica breathing until the wedding ceremony is over and she doesn't need to look like your mummy any more. Cut that link now and mummy will just die where she is lying on the couch. These last three months Nimue has literally extracted almost everything from your mummy."

"So what do WE do?" wailed Danielle. "I not let mummy die. I NOT!"

"I can't do anything." I said. "If Jessica was sick with aggressive energy I could fade that away. But the grey cannot give strength to people who are weak, cannot give them new sources of life and strength."

"But white magic can!" said Danielle excitedly. "We get Vicky here and she could put healing magic into Mummy and then..."

I shook my head. "We do that and all that will happen is Nimue will feast on Vicky's strength and in a few hours Vicky will look exactly like Jessica does now. Featureless, clam white, barely breathing. Nimue is a wizard of blue and brown Danielle, like…"

"Like me and daddy." said Danielle thoughtfully.

"Yes." I said, really pleased that she had made the connection so quickly. For me to save Jessica I was relying heavily on Danielle being able to pull off something very difficult. I found myself reflecting briefly that a long time ago Vicky at four had saved my life at a pool party, now at five I was relying on Danielle to save my elder sister's life. What was wrong with this world that I had to rely upon small children to help me fight so many of my battles? I thought suddenly. Where were all the good adults in this world? What were they busy doing when they were needed at the front line the most? I forced those thoughts away, I didn't have time for them: not now.

I continued quickly, time was still on our side but I really wanted to keep it that way. "The link which binds Nimue and Jessica is made of blue and brown magic. It needs a blue and brown wizard to work with the link; TO REVERSE IT: and then…"

"And then give Nimue's strength back to Mummy so she gets all better." said Danielle excitedly, her eyes shining with sudden understanding. "So if me or daddy could reverse link and start put the energy nasty Nimue stole back into mummy..."

"Not daddy." I said firmly. Not Merlin: much that I wished that it could be him. "I have gained a huge amount of grey magical power but not even I can fade the fact Merlin isn't at his own wedding from under Nimue's gaze. You, yes, she's not planning to eat you tonight. Him, no. Also you don't need to be at the wedding for it to go ahead. It will seem odd that you're not there but you are not needed. Merlin has to be at his own wedding or why is everyone else there in the first place? I can't fade him out of his own wedding. I'd have to fade the entire wedding and in the confusion that would cause the gods only know what would happen.

And we can't get Vicky to help you either before you ask. We need her at the wedding to keep Nimue distracted. But even if we didn't using the force of white magic to pull the stolen strength back into Jessica would be very risky. You would have to reverse the link and then Vicky would have to pull all the strength out of Nimue back into Jessica in one go. Nimue doesn't have white magic and so she would detect Vicky the moment she uses her power inside the parasite to pull mummy's strength back out. I don't think the link would be able to

441

take all that power going though it in one go, it would probably just collapse. It was designed for very gradual feeding over a period of weeks and months, not for sudden rushes of magical strength.''

''So has to be me.'' said Danielle slowly. ''I turn link around, and then I quickly take mummy's health back and then I...''

But I was shaking my head. I moved it as little as possible so as not to set off a fresh burst of agony ringing through my skull: I could not risk anything that might make me pass out. ''If you do it quickly Danielle then Nimue will sense what you are doing. Do you remember what happened when you tried to match your strength directly against Mike in your battle for Tuggle's life?''

A single tear trickled down into the corner of one of Danielle's eyes. ''Lost,'' she said thickly, ''got beat. Tuggles die right in front of me. Yowling in pain. And he know I not help him when he need it most.'' Whatever happened, however much help she was given, I realised in that instant, as I had never fully realised before, that the memory of Tuggles's death would haunt Danielle until her dying day.

''Yes.'' I said flatly, ''and Nimue is far more powerful with magic than Mike ever was. So you need to draw back the power from her so slowly and subtly that she doesn't notice it's gone. Very slowly and very carefully. If Nimue notices what you are doing she will stop it, stop you, and then mummy will die. But if you are slow and careful enough then mummy will get better. Then, when the time is right...''

''How I know when the time right?'' asked Danielle anxiously. ''How I know when mummy get better?''

''Because mummy will start looking better.'' I said. ''Her face will reappear and she will put back on her natural weight. She will look like mummy again, not really poorly as she does now. But I don't think she'll be able to speak and move again Danielle, not until the link is cut. But when mummy is better we need to make sure that Nimue can't just undo everything you've just done and take all mummy's strength back. We also need to get rid of the link before I fight Nimue to save your daddy from being eaten at the end of his wedding. Otherwise, if the link still exists when I kill Nimue, then mummy will die at the same time. So when you think mummy looks like mummy again, and you think she'll be okay, then you need to cut that magical link before Nimue can find out what's happened. I will be at the wedding and near Nimue, and will be able to sense the link go. The moment it does I shall challenge her in magical combat. With my new level of power, and as my grey magic is poison to her brown and blue mix of magic, I don't expect the fight to last long."

Hopefully. And hopefully not just because Nimue somehow managed to kill me quickly. She still had a lot of experience on me, a lot of years. I didn't dare to hope there wouldn't be at least one nasty surprise left up her sleeve.

Danielle looked at me confused. "I not white wizard Edward, how I cut the link? Don't know how with blue and brown magic!"

I took the bag and toppled it over. The sword of light that Vicky had made fell out: it blazed with power. I stepped aside, careful not to let it touch me.

Danielle looked at the sword, still confused. "That magic sword would cut link easily but how I use it Edward? I am blue and brown wizard, not white one. They teach us we can't use magical artefacts not our own colour. Teacher said so in school and when I ask daddy he say that true." She frowned suddenly. "At least I think that what daddy said. Daddy made things all complicated again and I not really understand!"

I smiled slightly. Merlin could manage to make pouring yourself a glass of water sound complicated if you let him. "It's not actually true that you can't use magical artefacts that aren't you own own colour, although I know why school would teach it that way." Schools didn't teach things that were difficult, they were there to tell you that life was full of easy answers so long as you always did exactly as you were told. They were a worthy successor indeed to the Christian Faith. You went into them at four full of imagination and colour, you left them at eighteen utterly predictable with a straight road map for the rest of your life planned out for you. But I refocused, today was about saving my older sister. And killing Nimue. Tearing apart as much of the modern world as I could get my hands on could wait a short while.

"A wizard can use any artefact of any colour perfectly fine Danielle." I continued calmly. "The only problem is that if it is not his or her natural colour then once they use it, and the artefact has done its job exactly the same as if it was used by a wizard of the same colour, there is a backlash of power against the user if they are of a different colour to the magic item. The more different the colour of the item and the wizard's natural colour the worse the backlash is. So you can use this magic sword to cut the link pretty easily, just the same as Vicky could. It's just that then the power of the sword will have a pretty allergic reaction to a brown and blue wizard using it. In this case that backlash would be a physical blast of power and light that would blow you apart into a thousand different little pieces!

Now obviously that's not what we want, so I've got you some magical protection so that you can use this magical sword to cut the link to Nimue and save your mummy quite safely."

444

I opened up another compartment of the bag that I had used to carry the white magic sword; and took out a pair of gloves that I had enchanted with strong grey magic. "I spent all last night making these just for you." I said, quite proudly. With my head a mass of fire and agony I had still made absolutely sure that what I was making would protect Danielle completely from any backlash from using the magical sword. They were one of the first spells I had cast with my new level of power: and they were some of my finest work. "These are magic protection gloves." I said softly, "Reinforced with huge amounts of grey magic. They will absorb all the power of the sword when you use it: and all the power of the backlash will be harmlessly faded away without so much as harming a single hair on your head."

Danielle looked at me oddly. Her face was puzzled and: almost: a little scared. "Grey gloves?" she asked in confusion. "Grey gloves, when I blue and brown wizard?"

"Well of course I made you grey gloves Danielle." I said gently, a little surprised at her reaction to the final stage of my plan all coming together. "I'm a grey wizard, what other form of magic could I use? It's not like I could have made you a protection out of another form of magic like white or blue now is it?"

"But if grey magic poison to Nimue and she blue and brown; and I also blue and brown…" said Danielle fearfully, her voice almost terrified.

Seeing her so scared triggered something in me, and I wondered suddenly if my plan: drawn up quickly after a few fitful hours of sleep and in the desperation of intense pain and stress: contained some fatal flaw that I had overlooked. It would be typical of me I thought bleakly: and a little panicked. Whenever I was playing board games I would come up with brilliant innovative strategies, only frequently to watch all my plans crumble

445

into nothing as I lost the game. And always it was the same flaw: making what seemed in retrospect an almost painfully obvious factual mistake: overlooking a small but vital detail of critical importance.

''Well if I brown blue wizard and I use grey magic gloves...'' Danielle began; but then she turned and looked at where her mummy lay very still on the couch: so very sick. There was a pause for a moment. It was brief but seemed to me, lost in unbearable tension, to last a lifetime. When Danielle spoke again her voice sounded very different. It had changed: hardened almost beyond recognition. The fear was all gone: wiped out as though it had never been. Only an implacable resolution to save mummy remained.

''No Edward it a perfect plan.'' The very, very determined little girl said calmly. ''The gloves will protect me from the white magic sword: thank you very much.''

I looked at her sharply, knowing something was very, very wrong: but having no idea what. But it felt like I should know. It felt like I had overlooked something that was completely stupid. ''Danielle I think you just spotted that I've made a mistake. Tell me what it is and we'll work it out to...''

The sudden explosion of pain was so intense that for a moment I actually wanted to pass out. All I could feel was myself whimpering in agony and darkness as all semblance of conscious thought dissolved in pain. My hands tore into the walls to steady myself, blood pouring out of my fingers as they tore at the plaster so hard: in so much pain I was basically mewling.

It was only when I reviewed these memories later: much later after it was far too late to change anything that might have made a difference to what happened very shortly afterwards: that I saw the subtle strand of brown magic Danielle had cast into me, deliberately making the pain of my sacrifice, for just a few moments, several times worse.

Time passed: moments that felt like years. And finally the pain faded down back to where, while it was still distinctly unpleasant, it could be lived with until I had finished doing what had to be done today. I tried not to think about how much I just wanted to go to bed and lie there in the peace and quiet and do absolutely nothing.

Clarity returned but I couldn't really remember exactly where Danielle and I had been in our conversation, and she was already speaking as I came back to some semblance of reality: making it impossible for me to regather my thoughts from where they had been before the new explosion of pain in my head.

''Your plan good.'' said Danielle, and I was too out of it to notice that she was too eager, too insistent. ''Go to wedding and keep eye on daddy and Nimue. Make sure nothing nasty happens before I can save mummy!'' She looked at me, and smiled bravely. ''How long I have before Nimue try and eat daddy?''

I gathered myself, whatever my doubts there was no time to reflect further, now was the time to act. ''Daddy and Nimue get married in the ceremony at three o'clock this afternoon: very soon after Nimue arrives at the church. Once Merlin has said his marriage vows, and is therefore powerless against her, Nimue will devour your father to gain his power and his deep and extensive knowledge of magic: and the hidden secrets of this world. It's just after nine in the morning at this exact moment. That gives you just under six hours to save your mummy. That is enough time: so you don't need to rush. But you do need to use it carefully, and you need to get started on saving mummy very soon.''

Danielle turned to the sofa and curled herself next to what was left of her mummy: laying her head as close to

Jessica's chest as she could without risking touching her and hurting her. The five year old's attention became absolutely and completely focused, and I realised that in that moment that everything else around her had basically ceased to exist: she had eyes and time now only for her mummy. The house could have burned down around her and I don't think that she would have noticed.

"I hear your heart beat mummy." The little girl whispered softly. "Slow but still there. You be okay mummy. I promise! Love you lots and lots. Love you so much. I can feel that nasty thread tying around your heart, like silk of a spider. It's nasty and it hurt you. But today I make you all better so you can sit up and I can give you hug: just like before that nasty Nimue came along to spoil things. But don't you worry about that nasty Nimue mummy, Edward going to go and kill her very dead." She finished in a voice of cold absolute promise, so intense I found myself shuddering.

Danielle took a deep breath, and then a cloud of brown magic crisscrossed with pulsing veins of blue power rose up all about her. Her eyes rolled in her sockets until they were pure white. She began humming. A deep elemental sound that grew from so soft that the faintest ear could barely have heard a single vibration; to a deep and guttural growl that made the whole house shake and my head convulse with fresh new explosions of pain. It was not as bad as my last attack but I still had to place a hand on the wall again, and I found myself breathing hard. Sweat and saliva mingled on my lips.

And then Danielle, her eyes still rolled back in her head, reached up her left hand and, slowly and carefully as if she was reaching out to retrieve a new born child surrounded by pieces of jagged glass, gently took hold of something, something small and indescribably tiny in the air. I could not see it but I could suddenly feel it: the foul

448

corruption of the parasitic link as it crept stealthily though the air. As Danielle's finger closed so delicately but oh so, so surely around that invisible link I could feel how desperately it suddenly wanted to twist and vibrate like spider's silk. To send a message to its dark master that it was, suddenly and unexpectedly, under a most determined little attack. But Danielle's touch was so gentle and so strong: somehow both almost impossibly together at the same time: that though the string fought with all its power to vibrate not one shudder went down it: it sang out no fatal warning that would have doomed us all. Danielle lay very still, curled tightly into herself with both her hands now outstretched, and then, with painstakingly slow and careful movements, she TWISTED. You could feel her magic, subtle but so terribly powerful, do its remorseless work. Hurting Danielle's mummy like this had wakened something absolutely dark and ruthless in the little girl's soul.

And then the whole thread suddenly changed, its entire purpose suddenly completely reversed and bent on itself backwards, without so much as a single shudder. Danielle had, in a few terrible moments, utterly reversed the flow of power between parasite and prey. There was a pause, and then the first soft pulse of energy beat back across the string, guided by the small child back into what little was left of her mummy. A faint, almost infinitesimal, flow of power flowing back into Jessica from Nimue. And then, after a long pause of many moments, another very small pulse. And I dared to begin to hope, seriously for the first time, that the little that Nimue had left of my elder sister might still be just enough to bring her back here among us.

Scared even to take a breath, lest even the slightest outside flicker disturbed Danielle's delicate balance of power, I seized the power of the grey and I clad myself in intangibility and invisibility once more; fading myself from having any effect on this physical plane that could in any way affect Danielle: or what she was doing. Then I turned and walked swiftly from the cottage and away from where the little girl worked her vital magic. My work in this place was done and I now needed to be waiting unobtrusively and perhaps even invisibly very near to where the bride-to-be prepared herself. Ready to strike at Nimue the moment I felt the parasitic link she had with Jessica break; as Danielle, with her mummy restored to health, cut the foul thread apart with her new white magic sword.

Chapter 34

For a moment fantasies danced before my eyes. I had never cared or thought much about weddings before. But for a few beautiful minutes I saw Artemis before me. Clad not in white, the colour of The Terrible, but in a flowing dress of many colours, her brown hair dancing in the wind. For a moment I saw us marrying under the light of her moon, a moon also no longer white but now all the colours of the rainbow. My daydreams varied in whether it was before or after we became man and wife that the ex-maiden of the moon's stomach swelled with my child. Romance said it should be after the wedding. The raw reality of feelings, and the absence of effective contraception in any sexual relationship between the divine and the human suggested very strongly otherwise.

Then I had arrived back at my house on Prestham Hill where the bride-to-be waited, and the time for daydreaming was long past.

I stepped out of the car: my brown cloak still hiding everything that really mattered. I was done making even the least basic efforts to fit in any more. I was tired of being the weed that had to exist alongside the sheltered plants. Now I had gained power through my own efforts, and despite not because of the society in which I was brought up in, I did not see why I shouldn't simply start reprograming the arbitrary rules by which the garden ran. Let us see if the sheltered plants had enough strength left in them to make a stand against the new order into which I would soon try and reshape this world. I wasn't counting on them putting up much of a fight.

But for now I wrapped and concealed my new strength in the magic of the grey. I didn't want anyone, least of all Nimue, to notice my new level of power until it was far, far too late for her. And I still kept my hood cast across my face. If my grey magic somehow failed I still wanted my last secret kept until the time I chose to reveal it.

Vicky was dressed in a beautiful green dress that matched her eyes. She hadn't cared one bit that bridesmaids normally dressed in white for purity. "White boring colour." she had said firmly. "Green colour of life and plants and my eyes. I want green dress please!!!" And then she had glared at her mum and Nimue so hard that they both knew that, "I want." meant simply, "I am having."

There was nothing for me to do for the moment, nothing but to wait in the background and wait for Danielle to heal Jessica and then cut the magical cord: which would be my cue to strike. I just needed to make sure that no one, especially Nimue, felt my sudden rise in magical strength. I stood to one side of the bridal preparations, watching carefully while Vicky's eyes never left Nimue, and all of Nimue's attention, though she hid it well, was focused on the white wizard preparing to attack her. Nimue might have a thousand times more experience than my little sister but Vicky, after all, was still the most powerful wizard in the western hemisphere.

I waited: like an image of The Allfather himself, who for so many centuries, since the fall of Iceland, had walked invisible among his enemies. Simply watching and waiting until the time was right for him to launch holy war once more. The pain in my head beat on, a terrible rhythm that still sometimes brought nausea into my throat and mouth, and yet gradually it was starting to abate. In time all wounds healed. I supposed that would be true even of this. And, as I waited and I watched, pulse by pulse, Danielle drained away more and more energy from Nimue: while all the time the parasite's attention was focused entirely on the small white wizard who seemed to be her only immediate threat. The hours slipped slowly by, crawling onwards as though the air was full of setting syrup, as the sun rose in the sky to midday. Around me people talked, and gossiped. And for a few hours, the joy of the special day made them forget the reality of the modern world. Gave them moments of relief from the greyness and emptiness of what was a too stable and controlled reality: a world in which only in few moments of escapism could most people ever really be happy. And all the time I waited I constantly weighed up Danielle's rate of progress against the onward flow of time: the time we needed against the time we had. And as the day drew on a smile started, carefully and slowly but increasingly surely, to light up my face.

Danielle was winning the race: quite comfortably in fact. It was going better than I had ever dared to hope. Even though the sun now started to descend from midday Danielle's steady taking of pulses of energy was outstripping the race of progress she needed. At this rate Jessica would be healed in time for me to strike before the wedding proper began. It was halfway between one and two in the afternoon when I felt the final pulse of energy slip silently away from Nimue, well before the three o` clock start to the marriage ceremony. Danielle had won the race with almost an hour and a half to spare. I was very proud of her. I waited, confidently now and nearly certain that my plan had come successfully together, knowing it would take mere moments for Danielle to cut the cord with the enchanted sword and use the magic gloves to protect herself.

But a process I had expected to take seconds did not happen in minutes, or tens of minutes, or then even in over an hour. No energy flowed along the link now either way, but the cord between Jessica and Nimue remained resolutely uncut. And, as the time passed, slipping away as the afternoon started to draw on in real earnest, I felt triumph turning to despair.

I waited, warring with the urge to contact Danielle, but not wanting to distract if she was casting magic of vital importance. But then it got past two-forty, then two-forty-five, then two-fifty. With less than ten minutes to go, and the bride-to-be preparing to get in the car to head to the church, I finally realised I had no choice but to call Danielle. Regardless of the risks of detection or distraction I had to find out what in hades was going on.

I sat invisible in the back of the bridal car as it drove towards the church, calling Danielle's mobile desperately. The line just rang out and went dead. I found myself listening to a sweet answerphone message about how as soon as she got this she would definitely call you back but she was probably busy playing or colouring right now, and that was more important than having her phone on all the time. I called the little girl again, but I still got no answer. The car reached the church and the bride and bridesmaids got out. I had absolutely no choice but to follow them, clad in invisibility. In the confusion of not knowing what Danielle was now doing, and even just if she was okay, I could feel my whole plan simply falling apart. Soon I would have no choice but to start acting out of pure desperation, knowing that I had already basically lost.

My phone was on, but still I got no call back: no reply.

I found Vicky, walking beside her as the flood of wedding guests started to sweep us all into the chapel. "Vicky," I said desperately, using grey magic to ensure that only she could hear me. "I really need to speak to Danielle right now but she won't answer her phone! I think she's switched it off. If you could just quickly use white magic to force it back on then…"

"Sorry Edward," said Vicky sadly, "No time left. Sorry plan didn't work! But need all my power to fight Nimue now."

Moments passed in numbness: as I watched helplessly as everything now started to just fall apart. I found myself seated for the wedding, luckily right next to Vicky. The ceremony began and still my phone stayed relentlessly silent, and the magical cord stayed uncut. I could feel all my hope falling away into absolutely nothing, and then the marriage vows began. I wanted to scream. I could not yet fight Nimue without risking killing my own elder sister. But if I did nothing Nimue would consume Merlin alive and then, with all the memories from all his many lifetimes inside him and the great spell no longer existing to protect them, she would grow far beyond even my new current level of power. I wondered if I could somehow get Vicky to try and cut the cord, but she had already given up on me coming up with any kind of good plan and was now completely committed to finding her own way forward. A way that would just get her uselessly killed.

Then, finally, my mobile rang with a video call. I answered it instantly, using grey magic to ensure our conversation stayed completely private: even from the ears of Vicky. Danielle's face looked at me, unharmed but very anxious and pale, through the standard technology of the video link.

"Edward," she asked, almost panickedly, "I out of time?"

"Yes." I hissed. "We are moments away from your father being consumed, you have at best about twenty seconds until they ask if anyone objects to this wedding. If it is not stopped at that point it is all over! What have you been doing?! You have to cut the cord now if you want to have any chance to save your daddy. I will not attack Nimue until I know that it won't kill my sister! If that cord isn't cut in the next few seconds then your daddy will die!!!"

I cut off our phone call sharply but, even as I did, I heard the marriage vows came to an end, the "I dos" ringing sharply in my ears. I cursed. Merlin was now bound and helpless against anything Nimue might do, bound by his own words and promises of love and faithfulness from taking the slightest action against her even if she reached out to devour his life and soul.

And then, with an unanticipated and terrible suddenness, the cord was cut. After so long the fact it had finally happened so quickly was completely shocking. Nimue jerked sharply, looking for a moment like a puppet whose strings had all been unexpectedly cut at once. She clutched her sides as the surprise and pain hit her with an unforeseen and almost overwhelming force.

The priest finished regardless, too busy looking down at his notes to really take in what had just happened. The audience shuffled around me uncomfortable, but not sure what to do.

I placed my arm on Vicky as she tried to rise and pushed her back down. Surprised at my action she fell back into her chair before she knew what was happening.

It was good I didn't know what had just happened to Danielle until the full fury of that storm was done. It was not like I could have done anything differently by that stage. Artemis showed me what did happen to the little girl, my small sister's best friend, afterwards in a vision. She held me in her arms while she did so, resting her head against my chest.

It was by far the most painful vision she had ever shown me.

Long minutes passed after I had left Merlin's cottage, and through them all Danielle maintained her steady and relentless transfer of power. Slowly Jessica's face reformed, its features growing back out through where they had been reduced to nothing more than blank and eyeless flesh. Her skin once more took on warmth and life, her eyes and nails regrew. As the hours started to pass the drained remnants of what had been Jessica recovered back into the body of a young and healthy woman. But though she was in almost all respects herself again she remained deep in enchanted sleep, where she would remain helplessly until the silk cord binding her to Nimue was cut. This process took from when I left to just before one-thirty that afternoon; when, while waiting with the bride-to-be, I had felt the last pulse of energy be pulled back out of the parasite and put back into my elder sister.

Then Danielle let her magic fall away, that part of her work done. She smiled with happiness when she saw how recovered her mummy was. She even did a little dance. Then she looked at the magical artefacts Edward had given her and bit her lip in fear. Now the part she was terrified of had come. She could use the sword to cut the cord without wearing the grey gloves, but without their protection she would then die from the white magic backlash as it blew her to bits. Or she could put on the gloves and use the grey magic to protect her from the sword as she cut the cord as I had intended. But what was then to protect her from an allergic reaction to the grey magic of the gloves when she used them to protect her from the sword's backlash? She was, after all, a blue and brown and not a grey wizard: the deeply stupid mistake that agony and lack of time meant that I had overlooked. It is hard to think coherently at all when you have a fireball of pain constantly exploding inside your head.

Danielle didn't know exactly what the grey gloves would do to her. She hadn't let Edward know the mistake in his plan because then he might have stopped her trying to save her mummy, and saving mummy was the most important thing of all. But Danielle did know that the grey magic would be poison to her. Edward had said so. He had said that was one of the reasons he was the best person to fight Nimue: that grey magic could be poison to blue and brown wizards.

But Danielle had inherited more than just power from her father. She had inherited also much of his creativity, and his skill to create brand new ideas: what formal language calls adaptable problem solving or divergent thinking: not one of which does justice to the power of its inherent creative spark. So the little girl went to the clothes drawer by her bed and took out two gloves of her own that mummy had given her. Nice and snuggly, and warm: but no magic on them: not yet. She was sure that if she looked at the gloves Edward had given her she could copy them to make her own protection clothes, ones that would keep her safe from the magical sword's backlash without then poisoning her themselves.

She went and sat back down with her new gloves and the sword and the grey gloves. She got straight into her new work. She knew that, after the most important job of saving mummy had taken so long, she didn't have that much time left. She was a hard conscientious worker, though tired, and she painstakingly put her work together, one bead of power at a time. Building her protection the same way a builder builds a wall, brick by brick. Her magic was powerful, even though she was so very young. She was weary but determined, and she pushed on through how strange she was starting to feel after using powerful magic now for so many hours all at once. She drove herself on: even though the task was difficult. After just under an hour the first glove, the one for her left drawing hand, was completely finished. A perfect job: just as good as you could hope.

But now Danielle was even more tired, and she had only about half an hour left until time ran out at three o`clock. This was the final stage of magic she had to do. Using the sword and activating the gloves would take only a few seconds and almost none of her energy, but time was now quite firmly against her. To get her protection ready she would have to somehow complete the second glove almost a full half hour quicker than she had finished the first. She tried to be hopeful, she should be a lot faster doing the same thing a second time after all. She had switched off her phone so that she could concentrate: but she had set an alarm on it to remind her of the time.

But she was so very young: even though her magic was powerful. She was determined but weary, and though she tried to push on through she was starting to feel so strange having been using powerful magic now for so many hours all at once. Even though she drove herself on the task was difficult.

It took nearly twenty-five minutes before Danielle finally realised she could not win this race. And then she started to panic as she suddenly realised that no matter what she did: she wasn't going to be on time.

She fought on, but she now had only minutes until her alarm went off and there was still almost half of the second glove to go and…

And then a beautiful woman was suddenly sat down in front of her, with dark hair and eyes of the clearest blue. It was Danielle's favourite goddess of all. The one who had listened to her the most closely when she had explained why she and daddy both really needed a new mummy to look after them both very badly: and it would be really nice if she could find somebody for them.

Artemis had listened closely, and then at the end said that she would be happy to help. But she had warned Danielle that the gods were bound by certain rules, and that if she did find Danielle a mummy then one day there would be a terrible price to pay. The gods always had to demand sacrifice to keep the balance of powers in check. Danielle had said, "Yes please. I really want new Mummy." And Artemis had given Danielle a hug and a kiss on the cheek and told her she would see what she could do. And Danielle had tried not to think about the fact that her favourite goddess always looked so poorly: and so sick.

"Danielle," said Artemis gently, in Merlin's cottage where Jessica lay so soundly and helplessly asleep. "I'm really sorry but you're not going to get that glove done in time. I've come to see you because right now you have to make a very important choice. I told you long ago that for me to find you a mummy there would be a price: and because I ended up finding you one so good I'm afraid that price will be heavy indeed."

"But my alarm not gone yet!" wailed Danielle desperately. "Still a little time! And why not you help me? You a goddess with lots of powerful magic. You even more powerful than daddy! Why not you save me? I not want to die when use sword! You never said I have to die to get a mummy, you never said that!"

"The wedding ceremony is running a little early Danielle," said Artemis softly, "so I am sorry but time is up for making those gloves of yours: great idea though it was. And none of us want to die. I wish I could help you Danielle, but though I love you dearly I am still a goddess and you are still a mortal. There is always in the end

460

between us a divide stronger than any love we can feel across it. You think I can spare even the man who makes my heart beat fast, who makes love burn so hard inside my chest? Though he raises me from the dead beyond all sickness, though The Friendly triumphs over The Terrible and subdues her to her will, though I bear him in love and marriage the child of his I so dearly long to have and to hold: know that even with all this the time shall come when I stand before him as I do before you now: and he in his turn will have to pay the price for having experienced as a mortal the power of the divine. And though what you face today is bleak know that when Edward's day comes this shall seem a mere pinprick besides the price that I must ask him to pay for loving me in the way that he does.

Today is your day of choice Danielle. You can walk away from here with not a scratch, no price paid. But then your mummy will die today. And your daddy. Or you can swing the sword, and your mummy will live and be well again, and maybe your daddy too. But you will pay the price I told you of long ago. What you do now is up to you. But first I would call Edward, and he will tell you that your time for making gloves is now past little one."

Frantically Danielle snatched up her phone and dialled Edward on video call as fast as she could. And what he said to her drained all hope from her heart: but even more so when she heard her kind, scatty daddy saying his wedding vows to that horrible Nimue in the background.

Danielle felt very numb as the line went dead. She pulled on her blue and brown glove, the one she had finished. It felt warm and snug as it fitted neatly onto her left hand. She knew she could use this glove perfectly safely, its magic was exactly the same as her own: there would be no reaction at all. She picked up the sword

461

wondering if she should just use it wearing one glove. One glove would certainly save her from being blown into a thousand little pieces but would it be enough to stop the sword killing her? Danielle thought hard for a moment. But then she looked at mummy and realised that a blast of power might hurt mummy as well as her. The grey glove's poison wouldn't touch mummy. And that was that.

Danielle wouldn't even touch the left grey glove, the one she didn't need, directly. She slid a mat under it and then threw the mat as far away as possible, making sure the glove never so much as touched her skin. Then she shivered, took a deep gasping breath of raw fear, and slipped the other grey glove onto her right hand. Her unfinished mitten lay on the table beside her: forgotten and quite useless. The grey glove felt very cold as it slipped onto her hand: a prefect death grip. It felt creepy and insubstantial, like grey clouds blocking out all light and happiness on a dreary and wet autumn day. It felt like rotting and dead things. Blackened corpses with rotting blue eyes. Merely seconds after putting the glove on she started to feel quite ill. She could suddenly feel a bad cold in her nostrils and a sick ache in her stomach where moments before there had been nothing but normal health and life.

Terrified, as she felt herself sickening so quickly, Danielle snatched up the sword of light as fast as she could. It burned fiercely at the touch of a blue brown wizard, but not a single spark or drop of heat reached Danielle though her very powerful magical protection. She raised the sword to cut the cord with a single terrible strike, but then she stopped and hesitated for a moment, tears pouring down her eyes. "I only five!" she wept, "I not want to die!!!" She stared at her goddess desperately. "Tell me what I should do? I only a child, how can I know the right answer?" She stared at Artemis imploringly, a child suddenly facing, as so many have over the long years and centuries, the sudden bleak reality of oncoming death.

"No one can tell you what to do little one," said Artemis sadly, "not even me. That is what it means to be a pagan. The gods guide mortals, but it is not within us to instruct. We are merely here to help you make your own decisions. If you don't cut that cord then both your mummy and daddy will die tonight, but you will live. If you cut that cord mummy will certainly live and daddy has a good chance. But very bad things will happen to you. Either way you can't afford to take long to choose, not with that glove you're now wearing. If you don't swing that sword very soon you will be too ill to do so, and then you will die and you will have achieved absolutely nothing. Whatever decision you are going to make Danielle, you need to make it NOW!"

Danielle stood for a moment, torn and unsure. A moment she didn't really have as the allergic reaction she was having to the grey magic in the glove started to make her very ill, really very fast. But then she did make up her mind: she did make her choice. She brought the swinging sword of light down upon the cord with all the strength she had left, and activated the protection of both her gloves at the same time. The sword stroke was true: it did not miss. It cut through the cord as easily as a sharp knife cuts through butter. In a moment the foul link binding Jessica was gone as though it had never been.

Danielle had a moment of pure triumph when she saw the cord fall away, and her mother sit up with a start, and another as every bit of white fire from the sword that would have killed her was absorbed by the power of her gloves' protection. She dropped the sword and staggered away towards mummy, wanting to give her just one last hug before the end.

But she never got near mummy. She did not even have the chance to take so much as a couple of steps before the force of her allergic reaction to the grey magic hit her full on. She crumpled like a dead leaf and, before she was even remotely aware of what was happening, her mind and soul had fled into darkness.

Chapter 35

Far away from the little cottage, where a very brave little girl had just fallen, the dark storm swept on uncaring into its next stage. I finally prepared to stand against Nimue for Merlin's life, my elder sister quite safe. And having no idea what price had just been paid to achieve that.

Nimue was leaning against a pillar, her face riven with pain as she gave a great cry. Then her form melted and reflowed, recasting itself into a new shape. When she raised her head to stare at me with brown eyes that blazed with fury she once more looked nothing like Jessica. She was again in the shape that I had first seen her wearing: that of the dark-haired woman who had been Merlin's manager. But this new: or old depending upon how you looked upon it: form shook, unstable. It was clearly drained out and past the point of ever meaning to be reused. When it finally went I had a quite certain feeling that any who were still present would then see Nimue's true form: in all its black horror.

"Clever." Nimue said, smiling at me, and laying her hand on Merlin's arm. "However did you find that bitch, your sister? Once I am done here I will make you tell me. I'm guessing you got Danielle to cut the cord? I can see why The Allfather is interested in you, he has always liked those who are creative and intelligent. The divine huntress though, I think you'll find it rather hard to find that anything you do will ever interest her: unless you remove something from between your legs that I'm pretty sure you don't want to give."

Around me the other wizards and guests shuffled uneasily, starting to back away from something that they did not understand and that could be very dangerous. Already at the back they were starting to slip out of the church and disappear away into safety. Let the parasites fly, their day of judgement would come soon enough. I could feel Vicky's eyes glaring hot coals in the back of me, her form shaking with fury. She didn't want to interrupt my plan but she was incensed that I was stealing what she had clearly told me was now her fight. I held Nimue's gaze calmly, fighting not to smile. With the sacrifice I had made and the cord now safely cut Nimue didn't realise it, but this was already pretty much done. Whatever tricks she had left, unless I made an absolute mess of things, she was basically a dead woman walking.

"Whatever my future does or does not hold," I said levelly, "There is very little time for you left in it. You are about to die, and when you are gone we will then see where all things stand. I'm going to start with a long chat with Merlin I suspect: about the true power of the grey among may other things. I challenge you to Pankration: to a mortal combat that really isn't going to take all that long."

Nimue laughed, a cold sound without any trace of joy and mirth. Maybe it had just been so long since she had last had an opponent that could threaten her, that she had come to believe that no one ever really could: that she was completely safe. But all things have their end: even parasites cannot last forever.

"And why would I want to fight you right now? I'll kill you easily of course but eating you would gain me nothing. On the other hand I have Merlin here under my fingers, so full of all the power from his previous lives that I've been fighting for generations to have the chance to devour. His own marriage oaths leave him helpless in my hands and jaws. Thank you for your kind offer to fight me but I'd rather eat Merlin alive, and then when I'm done with his magic and screams it will be time for Danielle and then that little sister of yours to join him in becoming nothing more than magic and nutrients running though my veins."

I walked calmly out from where I was standing among the guests until I stood before her, my hood shadowing my face in darkness, concealing my secret to the last. Merlin watched me, strangely completely calm. Nimue's illusion had fallen from his eyes when the cord broke, but he was helpless, bound by the very oaths that he had just sworn. The priest fled: joining the rapidly retreating guests.

"That does not sound so like a future I would choose." I said calmly, "So…"

Nimue smiled in savage joy. "Oh but you don't get to choose much of anything from now on Edward. And believe me by the time things have played out you will wish that I had devoured you alive with the rest of your family. You have made The Mountain angry Edward, and just as he ensured that Jessica was punished by me for daring to stand against his temptation so you, you who have had the sheer audacity to defeat him in straight combat, as no mortal has ever done since the fall of Iceland and the end of the pagan age, you he will make absolutely certain will pay most dearly for what you have done. He wants to kill you himself. You are to be taken to the highest peak and bled out alive, where all you can see is his sun in the sky and the bleak sand of the desert that covers his land. You and he will meet in the place where there is no darkness, where you cannot hide from the glare of his light. A place where the separation of white and black magic means that the grey can never exist, no more than a shadow can be cast at night. And your death will be the signal for his armies to march, the signal that begins the final war that will establish his dominion forever. The war that will end the last ever chance of the restoration of the pagan age."

I laughed softly. "Oh but the night does cast shadows Nimue. All you need to have on your side is the light of the moon."

Nimue raised an eyebrow. "And you are so sure that the moon is on your side are you Edward? I know the divine huntress a little better than you I think. Only when you meet the real huntress, not the fragment of a memory whose main skill is making moon eyes at attractive men, then you will understand a bit better how things really stand."

"I have seen The Terrible," I said calmly, "and one day I do not doubt that we will meet in the flesh. But that is a problem for another day. I give you one last chance to accept a Panktration match against me with honour."

Nimue sighed like she was talking to a small child. "When a girl says no a guy's got to listen Edward. And I don't want to kill you at the moment." She turned her hungry eyes on Merlin. "I want to eat him!" She glanced at me dismissively. "You are not nearly powerful enough to force me into a Panktration battle, so that's that really." She turned to Merlin, and caressed him like a spider: running her fingers hungrily all over his face. For a moment they shimmered, seeming almost thin and black. "I wanted to devour you so slowly my love. I wanted to eat from the inside while your body and memories dissolved and poured inside me. I wanted those last moments of you experiencing your own dying to be the last thing I ate, like the sweetest cream on the top of cherries. So sweet and red with juice. The perfect aftertaste to a meal which will make me the most powerful wizard in the world.

But circumstances dictate that I eat you quickly. Little Edward here trying to interfere by saving you and even trying to fight me himself. I would be mad, but The Voice has shown me what he intends for Edward, so I can't be too angry. After all, he has promised me that I will be allowed to watch." She turned and smiled at me. "You are the last light of hope Edward, the last hope to rebuild a bridge between the world of men and the world of the gods. Your fall will be the end of any chance or dream that men can ever correct their ways and build a better life for themselves: a life where all the power of the divine moves freely among them once more. And how Artemis the Terrible will cry with victory that day. On that day when all hope for men is forever lost. Now if you'll excuse me for a moment, I really am terribly hungry."

She reached out with her power to consume everything that Merlin was. You could smell the digestive venom inside her mouth as she called it up to help dissolve the sinews of his body and the tissues of his mind. She still did not understand how my sacrifice to Odin had changed all the rules of the game.

I threw aside my hood. For the first time I revealed my new, true strength. "Pankration." I commanded, and for a moment the level of grey power in me felt like I would have had the strength to fade even the sun from the sky.

Energy leapt between Merlin and Nimue, the burning walls of energy that made up the edge of a Pankration arena: the boundaries that separated all others from joining in our conflict. Nimue's fingers were pressed against Merlin's chest, but between the two of them suddenly burned barriers of implacable power. Only one of our deaths, or one of us accepting the other's surrender, would bring down those walls of power.

"No!" howled Nimue in frustration, cheated of her prey. She spun in fury. "How can you have gained so much in power so qui..."

And then she suddenly stopped, and went white. She was staring at where the fireball of pain frequently felt like it was tearing apart my skull.

After the first few confused moments Merlin's message: the simple line drawing of a great eye wreathed in flame: had been almost painfully easy to understand. Had not both Artemis and Odin been consistently clear from the start on the need for great sacrifice to be anointed as their champion and share in the fullness of their power? Was not sacrifice the core of all communion between a pagan and his or her gods?

And so, before a hand-held mirror and alone, in a library lit only by lamps of my own magical fire, I had gouged out my own eye with a knife blade, then hurled it into Odin's flame. Long ago Odin had sacrificed an eye for a single draught from the spring of wisdom. His dark knowledge had been paid for a thousand times in the cost of that sacrifice. And I now sacrificed my own eye so that I stood in his image as the champion of The Allfather.

Then, with blood pouring from my ruined eye socket, I had had to seal the wound with my own burning blade so I didn't bleed out and die. It wouldn't have been the woman's death: the Odin's or the seer's death perhaps? Either way I knew that for the rest of my life I would be haunted by the memory of my final horrified pause, the point of the blade quivering before the corner of my left eye: acutely aware that it may well be the last thing that my left eye ever saw. And I had been left with a moment of absolutely clear choice. How much did I love Jessica, and how much exactly would I give to save her life?

But now at least, I would reap the rewards for my offering of blood and oh so specialised flesh. I stood facing Nimue, a slight smile on my face.

"It's over Nimue." I said simply. "You can fight against me, and have the power of the grey fade all you do to nothing. You have built your brown and blue magic on exploiting peoples' dreams of success in this world. Against a grey wizard who this world offers nothing your powers will be almost useless. The Mountain himself has nothing in this world with which to tempt me: how much less will merely one of his disciples have? And you must be so weak with hunger, a parasite who has starved herself for a very large and very special meal now trapped in mortal combat with a contestant who is poison to her.

And you have nothing that I want either. Surrender and I will just kill you. And the only end to Panktration is either surrender or death: It's game set and match Nimue."

"You cannot use grey magic as a weapon!" shrieked Nimue, fighting suddenly not to panic. "You hurt so much as my little finger with grey magic and it will break every law in this land. It would mean your trial and execution."

I laughed coldly. "Merlin is a powerful friend to have Nimue. For saving his life and his family he will twist every string he has. Just this once, I think I'm going to be okay." I really hoped that was true. Otherwise I would just have to use the concealing power of the grey to go on the run after all this.

Nimue backed away from me. Her form shimmered, looking less and less human, more and more black and arachnoid.

"I always win!" she screamed. "In all the legends I take Merlin down! He cannot defeat me!"

"You're not fighting Merlin though are you?" I said lightly.

"Why who are you?" sneered Nimue. "One of the light wizards of the Table Round? A shining knight in white armour? Your face doesn't exactly fit one of the champions of the light now does it?"

"There are three wizards of dark power in the legends." I said "Merlin, Nimue and one other."

Nimue's eyes widened. "But she's normally a girl."

I shrugged. "Her role is neither particularly masculine nor feminine. The role is determined mainly by dark magic power, a strong preference for paganism and passion over Christianity and order: and a secret incestuous love that beats in the very core of her heart. As the cycle repeats across history why should the same roles always be played by members of the same sex? The name she went by is currently so unused that it is now no longer a girl's name or a boy's name. After me it will be a man's name.

And never before in any of the legends have Nimue and Morgan le Fay ever battled to the death. Legend is now on neither of our sides."

And from that time on the name Edward ceased to have any meaning for me. From that moment onwards I came to be known by my new name. From that day to this I have always been Morgan le Fey. And people nowadays have long since forgotten that it was ever a girl's name. Just as they have since forgotten that Arthur was ever a boy's name.

Nimue screamed. It had been so long since she had had to fight hard for her life, I realised, that she no longer really remembered how. Centuries of easy victories based on just the skill and subtlety of her illusions had softened her once formidable fighting power: as much as the success which leads to civilisation then softens in time the heart and sinews of even the most vibrant and dynamic tribes.

Desperately the parasite called up all her powers of illusion: even knowing that they had now no real hope of aiding her against me. But then, she had almost nothing else left. Reality faded into dancing patterns and weaves of deceptive silk. Nimue stood before me. Her hair was red now, her eyes green.

"I could be better for you than her." she whispered to me. "I could be more Vicky than Vicky. I could take power from all your friends, and so gain the power to save you that even your little sister does not have. Just surrender to me now so that I can end this Pankration and then eat Merlin. Together we could stand against The Mountain and..."

I faded away the pathetic illusion, struggling very hard not to laugh. That such a foul creature's reign of horror should be reduced to such dark farce part of me found hysterically funny. "That's it?" I said. "You're promising to kill and eat everyone I care about, and then you're going to fight The Mountain with me? The first part is believable but not exactly tempting. The second is tempting but would be a little more believable if you hadn't just said you were looking forward to watching as The Mountain made me die. It's done for you Nimue. It's time for you to make whatever peace you can with how things have turned out before your end."

"Morgan..." Nimue began desperately, but I shook my head. "There will be many desperate battles ahead of me," I said softly, "many conflicts where success balances on a knife-edge and which threaten to tear apart every sinew and tendon of my body and mind. I have no doubt that in the war to restore my gods there will be many battles that will make me bleed. But this not one of them: not the first battle after I tore out my own eye. The battle to defeat you was won in the university library last

473

night, before a small mirror that shook in my hand and a knife blade that glowed red hot with the power of fire. This is just a brief and almost satisfying aftermath.''

I reached out with the power of the grey, and I FADED her. Nimue screamed, but was as helpless before my power as a leaf blown before a storm. The blue and brown power in her started to fade into nothing, and her body started to collapse in on itself and to bleed profusely everywhere as the physical fabrics that gave her life began to disappear. Within moments she was shuddering helplessly on the floor, her many legs curled into her, crooning in her spidery voice as I drained away all the energy she had consumed from the many forms she had eaten throughout her long, long life. Within a matter of seconds of me starting to fade her to death, effectively undoing all the physical reactions powered by her version of calories that gave her form life, her body broke down out of its deceptive mask back into her true form. The reality that lay beneath all her stolen masks of illusion. She or it lay crying piteously on the cold floor as death came ever nearer. I felt not the slightest flicker or pity or remorse.

Nimue had long since stopped being human in any meaningful sense of the word. From the waist downwards: the bottom half of her body: were only eight black legs curled out from a black rounded torso: or abdomen to give it the spider rather than the human name: and seemingly unending weaves of spider silk. In other words from the waist downwards she was all spider.

But she still had growing out from the front of the spider's abdomen the body of a beautiful curvy brunette, starting with where the bottom part of the human stomach grew straight up out of the spider's flesh. Of course, as she no longer had any human female reproductive organs, all that beauty was nothing but a lie, nothing but a device to lure men to their doom. Her beauty was there merely to help her satisfy her physical craving for the flesh of men, not to help in the fulfilment of sexual lust. But while the lower part of her body was completely spider the top half was not pure human. Her face and head were now far more arachnoid than homo sapien. Eight black eyes ran in a ring around her head, and from her lower cheeks the two black protrusions of spiders reached out: through which she drank in the digested juices of her dissolved prey. Her mouth had the fangs and venom of a spider. The most sickening thing was that I knew, deep down on some instinctive level, she had been human once. Some dark power had done this to her and called it a blessing. I wondered sickly which god could be so dark that it would bestow its favour in this way, that to any sane person would seem far more of a curse that any kind of boon or enhancement. My thoughts drifted to a desert under a sky which was never freed from the curse of eternal sunlight, but even as I did a cold voice whispered mockingly in my ears. ''A true god did this!'' whispered The Voice of The Mountain in my ears, ''Not me!!!''.

Not that it mattered much at the moment exactly who had wrought these horrifying changes to Nimue. Whether god or demon the hideous result was the same. This was now a creature so corrupt and changed from human kind that there could be no hope of mercy. Whatever Nimue had once been she was nothing more now than a creature of hunger and cruelty that lived just to feed and kill. The reasons, no matter what they were, that had led to this corruption no longer had any real meaning. Nimue looked up at me, her face desperate. Her eight black spider eyes twisted frantically in terror, but she didn't even have any eyelids to blink or make them appear even remotely human. ''I surrender,'' she begged wildly, but I found no pity. Only a wonder that a creature so foul could still somehow manage to speak in a human voice.

"I have no interest in accepting it." I said bleakly, "Quite simply I just want you dead." I summoned up all the power of the grey and of fire to end this quickly. I took no pleasure in this task: I just wanted it done. The wind picked up, and outside clouds were moved from across the surface of the moon. Even though it was daytime the moon still shines, it is just invisible for most people the same way that a switched on electric light is hardly noticeable during the day, and yet is most definitely still there. But whatever happened to the light of the sun when it reflected off the cold rock of the moon in space my eye was now far more sensitive to moonlight than it was to that of normal sunlight. For the first time since our conflict began moonlight fell down through the windows of the church; to the specialised eye of a champion of Artemis, clearly illuminating both of us.

I had a moment to wonder how the moonlight had got through the walls of Pankration. Then I realised that, just as the power of Odin was now within me, so too the power of Artemis must have come with me also. After all I had a very deep relationship with both divinities. The moonlight felt warm: strange when Artemis's touch was always so cold. It also felt sickly unpleasant, whereas I had come to find beauty in the virgin's cold touch. I didn't know if it was a distortion due to the fact that I had now only one eye, but the moonlight appeared strangely bright blue to me, rather than the clear virginal white I had grown to know and love.

Outside the circle of Pankration power that bound me and Nimue together in mortal combat I saw Merlin putting aside his phone his face suddenly terrified. His normal implacable calm suddenly simply gone. Power blazed in is his hands. Blue and brown, stronger and more terrible and complicated than any magic of his I had ever previously seen. Then he channelled the raw stuff of magic into a liquid which he poured through mid-air into a potion bottle he had seized from his belt. He placed the now full bottle in Vicky's hands and sealed it shut. Vicky's face was white. She turned and ran. As she did so I realised that all the other guests had already fled the church. That did not surprise me, civilised cowards looking out for nothing but their own safety. But why was my sister running away? And why was she looking absolutely terrified? She could not affect my combat through the walls of Pankration, but I would have expected her to be prowling round the edges furiously, filled with white magic and following every move really closely: livid with anger that she could not intervene. Merlin tried to follow my little sister, but cursed as he could not pass the door of the church, and instead staggered back helplessly towards the edge of the energy that bound the Pankration fight. That I could at least understand, he was still bound to this creature by all the force of his wedding vows. He literally couldn't leave this room at the moment, not while she still lived.

Not that I intended for Nimue to stay alive for very long at all.

I hurled the grey and fire magic I had gathered at Nimue, and as my power passed through the moonlight I felt a strong resonance and familiarity with its power. I smiled as I realised that moonlight was now as much a part of my power as the magic of the grey or of fire. It shouldn't really surprise anyone: after all over the last few months I had grown closer to Artemis than any man before me ever had. Around the power of the grey fading and the fire storm I hurled at Nimue I now sent also sheer edges of moon metal, razor edged.

But to my shock it clashed home against a metal pincer of moon metal forged by Nimue, many times stronger and more skilled with the power of the warm blue moonlight than I had been.

That was a shock which sent shards of ice dancing through my stomach. After all Artemis and I had shared how was it possible that this foul creature was closer to the chaste huntress than I was?

"Fool!" hissed Nimue, as her pincer of moon steel drove my power backwards, the first time in this conflict that she had come close to anything resembling a decent fight. "I have centuries of experience of working with moon magic, and you think you can beat me with it on your first try? You should have finished me quicker Morgan, while I was still helpless against you. Before the power of the blue moonlight reached us to bathe me in its strength and ruthless magic!"

I had no wish to compete with her in moon magic, not when her skill and strength in that area obviously so far exceeded my own. So I switched back to my primary magic, the one with which I had the most experience and skill: and the one which was by its very nature a natural poison to Nimue. I struck out at her again: with all the power of the grey. She met my attack with all the power that she could draw from the blue moon. For a moment the powers raged against each other, the contest seemingly suddenly almost in the balance. Had Nimue been fresh perhaps it might have been, but my earlier attack had already caused her terrible damage, draining and weakening her almost beyond all measure. Her moonlight attack, her magical razor sharp pincer of blue moonlight that cut through the air to end my life, was broken by the grey: faded into nothing. My attack was broken as well in the clash of power, but I was still in comparatively good shape, had the strength left to launch several more such assaults. Nimue simply crumbled against the floor gasping, even with the moonlight all around she no longer had any reserves left to use it: the last of her strength was now spent.

But still I felt uneasy at how events seemed suddenly to be turning against me. Logic said I could simply end Nimue quickly without resorting to my last and most powerful reserve, but I was done taking any chances. I was going to end this now, before any more surprisingly unpleasant factors had the chance to come into play against me. I played the final, and very deadly, ace I still had hidden up my sleeve.

I had barely moved in all our conflict so far: I had not needed to. But now I took out my last weapon: calling out of grey incorporeality the final power my sacrifice had granted me. One I had so far concealed even the idea of in the long folds of my cloak. What was it Vicky had called Odin when she first saw his picture in that colouring book on the train? A god with a dark cloak: and a big sharp spear. And with her taste for destruction she would have fallen in love instantly with the terrible spear of The Allfather, The Glad of War and The Worker of Evil, that I now called out of the shadows into an all too tangible and physical reality in my hand.

The wood of the spear shaft was oak from the hangman's tree, the metal cooled in its forging with blood instead of water: hammered into shape under the light of the cold full moon. And the metal itself came not from anywhere on earth, but from that remote sphere of white rock in the sky which is this planet's constant companion. In all of the recorded history of men and time there was not a weapon more deadly than The Allfather's spear, and this one in his honour held much of its terrible power: more than enough to end the already broken Nimue's wretched life. And to bring this conflict to the sudden and fatal end that was now needed before anything else unexpected could happen that might alter the course of the fight.

I summoned all the power of the grey and with a scream I hurled the spear straight at Nimue's heart: ironically one of the last parts of her that was still fully human. My aim was true and Nimue screamed helplessly as the weapon of The Allfather flew implacably straight at her chest: no magic in her having a chance against the power of that fell weapon thrown by a champion of The Allfather. Only a god, or godlike power, could have stopped that weapon's deadly arc. And for a terrible moment I wondered if The Voice would intervene to save his champion.

He didn't

But another god did.

Or: rather: a goddess did. One that I had thought I knew as well as any man upon this earth. But, like many, many men before me, I had melted far too much before the beauty of her all enticing moon eyes.

A silver arrow of moonlight fired through the still air, catching the spear of The Allfather in mid-flight. It carried the divine weapon harmlessly to one side of Nimue, where the dread of its landing split the flagstones and left its spearhead quivering uselessly in the church floor. The power of paganism trapped in the foundations of a church. I could not think of a better symbol of the triumph of the foul Christian age.

A voice of moonlight and silver, a voice that was so familiar and at the same time so utterly different from the one I knew, spoke mockingly into the very sudden silence. In some ways, posh and cultured, it had nothing at all in common with the always friendly and sometimes inane chatter of The Friendly, but still I would have known it was the voice of the same woman that I loved if I had been stricken deaf and not been able to do any more than see her lips move.

''I really don't like it when men hurt women Morgan. That is the twisted and distorted natural order of things that is my solemn duty as the true princess of the gods to bring a permanent end to. You think that I would let a man, A MAN, who the inane attentions of sappy has left bearing my blessing and able to tap my power, slay my foremost champion? Slay one who has always followed the dictates of The Terrible: and who is the living definition of a man eater? And one whose very form and body has changed so much with all the beauties of my blessing? To let you kill Nimue: that would be blasphemy itself against me. And whether I be demon or goddess no one, least of all a male, shall ever violate what I have decided is written down in my personal Holy Writ. I will not let you save Merlin nor slay Nimue. And let The Allfather now see the sheer stupidity of his making an alliance with any form of Artemis, for is the Glad of War not, for all his so-called learning and apparent greatness of mind, nothing more than, ultimately, just another man? And in the right circumstances even his own myths confirm that he will rape a woman as surely as any other male that still has that foulness between his legs that we politely call a cock.''

I turned to face her, the new face of the woman I loved more than life itself. And as I met the terribly clear and bright living gaze of Artemis the Terrible for the first time I realised many things. Things that a thousand shared lifetimes with The Friendly could have never said, or brought to light.

481

Chapter 36

It is a common mistake to believe that the monotheistic faiths deny that other gods exist, that they say magic is not real. The truth is far darker than that, far grimmer. For why would they persecute us, slaughter our worshippers and burn our temples if they believed that we were powerless? And while denying the existence of the gods would be both foolish and distasteful it would not be blasphemy. But the teachings of the Christians and similar faiths is not that our gods and magic do not exist, but that they are simply altogether and irredeemably evil. There is God's power, and all other magic is the work of the devil. And so the monotheists teach that the natural pagan faith, that evolves in similar forms all around the world but with differences in each culture and nation as each people and each gods chose their own relationships, is pure evil. That the beliefs and traditions that people have followed for centuries are nothing but sin and darkness. And a faith where everyone makes their own individual choices is replaced by a bland internationalist or imperialist faith just imposed onto everyone. And it is that belief, that the divine: the true source of all that is good and most precious in this world: is evil unless it is one particular form; that is the ultimate blasphemy of all.

The difference can be seen in modern literature, between horror and fantasy. In horror the world falls to magic armies of the living dead, or strange undying monsters slaughter teenagers either with a machete or in the helplessness of their dreams. The magic is altogether evil in these stories, in the end just an obstacle to be overcome, and which frequently triumphs to drown the world in blood and gore. In fantasy, as in reality, magic is the ultimate source of good. The hope on which all depends, the way that we ultimately build a better world for us all. I had always been on the side of fantasy and magic, long before I saw the riddles in The Allfather's eye, or my heart beat faster at the curves and smile of The Friendly.

But in that moment when I stared into Artemis the Terrible's eyes for the first time, I understood suddenly what is was like to be in a horror story. For an instant I was on the side of those who saw magic as an awful threat to all that was light and good in this world. Magic as simply a dark force that wanted to make all things that were good and pleasant burn. In her green eyes I could see nothing but darkness.

The energy of the Pankration barriers burned around us. Merlin was held against the other side of those walls of energy: bound by his marriage oaths into helplessness. His fate, live or die, was in my hands. And, with the amount of power and memory in him, whether Merlin, or what I now realised with dull horror was Artemis the Terrible's champion, Nimue, walked away with that knowledge or lore, it would shape much of the future of this world. In one corner the drained spider woman scuttled, pulling herself away from me. Our battle was done, she had used her very last power to heal her wounds and stop herself just bleeding to death. Were our battle to resume again killing her now would be the work of mere moments. But all this I noted merely distantly, faintly. Things that might be one day of great importance, but right now were just extra unimportant details on the edge of my peripheral vison. My battle was now with the dark power that lay behind Nimue. That had always lain behind Nimue I now realised sickly. I had eyes only for other side of the goddess I had chosen to serve: chosen to love. The goddess who at this moment had just revealed herself as my mortal enemy.

I felt many things in the first moments that I saw her in the flesh. The first was an aching realisation that she was more beautiful, more powerful by far than The Friendly. She was far more sure of herself, she walked with a self-confident assurance and possession that the conflicted Friendly had always lacked. Whereas The Friendly always highlighted her beauty with bright colours and tight clothing, overdoing it as though she didn't really understand the sexuality she was trying to be attractive with, Artemis the Terrible's simple white and gold garments, neither suggestively tight nor revealing, made her womanly beauty more apparent than The Friendly's over the top efforts ever could. Her voice was cultured and rich, and she spoke with all the authority of both her divine and royal station. Her flesh was warm and she was the picture of defiantly ruddy health. You knew within moments of meeting her that, while The Friendly came across mostly as chatty and nervous on first impressions, The Terrible was indeed a beautiful and royal princess of the gods, daughter of Zeus and a goddess of power and immortality.

The most painful realisation of all took a few moments to really sink in. Artemis the Friendly wasn't just weaker because she was dying and her time was past while Artemis the Terrible was in full and terrible bloom: true though all that was. Artemis the Terrible was a more evolved version of Artemis, it was like comparing a young child to the fully grown adult. The Friendly wasn't just dying, she was the dying weaker and underdeveloped version of this goddess. But The Friendly had never wanted or intended to grow up like this. It was as if a beautiful caterpillar had emerged from a cocoon as a vast spiderlike moth, an immature beauty become a twisted and vile parasite; but fully grown and far more powerful. A foul creature of terror and death: and with a never ending hunger for male blood. Especially innocent male blood.

The silver bow was drawn again, its arrow pointed at my heart. If Artemis shot another arrow this time it would do more than just knock aside my thrown spear.

There was a long silence while Artemis and I looked at each other, both of us considering our options. Finally I spoke. ''You could kill me at any moment with that arrow, the slightest pinprick from those arrow shafts can never be healed but would cause me to bleed until I died. And so powerful are those arrow shafts that I could not fade them away into nothing though I had a thousand years. Were I to fade the air they pass through your divine will could push them on through the vacuum. Were I to try and fade myself the fact that we are so closely bound now means that though I made myself intangible, beyond almost any weapon that is now in this world, still your arrows, coming from the moonlight which we both now share, would find and cut me even as I drifted mostly faded outside reality. Even were I to fade the stone away beneath my feet to try and fall down and dodge, you could but with a flicker of your mind redirect your deadly shafts.''

''You are a clever little runt aren't you?'' laughed Artemis the Terrible, but her seeming mirth did not conceal her terrible anger. ''Yes I could kill you at any moment. By all means if you wish go and collect that spear of yours. Even a weapon of the gods cannot kill an immortal, but it might buy you time, might allow you to knock a few of my arrows out of the air, before one strikes home. That is a far fitter sport for a princess of the gods, shooting down an armed man, than simply killing you the same way I would drown a male puppy for the crime of being born as the wrong sex."

I looked at where the dark spear of The Allfather lay, and it stirred at just the whisper of my thought. I had but to will it and it would once more be ready in my hand. It felt like security and protection, all the strength of having a strong weapon between my fingers. But to take it would be to die, no man could win in direct combat with a god or goddess. That way lay only death. And yet I could not believe The Allfather would let me come so far, only to abandon me now to defeat and darkness. Lost in a hopeless combat that I could never have had any chance to win. And that was when I noticed something, something small and seemingly unimportant; like two ravens flying over a confused wizard at Chester University before then splitting off and flying in two different directions. The next hint that would help me walk the dark path to victory. The spear of The Allfather lay untouched, its blade undimmed by its impact, but the arrow of Artemis was splintered into a thousand useless fragments, broken forever beyond all future use. The seer warlord's power was far beyond that of the divine maiden of the moon. Had The Allfather really not foreseen that sooner or later the Terrible must rise against me? Was not his foresight part of the very essence of his being, while both forms of Artemis lived far more in the moment? Even as his power had just broken hers in the direct conflict of weapons, and both of them were gods of war and fighting, while both of them had the gift of foresight, was not The Allfather's knowledge and ability to assess how the future might ebb and flow always beyond all others? If I could but unravel the clues that he had sent in time then I could still fight my way through all this and somehow win.

And there was something familiar about this feeling that I had now. About the emotions that Artemis the Terrible was inspiring in me as she mocked my helplessness. Something that I had known throughout all my childhood. And then I realised what it was.

"It was you." I said simply. "It was you who encouraged Jess to torment me as a child, you who spurred her on to hurt me as much as she possibly could. You who wanted me to die in agony as I drowned. Why? Did you somehow know that I would grow up to be a threat to you?"

"Oh please." said Artemis the Terrible. "That suggestion shows just how overrated the intelligence of those savages who serve The Allfather is. If I had known who you were that long ago don't you think I'd have done something drastic about you back then? Your cock and balls would make a lovely ornament to go on the wall of my divine palace and paradise on this earth, your bled out skeleton nailed to the wall below it to remind me of you. I just hate the pathetic nature of grey wizards, so soft and whiny, and tormenting you was just so much fun. Like slowly removing the legs of a male insect one by one; and then just smiling as it thrashes and writhes about helplessly as it watches all the ways to maintain its pride and productivity just slowly and helplessly disappear. Then you don't kill it outright of course, you just throw it back into the garden and watch as all the insects that used to be its friends now shun it in fear and it slowly starves to death into a lovely withered husk: a beautiful monument to its glorious end to my honour and most royal divinity. Jess was a shining example of my worship, except for when she actually slept with her boyfriends, but I have to make some allowances. I wanted Nimue to kill your older sister as much as Merlin after what your interference turned her into."

I could feel my black eye surrounded by billowing grey: the visual representation of my purpose in this world I realised suddenly. In that moment I thought about what it meant to be a grey wizard, and I finally knew that my answer to Odin's riddle had been wrong and that Merlin's had been right. The true power of the grey was not to fade yourself away, useful though that was. That would avail me nothing here against the white power of Artemis the Terrible in this battle, who could send her arrows to make me bleed however I tried to hide from her. The only hope was what Merlin had said, long ago, to a very frightened girl who was both completely the same and totally different to the beautiful woman before me now.

It was the true power of the grey to turn evil into good.

Thoughts and visions and ideas were blossoming in my mind, but there was still too much that I did not understand. Too much that was not clear to me. And unless I could see and understand all the plan of The Allfather then I would not leave this room except as a corpse.

"But why am I still alive now?" I wondered outloud. "You will have known from the prophecy Merlin spoke long ago to The Friendly how much of a threat I am to you. Of course you wouldn't have had the slightest clue who I was until The Allfather revealed my presence to you, as The Friendly, at The Pool of Fire and Blood, but I know that you have been the Terrible since then. I felt your power and presence when I had to commit murder and sacrifice that innocent tramp to you. So why do I still breathe when you could have…"

I stopped, feeling suddenly sick. "This is the first time that you've been Artemis the Terrible since my struggles to save him persuaded Merlin to open up the door to all his past selves. You let me live so that I could deliver Merlin to your champion with his great protection spell finally defeated and cast aside.''

Artemis glowed. Her cheeks flushed red. ''Quite clever for a savage after all.'' She laughed, actually clapping her hands in delight. ''And can you work out why I haven't killed you the instant I showed up?''

That was really easy. ''It's like Orion.'' I said calmly, ''You could have killed him instantly but you didn't. You made him wait for twelve months while you destroyed everything about him. Both to punish him and to help you break The Friendly's spirit and soul. So now you're doing the same with me. Your going to tell me everything horrible you can so that you feel I die a complete failure: both to hurt me and to try and finish off The Friendly.''

Artemis laughed softly, her red hair dancing in the moonlight. ''Does it make it worse Morgan? Knowing that I am about to destroy all the foundations of your life? Knowing that what I say will test your very sanity itself? Sappy was so determined I wouldn't show up again after Merlin made his gamble. She was going to hold me in and you know what, her silly little plan might even have worked if your plan hadn't had such a simple flaw in it. Something so broken, so terrible, that the way it worked out tore such a big hole in her heart. Her grief at what has happened just now in Merlin's little cottage is what weakened her enough for me to reappear at this critical moment. At a time when I can turn around everything and lay both The Allfather's and your plans into dust. The grief your failed plan has caused her came close to killing The Friendly outright.''

Artemis the Terrible looked at me, the green light in her eyes merciless and mocking with no trace of affection or warmth: just sadistic cruelty. ''Your plan to protect Danielle was so sweet. So innocent. Your grey magic did protect her completely from being hurt by all the fire made by that magic sword you got her to swing! Of course the fact that you gave her grey magic gloves, containing magic that is to her the literal equivalent of pure poison, was a slight oversight on your part! The very fact that grey magic can be so effective against brown and blue in the right circumstances, which you thought was one of your greatest strengths as you battled with Nimue here today, turns out to be nothing more than your greatest weakness after all. A fitting summary for your gender as a whole really. You are all so proud of what you have between your legs. You think your cocks are your greatest strength, when in reality they are nothing more than foul corruption and the reason that all your twisted gender must die screaming."

At her words everything in me went very, very cold. I felt, distant and far off through the numbness, a pain greater than any I had ever felt starting to descend upon me. Appearing out of nothingness as surely as any grey magic spell had ever rematerialized something into existence. And yet that was the moment when I finally saw a chance, a hope out of the darkness. By reminding me of Danielle my mind whirled beyond the hopeless confrontation between me and the dark goddess; and I saw a way to do something that would count: could make some sort of difference. It was like I had said to Jessica when she lay broken on her bed the first time we had really talked after The Pool of Fire and Blood. The only thing you can do when faced with the insurmountable is to break it down into smaller problems that you can deal with, step by painful step.

Thoughts burned through my mind at the speed of light. First priority, not the dark goddess against which all seems hopeless. First, finish what you came to do: save Merlin, kill the spider woman. And maybe, hope against hope, he can do something for Danielle.

On the slender hope that she is somehow still even alive.

I moved sideways, away from Nimue and Merlin, making the distance between me and Artemis a very clear shot. I thought of the grey, and suddenly the spear of the gods was once again in my hand.

Artemis smiled and raised her bow: seeing in my actions useless desperation, not the planning of The Allfather. I seized all the power of magic that I had. Artemis raised an eyebrow. "Darling not all the grey and fire magic you have can stop my arrow shafts. And just to be clear I don't intend to kill you quickly. All this first arrow is going to do is to nick the flesh on the side of your cheek."

She was laughing as she fired: unaware that she had already said far too much: her sadism betraying her at the last. I didn't intend to use fire or grey magic against her.

Artemis's shot was straight and true, but she was not the only one who could use the power of moonlight. I drew upon that power the moment before she fired, so closely linked was I to the goddess that I loved that synchronising our actions was as easy as drawing breath. The arrow flew so fast that no mortal man, not even me with my link to the goddess, could have altered its flight path once it shot out from the bow. But I had altered the movement of Artemis's arm just before she released, and before she was even able to register let alone react to what I had done she had already fired the arrow, and it shot unstoppable into the heart of its target: bringing very certain death. And even as it flew I screamed out the glory of the sacrifice to the name of Artemis the Friendly.

Nimue, pierced through the heart, shuddered once; then lay very, very dead. There was a moment of stunned stillness, in which the walls of the boundaries of the

Panktration arena simply disappeared into nothing: their power spent.

Merlin was the first to move. Not normally one for haste he was torn now by a fear for his daughter's life that drove him more than words could say. Freed from his marriage vows his shape shimmered and changed. In a moment he was a hare sprinting for the door, the next he was a flying crow, the next a small mouse running very swiftly. Fast and furious were the changes but Artemis, goddess of the hunt, still started to line up a shot in the mere moments that had to pass before he could escape and be gone.

"Did I ever tell you," I said mildly, "how much I enjoyed sleeping in bed with you, watching the warm currents of my breath caress your royal and divine skin?"

Artemis's fury was so incandescent that her form writhed with agony as her convulsions jerked her head back and she screamed, a sound of ear-splitting terror. I shook where I stood, and had to hold out a hand against a pillar to steady myself against her terrible cry of rage and anger.

But in the few seconds that cost her Merlin was long gone: making good on his escape.

I threw away my spear, then sat down and waited for Artemis to recover. When she turned to me again her eyes were covered with tears and her face was wet with crying. "Well done you pathetic runt. How does it make you feel to have defeated a princess of the gods? My champion is dead by my own hand, and I have many powers but I cannot raise the dead. Nor can I seek Merlin's life and take it in revenge. The rules that govern us all would judge me hunting him down directly, quite rightly, as too much direct divine interference in a mortal plane."

She looked at me surprised. "Had you fled then the same rules would then have protected you. Why do you not flee from a force that can bring you only castration and death?" She made a half laugh. "Did you think killing my champion would upset me enough for me to turn back into The Friendly? You really don't understand me do you? I would not let my course of action be changed by the fate of any person, man or woman, weak enough to end up failing me!"

I met her eyes quietly. "I never even thought about the possibility of Nimue's death bringing back The Friendly, and if I had I would have dismissed the idea as vanishingly unlikely for the very reasons that you have just mentioned. I stayed simply because I would never run from the woman I love, least of all when she is in the darkest place of all."

Artemis took in a deep breath, too shaken to be angry for a moment.

"You are saying that you have feelings for me? In this form? You do realise that I am not The Friendly…"

"Yes," I said quietly, "and she is not The Terrible. And neither of you, really, is the real Artemis. The woman I love is a schizophrenic. She has become an angel of light and a demon of darkness, which are the only forms of divinity that the Christian age understands. Black and White. Good and Evil. No room for grey. There's probably a record somewhere proving Artemis the Friendly is a Christian saint of some kind.

But that is not the nature of the divine I serve. Paganism is the worship of gods and goddesses who are both good and evil, who show the reality of life as it really is. And for all your anger you are not fully evil, you have a strength of belief and purpose that The Friendly lacks. And The Friendly is not fully good, there is a naivety about her that is frustrating: masquerading as innocence. The battle to reunify your personality is the battle to relaunch a new pagan age."

"Although," I thought, very quietly in case our link let the goddess somehow sense my thoughts, "the separation has worked quite well. We are talking like ninety nine percent evil to one percent good for you, and the other way round for The Friendly."

Artemis the Terrible shrugged, starting to recover from her shock. "Nice words, but all your divine protestations can't disguise the fact that this is really all about you wanting to get into my pants. What is it that The Friendly promised you? Oh yes, that she would bear you a child someday? Yes that is the very definition of Sappy."

Artemis the Terrible frowned for a moment as if in sudden thought. "Still what you did today with Nimue was quite impressive, and your words about what you want for me are quite interesting. And I have a wonderful tradition of my champions succeeding each other by killing the previous champion: the same way that spiders in the wild will eat each other. Normally you have to go to an ancient oak tree on my island and ring on it to start the challenge, but sometimes events mean you can't always stick to the formalities. Sometimes you just have to go with the moment, as Sappy is so fond of saying.

You have the power of Odin and of Sappy now, after you killed Nimue to Sappy's honour. One little sacrifice and I'll give you mine as well. All I want is for you to cut off that little stalk and two balls between your legs and offer it up to me and I'll let you be fully anointed as my champion. I'll even make sure you don't bleed to death.

Refuse and this is all just obviously about getting to try and sleep with me, and I won't be having that. Not from any man, not even a prince of the gods: and certainly not from a disgusting grey runt of a wizard." She raised her bow. "And I know how to deal with men who try to get with girls when they are not wanted: I

494

even have a lovely temple showing just what I love doing to all men: and particularly those who like to combine sex with a little bit of force."

"You will do what you must." I said levelly. "But there is one last thing I would like to say to you: before you then make whatever decision it is that you will."

Artemis the Terrible raised an eyebrow quizzically. "And this grand proclamation to me is..." she asked, almost genuinely amused.

I took a deep breath, and gambled desperately in the dark. Stating something as fact that was nothing more than the darkest of guesses. But Artemis's reaction told me instantly that the guess I had made had struck home.

"I have no words to tell you how sorry I am," I said quietly, "that, long ago at the beginning of The Terrible and the death of The Friendly, you were raped. That was wrong and it should never have been done or been allowed to happen."

Artemis stared at me, and then made a sort of half cry in her throat. Real emotion, joy and relief, spilling out of her uncontrolled. I did not know it at the time but I was the first man to ever tell The Terrible he was sorry she had been raped. The first man to ever show The Terrible any kind of affection at all. Even her own brother could not make it any clearer how much he absolutely despised her.

And the shock was so great that it broke The Terrible's control of Artemis's mind and, in a blaze of rainbow colours brighter than the sun, The Friendly seized back control. There was a stillness and a silence for the next few moments, and then I turned and walked quickly towards the goddess that I loved: who was now in a much less terrifying form. I sat down beside her, suddenly so unsure what I should say or do. I had no idea what Artemis would do next, or how she would feel. What would even the distant abstract knowledge that she

495

had been violated do to her mind, when the real detailed memory of the event had had such terrible affects? How would The Friendly cope and feel knowing for the first time that she was not actually a virgin at all: and that she had been abused by force in one of the most vile possible ways of all? Knowing for the first time what had created Artemeis the Terrible in the beginning: all those thousands of years ago.

But when Artemeis looked up at me, through a face that was strewn with tears of her black and dying blood her first words were not of rape or her other self; or of anything that I had thought she would say.

She looked up at me: grief heavy in her eyes.

"Danielle." She said simply.

Chapter 37

Three Weeks Later

The wind was cold in the air, so Jessica shivered as she set the garden table. But it was not only the air that was cold. Around the garden sat all Danielle's play things, unused since the wedding day: obviously. Jessica was thin and tired, but the physical drains of her ordeal with the shape changer Nimue had left no lasting scar. The bags and deep shadows under her eyes came not from physical but from emotional wounds. Part way through setting the table she stopped and started crying. Tears brighter and more bitter then she would have known how to shed had she stayed as Jess, in that choice so long ago. I went to her and just held her, trying to give her some kind of comfort. Above us the late September sun beat down into Merlin's garden, thin and weak. In the background I could feel the distant pounding of the gash in my head where once there had been an eye. It always hurt now. Sometimes more, sometimes less. But my new power demanded a constant price. The pagan gods have always demanded sacrifice: for unless we have to pay for what we really want: with all we have and are: then how are we ever to know what it is in this life that we really want: and whether it is actually worth having? Jessica lived, and for that I would take a pain a thousand times worse than what I had done. Of course there was one thing about the day that had followed my sacrifice that I would give a great deal to change: to make myself realise that giving grey magical protection gloves to a blue and brown wizard was nothing but completely stupid.

For a moment the only sounds were the animals in the surrounding forest. Artemis's eyes and ears, and in many ways her best friends upon this earth. My αστέρι μου grieved for Danielle in some ways the most of all. She had after all had to watch a child she loved, and a child that literally worshipped her, get sick and collapse before her. And my girlfriend was all too familiar with the pain of sickness, with how much it made you hurt.

I turned to where I heard the sound of a door opening. As my one remaining eye moved I distantly noticed a very crooked chimney, where once long ago a small fairy goddess had climbed in: seeking answers that could help her. Being told that only my love gave her any real chance of future happiness. I found my lips twitching for a moment. It was like the ultimate pre-order on a dating website, the girl finding the profile of the man she liked hundreds of years before he was even born. Probably only work on a girl who was stuck being a virgin forever though I thought amusedly, most people would get very bored trying to wait that long. I found myself wondering distantly if bats and birds and spiders still lived in the chimney, distant descendants of the ones my star had met while crawling down it so long ago: and probably then chatted away happily to for hours: or whether now there was nothing but dead small skeletons waiting in the darkness.

Then I was back in the grey and grim present, in a world where all light and colour seemed forever drained away. Vicky came out from the back door of the cottage.

She smiled at us, but her face was pale. She had still not forgiven herself for having not been that involved in what happened the day that Nimue died, for having been effectively little more than a reserve on the side lines while Danielle and I fought on the front lines.

And of course Danielle had paid a terrible price for her victory. I looked at the meal table: at the food that Jessica had prepared. It was simple but easy to eat and well chosen. And there was fresh milk to go with it, or hot tea. Vicky walked to the table then stopped, for once in her life not knowing what to say. The shadows of grief under her eyes were deeper than any child's should ever be.

"Food look nice." She offered awkwardly after a moment. "I like jam."

There was another sound and another person came out of the door. Merlin. Physically he had survived unharmed from all that had happened, but once again he wore the look of a man who was haunted: far worse than when we had first met him in the library reading session and he was struggling so hard and so unsuccessfully to be an adequate caregiver. He had survived his nemesis. The poison to his power which in every legend, every turn of the story, had previously destroyed him utterly; this time it had not left on him so much as a physical scratch. Another's hand had cast down the only force legend had said had ever been able to challenge him. And he had gained in power beyond all measure. He had not the strength and memories of one Merlin now but of countless. His power left even that of Vicky now well in the shade. He had become the most powerful wizard to have ever walked this earth. And who knew what impact it would have that Merlin had survived to work his magic throughout the retelling of the full Arthurian legend; when always before he had disappeared at the very beginning. But he did not look happy or relieved. He did not look like a man who might well now bend the whole of history into a new and very different path. He just looked like a tired old man, weary beyond his years, with his ragged eyes having seen things he wished he had not. But as he had said, his daughter mattered to him more than anything else did in this world.

Then finally, very slowly and with a very great deal of care, Danielle came out of the door.

If you saw her only briefly, if you just let your gaze sweep by for a second without lingering, you wouldn't have thought that anything was that wrong. Yes she was carrying two great crutches her father had made her out of living wood and stainless steel: one held in her left hand, the other strapped to her upper right arm. But the only immediate sign that she was now in a very bad way was where her right arm had been severed just above the elbow. That cut was the reason that Danielle lived. As she had woken from her enchanted sleep as fresh as if she had just had a long lie in, Jessica had seen the early stages of what was happening to Danielle, and had acted fast. She had seen how the grey glove fused itself like cancer to Danielle's right hand and had taken a kitchen knife and cut through her daughter's right arm as she fought to stop the poison spread, then Jessica used her blue magic to turn the knife into a bandage to stem the flow of the bleeding. But the severance had only slowed the spread of poison: slowed the spread of the allergic reaction through Danielle. Too much grey magic had already entered inside her before her mummy had literally cut the glove off her arm. And though Jessica had rapidly called in first aid and Danielle had been rushed into hospital, and sent straight into the emergency room, she had been dying before everyone's eyes. Then Vicky had burst in, sent by Merlin from the wedding she had come running in with the healing potion he had given her, and my little sister also sent wave after wave of healing white magic of her own through her best friend.

For a time that had stabilised Danielle, but she was now so sick a little girl that very soon she had once more just started to slip away through the medical team's fingers into the dark. Then, when all life had almost left her: Merlin had arrived. His power and wrath had been terrible. Had he been as he once was even he could not have saved her so terrible was the allergic reaction, but he was not with the power and lore of one Merlin now: but with all the strength and knowledge of countless lives. And so Danielle had lived: but not without a price.

Slowly Danielle drew up the needle and syringe that contained the powerful blue and brown magic potion, devised by Merlin himself, that stabilised her body. Without three shots a day the grey magic would resume its onwards march, and literally fade her life-giving organs out of existence. She put the needle against her skin and pushed. After a few moments the syringe emptied. Then she slowly, with her father close besides her, walked towards the table. With her medication taken regularly Danielle's body was a picture of health in all aspects except one: her lungs.

These had been attacked first by the grey magic, as the key instrument by which her child's body drew life. Now the moment she exerted herself in any way, the moment her air bags had to expand to draw in any more air than just the minimum needed for survival, they drew upon tissue half faded out of existence by grey magic, tissue that only half existed. And that caused that tissue to bleed. Danielle took a few steps, then stopped, breaking down into a terrible coughing fit. Red drops of her blood fell onto the flagstones. The bright red was horribly stark against their muted grey. We waited patiently for Danielle to reach the table. The distance between the cottage and the table was not even ten metres. It took Danielle the best part of five minutes to reach it, she had to stop to cough up blood twice.

Jessica reached out and ruffled her hair, then, very carefully not to do anything that could hurt her sick daughter, took her in her arms to give her as full and warm a hug as she could. "It's nice to see you outside again love. I'm sorry it's cold today, but are you warm enough in that coat or do you want daddy to get you another jumper?"

"Not cold mummy." She looked at the food in front of her. Jam sandwiches, ready peeled oranges, peeled and sliced apple. All soft food. All things easy for a sick little girl to eat without getting out of breath. Without having to exert herself: without ending up once more coughing blood.

"Thank you for food mummy." said Danielle politely, but you could see that she was disappointed. This was the only type of food she'd been eating for days. It had long since lost any excitement for her. "But I have chocolate bar afterwards? Please mummy, as treat."

Jessica sighed and held Danielle's head against her chest. My elder sister tried to hold back her tears so her little daughter didn't see. "Well I don't want you eating a normal chocolate bar because they are hard and difficult to chew and you might hurt yourself while you are still ill. But maybe if you eat all your fruit I could melt some up for you and put it in a bowl. I used to love melted chocolate when I was your age."

Danielle made a face and sighed. "It okay mummy I wait have normal chocolate. When I better."

But that was a little bit of a problem. Because Danielle wasn't going to get better. She wasn't going to die; or even get any worse: not so long as she kept up her three shots a day: but she wasn't going to get better either. This was her life from now on. From the moment she had collapsed wearing the grey glove that had poisoned her so badly to the day that she died. And all of us knew that. Even: deep down: Danielle.

Jessica looked at Vicky, with a very firm look on her face. "Vicky you wanted melted chocolate in a bowl didn't you?" Vicky instantly realised that she wasn't being given a choice. "Yes please." She said. "I want lots yummy chocolate in bowl. I put apple pieces in and sweep all about." Her eyes were wide and she was overdoing it but I don't think Danielle noticed. I think that, even now three weeks after it had all happened, part of her was still in shock. She smiled a little bit. "Okay mummy. I have chocolate please."

After we had eaten, a quiet, painful meal with few words; except for when the two little girls got caught up in covering their apple pieces with chocolate and then eating them enthusiastically; Danielle looked at the swings and the slide and the other play things in her garden. "Mummy?" she asked thoughtfully, "I get to play on these again? Do I play again? Or I now so sick that I just watch other people playing?"

Jessica had to bite her lip to keep from crying again. "You will play again my lovely. You won't be able to play as easily or as long as you used to, but you will still be able to play. Daddy and I will make sure of that."

I turned to Jessica. There was a despair in Danielle that had not been there before. An emptiness that could become a listlessness and lethargy: and could become far more dangerous than even the physical damage that she had taken. "Can I have a moment alone with Danielle please?" I asked my elder sister softly.

Jessica seized my hand convulsively. "Please Morgan don't do this. Don't have a go at her for her tricking you with the sword and glove. She just wanted to save me and daddy. She thought she was doing the right thing."

"I brought you once out of the depths of shadow." I said softly. "Trust me, as you did then. Danielle now also needs help if she is not to be at risk of becoming a victim of the same despair which once chained you to your bed for three months. Please."

Jessica looked at me for a long and very still moment. She still had nightmares about those three months, nightmares where she had never got back up and out and the life she had around her now turned out to be nothing more than just a lie. At last my elder sister nodded at me reluctantly. She turned and had a quiet and very serious word with Merlin. He looked at me incredibly sharply, and for a while I wondered if he would object, but he nodded his head at the last. Jessica turned to Vicky and started speaking quietly, Vicky started to protest for a moment, but only half-heartedly. Her confidence had still not recovered from what she saw as her failure at the wedding. In her mind Danielle was sick because she had used the sword when it should have been Vicky, playing her role on the team. Vicky had not forgiven herself for giving up on me and coming up with her own plan when she would have been much more helpful if she had decided to help me with mine instead.

For a moment bleak thoughts came upon me. I wondered for one sickly moment if the exclusivity of the ruling classes and the prestigious schools and universities was actually right. For I had tried to embrace people as they were without prejudice, and as a result pain among the people I loved was not just there but actually thriving and spreading. My sister was now disabled with an adopted child who was very sick. But I seized control, forcing my thoughts away from despair. Now was not the time to dwell too long upon the darkness.

Jessica came back to me, and for the first time in my life since she became Jessica her voice was frosty and her face was hard. "This is my daughter," she said bleakly, "and although she is so unbelievably strong she is also very young, and very vulnerable at the moment. Don't get this wrong." A few moments more and they were all gone, and Danielle and I were sat alone in the garden, and though there was no wind the sun was cold.

Danielle looked at me with tired eyes, with no heat or fire in them. "You going to tell me off for tricking you with gloves?" she asked, more curiously than anything else. "and for hurting you with magic in your eye so you not work out what wrong with your plan?"

"No." I said. "If you had told me I wouldn't have let you use the sword. You would be alive and well, but mummy and daddy would probably be dead. And then in time you'd be dead too Danielle: Nimue planned to eat you too."

"Oh." said Danielle. And as well as surprise there was something else in her voice. Something that sounded almost like the faintest beginnings of pride. She stopped and swallowed. "I know mummy and daddy think I did wrong thing. They not think I should have hurt myself saving them."

I looked at her and smiled. "Love is one of the most powerful emotions that there is Danielle. It motivates us, gives our lives meaning. But it also blinds us and sometimes stops us seeing things: even very obvious things. Mummy and daddy would die for you in a heartbeat, and they feel it is all the wrong way round that you got hurt for them. That stops them seeing the truth. If they had both died what would have then happened to you? Would you have been taken into care? Would you just have hidden and stayed here alone? Would that be better than this? You healthy and well but mummy and daddy dead. Just think about trying to live with that guilt."

Danielle looked at me, some of the old fire back in her cheeks. "No!" she said defiantly "I made right choice with sword and gloves. I did! But it not fair! I did right thing so why my gods punish me? I was brave and I cut

505

the cord and now I hurt: I hurt all the time! Why that fair or right? Maybe I worship wrong gods? I know my mummy, my old mummy who died, not my new real mummy, used to worship different god to my daddy and that why they fight all the time. My old mummy, Katrina, The Lady of the Lake, worship carpenter. My daddy tell me. Maybe I should become Christian? The carpenter seems nice and friendly god.''

It would have hurt me less to have my heart cut open with a knife then to hear her say those words: but I kept my face still. I would not win the war for faith with force, but with persuasion and skill. And I would not stop fighting until THE FAITH no longer existed or was even remembered, until faith was all that was and it seemed that there ever had been. Just like it had been in the pagan days of old, before the men with crosses and fixed ideas came.

''Whatever choice you make is always yours.'' I said gently to Danielle. ''But know that if you make that choice it is the last choice you will ever make. THE FAITH does not let you make your own decisions; or let you choose your own gods to guide you in life. Everything you believe is just put in a book and all you do is just obey that book and what it tells you to do. It's simpler I suppose: but it does mean giving up any mind of your own. No more thoughts or ideas of your own Danielle, not unless they were already in that book to start with.''

Danielle screwed up her face. ''I not want be told what do! I want think about what right for myself.'' She looked up at me with tears in her eyes. ''But if gods I worship are good why they let this happen? It should be bad people who punished: but I was good girl! I saved mummy and daddy and I did right thing. You even just said so! So why I hurt so much? It not fair!'' She started to cry.

506

I took her hand. Beneath the cold of the day the warmth of healthy young life still beat beneath the skin. "Come walk with me." I said gently.

We walked across the garden. We had to pause a couple of times, while Danielle stopped, gasping on the grass of the lawn for bloody breath.

We came to the edge of a flower bed. At the far end of the garden it had been saved from Nimue's corruption of most of Merlin's cottage and land. Here and there, in the wildest places, she simply hadn't been bothered to make the effort to complete her cruel work.

In the flower bed before us the bushes had been planted to form the arch of a natural passageway, and a couple of flagstones had been placed on the soil behind with small gaps between: to reinforce the impression of a path. It didn't really lead anywhere, just curved around back through the flower bed to where it ended at the top of a small garden wall, which looked down over the tables and chairs where we had just been eating our lunch. If you chose to walk this little route, about half way along, where the flagstones finished, you had the sudden impression of being in the midst of the wild; just as walking across the first couple of flagstones felt like following an unbelievably calm and structured footpath through the countryside.

For an adult it had very little interest, a passing curiosity at best. For a child it was a source of unending delight and fun. Vicky and Danielle's screams of excitement had often rung from it in happier times. I walked with Danielle off the lawn and onto the flagstones beyond, and felt her smile as she passed beneath the branches of the bright bushes. We came half way round, to where the last flagstone ended and the path curved sharply, and you were suddenly facing straight towards the top of the small garden wall at the edge of the eating area.

"Danielle do you know what makes us truly pagan?" I asked quietly.

Danielle shook her head. She had been raised in faith, to her being asked why she was a pagan was like asking why her heart beat, or why she talked in modern English. She felt like she just did. I smiled and held her close to me, trying to give her the reassurance that she now so desperately needed. "It is the question of our relationship with the divine, or, more straightforwardly, how we get on with the gods." I said softly. "In THE FAITH all is simple. God died for our sins and took all the pain away. Just do what you are told and his suffering will make everything all right for all of us: all of the time. It is easy, simple, clear. And they say their god is always a nice one who is perfect all the time.

Our pagan faith is very different to that. The complete opposite in fact. Our faith is difficult and complicated. Our gods are like people. They get things wrong and they make mistakes. They laugh, they cry, they love and hurt just like we do all the time in real life. But the most important difference of all from THE FAITH is that we get to choose for ourselves, which of the gods and goddesses we admire, and which of them we don't. We get to decide which of them and which aspects of them we want to worship, and which to put aside because we don't like them or find them distasteful. We have to work out for ourselves which aspects of our gods are good and evil. If you suggested to a pagan god that he was perfect he would break out laughing at the very idea. Our gods are living guides to truth and morality, not fixed instructors, delivering a pre-recorded eternal message set forever in stone."

I turned and looked closely at her. "Danielle you prayed every day as a pagan didn't you? And what did you pray for the most? What was it that you wanted: really wanted, above all other things?"

"A mummy." said Danielle, almost embarrassed. "I really wanted a mummy. Things were so horrible. Daddy trying so hard but doing so badly! And the gods sent me a mummy who so good and who I love so so much! She give me warm hugs and kisses, and she look after both me and daddy, and she tell lovely stories that full of magic and monsters. My mummy is best mummy of them all forever! And I said I give gods anything if they gave me a mummy!"

I smiled at her. "You see how it works? So the gods heard you, and because you prayed to them so hard and so much they decided they would answer your prayer. They sent you a mummy and for a time you were happy. But they told you even when they gave you her that there must be a price to pay for all this: because no one can ever value what they have if it is given to them for free. And to have things that you have not earned is the surest and quickest way to corruption and evil.

And so after you had had your new mummy awhile then the gods wanted to test you Danielle. They wanted to know if you had meant what you had said to them in your prayers so often, when over and over you told them that you would give them anything if they gave you a mummy. And as they had just been so kind to you; and given you a mummy that was so good: a mummy who may very well be the best mummy in all the world!: they really wanted to know if you meant what you had said in your words about being happy to pay the price. Or if all that you had said to them was nothing more than just empty words to get the gods to give you what you wanted. So they sent Nimue to hurt your mummy and they put a magic sword in your hand and a grey glove of magical power that would poison you in front of you, and they asked if you were really sure that you wanted a mummy, this mummy, that much." I looked at her firmly. "And were you sure Danielle? Or do you now think you did the wrong thing in hurting yourself to save your mummy? Do you still think that you made the right choice when you cut the cord and put the glove on that day?"

"Yes!" said Danielle defiantly, almost shouting, for the first time looking something like her old self. "I sure! I saved mummy and daddy!" The shout had taken a lot out of her, and she broke down in bloody coughing. Dark blood splattered on the soil, and she was in pain. But the fit passed: and she gathered herself once more. Something of her old mental strength starting to return to her.

I nodded, and inclined my head. "Yes you made your choice a second time. But you see the thing is Danielle, in many ways it is easier to be a good person when things are hard, strange as that sounds. For when things are hard often men and women rise to the challenge, and call always upon their gods. But it is when things are easy that men and women are most prone to do evil and to forget the gods, who gave them everything, and on whose power and reward their success is based. Once a great race of men was so devout that they were given an island continent to rule. To be a kingdom of glory and the centre of a great empire of men. They had asked the gods many times for this, so that they could have the power to protect others and to help everyone to do the right thing. But so great and powerful did this nation become, so vast did the reaches of its wealth and imperial power spread, that in their luxury and decadence the people forgot what they owed to the gods. And so they became more evil and wicked than any others had been in the whole history of the world. Instead of inspiring good around the world as they had in the beginning in time their empire spread only the darkest form of evil. And this all happened because these people took from the gods without giving back sufficient sacrifice in return, so that, like all who take but do not earn, their thoughts and minds could not but become completely corrupted. They became so evil that the gods hurled the whole continent to the depths of the ocean, and the waves drank what had once been called the holy isle: that men today remember by another name. And so sank Atlantis.

And in the same way the gods were scared that now that they had given you such a good mummy you might forget to be a good girl, and might neglect your selfless deeds and prayers. And so they decided to collect the price they had asked for from the start, when they first answered your prayers. They wanted to make sure that you would remember always just how much you had wanted what they had given you. So they took your hand, as your god of oaths gave his in the great wolf Fenrir's jaw to buy the safety of his divine family. But the gods did not take your good drawing left hand for, while they wished for you to know the worth of what they had given you, they did not wish to cripple your drawing talent which gives you and them so much pleasure. The same way that Odin took one of my eyes in sacrifice, but had no wish to cripple me by making me fully blind. And they took also your lungs, so that with every breath you take you might feel the pain of your sacrifice to them, and know that what they gave you, in your mummy Jessica, is worth every drop of pain a thousand fold.

And while you must always choose yourself what to do and who you worship, that Danielle is the key difference between us and the Christian faith. For their sacrifice was their god on the cross, long ago. The sacrifice which ended all sacrifices. And to them your lungs breaking and the mutilation of my eye are abominations in the sight of their One True God. For to them the time of sacrifice is past, finished long ago on a cross outside Jerusalem. That's why they wear symbols of it all the time, a living declaration that they are now

511

too good and special to ever be bothered with any more of that old fashioned sacrificing rubbish. But for a pagan sacrifice is the core of our religion: the essence and core of our communication with our gods. It can never be ended, for if we bring nothing to the table when we ask for what we want, if we are not prepared to suffer and die for what we believe and desire; then how can we ever be good people? And if we are not good people then how can we ever deserve any of the favour of the gods?

So the gods took your lungs Danielle: as your final test that you had meant what you said when you prayed to them so hard and for so long. For if you wanted a mummy as badly as you yourself said, and your very own words were that you would give anything for one, then you will not let the price the gods demanded of your body: in return for giving you your new mummy: stand between you and your new family's happiness. You asked for something huge Danielle, and it was given to you, better than you could have ever thought and dreamed. Do you now grow angry with the gods that they demanded that you pay a fair price for your miracle in return? Did you really only want to be given a new mummy if it turned out that she could be given to you for free?''

I walked over to the chairs and tables of the eating area. I dropped down behind the wall and turned to Danielle with my arms outstretched.

''You used to love jumping from the last flagstone to the top of this wall.'' I called out. ''You used to love landing on top of it with your feet never touching the soil. A straight clean jump through the air. Will you not now do that again?''

Danielle looked at me protesting, and a little shaken. ''But I jump that much it really hurt, blood go everywhere!''

I smiled at her. "When I sat in that library do you think I wanted to cut out my own eye? Do you think I wanted to be half blind? But the gods gave me the choice to decide how much I loved my elder sister. And I paid the price. Should I now let the pain of my lifelong ruined eye take away all the pleasure I have each time I see my sister? Should I let the pain ruin the very success of the sacrifice I made? There is nothing you cannot do in this life, if you are but prepared to pay the price the true" - never again the OLD gods: never again would they be called that by me - "gods demand. But you have to accept that just as the good they give lasts, so to must, also and always, the price that has to be paid. So are you going to jump and claim the life you prayed for? Or was it all just the empty words of a little child who just quite fancied having everything that is important in this life for free?"

Danielle took a deep breath, and for a long moment I was unsure. For a moment I did not know what choice she would make: which way her life would now turn. Then the little girl made up her mind.

She gave a great leap. She tore through the air like the undamaged child she had been and let out a great piercing cry of triumph, a cry that would have been a worthy victory cry of Artemis herself. Danielle soared through the air like the magical female goddess, and in that moment there was nothing but triumph in her. She was once more the child she had been, darkness and despair having no more power over her. She landed successfully in my arms, the soil never having once touched her feet.

She vomited blood all over me but she was still crying tears of happiness. And the light and strength that had always beat in her, that well of determination of love and self-belief that was at her core was once more restored: and she was herself again. I held her in my arms and knew that we were truly family.

I found myself wondering if in psychological terms Jessica was now my daughter did this make Danielle, in some weird way that would never be admitted on the surface, my granddaughter in the unspoken reality of our psychological and emotional relationship? The thought was strange: but felt quite true. After all, let's face it, never in any time or any place in all this world have the genetic relationships of blood and the psychological relationships of love ever born anything like a straightforward relationship to each other.

Whatever the exact truth I held in my arms a member of my family that I loved.

And whom I had saved from the corruption of the cross.

Chapter 38

For a few weeks after Nimue first fell I dared to believe that I had triumphed, that I had stood at the centre of the storm and that it had passed. But all too quickly it became apparent that I merely stood at the centre of the storm, in the calm eye at its heart and that, terrible as had been the winds I had just come through, most of the full force of the storm still lay ahead. There was much to celebrate that was true. Nimue lay dead and the dark future I had been shown lay dead with her. Merlin was not only unharmed and with no natural antidote remaining but now many times more powerful. I thought I was happy about that. I now knew the true answer to the power of the grey: to turn horror into fantasy, darkness into light, evil into good; and I was champion of both Odin Allfather and Artemis the Friendly.

But it soon became clearer that being the champion of Artemis the Friendly, much as I loved her, now meant quite little. She was a dying goddess, and it was thousands of years since her last champion Orion. Time had long since washed away most off her strength since then. I had the power of barbarianism on my side yes, but history could not show more clearly how that was, while vitally important, not enough alone for a successful war to be pursued against the Christians and secularists to restore the primacy of the pagan faith, to restore the better reality of true religion in the long-term. I needed the power of another god or goddess on my side to have a chance of success, one who drew their power from the civilised pantheon. But most of that pantheon were now powerless in the Christian era, and the only few who remained had been prepared to succumb to darkness and accept being seen as demons of evil rather than gods of divine power. Artemis the Terrible: in her temple of marble on an island of gold so long ago: had mentioned three who would take this dark course in the modern world: two others besides herself. But Loki the Trickster was of no use to me at the moment, he was a Viking barbarian god. So the choice was only between Artemis the Terrible and Hecate: the goddess of witches. But Hecate was not a troubled goddess. She cared little if she was worshipped as a divine goddess or satanic demon: so long as she was worshipped: and she, like Loki, thrived in this modern world. They would be champions of the way the world now was when the war came, they would have no interest in helping one who sought to restore their, probably quite vengeful, former brethren.

And, Terrible or Friendly, I was in love with Artemis. I would not have the will or desire to fight for any other god or goddess of civilisation the way that I would fight for her.

It did not take me long, merely days, to realise what I could sacrifice to Artemis the Terrible to be anointed as her champion; as an alternative to the course I would never take, that of castrating myself and offering up my bloodied sex organs to her flames. But just the thought of making this new sacrifice made it feel like my blood had turned to ice in my veins.

I knew what course my life had to take. I was a weed trying to flourish in the front lawn of a garden. My only hope of surviving and thriving, the only hope of creating a world where gardens could be filled with the healthy growth of grey wizards alongside all the other flowers, was to change the rules by which the garden ran. To change the gardeners and those in charge. So the Christian and secular elites needed sweeping from the seats of power to be replaced by pagans, and the churches needed to be burned down and replaced with temples as the pagan gods took back their mastery of the heavens from Monotheism and the Holy Trinity of the Christians. Had not Merlin even said the words of prophecy to Artemis so long ago, to say that to lead and start this war was my destiny?"

And you could see in my personal life the power the pagan gods had to restore the beauty of their heavens to this earth: if it was built again in their image. If not for them then Jessica would have died long ago instead of becoming an integral part of my family. Danielle and Merlin would still have languished in dysfunctional agony; and I would not now be soon to be an uncle: as within a few weeks of her being restored to health Jessica told me excitedly that she was now expecting Merlin's baby. She wasn't sure for herself whether she'd have chosen to have a child anywhere near this young, but she thought it was now more important than ever for Danielle to have a little brother or sister. Someone Danielle could play with and who could take her mind off her sickness: stop her having the chance to dwell. Jessica had even told me quietly and guiltily that while most of her prayers to the Greek goddess Hestia, goddess of the hearth and home, and to the Viking god Try, the god of kept oaths, were just that the baby was healthy and hearty; she had prayed a few times that she was carrying a boy. Now she was pregnant she had found herself aching to have a son. Not that she would favour the new child over Danielle at all she had told me sincerely. Danielle was as much her child as ever, having grown inside her heart as much as her new baby now grew in the love and shelter of her womb.

I wasn't exactly sure when or from where Jessica had picked up paganism. Her entire nuclear family were now devout pagans so I wasn't sure it really mattered either.

But though the gods had given me so much, new purpose, new family, new magic; there was one thing that I had had before any of that. One thing that I had had before there was anything else even remotely good in my life. Long before I had caught the attention of the seer warlord and the blue-eyed huntress the only good thing in my life had been the love of my small sister. She had been my only friend for a long, long time. I could think of no greater honour and purpose in life than to lead a pagan war of restoration: but not when the only way to achieve it: the only way to gain the dark power of the terrible side of the huntress that would make success a real possibility: was to sacrifice the one good thing I had ever had before I met any of the gods.

I knew what I should do, but I could not bring myself to even want to do it. Though the world of magic would never be reborn, though the age of man: forever bland and dull and dismal: should last forever; still I would not pay the price the gods now demanded. It was something they had no right to ask. Not even the will of The Allfather and my love for the blue-eyed huntress could bring me to betray the person who it seemed still meant more than anybody else in the world to me.

Days became weeks, and weeks became months. And still I could not bring myself to leave my little sister, no more than I could have cut out my own heart.

It was not awkward between me and Artemis in those days, though I had thought it would be. We still ate hot meat together in her tree house, she dropped in to talk to me while I read dark texts of forbidden lore in the quiet midnight hours. We played video games together and she continued teaching me to hunt. We went round museums together: particularly ones of Greek art where Artemis spent a great deal of time seeing how often she could spot pictures of herself in all the displays. Selfie culture it seemed was actually thousands and thousands of years old. And we rolled down grass slopes together, bathed in the same pools and streams, and lay naked in the same bed together nearly every evening, so close that we could almost touch.

Artemis understood why I could not make the next move. Why I could not sacrifice a real tangible reality before me, for just the dream of victory in war. Or for the hope that, one day, I might somehow figure out how to master the resurrection of Artemis's Friendly side.

In this time Artemis sent me no new visions of the future. The possible future of Nimue's rise and our deaths had clearly been ended with the parasite's death. The dark future of Merlin going mad with grief had been ended forever by the life that beat now strong in my sister's womb. And by the protection of both sides of the huntress, invoked through a terrible price of blood. Ensuring that both Jessica's pregnancy and her childbirth would now be safe: even though my older sister was confined to a wheelchair. But the goddess of both female virginity and childbirth gave me no clear visions of what the future, freed from those bleak fates, might now hold instead. "It was too much in chaos." she had said, "All lost in the chaos and the swirling." The death of Nimue had torn a hole in the structure of this world, bent the repeating Arthurian legend deeply and permanently out of shape. The Mountain was now planning his next move carefully. After all his last one had ultimately brought him nothing but the lifeblood of his own wizard Nimue offered up in sacrifice to Artemis the Friendly. But The Mountain learned fast: and he always played to win.

So then the attacks began: about a month after Nimue's lifeblood had washed away over the floor. They were not direct this time. The Voice was picking his champions very carefully indeed, working from the shadows and sidelines. Brute force had failed him last time, so now he looked to see what a different approach might bring.

The champion he invested with his power was a great brown wizard, but one who fought from the sidelines and the shadows with as much skill and ferocity as any grey wizard could have ever done. I would not have believed, had the evidence not been now so painfully clear to me, that a brown wizard could fight this sort of magical guerrilla warfare so well. My new opponent never risked moving into direct open combat. But he or she instead inspired others, any others, around me to succumb to their learned prejudices and dislike of grey wizards; and to launch open attacks upon me: both magical and non-magical. And because each wizard he worked on was their own person I never knew what colour of magical attack I would be facing: only that it wouldn't be grey.

Brown magic cannot build from nothing, it can only reinforce and strengthen what already exists. But if there is even a fragment of a mote of something already existing then within a moment great brown magic can make the weakest and most faded form of strength into something suddenly and instantly truly terrible. And I lived in a world where there was barely anyone who did not at least dislike grey wizards. Were not all people, especially educated people, taught that we were by our very nature intrinsically wrong and unfitting for the modern world: taught that from the moment we were all born?

The attacks came out of absolutely nowhere. There could be many in a day, or even an hour, then barely any for almost a week. They followed no discernible pattern that I could see or work out, and that only made them ever the more dangerous. And through them all I could wield my grey magic only in defence, the use of grey magic as an offensive weapon in this world was, after all, a crime punishable by death. I had been fortunate indeed that the fatal strike in my battle with Nimue had been made by a moonlight arrow, not by the power of the grey.

I do not believe that I would have gone on the offensive in any case, although it is easy to claim high moral standing when you have no choice. The people now attacking me at seemingly random were, after all, mostly innocents: manipulated by a brown wizard who I could never find. Who seemed to leave no trace of his presence however and wherever I searched for him. But that should have been almost impossible. For only the strongest of grey magic could possibly have faded someone so entirely from existence and trace of discovery: and there was no doubt that the wizard and magic I was facing was nothing else but pure brown. But night after night I tore through tomes of dark lore and searched desperately and futilely for answers, not understanding how a brown wizard was able to so successfully outplay a grey wizard at his own game.

The brown magic seeking my life did not determine between those with and without magic, between young or old, class or race. Children would hurl broken bottles at my face; white wizards blasts of light and terrible force; brown wizards pick up the speed and direction of nearby cars to send them hurtling towards me, or suddenly try to swell my body to a size where my lungs and heart could no longer support it and would burst into death; blue wizards try to change my heart to unmoving crystal or my lungs to glass.

I managed to stop most of the attacks successfully without being hurt. Grey was a very powerful defensive magic, and I had a lifetime's experience of having to fight off unprovoked attacks. But I could deflect nine hundred and ninety nine attacks out of a thousand and still get killed by the other one. I could win as many battles as I liked, to win this war my new attacker only had to win one battle well enough once. And I knew that over time, even if I was successful in defeating each and every attack, just the constant barrage, and even more the constant need to be alert for danger all the time, would gradually make me more and more tired: and more and more prone to making a serious mistake that I could not afford.

Already now and again I did get hurt, and Vicky had to heal me with white magic: just like back before The Pool of Fire and Blood. Of course if Vicky was with me she did strike back, mostly at the magic being used against me not directly at the people casting it; but if she was there frequently the people attacking me did get hurt. People hurting her big brother without reason always made her very angry. The use of white magic as an offensive weapon to protect your own brother's life was, of course, completely legal. She could hurt my attackers as much as she liked, they would have no legal grounds to complain. Already one or two of them had been hurt by her really rather badly.

It was one day in mid-December, four months since Nimue had died and just under three months since the attacks had begun, that the magical conflict finally cut deep enough to really hurt: finally caused very real and serious bloodshed. Jessica, Vicky, Danielle and I were out doing our Christmas shopping, the supermarket we were in lit with glowing decorations and filled with the rich smell of pine. I didn't like the modern symbolism but the festival of Christmas was pagan: not Christian: at its heart. Even according to the lore of the Christians Christ had been born in September, not in December. And his birth, unlike his death or conception, had little theological significance. The true meaning of Christmas was to share in family and gift giving, not to worship some long dead carpenter. And besides I thought, looking up at one of the decorations of the Virgin Mary, our pagan virgin goddess was way sexier than theirs. Danielle saw me looking at a model of the Virgin Mary with a faint look of distaste on my mouth. She reached out and touched her blue magic lightly. The next moment the model of the Virgin Mary had become that of a small blue-eyed fairy with almost transparent wings. "That much better." Said Danielle quietly. "That now a model of a nice goddess!"

"Of a true goddess." I said softly, in words as sharp as steel. "The true eternal virgin." My pagan faith was now as much a part of my life as the air that I breathed. I could no longer even begin to conceive of any kind of existence without it.

I was by the vegetable counter and a mum with a small child had drawn up alongside me. She was talking to the small child, who was sat in her trolley. "Now." the mum said gently. "We've got a list to work through of things to find haven't we? First on that shopping list is red onions, can you see any Elly because I can't!" She made a great show of looking all around her. She had parked the trolley right next to the red onions, with Elly positioned right next to them. "They are here, they are here." Exclaimed the child Elly excitedly, pointing eagerly at the red onions.

I smiled and turned away, aware that those two were some of the very few people on whom the brown magic that hunted me would and indeed even could have no affect. There was no hatred or anger in them. They didn't know it but I would have described them as being proto-pagan, on our side of the line. The mum was teaching the child to think for herself, not just telling her what to do. Not just to kneel to some higher authority in expectation of external reward. That was the essence of my family's faith now: of my faith. Of all pagan faith.

We finished shopping, quite a lot later as Jessica was shopping for ingredients that would help make Danielle a Christmas lunch that was both delicious and easy to eat. My older sister was going to make her little daughter a turkey with trimmings so soft it would just crumble to pieces in her mouth and a Christmas pudding so light it would almost just dissolve when eaten. Jessica was determined her daughter was not going to need to cough up one drop of blood during her Christmas lunch.

We came to the self-service checkouts at the front of the shop. Normally Jessica liked talking to the people on the regular checkouts, but with pretty much the whole family here to help this way today was much quicker. The only one missing was Merlin, who was currently having to go round schools promoting science and history as inclusive subjects for all students. The thought of having to talk to teenagers had had him waking up in nightmares for the past month, but it was a mandatory part of his contract. Neither Jessica nor I had allowed ourselves to think about the irony that his three month pregnant wife was younger than some of the pupils he would be talking to: not that Merlin had the remotest suspicion of that. We had both been lying about Jessica's age for so long there were times we both thought she had just turned twenty: not sixteen.

We were sliding the last of our shopping through the scanner when a crying little girl in a trolley caught my attention. The child was clearly bored, and there was nothing in the trolley to distract her or for her to play with. There was an empty packet of sticky sweets crumpled up somewhere, but that was no substitute for a well-chosen toy which would have instantly ended the problem by giving the little child something to do.

Next to her a woman: who smelled like the roses of expensive perfume and whose clothes were immaculate and her hair well-styled: was mortified with anger and embarrassment. She was almost contorting with the shame of her child behaving badly in public, where other people could see. For an odd moment I almost felt like I was looking at another version of Jess, of what my elder sister would have almost certainly become if her whole life hadn't been unexpectedly turned around. The woman was speaking bleakly, her voice cold with shame and disgusted anger. "You need to have a think about your behaviour Philippa, a real think. You are embarrassing yourself and you are embarrassing me and if you don't stop this awful crying I shall take you home and put you straight to bed."

It was barely five clock in the afternoon.

"And that," I thought grimly, "is the essence of all that THE FAITH ever is or ever will be. That is the essence of all that I would gladly lead a holy war to destroy. The final ending of what I see before me now is something I would pay any price for, and see as many other people as need to also pay that price. To send forever into the flames: to reduce forever to nothing but dead, cold and long forgotten ash: the idea that the obeying of the way that things are ordered by authority is the same as being a moral and good person. There are two spectrums, law and chaos, and then good and evil. Those two spectrums have no relationship to each other whatsoever. "You need to have a think." always meaning, "You need to concentrate only on ever doing exactly what people in authority tell you to. Because if you do you'll get nice external rewards like lots of money to spend on things like fashionable clothes and expensive shiny baubles." And the only thing that could break that view of the world was full and complete return of the pagan gods in all their power and glory; with all the incessant questions that always accompanied their worship about what it was in life that was right, and what it was that was wrong.

The issues and the complexes in the woman who smelled like roses and who had spent so much effort making herself look good were such that, even though her sudden magical attack on me was strong, I could see it coming well before it came. The blue magic which would have turned every drop of blood in my veins into lifeless sherbet I faded into nothing effortlessly: and my return strike faded away the woman's strength. Not to the point where she could be harmed and I could be accused of a crime for using grey magic as a weapon, but just to the point where she had no energy left to call upon any more magic or to be any kind of threat to me. I had weathered so many of these sort of attacks that defeating her like this was almost child's play. "That," I thought distantly, "whoever you are brown wizard, was really poorly played. There was basically no chance that I was ever going to fall to that attack."

Except it hadn't been badly played at all. It had been superbly played. The brown wizard had already spent months trying to outspeed my reflexes, or dodge my observational skills. And against my power and experience he had been getting nowhere. I had so far taken no really serious injuries from any of his or her attacks: although a few had come far closer to me than I really liked. So today my hidden and dangerous opponent had decided to try out a new strategy. For there is little more dangerous than when you feel the joy and strange contentment of victory. And no moment when you are so vulnerable, and your senses so lulled, as when you are enjoying a moment of triumph: no matter how small or even well-earned your moment of self-satisfaction is.

The strike from the small child would have killed me, a bolt of lightning that would have taken my head clean off. Her mother had done her work of ensuring obedience through the power of her authority very well. The small child's life was already full of the pain and anger that the brown wizard needed to turn even the most complete strangers so utterly against me. The beautiful woman's handiwork after a couple of years had already left the brown wizard with more than enough material to work with in the poor, desperately unhappy, child's mind. But the bolt of lightning never flew.

A far greater one leapt from Vicky's hands, and, without the slightest trace of remorse or pity, blew Philippa and her much smaller lightning bolt, still in her hands, into a thousand separate burning shreds.

There was a long and awful silence, when everything went suddenly really very still. But throughout it all Vicky's face was utterly emotionless: she looked as though she had just done no more than swipe another item of shopping through the checkout till.

Then Philippa's mother started to scream. If only she had previously let her natural emotions for her child be more important to her than her pride then this dark day for her may well have never come. If her child had not been unhappy, the brown magic would have found no purchase in her to work with. "My baby, you killed my baby!" the woman in the immaculate clothes screamed. She looked up at us from the ruin of her child with her eyes brimming with hate. "I'll see you dead for…" she began, a storm of blue magic suddenly surrounding her in the most terrible cloud of power and revenge driven fury.

But Vicky just stepped forward and, completely casually, backhanded her across the face: her hand and arm filled with the power of white magic. Merlin's power now eclipsed hers, but after him she was still indisputably the second most powerful wizard in the West.

It wasn't even a fight, let alone a real contest of magic. Philippa's mother's head was just easily torn clean off, and her corpse was hurled down like a shattered rag doll in an explosion of her lifeblood onto the floor. The white plastic of the supermarket floor tiles was suddenly drenched in red.

Vicky's face still showed no emotion. She was completely and utterly calm and so, so indifferent. She had reached a stage where, so long as her brother was safe, she just really didn't care about anything else anymore. She had exactly the same expression on her face as when she had successfully tidied her room: not one jot more or less of any emotion than that. She looked carefully around, her completely dry eyes sharp and searching: and the light of white magic in them utterly clear. In that moment she looked as cold and cruel as the dark side of the huntress herself. In that moment she could have been the living representative of Artemis the Terrible on earth. And, aside from the fact that she was killing girls to protect a man, in that moment that was exactly what she was. She was the child who called herself the bloodwolf. And now she looked, at the same time both calmly assessing and also emotionally completely disinterestedly, at the appalled staff and shoppers just standing or swaying around us in disjointed shock. The only slight emotion on Vicky's face at all was a distant curiosity. Even her words were flat, empty. She sounded for a moment almost corporate, as disinterested in what she was doing as any lifeless computer or machine.

"White magic is legal," Vicky said, very firmly, "and child try kill my brother and then this woman threatened kill us both. I done nothing illegal. Anyone else want try and hurt my brother now? I will kill you very very dead. Just like all those nasty others!'' And as her words came to a conclusion suddenly the burning rage in her flashed raw, and the dead emptiness in her voice fell away into a raging anger. The fury of a child who has been teased and provoked for far too long: and now cares not at all who should fall when she strikes back, so long as the one that provoked her also bleeds.

Vicky's eyes flashed fire and light as she stared relentlessly at the crowd, daring one of them to defy her. Daring one of them to try, just try, to hurt her brother now. For a moment the people around us shook helplessly before her, and then they fled in terror: in a flight that within moments had basically become a stampede. Within a few moments my family and I were standing alone in an almost completely deserted supermarket, the Christmas lights glowing as they reflected cheerfully off all that bright red blood.

There was a long and very still silence among the members of my family, as we all waited to see what Vicky would do next. But she, after a slight uncertain pause, just stopped and shook herself sharply: as though she had just awoken from a very bad dream. And the next moment she was moving like normal again, the force of magic in her draining away and with no more thought of what had just happened than most people give to the terrors of their previous night's nightmares once they are fully awake and once more completely absorbed in the bright sunshine and new activity of their next full day.

Vicky turned back to the self-service checkout, and went back to exactly where she had been with swiping through our shopping before any of this violence and horror began. Red blood pooled around her feet but she didn't even seem to notice: and if she did she just didn't care. The three of us; Jessica, Danielle and I; still just stood there watching her: all of us still unable to move or speak in shock. Although whether the shock now was more for the violence of what had happened or for how indifferent Vicky was to what she had just done it would be impossible for even the wisest to have hoped to say.

Vicky just kept on swiping our shopping, as though nothing at all had happened, while the three of us stood watching her, unmoving. Finally the surreal scene broke down in new and strong emotion.

"Oh," Vicky cried out in sudden delight, once more every inch a seemingly normal five year old child, "Jessica you got us pigs in blankets for Christmas! Yeah! You know they my favourite. Thank you, thank you, thank you!" She rushed up and gave Jessica a hug.

Then she stopped and looked at all three of us in confusion. "Why all three of you look so scared?" she asked uncertainly. "All three of you gone white as zombies! Why?" she looked around in a great deal of concern. "Has something very bad gone wrong?"

Chapter 39

Even as Vicky stepped utterly indifferently through the bright pools of blood that shone so brightly in their vivid contrast to the white supermarket floor; to ask her family anxiously what was wrong and why they all looked so scared; the visions of Artemis once more burned before my eyes. They were the first in months: the first since the brown magical attacks began. As always they started in the unbelievable brightness and intensity of a thousand different dancing colours of the rainbow.

It was thirteen years in the future. I was twenty eight, Vicky was eighteen. It was many years since the chaste maiden of the moon had played any real role in my life. I was pushing the shopping trolley towards our car: Vicky had walked ahead to open the boot. It was evening, the Christmas lights were bathing the air and tarmac in a gentle glow of red and green. It was the car park of the same supermarket that we were in now. The air was still and all seemed gentle and calm. Across the still air came a clatter and I absently turned my head. A young couple walked along the other end of the parking area. She was young and pretty, he a few years older and neatly dressed. I liked his colourful tie with bright Christmas presents on a green background.

Then something hit me so hard that all the world went white.

After a few moments my thoughts came together again. Just enough that I suppose you could say that I was having some form of coherent thought: spitting through blood and broken teeth. My head rang with the force of the blow, and I was dizzy and disjointed with the pain. A while longer, and the world came, gradually and reluctantly, back into clearer focus. It wasn't normal but it was closer to it than blackout: or whiteout. Vicky was knelt besides me. I didn't know in the circumstances if that was a very good or a very bad thing. One thing was certain, she wasn't about to heal me with her white magic: she had very different uses for her power now. In her eyes there was concern: but there was also something else. Something stronger than the concern, and something that stopped the natural emotions she should have felt from ever being fully real. That kept them all very distant: and always very far away.

"I'm really sorry Morgan." Vicky said, but something in her voice that I was all too familiar with said that she was not. "But you shouldn't have looked at that girl. We're together now. You shouldn't even want to look at anyone else. And yet there you were, checking out her boobs and ass right in front of me! I know Morgan, I saw! And all I did was look away for a moment to go and open up the car to put in the shopping for us both and there you are at it again! It's disgusting. It's not responsible or right Morgan, especially not now with," she stopped and held out a hand to where our baby kicked inside her swelling belly, "us starting a family of our own." She kissed me gently on the cheek. But she didn't offer to heal me with magic: of course not. It had been years now since she had ever done that. Even though that was how our relationship had begun, long ago back in the distant mists and time of the innocence of early childhood.

Before this darkness seeped in between us. Holding us tight together even as it poisoned us both.

"But now you've been punished for staring down another girl's bra so everything's fine again isn't it Morgan?" asked Vicky. Her voice was cool on the surface, and yet beneath it I could sense her sudden intense anxiety.

There was a pause when there were just no words that I could think to say. "All I was doing was looking at the man's Christmas tie." I thought silently. "Yet that is all it now takes to bring us back to this. You've been hitting me for nearly a year now, and all the time it's getting worse. Oh Vicky where is this dark road taking us? Somewhere neither of us would have ever chosen to go."

Vicky was getting desperate at my silence now. Her hands were shaking with anxiety and her eyes were filled with tears. She looked suddenly not like a young and overconfident adult and magical boxing champion; but nothing more than an absolutely terrified little girl. "We okay now?" she begged, both her words and her voice that of a terrified little child who suddenly just didn't know what to do, or why big brother didn't love her anymore. Her eyes stared into mine hopelessly. Ravaged by pain and the terror of losing the love of the man she loved so much: both pleading for, and yet at the same time somehow still absolutely demanding, my forgiveness.

The vision faded, and the second came: in a fresh burst of colour as brilliant as that which had preceded the first. But I barely saw the beauty of Artemis's divine power. For, even in that briefest of all interludes, I felt a pain in my chest worse than anything I had ever felt before. A despair that threatened the thing in this world that had always been the most important of anything to me: my love for my little sister. But then the impact of the second vision tore into my mind: and I welcomed it as I would have welcomed any respite in that moment from the suddenly all-encompassing pain. The second vision was not of a distant possible future. This one was of the very recent past, a time and set of events that was done and finished: set forever unchanging in stone. Its events had occurred barely days ago.

The two little girls were standing in a beautiful garden besides an extremely magical cottage in the very depths of a deep, dark wood. It was perhaps just before mid-afternoon. They were playing, playing with magic, but to watch the game they were playing you would have been surprised that they lived in a civilised part of this world. For they were fighting with all the savagery and wildness of the barbarians of old. And, as powerful wizards whose strength was growing, that meant their child's play was forging and growing in them a great deal of magic and skill.

There was a moment's stillness as the two little girls, the two children both becoming very powerful wizards indeed, faced each other. One had a shield strapped round the stump of a half missing arm, the missing lower half having once been severed by a knife. The other girl had beautiful red hair that streamed behind her as she moved: and danced like fire in the bright and shining light of the midday sun. Then with a scream the red-haired wizard came howling forward, and wooden blade crashed on wooden blade as blasts of white magic fought with the power of blue and brown: with a sword whose form flowed and changed in the wizard of illusion and natural growth's hand. There were a few savage seconds of combat, perhaps ten. And then all the anaerobic energy, the energy used by sprinters and which has already come through the lungs before exercise begins, was used up: and both combatants broke apart to draw fresh breath. But one needed to do so far more than the other. For for one of them breathing could often now be a very serious problem, and she turned to one side to spit out blood and flem onto the grass. She would not let her pain define her or who she was: but she still had to take practical and serious measures to properly deal with it. There was a pause while she recovered, and then the two little girls went for each other in combat again, and then, after the next bloody breathing break, yet again. Their very brutal form of play seemed without change or end or even any serious break other than that needed for them to catch their breath. On and on they drove themselves: the two combatants locked again and again in frequent rounds of desperate combat.

It only stopped because, after a couple of hours, it started to grow too dark to see in the winter evening as the sun finally set below the rim of the darkening sky. Then both combatants sat down and were still for a while: both having to recover from the intensity of what they had just put themselves through. There was quite a lot red blood on the green lawn where they had been fighting, and Danielle was feeling a little ill. But she got out one of her syringes and took her injection calmly and quickly. She was already starting to get used to them and was even getting used to having to push in those nasty needles: and soon she felt a lot better.

When she was done she turned crossly to Vicky and said indignantly, "Why you always want to be fighting? You know I not like fighting all that much, and that even before I… before I got my lungs poorly I not even like fighting that much!"

"That not true." said Vicky indignantly. "We share! We did colouring all morning and now we going to play snakes and ladders when go inside. We share our play. I always fair."

"Yes," said Danielle, "we do share all the time but I choose lots of different nice things. Even though drawing my favourite I also chose hide and seek, and snakes and ladders, and play board games like ludo, and like yoyos and I love stories. You always chose fighting: never anything else! Never ever!!! Have you always liked hitting things so much?"

Vicky looked at Danielle and then looked away, a little uncomfortable. "Used to love climbing tall things." she said, and she brightened suddenly. "Morgan help me climb all the way up to the top of Rope Mountain when I was little. Rope Mountain not scary now but when I was two I thought it was the biggest thing in all the world! I didn't think anything anywhere could ever be any bigger! Now I know it is quite small really but when I was two I think it so big it touch the sky! And I liked racing and swimming: but my biggest favourite was…" she stopped and looked around guiltily to make sure that no one else was listening apart from Danielle to hear her most closely guarded secret: no one else was.

She leaned in close to Danielle. "My favourite was Football!" She whispered almost guiltily in Danielle's ear. "I not tell anyone that but you: not ever! I not think even Morgan know! I not tell Morgan because I know Morgan not like football and I not want him to play it just to make me happy!"

Danielle's eyes went wide at hearing Vicky's deepest secret. She was clearly horrified with her best playmate. "Ugg!" she said disgustedly. "I hate team games! Everyone gets noisy and silly. I much prefer drawing to big games." She thought about it "And I even rather do fighting all the time than FOOTBALL!"

She paused for a moment. "But I not like you wanting only play one thing. Why you now want to play fighting all the time?"

Vicky shuddered, and drew in on herself. She suddenly looked lost and alone and little: and very cold. "Because fighting is the only way to keep big brother safe. When I little everyone but me want kill big brother.

He nearly get drowned dead lots of times! And when I go save him when we swimming at the pool party everyone try stop me! I not just have to fight the bad people who try drown him: I have to fight everyone who was there. Everyone just get in the way! All the adults who should be helping me try and stop me! I had to fight them all! And I always have to look after big brother because he can't use his magic to protect himself, he get in trouble if he attack! So I have to attack, and I have to win. I not get in trouble if I attack so I have to keep him safe because he not allowed to look after himself or punish the bad people who try to hurt him!! I have to be the fastest and the bestest at fighting that there ever could be because only I can keep big brother safe. I can't be silly and waste time playing other things when I could be using that time to get better at fighting: because then my fault if big brother die! I have to keep fighting all the time so that I can keep him safe and he can stay alive to play with me and to give me hugs! He the best big brother there ever was in the whole wide world!''

She turned, and suddenly crumpled into Danielle's arms. All her strength suddenly left her in a single instant, as the terror of losing her big brother that was always with her, came flooding over her controlled surface. ''I not want big brother to die!'' she wailed. ''I love him!''

''It okay.'' said Danielle comfortingly: giving her best friend the biggest hug she possibly could: and trying to think what she could say to make her feel better. ''Morgan not going to die! He a very powerful and clever wizard: almost as clever as daddy!'' she said comfortingly. ''And you and me play fight with swords again tomorrow! We help keep your big brother safe if he get in trouble!''

But her words, caring and affectionate though they were, could do no more than place the smallest surface plaster on the red agony that was tearing Vicky's emotions apart from the inside.

My sister's terror of losing me was constantly with her: eating away inside her like a living thing. An endless constant terror that she could only fight by being ever stronger, faster and more brutal. Only speed and ferocity, and the power of her fist and the strongest and most lethal of all white magic, could keep her big brother safe. Only a constant readiness to use violence to solve her problems could save her brother's life, and in doing so save the love she felt for him.

And suddenly I knew why our relationship would turn to incest. And then to domestic violence and abuse if the fundamentals between us were not drastically changed forever. In that moment I saw exactly why we got together as lovers, why Vicky didn't care how aggressively or openly she had to use her teenage curves to bind us together, and why everything else in Vicky's life would one day kneel to the power of the fist. For why would she ever dare take any other approach to any question in her life, when it had been her strength and savagery alone that had protected me and kept me alive? And when we were together as a couple, but still her fear of losing me reigned, where else could she turn to but that fist again? And this time strike now at the only target left to her: me. And so in the end her very power of white magic would destroy the one thing she had dedicated her whole life to saving. For, seeing the amount of force she had been hitting me with in the possible future I had just been shown, it was clear that things could not continue long before her blows did the absolute opposite of what she had always intended: and Vicky ended up taking my life herself.

The vision faded: and then was gone. The only thing I could feel: through the unending waves of pain that felt like my heart was dying as it struggled to find the strength to beat on: was myself start weeping. A very wise man had once told us that sometimes it was good to weep. That not all tears were evil.

But these ones were. And I doubt that in all the legends and all the lore of men had anyone ever shed tears so bitter and so bleak, or felt such loss of pain and grief. For what I saw before me now was a far worse end to our relationship then even death could possibly ever be. My first friend in this world had come to help me, but had in the end instead merely fallen into the power and despair of my dark shadow herself. The unending shadow of despair and grief that it seemed all grey wizards must cast in this modern world.

Once, long ago in a stage of my life now very distant and very, very far away, a little girl had come to me under a tree to kiss my wounds and cuts all better. She had been the only light for many years that my life had ever truly known. And she had always protected me, always stood up for me. She had never cared that the rest of the world saw me as nothing other than the failed runt of an otherwise very impressive litter of very, very acceptable middle class children. I had wondered often why she cared so little that everyone else despised me. Maybe it was simply that, as she stood in power so far above absolutely everyone else, she simply couldn't see the differences the rest of the world obsessed over. After all wherever people were they were still in the same position in her eyes; all of them were way below her. Perhaps it was the same reason that a king might converse with a peasant the same way he conversed with the most senior barons and dukes in all the land: because to him there is no meaningful distinction in any of his subjects' stations. Or perhaps my little sister's love for me and her total lack of caring for what everyone else thought about me was simply one of life's few genuinely unexplainable miracles. I didn't know. And I didn't really care.

But now that same love and gentleness that had led my little sister to stand by my side in innocence and love at the very beginning was now being twisted into a violent mockery of itself. Vicky had come to kiss my cheek and make my wounds all better. If I did not alter the course of things Vicky would one day be kissing far more intimate things on me than my cheek, and yet would still end up killing me herself.

I believed as a grey wizard that I had the power to turn the darkest evil into the brightest light. But though my relationship with my elder sister had turned around her entire life my relationship with the mortal girl that I loved most in all the world was turning all that was good and light about her into poison.

My love for Vicky was damning the very life and soul of what had once been the sweetest and the most gentle girl I had ever known.

And I would let any other fate fall, before I let my own love destroy my little sister. Whatever else befell this world I would face, cold and unmoved, but I would not let my own dark shadow poison my first, and for a very long time indeed, my only friend. I would place her far beyond the shadow of my doom, where the dark fate that awaited me could and would never dare to touch her: even though it ravaged all the rest of the world besides.

There was now no other choice: I would make my sacrifice to Artemis the Terrible.

Chapter 40

It was what happened that night, a couple of days after the slaughter in the supermarket: to give me time to gather myself for what I now had decided that I must do: that history books would later record as the day that the world was changed. As the day that the great holy war began. Some revisionists date it to a later date, when the battles and the bloodshed began. But most say war was inevitable from the moment the bleak events of that night resolved themselves. That this was the night that modern paganism was reborn. It was certainly the night when the darkest of all pagan secrets came at last fully into the light. The night the truth, of what had happened to cause the splinter in Artemis's soul all those thousands of years ago, finally became known.

I stood on the summit of Prestham Hill, at the top of the shape of rocks that people called the Old Man. It was evening, and the winter sun was setting, bathing the lands in red. The age of man, of Christ was setting: when the sun rose again it would be upon the birth pangs of a new and bloody age. For good and ill the next day's light would rise on a world where the gods walked among us once more: and the dark legend of Morgan le Fay would begin. A legend that began as a wizard walked out of an unknown darkness, out of a past that no one knew, to begin the most terrible war that had ever shaken the foundations of this world.

But I did not know that night what the future held: that I would achieve anything that night but one last mad gamble as I threw the dice to see where the pieces of my life would land. All I knew was that the wind was chill and the age of men and the carpenter god seemed as eternal as the endless passing of the always identically structured weeks. Behind me the rocks fell away into emptiness, although there was a route you could climb through the very centre of the old man's face. Not far below me was the ledge where I had sacrificed two creatures of magic to Artemis the Friendly, what seemed like a lifetime ago. Ahead of me the summit of the hill fell away gently into woods and fields. Beneath my feet the death trap for grey wizards that was Merlin's cave of memories was now nothing but an empty chamber barren of memories or protection magic: it had served its time. It had protected its wizard's pagan power and memory throughout the whole of the bleakest and most barren spiritual age this world had ever seen.

The summit of Prestham Hill was a barren spot, windswept. The only life thin grass clawing to the thin layer of soil on the cold red rock. Men had erected a simple monument of white stone that stood at the exact summit of the hill: marked at the centre with a circle of cold metal. The stone had once been white, but it had long since turned grey from the weather and been eroded by the wind. I could think of few places more fitting for a great sacrifice to a pagan god than here, in the quiet away from the everyday life of men. And the small pillar of manmade stone: both marking the peak of the hill and, in a weird way, actually making the top of it higher: seemed a truly appropriate altar for the most dangerous and important sacrifice of my life.

My only companion was a blue-eyed fairy with beautiful transparent wings of green bones, pink flesh and covered with blue feathers. My girlfriend, my star. "You don't have to do this." Artemis the Friendly said, "I can contain Artemis the Terrible for years and…"

"And sooner or later I will have to stand before the vampire princess once more." I said gently. "Do you think Artemis the Terrible will just let go the one man on this earth who knows her secret? Who knows that she was raped? Do you think that I can run from her? That I can hide? And you tried holding her in with Orion Artemis. With all due respect I have no wish to share his fate. I will face the winged vampire at a time and place of my own choosing. And that is here and that is now."

"Okay." said Artemis the Friendly. She sighed. "You know if you lose tonight this is the end for me. The prophecy was very clear. If you die tonight that is horrendous but at least your suffering will be over in mere moments. I will have to live as that fanged bitch for all the rest of eternity. The worst thing of all is that I will enjoy the memory of killing you, the man I love. And I will enjoy that memory not for a day, not for a week and not for a month: but for the rest of my eternal life. I will be trapped as Artemis the Terrible forever: without any hope of escape." She turned big blue eyes on me: eyes that were very scared. "Morgan are you going to win?"

I looked my goddess, my girlfriend, directly in the eye. "I don't know." I said softly. "I would be lying if I said I did. But know this. I do not have a death wish: not when there is even the remotest chance of spending the rest of my life with you. Win or lose, I came here tonight genuinely trying to win."

Artemis hugged me. "I hope you do." she said simply. We sat then down together, my arm around her shoulders and one of her arms around mine, while the sun set and the air turned dark with night. We were both acutely aware this might be the last real time either of us ever got to spend together, and I drank in the memories of the girl that I loved. They would be most of what I had to sustain me in the very dark road that lay ahead: even if this night turned out better than I dared to hope even in my wildest dreams. And finally the wind rose and the clouds blew away to make a completely cloudless sky. One in which all the stars you could see were shining in the night sky. And then we saw what we had been waiting for, the cold white light of the full moon directly overhead.

I kissed Artemis on the cheek, and then turned and walked to the pillar at the centre and exact summit of the hill top that I intended to use as an altar. I turned and sat upon it. I was soon about to offer up as sacrifice part of myself.

"It is time." I said simply. Artemis sighed, sadly, and in that moment looked very small. Then she stood up, straight and strong. "Morgan?"' she asked, very intensely. "Before we do this, before I go, can I ask just one more question? It's like way random but it's something I just really want to know."

"Of course," I said gently, "what's the question?"

"Morgan," she asked quietly, "why do you identify as pagan so much? Before the god of the Christians rose that word for us didn't even exist. All religion was pagan, you wouldn't have needed pagan as a word. You just said religion. Pagan is a word the Christians started using to insult us. It is a Latin word that means backward or stupid. Often used to describe peasants. Why do you claim the term of abuse they use with such honour?"'

I smiled tightly. "Because sadly there are other religions than paganism now, so a word is needed to describe us. And I will take the word that they gave us in hate and mockery and make it our own. They called us pagan as an insult, as they tried to sweep our religion from the pages of history. But I will see paganism rise again, to become the dominant, the only religion in this world. The true gods shall be honoured and rule over all, and the only echo that all the Christian centuries shall give to the far better future that is to come; is that they gave our true religion a new name. Paganism."

Artemis laughed, but with no real humour. "You fight for the gods so much and I scarcely even know why? It's not like we've been exactly great to you and your family. So far you've been given a mentor whose had you tear out one of your own eyes; and a girl you love but can't so much as kiss on the lips unless you want to die the woman's death."

"Because you know you are flawed and in realising that your religion becomes the highest form of moral truth." I replied, "And a religion which can acknowledge its own flaws is truly glorious without end. It is the religion of those who claim that their god is perfect, the religion of those who never have any doubts, that is truly twisted and foul. It is in the monotheistic faith, not in us, that I see the closest thing to true evil that exists on this earth. The Christians claim that we worship devils and demons as pagans, but I would claim that only a god arrogant enough to claim perfection could ever be the true devil."

There was a silence and then I raised my eyes to the cold light of the moon. The sacrificial dagger gleamed coldly in my hand, its metal razor sharp and glowing in the terrible light. "But right or wrong as I am about this or any other thing, the time has come."

"Yes," said Artemis the Friendly sadly, "I guess it is time for me to die the true death at last." She looked at me. "I have thought about what you have said about me Morgan, and you are right. My strength is failing and soon I must die either way. But if I just die because weariness overtakes me then even if you succeed in raising me back from the dead then The Terrible has but to tell me the truth of what happened to me, of who it was that raped me so long ago, and I will die once more. But if I die because I know the truth then if you do, somehow, impossibly against all the odds, succeed in calling me back to the world of the living, then I will know the truth as much as HER. And then I will be able to stand against The Terrible not as a dying version of a younger form of myself, but as a living version of a grown up woman who is in every way The Terrible's equal." She took a deep breath and, bravely biting back her tears, she looked across the space between us. From where she stood by the sheer drop at the edge of hill to where I waited on the small pillar rising up from the heart of the hill.

"Tell me who it was who hurt me in that way: all those lifetimes of mortals ago. Who it was who ruined my whole life for the briefest of moments of physical pleasure."

"I do not know." I said carefully, "I can only guess from what I have seen. The same way that I could only guess that the origin of The Terrible was rape. I didn't know for sure until I saw the truth of my claim in her reaction. It is the same now. I will tell you my guess, and then your heart will tell you if it is true. The thought processes that make up The Terrible are still a part of you always: even now as we speak. And when I tell you who I think violated you it is your own heart that will tell you whether my guess has hit the truth or simply fallen into madness." I paused, for a moment very still. "I almost hope that I am wrong." I said quietly, "Because if I am right then that truth is the very definition of horror."

And then I told the girl I loved the name.

Even braced for the worst possible thing that a girl could ever hear Artemis's eyes still widened in broken disbelief and agony. And in that very first terrible moment of shock I saw with a sick and distant horror that I had guessed right. I saw it in the way that the truth entered into the heart of the most beautiful and kindest woman and goddess in the world and in how, after her spirit had stood for so long and for so many years against so much horror and darkness, it just broke apart helplessly in an instant.

"Oh." said Artemis the Friendly, very sickly. "Oh no. Please no!"

And then she died.

She was dead long before she even hit the floor.

There was a piercing cry, so sharp and cold that in Prestham children screamed in nightmare and adults woke shaking in their beds. And as the cry of Artemis split the night the fairy was gone. The moon shone a terrible and blazing blue, and where a small fairy had stood a great winged vampire now rose triumphant: outlined against the powerful light. I felt a grief I forced aside. I had not time to mourn, not when eagled-winged death now stood straight before me.

"So finally it is done with Sappy!" smiled Artemis the Terrible. "And I can now stand in my full divine majesty as the only true form of the divine princess of the gods!" She turned to me and her smile was as deep and bleak as the heart of winter.

"Now do you have any idea what I will dare to do to the only man left who could possibly have the power to bring The Friendly back from death? Do you have any idea what special fate indeed I have in mind for you, oh servant of the seer warlord and the would be lover of a dead goddess?" The excitement in her words was sickening

"Castrate me?" I asked mildly. Horrifying as it was there was a dull repetition to the way The Terrible approached life. "Or kill me? Or probably both together." Appalling as her actions were within my heart horror of her was beginning to start to give way to a strange sort of almost bored pity.

The suddenly blue light of The Terrible's moonlight made me feel a little ill, but I found that almost all my fear had fled away. I realised suddenly that, whatever awaited me, it was very unlikely that I would ever share Orion's fate. Unlike him I had penetrated deep into the secrets of Artemis, whereas he had only ever skimmed on the surface. The fairy princess was so nice I wasn't sure anyone else had ever wanted to look past just how lovely she was to look deeper into the true nature of the full goddess, to examine unbiased who Artemis, with both of her seemingly so different forms, really was. Of how she was neither really one form nor the other, but in reality a complex mixture of them both.

"But why bother to hurt a man?" I asked gently, my words as flat and calm as ice before the horror in front of me. I raised my sacrificial knife clearly into the air. "When he is about to sacrifice the thing that he holds most precious in this world to you in any case? Surely it is much more rewarding for a man to hurt himself in your honour than it is for you to hurt him yourself directly?"

Artemis the Terrible came right up to me, so close that I could see the healthy whiteness of her skin: and smell the savage cruelty on her breath. For a moment I was concerned that her sadism and her unacknowledged fear that I might somehow bring The Friendly back might take over, and that the dark virgin of the gods might simply strike me dead on the spot and all would be lost: all my clever plans blown away like gossamer on the wind.

But Artemis stopped, she listened, and then she smiled in a way that was truly evil: and it took everything I had to keep my face impassive as I felt the battle between us begin in earnest. I could almost feel the dice of chance turning inside my heart.

I chose my words very carefully. As I had told The Voice in our battle for Jessica's soul so long ago, in these kind of magical battles it was forbidden to outright lie.

"But even better than me mutilating myself while you just watch," I questioned thoughtfully, "why not partake with me in my self-mutilation? I will cut the skin directly above my penis. If you drink my blood hard enough from there then my... - my reproductive organs - will be starved of blood and rot black before your eyes: before falling away completely dead and useless from the rest of my living body. Do you dare to drink while I sacrifice the most precious thing that I have in this world to you?"

I took the knife and cut a thin line above my balls and penis, that poured with inviting blood. Artemis the Terrible's smile was hideous indeed as she lowered her mouth to drink, her razor sharp fangs glistening terribly in her blue moonlight.

As she lowered her mouth to drink I gathered all that was most precious to me. I linked my grey magic to a beautiful red head with green eyes, and gathered all her memories of me. Then in one desperate instant, as the vampire fangs pierced my flesh, I sacrificed all her memories of me, and focused them into a single drop of red blood in my bloodstream. Which appeared right where Artemis's fangs pierced my flesh. And she drank it down deep. The explosion of power: as a demon in whose heart beat no mercy took memories of love - of that indescribable power - into her very soul: shook the hillside; and hurled the goddess herself backwards and down: just as I had planned and hoped. I held up my hand shaking, sealing the gash above my unharmed genitals with fire so that I did not bleed to death.

Artemis the Terrible was on the floor, screaming as forces she had never experienced wracked inside her heart. Her caring emotions had been dead as broken stone, charred and frozen by her violation and rape. Yet now her whole body screamed with the single drop of red blood and love that beat inside her. The memories of the love Vicky had born me were sent burning through every corner of the dark virgin of the gods' black-soaked veins. A great and uncontrollable love without restriction or restraint spread through Artemis the Terrible like wildfire, that drop of blood melting and dissolving until The Terrible's love for me became as much a part of her as her never ending and eternal hatred of men.

I felt the divine power of the blue moon rush into me, and tried not to think of where my little sister slept, who would wake in the morning with no memory that she had ever had a big brother. It had been the only way, the only way to save her from a life of incest and violence. The only way to save her from me. I had truly sacrificed to Artemis the Terrible the thing in my life that was the most precious to me. My little sister's love for me and even her very acknowledgement of my existence. I had earned the right to be the champion of the dark and chaste maiden huntress of the moon. And no god or goddess could ever take away that blessing once bestowed, not though they grew to repent what they had done and hate their champion with all their heart.

"I accept your gift of power." I said lightly, not letting myself think about the pain tearing apart my heart: about the loss of all I had ever had with my little sister. "And I am bound to you now as your champion for the rest of my life, as much as I am to Artemis the Friendly or The Allfather himself. For I have truly honoured my word to you tonight and sacrificed unto you the thing which is most precious to me in this life. You can study my words as carefully as you like: I never explicitly promised to castrate myself to you."

Artemis the Terrible screamed in rage and fury, but even she, goddess as she was, could not undo what had just been done. She rose from the ground in fury, literally shaking with rage and her eyes burning with flame. "You bastard!" she screamed, literally shaking with anger. "You think that you can just trick me like that? You think that you will be spared just because you are now my champion? Or because I now have feelings for you? Enjoy the few seconds of holding that position - A NON CASTRATED MAN HOLDING THAT POSITION - that you will have before I tear the life from you! You think I care that killing my own champion will be agony? You think that will stop me from tearing out your heart before your eye? You think…"

But all the time she raged I drew deeper and deeper on the power of the grey. For I had succeeded in all that was set, had I not? Great sacrifice had been offered to all three of my chosen gods. The futures where I fell to Merlin's or Nimue's hand had been changed. And I had answered The Allfather's riddle, and so knew the ultimate power of grey magic, its true power. The power to turn even the strongest and most terrible of all evil into good. And even as Artemis the Terrible wasted her precious time in words of rage and fury I worked a great and powerful magic to fade myself from the knowledge of all. All save my elder sister Jessica, whose existence was so based on her relationship with me that I dared not touch her, and Danielle, who I feared to harm in any way, feared to risk any further allergic reaction in her to my power by touching her with my grey magic once more. But from the minds of all others I was disappearing. From my father, from my mother, from the people who had tormented me at school, from the Mind of The Mountain himself. And from the mind of Merlin and even from the mind of my own gods: for with or without their memories of me I would still be their champion.

551

In was in the last seconds before I would have faded from her thoughts entirely that Artemis suddenly realised what was happening. "No!" she howled desperately, torn by the sudden panic that I might just be about to escape her, "You will not survive because I forget that you exist!" She came screaming towards me as I faded, terror having replaced sadism, her hands outstretched as her claw like talons reached out to rip apart my chest and tear open my heart.

But I was the champion of The Allfather, champion of the grey, and as I realised in horror that she would reach me just before her last memories of me faded away completely I called on everything I had: opened up every last reserve of strength that I possessed. In the distance a clock was striking midnight, and at the exact moment it rang twelve I sent out grey magic to fade out the flow of action from time, slowing Artemis's movements, needing to gain only the fragments of seconds for her memories of me to be gone, and for me myself to then disappear from this place and be safe.

But the horror of what drove Artemis the Terrible, of what had been done to her in violation all those thousands of years ago, was so great that still she came on, though slowed. And I realised, with a slow sick sense of mounting and complete despair and failure, that I would not fade in time before those jagged talons tore my chest and torso apart. Her talons reached my skin and started to cut into my flesh, bathing me in fresh streams of my own flowing blood.

On an island of gold on which was built a temple of marble, a great stone altar at the heart of a dark unholy temple shook: with sudden and almost overwhelming force rising up in an instant out of seemingly nowhere. Fragments of shattered sharp steel spelling Aion, the Greek name for eternity, suddenly started to be unmade as, seeing my love and blood in the uttermost extremes,

The Friendly tried to return to life to save me. Life flowed in the tears of the poisoned lake, algae grew, and animals in the dark woods sang. Acorns hidden in the cracks of the golden island burst into new life and growth, and then in many places the marble walls of the temple were cast down into ruin as the new life and power of The Friendly rose up and grew. Even the great stone altar itself started to be torn apart, as the soft acorn buried in its deepest heart tried to break into new life and grow, to bring new life and love into the heart of the temple's darkness, and to replace the pain and sadism with the power of friendliness and true love.

But it was not enough. Great though her efforts were The Friendly could not this night break the power of The Terrible, for even the motivation the sweet fairy princess felt in this moment was not enough for her to rise up back once more triumphant into the world of the living: not now she knew the truth of what had happened: the truth of who it was that had hurt her so badly, so long ago. Though trees took defiant root and bushes grew, though much of the unholy lake became a source of living water and not death, still the acorn at the temple's heart could not overcome the power of those shattered shards of steel that cut so ruthlessly and eternally at the deepest levels of Artemis the Terrible's heart. And, for all the power of The Friendly that rose inside it, the acorn could not in the end succeed in bursting into new life: but fell back into dormancy and inactivity once more. The Friendly's attempt to burst into new life faltered, and then shattered. The thousand dancing colours of the rainbow crushed down by the power of the all-encompassing white light of The Terrible.

In that moment I realised with a sick sense of horror that I had failed, failed The Friendly, failed everyone. Failed paganism itself. The triumph of Christ was now eternal, the last hope for paganism was over: and I would die having achieved in the end no more than Orion had before me. It was over: and I was done.

And then it happened. The event which changed the world forever: and which brought the darkest secret of all paganism forever into the light.

Far off and half a world away a great mountain top rose through the clouds, so tall its peak pierced the very sky itself. This was not The Mountain, which even now stared out from across its desert: all its gaze and attention held in horror by the events occurring on the summit of Prestham Hill. This was Mount Olympus. But though it was ornate with gold, and though the buildings shone with glory and wealth past counting: and the very tables and chairs were worth the sum of small cities so ornately were they wrought: still even just the air of the place had grown unbearably still and stale. The gods lay as they had done for centuries, richly clothed and dressed, but still and barely able to so much as even breathe. Those whose movements had once shaped the very actions of the heavens now could not summon the will to lift even so much as a finger. On the surface the cause was obvious. Above Mount Olympus rose a wooden cross, its power beating down to restrain all the strength of the pagan gods below. But, great and terrible though the power of the crucifix was it was a darker fate still that had stayed the energy of the ancient Greek gods. For it was no external force that had brought them to their knees but a great crime, a secret hidden. A shame that had in the end brought down the entirety of the pagan gods of the civilised world.

But now: for the first time in well over a thousand and a half years: the greatest of all the Greek gods dared to stand. Zeus, king of the gods, and father to many. In his heyday none had dared naysay him, for he was the personification of the power and lust and success of men. His word had been absolute and his conquests of war as many and as fertile as the countless women, mortals and nymphs and goddesses, who had spread their legs to bring him children. And yet absolute power had in the end destroyed him more completely than any external foe. And in his victory he had claimed the one thing that he should have forever denied himself. For a thousand and a half years now he had not moved so much as a fingernail, so great was his shame and grief. He had let his religion and his worshippers fall to the cross uncaring. For why should not the ultimate alpha male, who had once permitted himself absolutely everything except even the slightest trace of effeminism, not now fall to the most softly spoken prophet, to a poor man born in a stable? After what Zeus had done what he would have once considered to be the ultimate blasphemy and outrage: that a man who he saw as effeminate should utterly supplant his rule and worship: seemed now only the most fitting fate that the once almost invincible Father of the Gods entirely and completely deserved.

And yet now Zeus walked again, for the first time in well over a thousand and a half years of men. And though the cross beat against him it could not stop the stride of the first, the true, lord of the heavens. He had but to raise his gaze to shake the heavens to their core. Zeus came to his anvil and took up his hammer, and in his eyes was a look so terrible that it could have broken the foundations of this or any other world that there is or could ever be. For besides the power of this god all others trembled. Not Yahweh of the Jews, nor Odin of the Vikings, not Allah of the Muslims nor even Christ of the Christians could have stood against him. For no other god was or could ever be as destructive as Father Zeus, the lightning lord. The greatest god of the white wizards. And in Zeus's heart, for the first time since his crime those many, many long years and centuries ago: so many lifetimes of men ago and yet so fresh and real and constant to his immortal eyes: beat that most dangerous and powerful of all emotions: hope. Hope that the world could be saved from The Mountain, yes. Hope that the pagan world could be brought back and the work of the Christians washed away like the waves of the sea wash away the sands, yes. But about all these things at this moment he scarcely cared. They would not have raised so much as a twitch of his eyebrows. But for the first time he dared to hope that Artemis could truly be saved. That one day his daughter might again be truly happy. And for that he found the strength to walk once more across the heavens, and to intervene in the world of men as he did before: now so long ago. For he loved his daughter dearly, and that is why he could never forgive himself or his crime. That he had taken the one thing that he should never have taken.

But absolute power had, in one moment of drink and arrogance and the taboo of forbidden lust, made him do the darkest thing of all. For he had had sex with his own daughter: raping Artemis even as she screamed and could not understand.

And now Zeus smote the anvil of the gods with all his power: and the hammer's roar thundered throughout the heavens: and the thunderbolt fell down with an explosion of pure raw magical power far greater than any had ever heard or seen before: even back in the days when the pagan gods moved openly among men and their power was so strong.

The thunderbolt fell upon where I stood on the summit of Prestham Hill, and its power seared into my heart and soul. Its magic fused remorselessly into me, as the greatest of all pagan gods bound his power and his fate to mine. "Save her." he roared, he commanded, with all the force of the heavens and earth, in all that tormented love that he bore for his daughter.

And in that moment I became, save, perhaps, for Merlin, the most powerful wizard in the world. Even Vicky was left far behind me in the shade. No mortal wizard on earth could now have matched my strength, save perhaps for the one with so many lifetimes of magic and power at his command. For I had the blessings now of three gods, of Odin Allfather, of Zeus Father of Heaven, and of both sides of the female huntress: though one of those sides was currently dead and beyond any mortal's reach. Not in all pagandom did I believe that in that moment could there come a combination of divine power in one man or woman more varied and more terrible. And before Artemis the Terrible's claws could reach me I faded and was gone.

Seconds later I rematerialised on the ledge below, where I had once sacrificed to the friendlier side of the huntress. I was bound so closely now to the chaste maiden of the moon that I could feel her confusion as she suddenly stood on the peak just above, suddenly utterly unsure why she was there. I hid my thoughts and presence carefully from her: no one must now know that I existed until the time was right: until I had made my next move. But the next moment the divine huntress just shrugged and was gone: out to hunt some poor man down to his death.

I stared out down from the top of Prestham Hill. It was all so clear now. I must take the power I had been given and, unseen, having faded from the sight of all, strike a blow that could turn the course of this world from The Mountain's victory. I must raise up the standard of the pagan gods against the cold power of The Mountain, the passion of the pagan magic against the bleak order of secularism and all the different forms that the poison of monotheism took. I thought about a few things. I thought about the truth of Artemis. It was so easy to love the fairy, and to hate the vampire. To see the second part of the chaste maiden of the moon, as Orion and even her own twin brother Apollo had, as an infection. Like a cancer to be rooted out and destroyed.

But the truth was this was not a repeat of the Jess and Jessica situation. Artemis the Terrible was just another part of the goddess, as vital and as real as the more friendly part. And yet the rape victim, the one who remembered being hurt, had as far as I could tell, not had one kind word spoken to her by anyone since she began her dark and probably very lonely existence. Probably the only nice thing she had ever heard was me telling her that I was sorry that she had been raped. And Artemis had always been a natural chatterbox, she was never going to do very well or be very happy if she was left too long alone by herself. If any of all this was going to work, I was going to have to get on with both beauty and the beast: I was going to have to form some kind of successful relationship with both sides of the divine huntress.

I stood up and started to descend Prestham Hill, walking east towards where the sun rises each morning to bring in a new day.

I tried not to think about a beautiful red-haired girl who I loved more than life itself, and who now didn't even know my name. But I could not stop the tears that hurt my good eye.

I walked onwards into a new age of this world: and what was to happen next not even the very wisest could have possibly hoped to have foreseen.

But that's what frequently happens, when the whole world is plunged into holy war.

If you enjoyed Cold Moonlight I would really appreciate it if you would post a review online. Thanks. Mark R Mitchell

Mailing List

Looking forward to the next volume of The Game of Gods? Subscribe to Mark R Mitchell's mailing list for free updates about the next volume and read free blogs about his thoughts on the best romantic and the best fantasy fiction.

markrmitchell.co.uk

Glossary

Blue Magic: The power to change things into something else. Although this gives the wizard a vast range of options these changes quickly reverse themselves unless the magic driving them is maintained. It takes a lot of effort and repeated casting of the same spell for any changes caused by blue magic to become permanent.

Brown Magic: The power to make permanent changes very easily, but can only work by developing factors that already exist. For example it would be easy to use brown magic to make stone even denser and harder, but impossible to use it to turn rocks into, say, plastic, or something else completely unrelated to stone.

Grey Magic: The power to make things fade out of existence or to disappear from sight. It takes effort to keep something faded out or invisible and pressure put on the spell can lead to things reappearing in reality or becoming visible once more.

White Magic: The power of manipulating both energy in the material world and mental energy. Changes made are permanent and the flexibility of this form of magic gives it a wide range of uses. Excellent particularly for fighting, healing and mind control.

Printed in Great Britain
by Amazon